**All New Works of Horror
and the Supernatural**

Masques

Edited by J.N. Williamson

MACLAY & ASSOCIATES INC.
Baltimore/1984

FIRST EDITION

Contents

Introduction and
Acknowledgments

J.N. Williamson

Why Masques *as the title for this anthology of all-new horrific, occult, and supernatural material?*

I have my reasons and you shall have them, too. . .

1. Most readers of such writing get all the trivia questions right when the subject is Edgar Allan Poe, and Masques *swiftly conjures EAP's "Masque of the Red Death" (1842); titles are said to be best when the recognition factor is high;*

2. There may be a subliminal evocation of the cherished Black Mask *magazine but with — as Ray Russell observed — more dignity;*

3. A "masque" was an elaborate dramatic performance popular in England during the 16th and 17th centuries, and the focus of the form was a lusty witches' cauldron of horror, terror, revenge. One encyclopedia even reminds us that English tragedy "customarily probed the roots of evil."

What with Galileo having recently observed moon craters and Michael of Wallachia conquering Transylvania, the period was ideal for such a man as Ben Jonson to "court favor" with his Masque of Blackness *and* The Alchemist. *It was Ben, actor as well as playwright — Russell, Fritz Leiber, Richard Matheson, Mort Castle, and editor Williamson later trod the boards, as well — who organized masques for his king.*

Old Ben's creations (my encyclopedia insists) had a "controlled style," "incisiveness," and "sure sense of structure," characteristics of most who prune the roots of evil for fictive delights. He enjoyed gathering with his admiring followers in the Apollo room. . .of the Devil Tavern. Among them were two young dramatists of inventive imagination who guided a masque, disquietingly yet with humor, toward a preconceived point. One of the two was named — Beaumont.

It's fairly standard practice in introductions such as this to whet your appetite with cheers for the material to come. Considering the wordsmiths of rue assembled here for your pleasure, I cannot imagine such a need exists. Instead, my individual asides preceding each piece may provide you with information that humanizes and "sketches in a little background, as it were" (as memory tells me satirist Stan Freberg once put it).

Consider: One of the fine post-*Lovecraft anthologies of weird fiction was* The Playboy Book of Horror and The Supernatural *(1967). Six authors were represented by more than one short story, each reprinted from the magazine: Robert Bloch; Ray Bradbury; Richard Matheson; Ray Russell; Gahan Wilson; and Charles Beaumont. All, nearly two decades later, are here — despite Beaumont's tragically untimely demise — with* new writing. *William F. Nolan was present, too; Nolan, as well, is back with a finely-honed, frightening yarn.*

And they are joined by more than a dozen other tellers of terror who'd surely have deserved space in that 1967 anthology had they emerged — talent-wise, or in life — earlier. Deserved, and probably won it.

H. P. Lovecraft preached it right even when he didn't always practice it: "I believe that weird writing offers a serious field not unworthy of the best literary artists" (Some Notes on a Nonentity). *You'll meet the best in the pages ready to be turned, whether any of them ever see Stockholm or not. I believe that at least twelve contributors have rarely, if ever, achieved the heights they scale in* Masques; *four have ascended to new levels of personal accomplishment. And except for one beautiful and necessary tribute to Beaumont, which has never before appeared in book form but ran many years ago in a magazine, it's all heretofore unpublished work — masterworks, if you will.*

Ladies and gentlemen, whether you watch from your royal throne or peer enigmatically through the slits in your domino, prepare yourself for shock, suspense, surprisingly stimulating ideas, and wonder. Let the masque begin!

J. N. Williamson
May 1984

This book is an achievement of cooperative attitudes on the part of the present authors and poets, others who are integral to the free exchange of supportive ideas and information, and the encouragement of friends, eager readers-to-be, and people within the writing and publishing communities who are not present in the pages of *Masques*. More specific gratitude must be expressed to those whose unflagging willingness to Point the Way was utterly indispensable, particularly Dr. Milton L. Hillman for the title; William F. Nolan; Stuart David Schiff of *Whispers;* Ray Russell; Peter Heggie, Executive Secretary of Authors Guild; Richard Matheson; Ardath Mayhar; Nancy R. Parsegian, long-time Playboy editor; Mike Ashley; Dennis Etchison; Joe R. Lansdale; Robert Collins, Editor, *Fantasy Review;* Karl Edward Wagner; the late Charles Beaumont, whose undiminished spirit increasingly became our inspiration; Joyce Maclay, Ethel T. Cavanaugh, and Mary T. Williamson. Not to mention the publisher, John Maclay, whose idea it was in the first place.

Design and production: John Maclay
Composition and mechanical artwork: Madison Graphic Services, Inc.
Printing and binding: BookCrafters, Inc.
Dustjacket design: Stanley Mossman
Dustjacket illustration: Allen Koszowski

Nightcrawlers

Robert R. McCammon

*In 1978, an Avon novel—*Baal—*marked the arrival of another author who hoped to survive the indiscriminate horror "boom." It was a time when many publishers sought to capitalize upon the successes of Levin, Blatty, and King, plus film producers as well—eager, as Douglas E. Winter wrote in* Shadowings *(Starmont House, 1983), to "snap up seemingly every property in sight and feed them to the momentarily insatiable appetite of the reading and viewing public."*

Occult readers were more selective than viewers. Five years later, most of those writers who could not advance culled out, Robert R. McCammon had benefited from the demanding nucleus of steadfast horror readers which had learned to recognize the names of top professionals. He'd followed up with Bethany's Sin, They Thirst, Night Boat, *and, in 1983,* Mystery Walk. *It became a book club selection and genuine best seller both in hardcover and in paperback.*

Yet Rick McCammon had been only 26 years old when Baal *was published! Born July 17, 1952, another gifted Southern wordsmith, he lives in Birmingham and speaks courteously with but a hint of his regional origin. McCammon novels typically begin on a note of suspense (with some of the more intriguing characters in modern fiction), skip quickly to all-out Terror Alert, then charge at the reader as forcefully as an old Bear Bryant front line.*

His latest novel continues the saga of Poe's tormented Ushers and he plans The Lady *next, a supernatural novel set in surroundings familiar to Rick. Your immediate concern is the following, rare Robert R. McCammon novelette, "Nightcrawlers," arguably his most mature yet terrifyingly typical shocker. If you read it by night, or alone, "in the light" will be a phrase that makes your skin crawl whenever you see a red neon sign . . .*

"Hard rain coming down," Cheryl said, and I nodded in agreement.

Through the diner's plate-glass windows, a dense curtain of rain flapped across the Gulf gas pumps and continued across the parking lot. It hit Big Bob's with a force that made the glass rattle like uneasy bones. The red neon sign that said BIG BOB'S! DIESEL FUEL! EATS! sat on top of a high steel pole above the diner so the truckers on the interstate could see it. Out in the night, the red-tinted rain thrashed in torrents across my old pickup truck and Cheryl's baby-blue Volkswagen.

"Well," I said, "I suppose that storm'll either wash some folks in off the interstate or we can just about hang it up." The curtain of rain parted for an instant, and I could see the treetops whipping back and forth in the woods on the other side of Highway 47. Wind whined around the front door like an animal trying to claw its way in. I glanced at the electric clock on the wall behind the counter. Twenty minutes before nine. We usually closed up at ten, but tonight—with tornado warnings in the weather forecast—I was tempted to turn the lock a little early. "Tell you what," I said. "If we're empty at nine, we skedaddle. 'Kay?"

"No argument here," she said. She watched the storm for a moment longer, then continued putting newly-washed coffee cups, saucers and plates away on the stainless steel shelves.

Lightning flared from west to east like the strike of a burning bullwhip. The diner's lights flickered, then came back to normal. A shudder of thunder seemed to come right up through my shoes. Late March is the beginning of tornado season in south Alabama, and we've had some whoppers spin past here in the last few years. I knew that Alma was at home, and she understood to get into the root cellar right quick if she spotted a twister, like that one we saw in '82 dancing through the woods about two miles from our farm.

"You got any Love-Ins planned this weekend, hippie?" I asked Cheryl, mostly to get my mind off the storm and to rib her, too.

She was in her late-thirties, but I swear that when she grinned she could've passed for a kid. "Wouldn't *you* like to know, redneck?" she answered; she replied the same way to all my digs at her. Cheryl Lovesong—and I *know* that couldn't have been her real name—was a mighty able waitress, and she had hands that were no strangers to hard work. But I didn't care that she wore her long silvery-blond hair in Indian braids with hippie headbands, or came to work in tie-dyed overalls. She was the best waitress who'd ever worked for me, and she got along with everybody just fine—even us rednecks. That's what I am, and proud of it: I drink Rebel Yell whiskey straight, and my favorite songs are about good women gone bad and trains on the long track to nowhere. I keep my wife happy, I've raised my two boys to pray to God and to salute the flag, and if anybody don't like it he can go a few rounds with Big Bob Clayton.

Cheryl would come right out and tell you she used to live in San Francisco in the late 'sixties, and that she went to Love-Ins and peace marches and all that stuff. When I reminded her it was nineteen eighty-four and Ronnie Reagan was president, she'd look at me like I was walking cow-flop. I always figured she'd start thinking straight when all that hippie-dust blew out of her head.

Alma said my tail was going to get burnt if I ever took a shine to Cheryl, but I'm a fifty-five-year-old redneck who stopped sowing his wild seed when he met the woman he married, more than thirty years ago.

Lightning crisscrossed the turbulent sky, followed by a boom of thunder. Cheryl said, "Wow! Look at that light-show!"

"Light-show, my ass," I muttered. The diner was as solid as the Good Book, so I wasn't too worried about the storm. But on a wild night like this, stuck out in the countryside like Big Bob's was, you had a feeling of being a long way off from civilization—though Mobile was only twenty-seven miles south. On a wild night like this, you had a feeling that anything could happen, as quick as a streak of lightning out of the darkness. I picked up a copy of the Mobile *Press-Register* that the last customer — a trucker on his way to Texas — had left on the counter a half-hour before, and I started plowing through the news, most of it bad: those A-rab countries were still squabbling like Hatfields and McCoys in white robes; two men had robbed a Quik-Mart in Mobile and had been killed by the police in a shootout; cops were investigating a massacre at a motel near Daytona Beach; an infant had been stolen from a maternity ward in Birmingham. The only good things on the front page were stories that said the economy was up and that Reagan swore we'd show the Commies who was boss in El Salvador and Lebanon.

The diner shook under a blast of thunder, and I looked up from the paper as a pair of headlights emerged from the rain into my parking-lot.

II

The headlights were attached to an Alabama State Trooper car.

"Half alive, hold the onion, extra brown the buns." Cheryl was already writing on her pad in expectation of the order. I pushed the paper aside and went to the fridge for the hamburger meat.

When the door opened, a windblown spray of rain swept in and stung like buckshot. "Howdy, folks!" Dennis Wells peeled off his gray rainslicker and hung it on the rack next to the door. Over his Smokey the Bear trooper hat was a protective plastic covering, beaded with raindrops. He took off his hat, exposing the thinning blond hair on his pale scalp, as he approached the counter and sat on his usual stool, right next to the cash-register. "Cup of black coffee and a rare — " Cheryl was already sliding the coffee in front of him, and the burger sizzled on the griddle. "Ya'll are on the ball tonight!" Dennis said; he said the same thing when he came in, which was almost every night. Funny the kind of habits you fall into, without realizing it.

"Kinda wild out there, ain't it?" I asked as I flipped the burger over.

"Lordy, yes! Wind just about flipped my car over three, four miles down the interstate. Thought I was gonna be eatin' a little pavement tonight." Dennis was a husky young man in his early thirties, with thick blond brows over deep-set, light brown eyes. He had a wife and three kids, and he was fast to flash a wallet-full of their pictures. "Don't reckon I'll be chasin' any speeders tonight, but there'll probably be a load of accidents. Cheryl, you sure look pretty this evenin'."

"Still the same old me." Cheryl never wore a speck of makeup, though one day she'd come to work with glitter on her cheeks. She had a place a few miles away, and I guessed she was farming that funny weed up there. "Any trucks moving?"

"Seen a few, but not many. Truckers ain't fools. Gonna get worse before it gets better, the radio says." He sipped at his coffee and grimaced. "Lordy, that's strong enough to jump out of the cup and dance a jig, darlin'!"

I fixed the burger the way Dennis liked it, put it on a platter with some fries and served it. "Bobby, how's the wife treatin' you?" he asked.

"No complaints."

"Good to hear. I'll tell you, a fine woman is worth her weight in gold. Hey, Cheryl! How'd you like a handsome young man for a husband?"

Cheryl smiled, knowing what was coming. "The man I'm looking for hasn't been made yet."

"Yeah, but you ain't met *Cecil* yet, either! He asks me about you every time I see him, and I keep tellin' him I'm doin' every-thing I can to get you two together." Cecil was Dennis' brother-in-law and owned a Chevy dealership in Bay Minette. Dennis had been ribbing Cheryl about going on a date with Cecil for the past four months. "You'd like him," Dennis promised. "He's got a lot of my qualities."

"Well, that's different. In that case, I'm *certain* I don't want to meet him."

Dennis winced. "Oh, you're a cruel woman! That's what smokin' banana peels does to you — turns you mean. Anybody readin' this rag?" He reached over for the newspaper.

"Waitin' here just for you," I said. Thunder rumbled, closer to the diner. The lights flickered briefly once...then again before they returned to normal. Cheryl busied herself by fixing a fresh pot of coffee, and I watched the rain whipping against the windows. When the lightning flashed, I could see the trees swaying so hard they looked about to snap.

Dennis read and ate his hamburger. "Boy," he said after a few minutes, "the world's in some shape, huh? Those A-rab pig-stickers are itchin' for war. Mobile metro boys had a little gunplay last night. Good for them." He paused and frowned, then tapped the paper with one thick finger. "This I can't figure."

"What's that?"

"Thing in Florida couple of nights ago. Six people killed at the Pines Haven Motor Inn, near Daytona Beach. Motel was set off in the woods. Only a couple of cinderblock houses in the area, and nobody heard any gunshots. Says here one old man saw what he thought was a bright white star falling over the motel, and that was it. Funny, huh?"

"A UFO," Cheryl offered. "Maybe he saw a UFO."

"Yeah, and I'm a little green man from Mars," Dennis scoffed. "I'm serious. This is weird. The motel was so blown full of holes it looked like a war had been going on. Everybody was dead — even a dog and a canary that belonged to the manager. The cars out in front of the rooms were blasted to pieces. The sound of one of them explodin' was what woke up the people in those houses, I reckon." He skimmed the story again. "Two bodies were out in the parkin'-lot, one was holed up in a bathroom, one had crawled under a bed, and two had dragged every piece of furniture in the room over to block the door. Didn't seem to help 'em any, though."

I grunted. "Guess not."

"No motive, no witnesses. You better believe those Florida cops are shakin' the bushes for some kind of dangerous maniac — or maybe more than one, it says here." He shoved the paper away and patted the service revolver holstered at his hip. "If I ever got hold of him — or them — he'd find out not to mess with a 'Bama trooper." He glanced quickly over at Cheryl and smiled mischievously. "Probably some crazy hippie who'd been smokin' his tennis shoes."

"Don't knock it," she said sweetly, "until you've tried it." She looked past him, out the window into the storm. "Car's pullin' in, Bobby."

Headlights glared briefly off the wet windows. It was a station-wagon with wood-grained panels on the sides; it veered around the gas pumps and parked next to Dennis' trooper car. On the front bumper was a personalized license plate that said: *Ray & Lindy.* The headlights died, and all the doors opened at once. Out of the wagon came a whole family: a man and a woman, a little girl and boy about eight or nine. Dennis got up and opened the diner door as they hurried inside from the rain.

All of them had gotten pretty well soaked between the station wagon and the diner, and they wore the dazed expressions of people who'd been on the road a long time. The man wore glasses and had curly gray hair, the woman was slim and dark-haired and pretty. The kids were sleepy-eyed. All of them were well-dressed, the man in a yellow sweater with one of those alligators on the chest. They had vacation tans, and I figured they were tourists heading north from the beach after spring break.

"Come on in and take a seat," I said.

"Thank you," the man said. They squeezed into one of the booths near the windows. "We saw your sign from the interstate."

"Bad night to be on the highway," Dennis told them. "Tornado warnings are out all over the place."

"We heard it on the radio," the woman — Lindy, if the license was right — said. "We're on our way to Birmingham, and we thought we could drive right through the storm. We should've stopped at that Holiday Inn we passed about fifteen miles ago."

"That would've been smart," Dennis agreed. "No sense in pushin' your luck." He returned to his stool.

The new arrivals ordered hamburgers, fries and Cokes. Cheryl and I went to work. Lightning made the diner's lights flicker again, and the sound of thunder caused the kids to jump. When the food was ready and Cheryl served them, Dennis said, "Tell you what. You folks finish your dinners and I'll escort you back to the Holiday Inn. Then you can head out in the morning. How about that?"

"Fine," Ray said gratefully. "I don't think we could've gotten very much further, anyway." He turned his attention to his food.

"Well," Cheryl said quietly, standing beside me, "I don't guess we get home early, do we?"

"I guess not. Sorry."

She shrugged. "Goes with the job, right? Anyway, I can think of worse places to be stuck."

I figured that Alma might be worried about me, so I went over to the payphone to call her. I dropped a quarter in — and the dial tone sounded like a cat being stepped on. I hung up and tried again. The cat-scream continued. "Damn!" I muttered. "Lines must be screwed up."

"Ought to get yourself a place closer to town, Bobby," Dennis said. "Never could figure out why you wanted a joint in the sticks. At least you'd get better phone service and good lights if you were nearer to Mo—"

He was interrupted by the sound of wet and shrieking brakes, and he swivelled around on his stool.

I looked up as a car hurtled into the parking-lot, the tires swerving, throwing up plumes of water. For a few seconds I thought it was going to keep coming, right through the window into the diner — but then the brakes caught and the car almost grazed the side of my pickup as it jerked to a stop. In the neon's red glow I could tell it was a beatup old Ford Fairlane, either gray or a dingy beige. Steam was rising off the crumpled hood. The headlights stayed on for perhaps a minute before they winked off. A figure got out of the car and walked slowly — with a limp — toward the diner.

We watched the figure approach. Dennis' body looked like a coiled spring, ready to be triggered. "We got us a live one, Bobby boy," he said.

The door opened, and in a stinging gust of wind and rain

a man who looked like walking death stepped into my diner.

III

He was so wet he might well have been driving with his windows down. He was a skinny guy, maybe weighed all of a hundred and twenty pounds, even soaking wet. His unruly dark hair was plastered to his head, and he had gone a week or more without a shave. In his gaunt, pallid face his eyes were startlingly blue; his gaze flicked around the diner, lingered for a few seconds on Dennis. Then he limped on down to the far end of the counter and took a seat. He wiped the rain out of his eyes as Cheryl took a menu to him.

Dennis stared at the man. When he spoke, his voice bristled with authority. "Hey, fella." The man didn't look up from the menu. "Hey, I'm talkin' to *you*."

The man pushed the menu away and pulled a damp packet of Kools out of the breast pocket of his patched Army fatigue jacket. "I can hear you," he said; his voice was deep and husky, and didn't go with his less-than-robust physical appearance.

"Drivin' kinda fast in this weather, don't you think?"

The man flicked a cigarette lighter a few times before he got a flame, then he lit one of his smokes and inhaled deeply. "Yeah," he replied. "I was. Sorry. I saw the sign, and I was in a hurry to get here. Miss? I'd just like a cup of coffee, please. Hot and *real* strong, okay?"

Cheryl nodded and turned away from him, almost bumping into me as I strolled down behind the counter to check him out.

"That kind of hurry'll get you killed," Dennis cautioned.

"Right. Sorry." He shivered and pushed the tangled hair back from his forehead with one hand. Up close, I could see deep cracks around his mouth and the corners of his eyes and I figured him to be in his late thirties or early forties. His wrists were as thin as a woman's; he looked like he hadn't eaten a good meal for more than a month. He stared at his hands through bloodshot eyes. Probably on drugs, I thought. The fella gave me the creeps. Then he looked at me with those eyes — so pale blue they were almost white — and I felt like I'd been nailed to the floor. "Something wrong?" he asked — not rudely, just curiously.

"Nope." I shook my head. Cheryl gave him his coffee and then went over to give Ray and Lindy their check. The man didn't use either cream or sugar. The coffee was steaming, but he drank half of it down like mother's milk. "That's good," he said. "Keep me awake, won't it?"

"More than likely." Over the breast pocket of his jacket was the faint outline of the name that had been sewn there once. I think it was *Price*, but I could've been wrong.

"That's what I want. To stay awake, as long as I can." He finished the coffee. "Can I have another cup, please?"

I poured it for him. He drank that one down just as fast, then he rubbed his eyes wearily.

"Been on the road a long time, huh?"

Price nodded. "Day and night. I don't know which is more tired, my mind or my butt." He lifted his gaze to me again. "Have you got anything else to drink? How about beer?"

"No, sorry. Couldn't get a liquor license."

He sighed. "Just as well. It might make me sleepy. But I sure could go for a beer right now. One sip, to clean my mouth out."

He picked up his coffee cup, and I smiled and started to turn away.

But then he wasn't holding a cup. He was holding a Budweiser can, and for an instant I could smell the tang of a newly-popped beer.

The mirage was only there for maybe two seconds. I blinked, and Price was holding a cup again. "Just as well," he said, and put it down.

I glanced over at Cheryl, then at Dennis. Neither one was paying attention. Damn! I thought. I'm too young to be either losin' my eyesight or my senses! "Uh . . ." I said, or some other stupid noise.

"One more cup?" Price asked. "Then I'd better hit the road again."

My hand was shaking as I picked it up, but if Price noticed

he didn't say anything.

"Want anything to eat?" Cheryl asked him. "How about a bowl of beef stew?"

He shook his head. "No, thanks. The sooner I get back on the road, the better it'll be."

Suddenly Dennis swivelled toward him, giving him a cold stare that only cops and drill sergeants can muster. "Back on the *road?*" He snorted. "Fella, you ever been in a tornado before? I'm gonna escort those nice people to the Holiday Inn about fifteen miles back. If you're smart, that's where you'll spend the night, too. No use tryin' to—"

"*No.*" Price's voice was rock-steady. "I'll be spending the night behind the wheel."

Dennis' eyes narrowed. "How come you're in such a hurry? Not runnin' from anybody, are you?"

"Nightcrawlers," Cheryl said.

Price turned toward her like he'd been slapped across the face, and I saw what might've been a spark of fear in his eyes.

Cheryl motioned toward the lighter Price had laid on the counter, beside the pack of Kools. It was a beat-up silver Zippo, and inscribed across it was *Nightcrawlers* with the symbol of two crossed rifles beneath it. "Sorry," she said. "I just noticed that, and I wondered what it was."

Price put the lighter away. "I was in 'Nam," he told her. "Everybody in my unit got one."

"Hey." There was suddenly new respect in Dennis' voice. "You a *vet?*"

Price paused so long I didn't think he was going to answer. In the quiet, I heard the little girl tell her mother that the fries were "ucky." Price said, "Yes."

"How about that! Hey, I wanted to go myself, but I got a high number and things were windin' down about that time, anyway. Did you see any action?"

A faint, bitter smile passed over Price's mouth. "Too much."

"What? Infantry? Marines? Rangers?"

Price picked up his third cup of coffee, swallowed some and put it down. He closed his eyes for a few seconds, and when they opened they were vacant and fixed on nothing. "Night-crawlers," he said quietly. "Special unit. Deployed to recon Charlie positions in questionable villages." He said it like he was reciting from a manual. "We did a lot of crawling through rice paddies and jungles in the dark."

"Bet you laid a few of them Vietcong out, didn't you?" Dennis got up and came over to sit a few places away from the man. "Man, I was behind you guys all the way. I wanted you to stay in there and fight it out!"

Price was silent. Thunder echoed over the diner. The lights weakened for a few seconds; when they came back on, they seemed to have lost some of their wattage. The place was dimmer than before. Price's head slowly turned toward Dennis, with the inexorable motion of a machine. I was thankful I didn't have to take the full force of Price's dead blue eyes, and I saw Dennis wince. "I *should've* stayed," he said. "I should be there right now, buried in the mud of a rice paddy with the eight other men in my patrol."

"Oh," Dennis blinked. "Sorry. I didn't mean to—"

"I came home," Price continued calmly, "by stepping on the bodies of my friends. Do you want to know what that's like, Mr. Trooper?"

"The war's over," I told him. "No need to bring it back."

Price smiled grimly, but his gaze remained fixed on Dennis. "Some say it's over. I say it came back with the men who were there. Like me. *Especially* like me." Price paused. The wind howled around the door, and the lightning illuminated for an instant the thrashing woods across the highway. "The mud was up to our knees, Mr. Trooper," he said. "We were moving across a rice paddy in the dark, being real careful not to step on the bamboo stakes we figured were planted there. Then the first shots started: *pop pop pop*—like firecrackers going off. One of the Nightcrawlers fired off a flare, and we saw the Cong ringing us. We'd walked right into hell, Mr. Trooper. Somebody shouted, 'Charlie's in the light!' and we started firing, trying to punch a hole through them. But they were everywhere. As soon as one went down, three more took his place. Grenades were going off, and more flares, and people were screaming as they got hit. I took a bullet in the thigh and another through the hand. I lost my rifle, and somebody fell on top of me with half his head missing."

"Uh...listen," I said. "You don't have to—"

"I *want* to, friend." He glanced quickly at me, then back to Dennis. I think I cringed when his gaze pierced me. "I want to tell it all. They were fighting and screaming and dying all around me, and I felt the bullets tug at my clothes as they passed through. I know I was screaming, too, but what was coming out of my mouth sounded bestial. I ran. The only way I could save my own life was to step on their bodies and drive them down into the mud. I heard some of them choke and blubber as I put my boot on their faces. I knew all those guys like brothers...but at that moment they were only pieces of meat. I ran. A gunship chopper came over the paddy and laid down some fire, and that's how I got out. Alone." He bent his face closer toward the other man's. "And you'd better believe I'm in that rice paddy in 'Nam every time I close my eyes. You'd better believe the men I left back there don't rest easy. So you keep your opinions about 'Nam and being 'behind you guys' to yourself, Mr. Trooper. I don't want to hear that bullshit. Got it?"

Dennis sat very still. He wasn't used to being talked to like that, not even from a 'Nam vet, and I saw the shadow of anger pass over his face.

Price's hands were trembling as he brought a little bottle out of his jeans pocket. He shook two blue-and-orange capsules out onto the counter, took them both with a swallow of coffee and then recapped the bottle and put it away. The flesh of his face looked almost ashen in the dim light.

"I know you boys had a rough time," Dennis said, "but that's no call to show disrespect to the law."

"The law," Price repeated. "Yeah. Right. Bull*shit*."

"There are women and children present," I reminded him. "Watch your language."

Price rose from his seat. He looked like a skeleton with just a little extra skin on the bones. "Mister, I haven't slept for more than thirty-six hours. My nerves are shot. I don't mean to cause trouble, but when some fool says he *understands*, I feel like kicking his teeth down his throat—because no one who wasn't there can pretend to understand." He glanced at Ray, Lindy, and the kids. "Sorry, folks. Don't mean to disturb you. Friend, how much do I owe?" He started digging for his wallet.

Dennis slid slowly from his seat and stood with his hands on his hips. "Hold it." He used his trooper's voice again. "If you think I'm lettin' you walk out of here high on pills and needin' sleep, you're crazy. I don't want to be scrapin' you off the highway."

Price paid him no attention. He took a couple of dollars from his wallet and put them on the counter. I didn't touch them. "Those pills will help keep me awake," Price said finally. "Once I get on the road, I'll be fine."

"Fella, I wouldn't let you go if it was high noon and not a cloud in the sky. I sure as hell don't want to clean up after the accident you're gonna have. Now why don't you come along to the Holiday Inn and—"

Price laughed grimly. "Mister Trooper, the last place you want me staying is at a motel." He cocked his head to one side. "I was in a motel in Florida a couple of nights ago, and I think I left my room a little untidy. Step aside and let me pass."

"A motel in Florida?" Dennis nervously licked his lower lip. "What the hell you talkin' about?"

"Nightmares and reality, Mr. Trooper. The point where they cross. A couple of nights ago, they crossed at a motel. I wasn't going to let myself sleep. I was just going to rest for a little while, but I didn't know they'd come so *fast*." A mocking smile played at the edges of his mouth, but his eyes were tortured. "You don't want me staying at that Holiday Inn, Mr. Trooper. You really don't. Now step aside."

I saw Dennis' hand settle on the butt of his revolver. His fingers unsnapped the fold of leather that secured the gun in the holster. I stared at him numbly. My God, I thought. What's goin' on? My heart had started pounding so hard I was sure everybody could hear it. Ray and Lindy were watching, and Cheryl was backing away behind the counter.

Price and Dennis faced each other for a moment, as the rain whipped against the windows and thunder boomed like shell-fire. Then Price sighed, as if resigning himself to something. He said, "I think I want a t-bone steak. Extra-rare. How 'bout it?" He looked at me.

"A steak?" My voice was shaking. "We don't have any t-bone—"

Price's gaze shifted to the counter right in front of me. I heard a sizzle. The aroma of cooking meat drifted up to me.

"Oh...wow," Cheryl whispered.

A large t-bone steak lay on the countertop, pink and oozing blood. You could've fanned a menu in my face and I would've keeled over. Wisps of smoke were rising from the steak.

The steak began to fade, until it was only an outline on the counter. The lines of oozing blood vanished. After the mirage was gone, I could still smell the meat—and that's how I knew I wasn't crazy.

Dennis' mouth hung open. Ray had stood up from the booth to look, and his wife's face was the color of spoiled milk. The whole world seemed to be balanced on a point of silence—until the wail of the wind jarred me back to my senses.

"I'm getting good at it," Price said softly. "I'm getting very, very good. Didn't start happening to me until about a year ago. I've found four other 'Nam vets who can do the same thing. What's in your head comes true—as simple as that. Of course, the images only last for a few seconds—as long as I'm awake. I mean, I've found out that those other men were drenched by a chemical spray we call Howdy Doody—because it made you stiffen up and jerk like you were hanging on strings. I got hit with it near Khe Sahn. That shit almost suffocated me. It fell like black tar, and it burned the land down to a paved parking lot." He stared at Dennis. "You don't want me around here, Mr. Trooper. Not with the body count I've still got in *my* head."

"You...were at...that motel, near Daytona Beach?"

Price closed his eyes. A vein had begun beating at his right temple, royal blue against the pallor of his flesh. "Oh Jesus," he whispered. "I fell asleep, and I couldn't wake myself up. I was having the nightmare. The same one. I was locked in it, and I was trying to scream myself awake." He shuddered, and two tears ran slowly down his cheeks. *"Oh,"* he said, and flinched as if remembering something horrible. "They...they were coming through the door when I woke up. Tearing the door right off its hinges. I woke up...just as one of them was pointing his rifle at me. And I saw his face. I saw his muddy, misshapen face." His eyes suddenly jerked open. "I didn't know they'd come so fast."

"Who?" I asked him. *"Who* came so fast?"

"The Nightcrawlers," Price said, his face void of expression, masklike. "Dear God...maybe if I'd stayed asleep a second more. But I ran again, and I left those people dead in that motel."

"You're gonna come with me." Dennis started pulling his gun from the holster. Price's head snapped toward him. "I don't know what kinda fool game you're—"

He stopped, staring at the gun he held.

It wasn't a gun anymore. It was an oozing mass of hot rubber. Dennis cried out and slung the thing from his hand. The molten mess hit the floor with a pulpy *splat*.

"I'm leaving now." Price's voice was calm. "Thank you for the coffee." He walked past Dennis, toward the door.

Dennis grasped a bottle of ketchup from the counter. Cheryl cried out, *"Don't!"* but it was too late. Dennis was already swinging the bottle. It hit the back of Price's skull and burst open, spewing ketchup everywhere. Price staggered forward, his knees buckling. When he went down, his skull hit the floor with a noise like a watermelon being dropped. His body began jerking involuntarily.

"Got him!" Dennis shouted triumphantly. "Got that crazy bastard, didn't I?"

Lindy was holding the little girl in her arms. The boy craned his neck to see. Ray said nervously, "You didn't kill him, did you?"

"He's not dead," I told him. I looked over at the gun; it was solid again. Dennis scooped it up and aimed it at Price, whose body continued to jerk. Just like Howdy Doody, I thought. Then Price stopped moving. "He's dead!" Cheryl's voice was near frantic. "Oh God, you killed him, Dennis!"

Dennis prodded the body with the toe of his boot, then bent down. "Naw. His eyes are movin' back and forth behind the lids." Dennis touched his wrist to check the pulse, then abruptly pulled his own hand away. "Jesus Christ! He's as cold as a meat-locker!" He took Price's pulse and whistled. "Goin' like a racehorse at the Derby."

I touched the place on the counter where the mirage-steak had been. My fingers came away slightly greasy, and I could smell the cooked meat on them. At that instant, Price twitched. Dennis scuttled away from him like a crab. Price made a gasping, choking noise.

"What'd he say?" Cheryl asked. "He said something!"

"No he didn't." Dennis stuck him in the ribs with his pistol. "Come on. Get up."

"Get him out of here," I said. "I don't want him—"

Cheryl shushed me. "Listen. Can you hear that?"

I heard only the roar and crash of the storm.

"Don't you *hear* it?" she asked me. Her eyes were getting scared and glassy.

"Yes!" Ray said. "Yes! Listen!"

Then I did hear something, over the noise of the keening wind. It was a distant *chuk-chuk-chuk,* steadily growing louder and closer. The wind covered the noise for a minute, then it came back: CHUK-CHUK-CHUK, almost overhead.

"It's a helicopter!" Ray peered through the window. "Somebody's got a helicopter out there!"

"Ain't nobody can fly a chopper in a storm!" Dennis told him. The noise of the rotors swelled and faded, swelled and faded...and stopped.

On the floor, Price shivered and began to contort into a fetal position. His mouth opened, his face twisted in what appeared to be agony.

Thunder spoke. A red fireball rose up from the woods across the road and hung lazily in the sky for a few seconds before it descended toward the diner. As it fell, the fireball exploded soundlessly into a white, glaring eye of light that almost blinded me.

Price said something in a garbled, panicked voice. His eyes were tightly closed, and he had squeezed up with his arms around his knees.

Dennis rose to his feet; he squinted as the eye of light fell toward the parking-lot and winked out in a puddle of water. Another fireball floated up from the woods, and again blossomed into painful glare.

Dennis turned toward me. "I heard him." His voice was raspy. "He said...'Charlie's in the light.'"

As the second flare fell to the ground and illuminated the parking-lot, I thought I saw figures crossing the road. They walked stiff-legged, in an eerie cadence. The flare went out.

"Wake him up," I heard myself whisper. "Dennis...dear God...*wake him up.*"

IV

Dennis stared stupidly at me, and I started to jump across the counter to get to Price myself.

A gout of flame leaped in the parking-lot. Sparks marched across the concrete. I shouted, "Get down!" and twisted around to push Cheryl back behind the shelter of the counter.

"What the *hell*—" Dennis said.

He didn't finish. There was a metallic thumping of bullets hitting the gas pumps and the cars. I knew if that gas blew we were all dead. My truck shuddered with the impact of slugs, and I saw the whole thing explode as I ducked behind the counter. Then the windows blew inward with a Godawful crash, and the diner was full of flying glass, swirling wind and sheets of rain. I heard Lindy scream, and both the kids were crying and I think I was shouting something myself.

The lights had gone out, and the only illumination was the

reflection of red neon off the concrete and the glow of the fluorescents over the gas pumps. Bullets whacked into the wall, and crockery shattered as if it had been hit with a hammer. Napkins and sugar packets were flying everywhere.

Cheryl was holding onto me as if her fingers were nails sunk to my bones. Her eyes were wide and dazed, and she kept trying to speak. Her mouth was working, but nothing came out.

There was another explosion as one of the other cars blew. The whole place shook, and I almost puked with fear.

Another hail of bullets hit the wall. They were tracers, and they jumped and ricocheted like white-hot cigarette butts. One of them sang off the edge of a shelf and fell to the floor about three feet away from me. The glowing slug began to fade, like the beer can and the mirage-steak. I put my hand out to find it, but all I felt was splinters of glass and crockery. A phantom bullet, I thought. Real enough to cause damage and death— and then gone.

You don't want me around here, Mr. Trooper, Price had warned. *Not with the body count I've got in my head.*

The firing stopped. I got free of Cheryl and said, "You stay right *here.*" Then I looked up over the counter and saw my truck and the station-wagon on fire, the flames being whipped by the wind. Rain slapped me across the face as it swept in where the windowglass used to be. I saw Price lying still huddled on the floor, with pieces of glass all around him. His hands were clawing the air, and in the flickering red neon his face was contorted, his eyes still closed. The pool of ketchup around his head made him look like his skull had been split open. He was peering into Hell, and I averted my eyes before I lost my own mind.

Ray and Lindy and the two children had huddled under the table of their booth. The woman was sobbing brokenly. I looked at Dennis, lying a few feet from Price: he was sprawled on his face, and there were four holes punched through his back. It was not ketchup that ran in rivulets around Dennis' body. His right arm was outflung, and the fingers twitched around the gun he gripped.

Another flare sailed up from the woods like a Fourth-of-July sparkler.

When the light brightened, I saw them: at least five figures, maybe more. They were crouched over, coming across the parking-lot—but slowly, the speed of nightmares. Their clothes flapped and hung around them, and the flare's light glanced off their helmets. They were carrying weapons—rifles, I guessed. I couldn't see their faces, and that was for the best.

On the floor, Price moaned. I heard him say "light...in the light..."

The flare hung right over the diner. And then I knew what was going on. *We* were in the light. We were all caught in Price's nightmare, and the Nightcrawlers that Price had left in the mud were fighting the battle again—the same way it had been fought at the Pines Haven Motor Inn. The Nightcrawlers had come back to life, powered by Price's guilt and whatever that Howdy Doody shit had done to him.

And we were in the light, where Charlie had been out in that rice paddy.

There was a noise like castanets clicking. Dots of fire arced through the broken windows and thudded into the counter. The stools squealed as they were hit and spun. The cash register rang and the drawer popped open, and then the entire register blew apart and bills and coins scattered. I ducked my head, but a wasp of fire—I don't know what, a bit of metal or glass maybe—sliced my left cheek open from ear to upper lip. I fell to the floor behind the counter with blood running down my face.

A blast shook the rest of the cups, saucers, plates and glasses off the shelves. The whole roof buckled inward, throwing loose ceiling tiles, light fixtures and pieces of metal framework.

We were all going to die. I knew it, right then. Those things were going to destroy us. But I thought of the pistol in Dennis' hand, and of Price lying near the door. If we were caught in Price's nightmare and the blow from the ketchup bottle had broken something in his skull, then the only way to stop his dream was to kill him.

I'm no hero. I was about to piss in my pants, but I knew I was the only one who could move. I jumped up and scrambled over the counter, falling beside Dennis and wrenching at that pistol. Even in death, Dennis had a strong grip. Another blast came, along the wall to my right. The heat of it scorched me, and the shockwave skidded me across the floor through glass and rain and blood.

But I had that pistol in my hand.

I heard Ray shout, "Look out!"

In the doorway, silhouetted by flames, was a skeletal thing wearing muddy green rags. It wore a dented-in helmet and carried a corroded, slime-covered rifle. Its face was gaunt and shadowy, the features hidden behind a scum of rice-paddy muck. It began to lift the rifle to fire at me — slowly, slowly...

I got the safety off the pistol and fired twice, without aiming. A spark leapt off the helmet as one of the bullets was deflected, but the figure staggered backward and into the conflagration of the station-wagon, where it seemed to melt into ooze before it vanished.

More tracers were coming in. Cheryl's Volkswagen shuddered, the tires blowing out almost in unison. The state trooper car was already bullet-riddled and sitting on flats.

Another Nightcrawler, this one without a helmet and with slime covering the skull where the hair had been, rose up beyond the window and fired its rifle. I heard the bullet whine past my ear, and as I took aim I saw its bony finger tightening on the trigger again.

A skillet flew over my head and hit the thing's shoulder, spoiling its aim. For an instant the skillet stuck in the Nightcrawler's body, as if the figure itself was made out of mud. I fired once...twice...and saw pieces of matter fly from the thing's chest. What might've been a mouth opened in a soundless scream, and the thing slithered out of sight.

I looked around. Cheryl was standing behind the counter, weaving on her feet, her face white with shock. "Get down!" I shouted, and she ducked for cover.

I crawled to Price, shook him hard. His eyes would not open.

"Wake up!" I begged him. "Wake up, damn you!" And then I pressed the barrel of the pistol against Price's head. Dear God, I didn't want to kill anybody, but I knew I was going to have to blow the Nightcrawlers right out of his brain. I hesitated — too long.

Something smashed into my left collarbone. I heard the bone snap like a broomstick being broken. The force of the shot slid me back against the counter and jammed me between two bullet-pocked stools. I lost the gun, and there was a roaring in my head that deafened me.

I don't know how long I was out. My left arm felt like dead meat. All the cars in the lot were burning, and there was a hole in the diner's roof that a tractor-trailer truck could've dropped through. Rain was sweeping into my face, and when I wiped my eyes clear I saw them, standing over Price.

There were eight of them. The two I thought I'd killed were back. They trailed weeds, and their boots and ragged clothes were covered with mud. They stood in silence, staring down at their living comrade.

I was too tired to scream. I couldn't even whimper. I just watched.

Price's hands lifted into the air. He reached for the Night-crawlers, and then his eyes opened. His pupils were dead white, surrounded by scarlet.

"End it," he whispered. "End it..."

One of the Nightcrawlers aimed its rifle and fired. Price jerked. Another Nightcrawler fired, and then they were all firing, point-blank, into Price's body. Price thrashed and clutched at his head, but there was no blood; the phantom bullets weren't hitting him.

The Nightcrawlers began to ripple and fade. I saw the flames of the burning cars through their bodies. The figures became transparent, floating in vague outlines. Price had awakened too fast at the Pines Haven Motor Inn, I realized; if he had remained asleep, the creatures of his nightmares would've ended it there, at that Florida motel. They were killing him in front of me — or he was allowing them to end it, and I think that's what he must've wanted for a long, long time.

He shuddered, his mouth releasing a half-moan, half-sigh. It sounded almost like relief.

I saw his face. His eyes were closed, and I think he must've found peace at last.

V

A trucker hauling lumber from Mobile to Birmingham saw the burning cars. I don't even remember what he looked like.

Ray was cut up by glass, but his wife and the kids were okay. Physically, I mean. Mentally, I couldn't say.

Cheryl went into the hospital for awhile. I got a postcard from her with the Golden Gate Bridge on the front. She promised she'd write and let me know how she was doing, but I doubt if I'll ever hear from her. She was the best waitress I ever had, and I wish her luck.

The police asked me a thousand questions, and I told the story the same way every time. I found out later that no bullets or shrapnel were ever dug out of the walls or the cars or Dennis' body — just like in the case of that motel massacre. There was no bullet in me, though my collarbone was snapped clean in two.

Price had died of a massive brain hemorrhage. It looked, the police told me, as if it had exploded in his skull.

I closed the diner. Farm life is fine. Alma understands, and we don't talk about it.

But I never showed the police what I found, and I don't know exactly why not.

I picked up Price's wallet in the mess. Behind a picture of a smiling young woman holding a baby there was a folded piece of paper. On that paper were the names of four men.

Beside one name, Price had written DANGEROUS.

I've found four other 'Nam vets who can do the same thing, Price had said.

I sit up at night a lot, thinking about that and looking at those names. Those men had gotten a dose of that Howdy Doody shit in a foreign place they hadn't wanted to be, fighting a war that turned out to be one of those crossroads of nightmare and reality. I've changed my mind about 'Nam, because I understand now that the worst of the fighting is still going on, in the battlefields of memory.

A Yankee who called himself Tompkins came to my house one May morning and flashed me an ID that said he worked for a veterans' association. He was very soft-spoken and polite, but he had deep-set eyes that were almost black, and he never blinked. He asked me all about Price, seemed real interested in picking my brain of every detail. I told him the police had the story, and I couldn't add any more to it. Then I turned the tables and asked him about Howdy Doody. He smiled in a puzzled kind of way and said he'd never heard of any chemical defoliant called that. No such thing, he said. Like I said, he was very polite.

But I know the shape of a gun tucked into a shoulder-holster. Tompkins was wearing one, under his seersucker coat. I never could find any veterans' association that knew anything about him, either.

Maybe I should give that list of names to the police. Maybe I will. Or maybe I'll try to find those four men myself, and try to make sense out of what's being hidden.

I don't think Price was evil. No. He was just scared, and who can blame a man for running from his own nightmares? I like to believe that, in the end, Price had the courage to face the Nightcrawlers, and in committing suicide he saved our lives.

The newspapers, of course, never got the real story. They called Price a 'Nam vet who'd gone crazy, killed six people in a Florida motel and then killed a state trooper in a shootout at Big Bob's diner and gas stop.

But I know where Price is buried. They sell little American flags at the five-and-dime in Mobile. I'm alive, and I can spare the change.

And then I've got to find out how much courage *I* have.

Somebody Like You

Dennis Etchison

Even allowing for hyperbole and other factors you might cite to suggest something less than absolute accuracy, what can you do about a writer who gets this *kind of praise:* Whispers' *Stuart David Schiff: "The only author who has appeared in all... my anthologies." Novelist Ramsey Campbell: "The finest writer of short stories now working in this field..." Reviewer Karl Wagner: "May well be the finest writer of psychological horror this genre has seen." Critic Doug Winter: "Perhaps America's premier writer of horror short stories." Anthologist Charles L. Grant: "The best short story writer in the field today, bar none." Your editor, scribbling in the guy's name, one of the first five he sought for* Masques?

I'll tell you what you can do about him. You can read Dennis Etchison's writing, short and *long form, sometimes "by Jack Martin," as often as your various emotions can take it. Because the praise is accurate.*

A clue to enjoying the work of this pleasant Californian (born in Stockton, March 30, 1943) is found in my careful use of the term "various emotions," since Etchison has a knack for arousing emotions ostensibly restricted to "mainstream" fiction. Read his handsome collection, The Dark Country. *His characters become evocatively involved in situations which do more than scare, appal, caution, revulse or shock you. In common with people you know, they, or their circumstances, elicit reactions that concern, bewilder, surprise or "inevitabilitize" you. You feel their loneliness, differentness, ignorance, unpredictability or apartness, by turn—turn of some nightmarish tool the nerve-jabbing dentist never quite lets you see.*

At least several of your various emotions are about to be probed in this new Dennis Etchison story, "Somebody Like You." P.S.: You'll reread *it...*

One morning they were lying together in his bed.

"Hi," she said.

Then her lids closed, all but a quarter of an inch, and her eyes were rolling and her lips were twitching again.

Later, when her pupils drifted back into position, he saw that she was looking at him.

"What time is it?"

He kept looking at her.

She kept looking at him.

"I was watching you sleep," he said.

"Mm?"

With some difficulty she turned onto her back. He saw her wince.

Finally she said, "How long?"

"A couple of hours," he guessed.

They waited. Within and without the room there was the sound of the ocean. It was like breathing.

"Sometimes I talk in my sleep," she said.

"I know."

"Well?"

"Well what?"

"Aren't you going to tell me?"

She tried to turn her face to him. He watched her long, slender fingers feel for the pillow. She made a frown.

"Hurt?" he said.

"Why won't you tell me what I said?"

"That's it," he said. "You said that it hurts."

"It does," she said.

"What does?"

"The place where they cut us apart."

He said, "Are you sleeping?"

"Mm," she said.

He never knew.

*   *   *

She did not come back.

He tried calling her for several days running, but could not get through.

Then one afternoon she phoned to say that it would be nice if he were there.

He agreed.

When she did not answer his knock, he pried loose the screen and let himself in.

The cat was dozing on the bare boards in the living room, its jowls puffed and its eyes slitting in the heat. The bedroom door was ajar, and as he walked in he saw her curled there on the blue sheets. One of her hands was still on the telephone and the other was wrapped protectively around her body.

He sat down, but she did not see him.

More than once he climbed over her and opened and closed the door to draw air into the room. He ran water, tuned the television so that he could hear it and bunched the pillows behind him on the bed, but she did not want to wake up.

When the sun fell low, he drew the thin curtains so that it would not glare on her and leaned forward and fanned her face for a long time with the folded TV log. Her hair was pasted to the side of her head in damp whorls, and her ears contained the most delicate convolutions.

It was dark when she finally roused. Her eyes were glazed over, so that they appeared to be covered with fine, transparent membranes.

She smiled.

"How are you?" she said.

"What was it this time?" he asked. "You were breathing hard and your mouth was going a mile a minute, but I couldn't understand anything." He waited. "Do you remember?"

She seemed to founder, feeling for the thread that would lead her back into it before it dissolved away.

"I thought we were at *his* place," she said, "and I kept trying to tell you that you had to get out of there before he came home. I couldn't wake up."

She lay there smiling.

"Isn't that funny?" she said.

"Who?" he said. But already it was too late.

* * *

He spent the next morning rearranging his place.
Perhaps that would work.

He tied back the frayed blue curtains, cleaned the glass all the way to the low ceiling, spread an animal skin over the divan and moved it close to the bay window; she had liked to sit, sometimes for hours, staring out into the haze that came to settle over the water this time of year. He plumped up the cushions on the long couch and positioned it against the opposite wall, so that they would be able to be together later as they watched the glow.

He washed dishes, piled newspapers in the closet, hid his socks, and even found a small notions table and placed it next to the window so that she would not have to get up so often. Then he got out the plywood he had bought and slipped it between the mattress and box springs. She was right; it was too soft a bed in which to sleep comfortably, though he had not realized that until she mentioned it.

He found himself padding from room to room, trying to see, to feel as she would. *Yes*, he thought, *it will be better this way, much better, and nothing will hurt.*

And yet there was something that was not quite right, something somewhere that was still off-center, vaguely out of place or missing altogether. But the morning passed and, whatever it was, he did not spot it.

The afternoon came and went, but she did not show.

He tried calling. Each time the girl at the answering service screened his ring. She had strict instructions, she admitted at last, to let only one person through, and did not even wait to take his message.

* * *

It was twilight when he got there. There were the sounds of

unseen people within their separate houses, and he seemed to hear music playing nearby.

I sing this song of you, he thought.

He knocked, but there was no answer.

He shook his head, trying to remember her.

When he began to pry his way in, he discovered that it was not locked.

The living room was warm and the air stale, as though the door and windows had not been opened in a long time. He was nearly to the bedroom when he noticed her stretched out on the old pillows, almost hidden behind the front door.

He saw that her eyes were only partly closed, her corneas glistening between the lids. Her hands and arms were wrapped around herself, her head and neck this time, in the manner of a child in a disaster drill.

"Didn't you hear me knocking?" he said to her.

Her eyes popped open and she looked up, startled, almost as if she expected to see herself. Then she sank back again.

He went to her.

He moved his hand up to her face, ran his finger along her cheek. She made a sleepy sound.

"Hm?" he asked again.

"What?" she said. "Oh, I thought the sound was coming from the other place."

"What other place?" he said.

When she did not answer, he bent to kiss her.

I sing this song of you.

*   *   *

The receiver had time to warm in his hand before he tried again.

The girl at the answering service cut in.

He muffled his voice this time, trying to disguise it. "Let it ring through," he said forcefully.

"Who's calling, please?"

"Who do you think?" he said. "I'm sure she told you to expect my call."

A surprised pause, a rustling of papers. "Let me see, this must be. . ."

She mentioned a name he had never heard before.

"Of course it is. Are you new there?"

She hesitated. In the background he heard buzzes, voices interrupting other calls and messages being taken and posted.

"I'm going to dial again now, and I want you to let it ring through," he said. "Do you understand?"

"Yes, of course," the girl said quickly. "Um, wait a sec," she added, reading from a paper. "I — I'm afraid she's not in this afternoon. I'm sorry."

He darkened. Then, "She did leave a reference number, didn't she?"

"I'll check. Yes, here it is. Well, not exactly. She said to tell you she'll be at 'the other place.' She said you'll know."

He almost gave up. Then he said, "Right. But which one? It could be either of two. Now don't tell me she's going to hang me up with one of her guessing games again."

It was hopeless, but he waited.

"Look," he said, "this is an emergency, for God's sake, and I really don't have time for her to get back to me."

"Um, I'll see. I'm not the one who took the call. Hold, please, and I'll see if I can locate the girl who worked that shift."

The phone went dead for a moment.

I don't believe it, he thought. *It's working.*

She came back on the line.

"It was someone on the late shift," she announced. "I guess she's left messages for you several times in the last week or so. It looks like it was always in the middle of the night, and since you didn't call they're all still on the board. The first one I have here — I'll just read it to you. It says, 'Tell him to meet me at the studio on Ocean Front.' Okay? That might be the place, do you suppose?"

"All right," he said.

"I'm sorry. We aren't usually so confused around here. It's just that — well, she's left so many messages for you, and when you never called, I guess the other girl stuck them in with last week's."

"Thanks," he said.

"Thank you for calling. We were beginning to wonder if you'd ever — "

He hung up.

* * *

She was having a hard time waking up.

Her lips were parted very slightly, and a narrow, opaque crack of whiteness shone between her eyelids. She resisted the hand on her shoulder, her neck, her head with faint, inarticulate protest until she could stand it no longer.

Her face twisted and she tried to rise, struggling to focus her vision.

"What's the matter?" she managed to say.

"You were asleep a long time," he told her, his voice more gentle and tender than it had ever been before. "I've been waiting a couple of hours. It's starting to get pretty late."

He caressed the back of her head, his thumb behind her ear.

"The way your eyes were jerking around, you must have been dreaming."

She shook her head, trying to clear it.

"It seemed like someone was outside, trying to get in," she said.

"That was me, I'm afraid."

"Oh. Then that part was true, after all." Her eyes swam, then held on him. "But why would it be you? This is your place. Didn't you have your key?"

"I — forgot it."

"Oh." She stretched. "Never mind. It was just so strange. So real. I thought someone else was here with me. And you know what? He looked a lot like you."

"So where is he, in the closet?"

"Don't worry — he wasn't as good looking. Only he wouldn't leave, even though he knew you were going to get here any minute. Isn't that funny?"

"Like an open grave," he said uneasily.

"I know," she said, as if it really mattered.

She looked at him, unblinking, in that way she had, until he said something.

"So?"

"So that's all, I guess. I don't know why, but I think I'd like to remember it." And, quite suddenly, tears sprang from her eyes. "All of it."

"Take it easy, will you?"

He moved to her.

"He was trying to be so good to me. Except that it was you, all the time it was you."

"I love you," he said.

"And you know I need you, too, don't you? So much. I don't know what's wrong with me, I really don't. I promise I'll try—"

He stood and quieted her by pressing her head to his body. Her arms went around his waist and they held each other.

"I know you will," he said. "Don't worry about anything. I'm here with you now, and I wouldn't want you any other way."

* * *

He went down the stairs from the loft bedroom.

The thick blue drapes, the richest blue he had ever seen, were set off perfectly by the white walls and ceiling, and as he passed them he considered drawing the cord on the magnificent view of the Pacific he knew they would reveal.

Instead he turned and stood for a moment before the mirror that was mounted below the loft, angled to provide a view of the entire room.

In it he saw the cat arising peacefully from a nap on the deep carpeting. He smiled, his lips curling with satisfaction at the couches, the chairs, the superb appointments.

He stood transfixed, listening to the surf as it washed in around the supports of the house. He almost leaned over to activate the custom stereo system, but could not bring himself to break the spell of the gentle rushing, breathing sound. It almost seemed to be coming from within the house, as well, and it made him remember.

The earliest parts of the dream were already beginning to fade.

Still he recalled tossing in a bed somewhere, a lonely bed to which no one ever came. There had been the sound of waves there, too. He had been dreaming of a girl who would need him as much as he needed her. And when he was finished she did; she needed someone; she needed to be taken care of, and that part had come out right, had been easy enough. . . .

He had forgotten, of course, that she would have dreams of her own.

Soon she needed other things, like more and more time away from the hot little house he had imagined for her. In fact she needed something even better than his own modest beach cottage. It was always the way. Except that this time he had found the street of her dreams, had driven up and down until he saw her car parked here in the shade of the port. . .

The carport of a house where someone lived. Someone even better suited to her needs.

This time it would take.

He shut his eyes as he dreamed the feel of fine knit against his legs, the designer shoes with the high-rise heels, the hand-tailored shirt of imported silk, the styled hair and the rest of it, all of it, the way she wanted it to be, the look. There would be more details. But they could be arranged, too. Of course they could. Why not? It was worth the effort.

She needed him, didn't she?

She needs somebody, he thought.

Wavering before the mirror as he tossed and turned, he opened his eyes. He smiled.

Somebody like you.

Samhain: Full Moon   and
I Have Made My Bones Secure

Ardath Mayhar

Can you identify these writers? (1) Author of 12 published novels, including one that was Number 1 on the Locus *best-seller lists for three months and another which made the* American Library Association Best Books for Young Adults *list* in the same year; *(2) a poet who took top regional prizes for eight years in succession and won awards from half a dozen other major competitions; (3) the writer of imaginative horror and fantasy yarns published in* Weirdbook, Twilight Zone, Asimov's SF *and in such anthologies as* Swords Against Darkness #4 *and* Alfred Hitchcock's Stories to be Read with the Lights On; *(4) the prose-writer/poet with a name that sounds straight out of "Star Wars"?*

Yes; you guessed they were all one person. And the novels cited were Golden Dream: A Fuzzy Odyssey *and* Soul-Singer of Tyrnos.

But now you have a better idea of how supremely talented Ardath Mayhar is.

Whether it's because Texan Ardath (born February 20, 1930) belongs to both MENSA and Small Press Writers & Artists Organization, mother of two and stepmother of another pair, or because those who can't *look dubiously at those writers who produce prodigiously, her light has been hiding under a bushel on her Chireno farm far too long.*

Cases in point: the critically-acclaimed Khi to Freedom *and her newest novel,* The Saga of Grittel Sundotha. *More immediately: the eerie, accepting horror of "Samhain: Full Moon"*—Mayhar: *"So last night I sat down after supper... and it's what got pulled out of the somewhere into the here"*—*and "I Have Made My Bones Secure." In common, extra-ordinary beauty and a spellbinding, human realism which suggest, far better than I can, the distinct likelihood that Ardath Mayhar is one of the major writing talents of our time.*

She sat, hands busy with a homely task,
and watched a cold white moon trail wisps of cloud
across the east. The last light died away,
leaving the meadows shadowed, ghostly trees
lurking about her house, and crawling mist
in chilly layers between hill and hill.
She shuddered—it's not good to be alone
by night at any time, but at Samhain—
oh, infinitely worse!
                        A rasping breeze
rattled its fingers in the frost-killed vines.
She put away her sewing, took a plate
of bread, a cup of milk, and set them out
upon the doorstone, keeping her eyes turned
up to the stone-crowned hilltop.
                                  "Let them stay!"
she whispered. "Let them keep their place tonight,
but if they come, let me not be aware!"

She barred the door, but still the mocking moon
peered through a crevice with its frozen eye,
reminding her of gravestones slipped aside,
of tattered flesh, stark bone, and flapping rags
that might come down the hill, scratch at her door,
plead for a place beside her tiny fire.
A year ago her man had barred the door,
made up the fire, poured spirits in the tea,
and they had huddled, warm and comforted
against the pleas and mewlings in the night:
but now he lay above—up there with them—
and all the children made their lives afar.
She pulled her shawl about her scrawny arms,
drawn to the window, staring up the hill
at all those stones, stark black against the moon...
they moved in eery dance!
                          A strangled cry
squeezed from her throat; her hands clenched at her breast

until the ancient fabric of her gown
was crushed by frantic fingers, and it tore.
Dark shapes moved there, above, to turn their steps
down to the foot-worn path; she moved away,
knelt by her bed, pulled pillows to her ears,
and waited, pulses hammering with fear.

Cloud crossed the moon; a sleepy raven croaked
a protest as the shuffling footsteps passed
its roosting-place. A file of misty shapes
drifted across the path, borne on the wind,
but not one face was turned to watch them go,
not one looked up to see the flying cloud,
or bat-shapes wheeling over mouldy skulls.
They stalked, the ancient dead, the newly-dead,
to find a warmth that, dimly, they recalled
one time a year to send them striding down
to find a hearthfire and the smell of food,
a homely comfort, lost among the stones:
just once a year some power called them home.

They crossed the frosted garden. Nora's cat
hissed curses and retreated up a tree,
sat staring, moon-eyed, after that strange band
upon the brittle grass.
                        They saw the milk,
the bread beside the door; the bone-white heads
bent, grinning, over plate and cup, inhaled
the scents of life into their rotten lungs,
but didn't linger long. One claw-nailed hand
reached out to touch the door; the fingers moved
mouse-quiet, but the scritching filled the night,
sent Nora trembling on her aching knees.

She *would not rise*, unbar that door, admit
the grisly crew, all family perhaps,
but terrifying, changed.

And one her man!
That was the hardest fact: the face she knew
would be a fleshless blur, the well-loved hands
reduced to bone.
        Her tears came freely now:
both loss and pain were standing at her door,
returned tonight to something like a life;
how could she leave him there amid the chill,
locked from his home, rejected by his spouse,
to plead the night away?
        There was his voice,
hoarser, perhaps, but welcome to her ear:
"Nora! Oh, let us in, for Pity's sake,
to warm our bones once more before your hearth,
remembering we once were living men!"

She rose and dried her eyes, took down the bar,
and opened wide the door; her chamber filled
with scents of earth, decay, and harsher things,
but Kevin came the last. She stared at him
and saw, through shrunken skin, the face she knew.
Reaching to take his bony hand, she led
him over to the fire, to join the rest
and sit in his old chair.
        It was a night
of strangeness; dryest whispers passed among
that group, but there was little they could tell
save tales of cold and darkness, damp and stone
that chilled her spirit, set a seal of fear
upon her heart.
        And yet she knew one thing,
incredible and perverse. When dawn drew near
she straightened up the room and quenched the fire,
looked once about her long-familiar home,
then followed as her guests moved up the hill.
The gravestones shifted, and they all were gone
to rest again, and yet they left no track

on path or turf.

One set of footprints marked
the earth—a woman's, leading to a stone
unweathered, new...and ending at its base.

All-Hallows dawned, and darkness drew away.

The rocks rolled under my moccasins
and my knees trembled with climbing, but I am here,
and none save my father the wind
and my mother the sun
knows where my bones will lie.

The stone of the mountain holds my back,
man-bone to mountain-bone;
I sit proudly, as of old, looking across the dry places
toward the White One.
Long has he stood in the sun
with the cold upon his head,
and long will he stand
when none sits here save the stone.
It is fitting that he share my vigil
as he has shared all the seasons of my life.
I will go away into the Other Place
with his shape in my eyes.

With the coming of spring
I knew this time was near.
The face of the sun brought no warmth,
and night brought shadows my eyes could not pierce.
I looked at my woman, and she was bent,
brittle as a winter weed.
I looked at my sons and they were warriors,
at my daughters, and they were mothers.
I looked at my tribe
and found the people strong and fat,
and the deer were many, the streams full.
So I called to the warriors and the women
and told them to find another to lead them.
They chose one of my sons, and we were glad together,
then I bade them goodbye.

Many days, many weeks I walked toward the White One,
stopping when I wearied or hungered.

When I held my bow in my hands
and brought down the antelope
I rejoiced that all my skills
were not lost to me.
But when I looked to my bow
it was pale as mist, and the arrows
were as shadows on the sand.
Then I knew that I moved
in the ways of the spirits,
and I laid out the heart of the antelope
that they might be joyful.

My fire sent pungent smoke, though it was small,
yet I had no fear,
for one who goes a spirit-journey
fears no man.
And the flesh of the beast was sweet,
and my sleep was dreamless.

So I came, across dry lands and wooded lands,
stone and sand and ash,
to the beginning of the mountains
where I was born.
I felt the White One, though I could not see him,
rising cold behind the ridges.
My limbs seemed young and full of strength,
and I went up into the forest upon the slopes,
coming home after many years.
As a spirit I moved: the beasts did not hear me,
the birds did not fly from my presence,
and I knew that I walked upon the edge
of the Other Place;
my spirit grew greater, as the flesh shrank,
and strength did not leave me.

The face of my father greeted me from the mists,
and the voices of my brothers

shouted among the rocks and in the wind.
I put my hands to my face,
feeling the tracks of years,
and wondered that they knew me still.
The air grew thin, the trees thin;
I walked above and watched my old self
struggle among the stones, gasping and trembling.
I laughed with a great HO! HO!
and my father the wind bore the echoes away among the mountains
and brought them back as many echoes.

So the old man that I was and the young man I am becoming
made their way up the slopes,
panting in the shadows of rocks,
but moving up, up, and I who was above wondered
that I who was below did not thirst or weary.
Flesh was becoming light...
no need came near it.

Now we are settled against the stone,
warmed by my mother the sun.
The White One shines on the edge of the sky,
and my father the wind is gentle.
The chants are done, and the prayers.
The spirits are very near...
I hear their whispers about me.

My legs are crossed in the old way:
I have made my bones secure against the rock.
When my spirit goes, they will not fall.

I am waiting.

Third Wind

Richard Christian Matheson

To set the record straight: Richard Christian Matheson isn't a teenager; he was born October 14, 1953. He isn't a carbon copy of his father nor is he trying to be. His appreciation for the author of I Am Legend is profound—even while, in the fairest of possible ways, he asserts merit as an individual.

And why not? Richard's record includes work as an ad account exec and copywriter, as ghostchaser for the UCLA Parapsychology Department, gigs as a drummer. He sold a TV pilot to Lorimar Productions at age 20, eventually wrote for more than a dozen programs including The Phoenix, Battlestar Galactica, and Quincy.

We can't inherit the talent to use arising opportunity fully. Made story-editor of The A-Team, he will, by point of syndication, have written upwards of 50 episodes on a seven-days-a-week schedule. It's "akin to trying to eat a picnic on the end of a runway," R. C. remarks—yet he's also writing a horror novel with a show biz setting in his nonexistent spare time!

"Third Wind," one of his "all time favorite writing efforts," is a shocking jewel of a yarn which, in its perceptive handling of a man who finds his hardest competitor is himself, gives evidence of another ambition dear to young Matheson's heart: completing his education and earning a doctorate in psychology. If he winds up like Michael in this splendid tale, we'll recognize Richard's scream: "It'll be the fatigued one just west of Hollywood and Vine...Business as usual in lotusland."

Michael chugged up the incline, sweatsuit shadowed with perspiration. His Nikes compressed on the asphalt and the sound of his inhalation was the only noise on the country road.

He glanced at his waist-clipped odometer: Twenty-five, point seven. Not bad. But he could do better.

Had to.

He'd worked hard doing his twenty miles a day for the last two years and knew he was ready to break fifty. His body was up to it, the muscles taut and strong. They'd be going through a lot of changes over the next twenty-five miles. His breathing was loose; comfortable. Just the way he liked it.

Easy. But the strength was there.

There was something quietly spiritual about all this, he told himself. Maybe it was the sublime monotony of stretching every muscle and feeling it constrict. Or it could be feeling his legs telescope out and draw his body forward. Perhaps even the humid expansion of his chest as his lungs bloated with air.

But none of that was really the answer.

It was the competing against himself.

Beating his own distance, his own limits. Running was the time he felt most alive. He knew that as surely as he'd ever known anything.

He loved the ache that shrouded his torso and he even waited for the moment, a few minutes into the run, when a dull voltage would climb his body to his brain like a vine, reviving him. It transported him, taking his mind to another place, very deep within. Like prayer.

He was almost to the crest of the hill.

So far, everything was feeling good. He shagged off some tightness in his shoulders, clenching his fists and punching at the air. The October chill turned to pink steam in his chest, making his body tingle as if a microscopic cloud of needles were passing through, from front to back, leaving pin-prick holes.

He shivered. The crest of the hill was just ahead. And on the down side was a new part of his personal route: a dirt road, carpeted with leaves, which wound through a silent forest at the peak of these mountains.

As he broke the crest, he picked up speed, angling downhill toward the dirt road. His Nikes flexed against the gravel, slipping a little.

It had taken much time to prepare for this. Months of meticulous care of his body. Vitamins. Dieting. The endless training and clocking. Commitment to the body machine. It was as critical as the commitment to the goal itself.

Fifty miles.

As he picked up momentum, jogging easily downhill, the mathematical breakdown of that figure filled his head with tumbling digits. Zeroes unglued from his thought tissues and linked with cardinal numbers to form combinations which added to fifty. It was suddenly all he could think about. Twenty-five plus twenty-five. Five times ten. Forty-nine plus one. Shit. It was driving him crazy. One hundred minus—

The dirt road.

He noticed the air cooling. The big trees that shaded the forest road were lowering the temperature. Night was close. Another hour. Thirty minutes plus thirty minutes. This math thing was getting irritating. Michael tried to remember some of his favorite Beatle songs as he gently padded through the dense forest.

Eight Days A Week. Great song. Weird damn title but who cared? If John and Paul said a week had eight days, everybody else just added a day and said. . .yeah, cool. Actually, maybe it wasn't their fault to begin with. Maybe George was supposed to bring a calendar to the recording session and forgot. He was always the spacey one. Should've had Ringo do it, thought Michael, Ringo you could count on. Guys with gonzo noses always compensated by being dependable.

Michael continued to run at a comfortable pace over the powdery dirt. Every few steps he could hear a leaf or small branch break under his shoes. What was that old thing? Something like, don't ever move even a small rock when you're at the beach or in the mountains. It upsets the critical balances. Nature can't ever be right again if you do. The repercussions can start wars if you extrapolate it out far enough.

Didn't ever really make much sense to Michael. His brother

Eric had always told him these things and he should have known better than to listen. Eric was a self-appointed fount of advice on how to keep the cosmos in alignment. But he always got "D's" on his cards in high school unlike Michael's "A's" and maybe he didn't really know all that much after all.

Michael's foot suddenly caught on a rock and he fell forward. On the ground, the dirt coated his face and lips and a spoonful got into his mouth. He also scraped his knee; a little blood. It was one of those lousy scrapes that claws a layer off and stings like it's a lot worse.

He was up again in a second and heading down the road, slightly disgusted with himself. He knew better than to lose his footing. He was too good an athlete for that.

His mouth was getting dry and he worked up some saliva by rubbing his tongue against the roof of his mouth. Strange how he never got hungry on these marathons of his. The body just seemed to live off itself for the period of time it took. Next day he usually put away a supermarket but in running, all appetite faded. The body fed itself. It was weird.

The other funny thing was the way he couldn't imagine himself ever walking again. It became automatic to run. Everything went by so much faster. When he did stop, to walk, it was like being a snail. Everything just...took...so...damn ...looooonnnngggg.

The sun was nearly gone now. Fewer and fewer animals. Their sounds faded all around. Birds stopped singing. The frenetic scrambling of squirrels halted as they prepared to bed down for the night. Far below, at the foot of these mountains, the ocean was turning to ink. The sun was lowering and the sea rose to meet it like a dark blue comforter.

Ahead, Michael could see an approaching corner.

How long had he been moving through the forest path? Fifteen minutes? Was it possible he'd gone the ten or so mile length of the path already?

That was one of the insane anomalies of running these marathons of his. Time got all out of whack. He'd think he was running ten miles and find he'd actually covered considerably more ground. Sometimes as much as double his estimate. He couldn't ever figure that one out. But it always happened and he always just sort of anticipated it.

Welcome to the time warp, Jack.

He checked his odometer: Twenty-nine point eight.

Half there and some loose change.

The dirt path would be coming to an end in a few hundred yards. Then it was straight along the highway which ran atop the ridge of this mountain far above the Malibu coastline. The highway was bordered with towering streetlamps which lit the way like some forgotten runway for ancient astronauts. They stared down from fifty-foot poles and bleached the asphalt and roadside talcum white.

The path had ended now and he was on the deserted mountain-top road with its broken center line that stretched to forever. As Michael wiped his glistening face with a sleeve, he heard someone hitting a crystal glass with tiny mallets, far away. It wasn't a pinging sound. More like a high-pitched thud that was chain reacting. He looked up and saw insects of the night swarming dementedly around a kleig's glow. Hundreds of them in hypnotic self-destruction dive-bombed again and again at the huge bulb.

Eerie, seeing that kind of thing way the hell out here. But nice country to run in just the same. Gentle hills. The distant sea, far below. Nothing but heavy silence. Nobody ever drove this road anymore. It was as deserted as any Michael could remember. The perfect place to run.

What could be better? The smell was clean and healthy, the air sweet. Great decision, building his house up here last year. This was definitely the place to live. Pastureland is what his father used to call this kind of country when Michael was growing up in Wisconsin.

He laughed. Glad to be out of *that* place. People never did anything with their lives. Born there, schooled there, married there and died there was the usual, banal legacy. They all missed out on life. Missed out on new ideas and ambitions. The doctor slapped them and from that point on their lives just curled up like dead spiders.

It was just as well.

How many of them could take the heat of competition in Los Angeles? Especially a job like Michael's? None of the old friends he'd gladly left behind in his home town would ever have a chance going up against a guy like himself. He was going to be the head of his law firm in a few more years. Most of those yokels back home couldn't even *spell* success much less achieve it.

But to each his own. Regardless of how pointless some lives really were. But *he* was going to be the head of his own firm and wouldn't even be thirty-five by the time it happened.

Okay, yeah, they were all married and had their families worked out. But what a fucking bore. Last thing Michael needed right now was that noose around his neck. Maybe the family guys figured they had something valuable. But for Michael it was a waste of time. Only thing a wife and kids would do is drag him down; hold him back. Priorities. First things first. *Career.* Then everything else. But put that relationship stuff off until last.

Besides, with all the inevitable success coming his way, meeting ladies would be a cinch. And hell, anyone could have a kid. Just nature. No big thing.

But *success.* That was something else, again. Took a very special animal to grab onto that golden ring and never let go. Families were for losers when a guy was really climbing. And he, of all the people he'd ever known, was definitely climbing.

Running had helped get him in the right frame of mind to do it. With each mileage barrier he broke, he was able to break greater barriers in life itself, especially his career. It made him more mentally fit to compete when he ran. It strengthened his will; his inner discipline.

Everything felt right when he was running regularly. And it wasn't just the meditative effect; not at all. He knew what it gave him was an *edge.* An edge on his fellow attorneys at the firm and an edge on life.

It was unthinkable to him how the other guys at the firm didn't take advantage of it. Getting ahead was what it was all about. A guy didn't make it in L.A. or anywhere else in the world unless he kept one step ahead of the competition. Keep moving and never let anything stand in the way or slow you down. That was the magic.

And Michael knew the first place to start that trend was with himself.

He got a chill. Thinking this way always made him feel special. Like he had the formula; the secret. Contemplating success was a very intoxicating thing. And with his running now approaching the hour and a half mark, hyperventilation was heightening the effect.

He glanced at his odometer: Forty-three, point six.

He was feeling like a champion. His calves were burning a little and his back was a bit tender but at this rate, with his breathing effortless and body strong, he could do sixty. But fifty was the goal. After that he had to go back and get his briefs in order for tomorrow's meeting. Had to get some sleep. Keep the machine in good shape and you rise to the top. None of that smoking or drinking or whatever else those morons were messing with out there. Stuff like that was for losers.

He opened his mouth a little wider to catch more air. The night had gone to a deep black and all he could hear now was the adhesive squishing of his Nikes. Overhead, the hanging branches of pepper trees canopied the desolate road and cut the moonlight into a million beams.

The odometer: Forty-six, point two. His head was feeling hot but running at night always made that easier. The breezes would swathe like cool silk, blowing his hair back and combing through his scalp. Then he'd hit a hot pocket that hovered above the road and his hair would flop downward, the feeling of heat returning like a blanket. He coughed and spit.

Almost there.

He was suddenly hit by a stray drop of moisture, then another. A drizzle began. Great. Just what he didn't need. Okay, it wasn't raining hard; just that misty stuff that atomizes over you like a lawn sprinkler shifted by a light wind. Still, it would have been nice to finish the fifty dry.

The road was going into a left hairpin now and Michael leaned into it, Nikes gripping octopus-tight. Ahead, as the curve broke, the road went straight, as far as the eye could see. Just a two-lane blacktop laying in state across these mountains. Now that it was wet, the surface went mirror shiny, like a ribbon on the side of tuxedo pants. Far below, the sea reflected a fuzzy moon, and fog began to ease up the mountainside, coming closer toward the road.

Michael checked the odometer, rubbing his hands together for warmth. Forty-nine, point eight. Almost there and other than being a little cold, he was feeling like a million bucks. He punched happily at the air and cleared his throat. God, he was feeling great! Tomorrow, at the office, was going to be a victory from start to finish.

He could feel himself smiling, his face hot against the vaporing rain. His jogging suit was soaked with sweat and drizzle made him shiver as it touched his skin. He breathed in gulps of the chilled air and as it left his mouth it turned white, puffing loosely away. His eyes were stinging from the cold and he closed them, continuing to run, the effect of total blackness fascinating him.

Another stride. Another.

He opened his eyes and rubbed them with red fingers. All around, the fog breathed closer, snaking between the limbs of trees and creeping silently across the asphalt. The overhead lights made it glow like a wall of colorless neon.

The odometer.

Another hundred feet and he had it!

The strides came in a smooth flow, like a turning wheel. He spread his fingers wide and shook some of the excess energy that was concentrating and making him feel buzzy. It took the edge off but he still felt as though he was zapped on a hundred cups of coffee. He ran faster, his arms like swinging scythes, tugging him forward.

Twenty more steps.

Ten plus ten. Five times. . .Christ, the math thing back. He started laughing out loud as he went puffing down the road, sweat pants drooping.

The sky was suddenly zippered open by lightning and Michael gasped. In an instant, blackness turned to hot white and there was that visual echo of the light as it trembled in the distance, then fluttered off like a dying bulb.

Michael checked his odometer.

Five more feet! He counted it: Five/breath/four/breath/three/breath/two/one and there it was, yelling and singing and patting him on the back and tossing streamers!

Fifty miles! Fifty goddamn miles!

It was fucking incredible! To know he could really, actually *do* it suddenly hit him and he began laughing.

Okay, now to get that incredible sensation of almost standing still while walking it off. Have to keep those muscles warm. If not he'd get a chill and cramps and feel like someone was going over his calves with a carpet knife.

Hot breath gushed visibly from his mouth. The rain was coming faster in a diagonal descent, back-lit by lightning, and the fog bundled tighter. Michael took three or four deep breaths and began trying to slow. It was incredible to have this feeling of edge. The sense of being on *top* of everything! It was an awareness he could surpass limitations. Make breakthroughs. It was what separated the winners from the losers when taken right down to a basic level. The winners knew how much harder they could push to go farther. Break those patterns. Create new levels of ability and confidence.

Win.

He tried again to slow down. His legs weren't slowing to a walk yet and he sent the message down again. He smiled. Run too far and the body just doesn't want to stop.

The legs continued to pull him forward. Rain was drenching down from the sky; he was soaked to the bone. Hair strung over his eyes and mouth and he coughed to get out what he could as it needled coldly into his face.

"Slow down," he told his legs; "*Stop,* goddamit!"

But his feet continued on, splashing through puddles which laked here and there along the foggy road.

Michael began to breathe harder, unable to get the air he needed. It was too wet; half air, half water. Suddenly, more lightning scribbled across the thundering clouds and Michael reached down to stop one leg.

It did no *good.* He kept running, even faster, pounding harder against the wet pavement. He could feel the bottoms of his Nikes getting wet, starting to wear through. He'd worn the old ones; they were the most comfortable.

Jesus fucking god, he really *couldn't stop!*

The wetness got colder on his cramping feet. He tried to fall but kept running. Terrified, he began to cough fitfully, his legs continuing forward, racing over the pavement.

His throat was raw from the cold and his muscles ached. He was starting to feel like his body had been beaten with hammers.

There was no point in trying to stop. He knew that, now. He'd trained too long. Too precisely.

It had been his single obsession.

And as he continued to pound against the fog-shrouded pavement all he could hear was a cold, lonely night.

Until the sound of his own pleading screams began to echo through the mountains, and fade across the endless gray road.

Redbeard

Gene Wolfe

In Birmingham, England, October 1983, a New York-born American writer of fantasy was honored as the sole Guest of Honor at the eighth annual British Fantasycon. He was one of three Guests of Honor at WorldFanCon 1983. The same alopecian author extraordinaire won the British Fantasy Award for Best Novel of 1982. The book was Sword of the Lictor —

And the writer was that gifted working pro (born May 7, 1931), Illinois resident Gene Wolfe.

Who has also written Peace, The Shadow of the Torturer, The Fifth Head of Cerberus, *and a must-read story feast entitled* Gene Wolfe's Book of Days — *and who won the Science Fiction Writers of America's yearned-for Nebula Award.*

*Wolfe, called "un Proust de l'espace" (*L'Express, *Paris) as well as "one of the finest modern sf writers"* (The Science Fiction Encyclopedia), *"served a hitch in the army during the Korean War" and "got the Combat Infantry Badge." He has a bachelor's degree in mechanical engineering from the University of Houston and married Rosemary upon graduation in 1956. "Now I'm a full-time writer," he adds.*

For your pleasure, amiable Gene has created one of those lazily-read yarns which lean back and pull you in, then set about telling you things you need to know — or remember — while munching on your nerves and surprising you all the way. It would be against common decency to tell you more about Gene Wolfe's chilling-but-human "Redbeard."

It doesn't matter how Howie and I became friends, except that our friendship was unusual. I'm one of those people who've moved into the area since. . .Since what? I don't know; some day I'll have to ask Howie. Since the end of the sixties or the Truman Administration or the Second World War. Since something.

Anyway, after Mara and I came with our little boy, John, we grew conscious of older strata. They are the people who were living here before. Howie is one of them; his grandparents are buried in the little family cemeteries that are or used to be attached to farms — all within twenty miles of my desk. Those people are still here, practically all of them, like the old trees that stand among the new houses.

By and large we don't mix much. We're only dimly aware of them, and perhaps they're only dimly aware of us. Our friends are new people too, and on Sunday mornings we cut the grass together. Their friends are the children of their parents' friends, and their own uncles and cousins; on Sunday mornings they go to the old clapboard churches.

Howie was the exception, as I said. We were driving down U.S. 27 — or rather, Howie was driving, and I was sitting beside him smoking a cigar and having a look around. I saw a gate that was falling down, with a light that was leaning way over, and beyond it, just glimpsed, a big, old, tumbledown wooden house with young trees sprouting in the front yard. It must have had about ten acres of ground, but there was a boarded-up fried-chicken franchise on one side of it and a service station on the other.

"That's Redbeard's place," Howie told me.

I thought it was a family name, perhaps an anglicization of Barbarossa. I said, "It looks like a haunted house."

"It is," Howie said. "For me, anyway. I can't go in there."

We hit a chuck hole, and I looked over at him.

"I tried a couple times. Soon as I set my foot on that step, something says, 'This is as far as you go, Buster,' and I turn around and head home."

After a while I asked him who Redbeard was.

"This used to be just a country road," Howie said. "They made it a Federal Highway back about the time I was born, and it got a lot of cars and trucks and stuff on it. Now the Interstate's come through, and it's going back to about what it was.

"Back before, a man name of Jackson used to live there. I don't think anybody thought he was much different, except he didn't get married till he was forty or so. But then, a lot of people around here used to do that. He married a girl named Sarah Sutter."

I nodded, just to show Howie I was listening.

"She was a whole lot younger than him, nineteen or twenty. But she loved him—that's what I always heard. Probably he was good to her, and so on. Gentle. You know?"

I said a lot of young women like that preferred older man.

"I guess. You know where Clinton is? Little place about fifteen miles over. There had been a certain amount of trouble around Clinton going on for years, and people were concerned about it. I don't believe I said this Jackson was from Clinton, but he was. His dad had run a store there and had a farm. The one brother got the farm and the next oldest the store. This Jackson, he just got some money, but it was enough for him to come here and buy that place. It was about a hundred acres then.

"Anyhow, they caught him over in Clinton. One of those chancy things. It was winter, and dark already, and there'd been a little accident where a car hit a school bus that still had quite a few kids riding home. Nobody was killed as far as I heard or even hurt bad, but a few must have had bloody noses and so forth, and you couldn't get by on the road. Just after the deputy's car got there this Jackson pulled up, and the deputy told him to load some of the kids in the back and take them to the Doctor's.

"Jackson said he wouldn't, he had to get back home. The deputy told him not to be a damned fool. The kids were hurt and he'd have to go back to Clinton anyhow to get on to Mill Road, because it would be half the night before they got that bus moved.

"Jackson still wouldn't do it, and went to try and turn his pickup around. From the way he acted, the deputy figured there was something wrong. He shined his flash in the back, and there was something under a tarp there. When he saw that, he hollered for Jackson to stop and went over and jerked the tarp away. From what I hear, now he couldn't do that because of not having a warrant, and if he did, Jackson would have got off. Back then, nobody had heard of such foolishness. He jerked that tarp away, and there was a girl underneath, and she was dead. I don't even know what her name was. Rosa or something like that, I guess. They were Italians that had come just a couple of years before." Howie didn't give *Italians* a long *I*, but there had been a trifling pause while he remembered not to. "Her dad had a little shoe place," he said. "The family was there for years after.

"Jackson was arrested, and they took him up to the county seat. I don't know if he told them anything or not. I think he didn't. His wife came up to see him, and then a day or so later the sheriff came to the house with a search warrant. He went all through it, and when he got to going through the cellars, one of the doors was locked. He asked her for the key, but she said she didn't have it. He said he'd have to bust down the door, and asked her what was in there. She said she didn't know, and after a while it all came out—I mean, all as far as her understanding went.

"She told him that the door had been shut ever since she and Jackson had been married. He'd told her he felt a man was entitled to some privacy, and that right there was his private place, and if she wanted a private place of her own she could have it, but to stay out of his. She'd taken one of the upstairs bedrooms and made it her sewing room.

"Nowadays they just make a basement and put everything on top, but these old houses have cellars with walls and rooms, just like upstairs. The reason is that they didn't have the steel beams we use to hold everything up, so they had to build masonry walls underneath; if you built a couple of those, why you had four rooms. The foundations of all these old houses are stone."

I nodded again.

"This one room had a big, heavy door. The sheriff tried to knock it down, but he couldn't. Finally he had to telephone around and get a bunch of men to help him. They found three girls in there."

"Dead?" I asked Howie.

"That's right. I don't know what kind of shape they were in, but not very good, I guess. One had been gone over a year. That's what I heard."

As soon as I said it, I felt like a half-wit; but I was thinking of all the others, of John Gacy and Jack the Ripper and the dead black children of Atlanta, and I said, "Three? That was all he killed?"

"Four," Howie told me, "counting the Italian girl in the truck. Most people thought it was enough. Only there was some others missing too, you know, in various places around the state, so the sheriff and some deputies tore everything up looking for more bodies. Dug in the yard and out in the fields and so on."

"But they didn't find any more?"

"No they didn't. Not then," Howie said. "Meantime, Jackson was in jail like I told you. He had kind of reddish hair, so the paper called him Redbeard. Because of Bluebeard, you know, and him not wanting his wife to look inside that cellar room. They called the house Redbeard's Castle.

"They did things a whole lot quicker in those times, and it wasn't much more than a month before he was tried. Naturally, his wife had to get up in the stand."

I said, "A wife can't be forced to testify against her husband."

"She wasn't testifying against him, she was testifying for him. What a good man he was, and all that. Who else would do it? Of course when she'd had her say, the district attorney got to go to work on her. You know how they do.

"He asked her about that room, and she told him just about what I told you. Jackson, he said he wanted a place for himself and told her not to go in there. She said she hadn't even known the door was locked till the sheriff tried to open it. Then the district attorney said didn't you know he was asking for your help, that your husband was asking for your help, that the whole room there was a cry for help, and he wanted you to go in there and find those bodies so he wouldn't have to kill again?"

Howie fell silent for a mile or two. I tossed the butt of my cigar out the window and sat wondering if I would hear any more about those old and only too commonplace murders.

When Howie began talking again, it was as though he had never stopped. "That was the first time anybody from around here had heard that kind of talk, I think. Up till then, I guess everybody thought if a man wanted to get caught he'd just go to the police and say he did it. I always felt sorry for her, because of that. She was — I don't know — like an owl in daylight. You know what I mean?"

I didn't, and I told him so.

"The way she'd been raised, a man meant what he said. Then too, the man was the boss. Today when they get married there isn't hardly a woman that promises to obey, but back then they all did it. If they'd asked the minister to leave that out, most likely he'd have told them he wouldn't perform the ceremony. Now the rules were all changed, only nobody'd told her that.

"I believe she took it pretty hard, and of course it didn't do any good, her getting in the stand or the district attorney talking like that to her either. The jury came back in about as quick as they'd gone out, and they said he was guilty, and the judge said sentencing would be the next day. He was going to hang him, and everybody knew it. They hanged them back then."

"Sure," I said.

"That next morning his wife came to see him in the jail. I guess he knew she would, because he asked the old man that swept out to lend him a razor and so forth. Said he wanted to look good. He shaved and then he waited till he heard her step."

Howie paused to let me comment or ask a question. I thought I knew what was coming, and there didn't seem to be much point in saying anything.

"When he heard her coming, he cut his throat with the razor blade. The old man was with her, and he told the paper about it afterwards. He said they came up in front of the cell, and Jackson was standing there with blood all running down his shirt. He really was Redbeard for true then. After a little bit, his knees gave out and he fell down in a heap.

"His wife tried to sell the farm, but nobody wanted that

house. She moved back with her folks, quit calling herself Sarah Jackson. She was a good looking woman, and the land brought her some money. After a year or so she got married again and had a baby. Everybody forgot, I suppose you could say, except maybe for the families of the girls that had died. And the house, it's still standing back there. You just saw it yourself."

Howie pronounced the final words as though the story were over and he wanted to talk of something else, but I said, "You said there were more bodies found later."

"Just one. Some kids were playing in that old house. It's funny, isn't it, that kids would find it when the sheriff and all those deputies didn't."

"Where was it?"

"Upstairs. In her sewing room. You remember I told you how she could have a room to herself too? Of course, the sheriff had looked in there, but it hadn't been there when he looked. It was her, and she'd hung herself from a hook in the wall. Who do you think killed her?"

I glanced at him to see if he were serious. "I thought you said she killed herself?"

"That's what they would have said, back when she married Jackson. But who killed her now? Jackson—Redbeard—when he killed those other girls and cut his throat like that? Or was it when he loved her? Or that district attorney? Or the sheriff? Or the mothers and fathers and brothers and sisters of the girls Jackson got? Or her other husband, maybe some things he said to her? Or maybe it was just having her baby that killed her— baby blues they call it. I've heard that too."

"Postnatal depression," I said. I shook my head. "I don't suppose it makes much difference now."

"It does to me," Howie said. "She was my mother." He pushed the lighter into the dashboard and lit a cigarette. "I thought I ought to tell you before somebody else does."

For a moment I supposed that we had left the highway and circled back along some secondary road. To our right was another ruined gate, another outdated house collapsing slowly among young trees.

The Turn of Time

David B. Silva

One reason editors say "No," even when they might derive joy from discovering a promising new writer, is that tiny botches by a professional, which they'd ignore or correct, look glaring in a beginner's yarn — and explaining proposed changes is time-consuming. Unless the PNW (promising new writer) has done a mistake-proof, original, uncontroversial minor masterwork, editors fear it will go unread in a magazine or anthology displaying the safer efforts of familiar pros. "The Turn of Time" should not go unread.

David B. Silva, born July 11, 1950, influenced by Bradbury and King, the writer of 15 tales published the small-press route, is one of three PNWs who became a part of Masques. *They don't know each other but they achieved the near-impossible in similar ways: Their premises were either highly original or left the indefinable haunting impression all good stories share; each PNW was the soul of cooperation; and each story filled a need that seemed otherwise to go unfulfilled — need for a certain style or kind of horrific or supernatural yarn.*

Silva, editor of the inexpensive, usually-readable The Horror Show *for two years, worked in gerontology — a vocational background that, we think, had much to do with the evolution of our next story, the moody, slowly-building, eventually terrifying "The Turn of Time."*

"Must you, Father?"

"I'll only be a minute." Harley James Mann smiled distantly, almost feebly, as he edged himself from the confines of his son's small Datsun. He pulled a cane from behind the seat. "Only a minute," he repeated.

The February day had arrived cold and dry, sharp as a shard of ice against the old man's soft flesh. With one hand, Harley kept the collar of his coat tight against his neck. He stepped carefully through the thin carpet of snow, using the cane first as a probe in quest of solid ground, then as his only means of stable balance. His steps were small.

A white picket fence, older than Harley Mann, guarded the house. The gate was partly open, caught against the packed and frozen earth, hinges rusted stiff and inoperative.

Harley paused, his back to where Daniel waited in the Datsun. He raised his face to the bitter wind, to the old Victorian house, and a tear filled one eye. He knew his son could not see his face but he wiped it away. *How long?* he wondered. It did not seem so far in the past. But it had been a lifetime, hadn't it? *Yes,* he admitted to himself. *A lifetime.*

Harley shuffled past the snow-laced grotesqueries of the topiary garden which lined the walkway. He stopped to stand before one, then moved onto the porch steps where he gripped the rail, let his cane dangle freely from two fingers stiff with arthritis. White paint flaked from the rail at his touch and he felt the rawness of the wood. *It shouldn't be like this.* In places, the porch boards sagged, more beneath the weight of time than the old gentleman's frail weight. One of the front windows, boarded over, seemed a dark-patched eye upon the aged Victorian. Although the lean of the walls was still slight, the house was clearly beginning to collapse in upon itself. The door remained padlocked, appeared rusted; thinking, *It should* not *be like this,* Harley stooped to an unbroken, unpatched window at the front.

A curtain of grime was brushed back by the sleeve of his heavy coat. He cupped one hand above his eyes to peer beyond the glass, saw long tails of light filtering into the house from a line of windows on the south side.

The room was empty. The mantel over the stone fireplace, where once a family portrait painted by his father had hung, was featureless. To the left side of the large room, a stairway led into darkness, seemingly skyward. Beyond it, Harley could not see the dining room.

A sigh fogged the windowglass. The wind was picking up, but Harley scarcely noticed it. "There, it was *there*," he said softly, to no one listening. "Where I grew up — right there." He straightened, blinking. *Here.*

The cold wind whistled under the porch boards as if seeking something.

Awkwardly, old fingers chipped at windowsill paint; splintering had left cracks, grave-deep in the wood. As a boy, he'd used a gift of his father — a pocket knife — to carve his name into this sill. Now he wondered if his mark remained and picked at the whiteness with his nails. With each falling chip, his heart sank deeper. Perhaps, he thought, even old windowsills are not safe from the inroads of time. And he knew it was true even when the last falling flake revealed *HARLEY* scratched, with schoolboy precision, into the wood. He knew the time was near when the old house could no longer care for itself.

Almost time for bed, Harley.

But it's only eight o'clock, Mother.

There's school tomorrow, young man, remember?

"What?" Harley, startled, turned back to the street where his son tapdanced impatient fingers upon the Datsun steering wheel. The sidewalk was deserted; a sleeve of newspaper was caught by a gust of wind and flapped off into the stillness.

Harley, put your toys away now!

"W-What is it?" Turning back to the house, from which the voices had seemed to emanate, he saw that the window was clean, clear, welcoming him. Now there was light from the interior of the aged house. And when Harley leaned closer, he saw flames burning blue-yellow in the fireplace. *"How?"* He scrubbed the sleeve of his coat over the pane again but the fire remained, summoningly. And above the fireplace, his childhood recollection vivid and true, the family portrait beamed back at him.

...*A lifetime ago.*

Eagerly, Harley hooked his cane to the projecting sill, again cupped hands over eyes, and watched the boy sit cross-legged upon the thick, oval scatter rug—watched him come to life. Twelve, perhaps. New-pup scrawny. Clad in knickerbockers and knee-high socks, all gray, black, and diamond print. Playing half-heartedly, it seemed, with a locomotive carved of wood. When he glanced up, attention apparently directed to Harley, it was to the old man as if they sent silent confirmations across the strange turn of time which separated and yet linked them— young from old, yesterday from today. He sensed the words: *I know you're there, looking back.*

"Do you; did I?" Harley asked of himself, past and present. "At this instant, do you perceive your future as well as I perceive my past? Your tomorrow, my yesterday?"

A smile upon the boy's face; as if to say, *The answer is in the question.* Then, spell broken, the twelve-year-old turned from the window where Harley stood waiting, anticipating perhaps, remembering what had next transpired—a lifetime ago. And the man entered the room from the shadows beside the stairway.

"My Father," the old man whispered, breath clouding the window.

The man smiled for the boy with faraway sadness, dulled eyes a granite grey, hands first tucked neatly into pockets and then out, helping him settle into the chair Harley knew was his father's alone. It was the chair that belonged to the man of the house, and, while he looked tired, depleted, he seemed comfortable in the warmth from the fireplace. It was as if the day had drained from him more than he'd been capable of giving, short of a surrender. Yet he was so much *younger* than Harley had remembered! Not fifty, sixty, with grey sprinkled at the temples; early thirties, round-faced, engaging, unsophisticated. Yet so grave of manner.

Father leaned forward, resting elbows on knees, looking down upon the young son. Appearing hesitant, at first, to speak, he swallowed hard and quietly began whispering—his words drawing the boy into a sitting position of alert attention. The locomotive tumbled to the floor. The boy, frozen, listened.

Harley himself sought a fragment of what the man said but silence greeted him, except for the distant moan of a train. Those *words*—so long ago uttered that they were soundless to memory, banished—the best he could—decades ago.

Then the man glanced away, shaking his head. Tears fell from the boy's eyes.

And tears spilled from the eyes of the grown, the old Harley. "I loved you, Father," he whispered.

From around his neck, the man who had been Harley's father removed a gold chain. A pendant dangled—bright and firelit— from the chain, twirling and twisting on an unseen cushion of air. The boy's eyes grew wide, wondrous; he took gentle hold of the pendant, his father making sure of his grasp.

Take it, Harley.

The mature Harley's fingers touched the talisman round his own throat, tested its lines, all fine and cold and shaped from soft gold in the likeness of strawberry shrub. So quickly the years had gone, days to months, months to years. Winters, in biting, Alaskan cold fronts. Summers turned heavy, and drooling from unsought humidities. So quickly, now, they were drawing to an end.

Gently, the man encircled his son's head with the chain, still holding the pendant in his palm as if he were reluctant to let it pass from his possession. The instant of his release brought a black sense of loss that stilled time and scented the air. *It will protect you, boy.* The quiet, cautioning words were familiar to the old man who listened. *Always keep it in your possession.*

"I will, Father," Harley whispered, synchronous with the boy.

Then a tongue of blue flame rose high and hot from the fireplace, seemed to fan out, to lap the air of past-become-present...

And an old man's reverie was washed with blue yesterdays—

And a hand caught Harley Mann's elbow, pulled him away

from the window, blinking.

"Father, it's time to go!"

"Wait, wait." Harley tried to avoid begging. "Just another moment."

"Father, *please.*"

"No!" Harley wrenched his elbow free. But when he turned back to the window, back to the viewing-glass that had spanned the years, it was different again: the fire was less than smouldering embers, the voices silent, the room itself dark, emptied. He found himself facing a grimy window, transparent only where he had used his own sleeve to effect a small peephole; and already, it was microscopically closing over...

"Damn it, Father!" The son's hold on his arm once more. "You'll be *late.*"

"No, I won't. Because I'm not going back." Whispering, Harley stared into the chilly bleakness of his long-ago living room. "It ends — *here.*"

"Please! Don't behave as if you're senile." The youth, inhaling sharply, impatient and anxious to be gone from there.

It wasn't the first time Harley's son had said such a terrible, casual thing, as if verbally slapping the hand of a child groping for forbidden chocolate. "Do I seem...so *old*...to you?" he inquired. Their eyes met briefly before the son looked away, studying the empty, snow-silenced street. He sighed heavily without answering. "Do I, my son, truly seem to have become so pathetically ancient?"

"It's only that they'll be waiting dinner." He said it flatly, leaving Harley's question unanswered.

"They don't wait meals." Harley frowned. "Didn't do it for Amanda when she slipped in the tub and struck her head. She was absent for a goddamned *day,* before anybody even noticed she was missing." Looking past his son, watching the lazy descent of fresh snow, his passion began to dissipate. "Didn't wait breakfast for her, or lunch. And they won't be waiting dinner for me."

"*Please,* Father!"

"Snow's starting up again," Harley said, eyes round in his

seamed face.

"All the more reason to get you back to the home."

The old gentleman braced himself, at the back, against the house of his own youth. It was suddenly so clear, so fully *reclaimed.* "It snowed that night, too. I looked out the window, saw flakes floating down like weightless angels. And I imagined they'd come to take your grandfather's soul, and escort him back to heaven. He belonged there; in heaven."

"I'm sure he did, Father. But—"

"I was sitting on the floor in the living room." He turned slightly, pointed inside with his cane. "And he sat in his chair, so large even seated that he seemed like a giant. *My* giant. And then he told me he was going to die."

"That's ancient history, it was a long time ago."

"He told me he was going to die," firmly repeated, purpose girding his tones; "and he lifted a chain with a pendant from over his own head and placed it round my neck. 'This will protect you,' he said. 'From evil.'"

The familiar boredom, despite Harley's message, the jaded expression of Get-on-with-it-*please* that had characterized the son since childhood, was apparent.

But Harley touched one finger to the pendant that was now displayed outside his shirt and the winter coat. "Because I was a boy and knew no better, I asked him, in my own childish fashion, about the evil that would be repelled. The nature of it. Do you think for a moment that I, then so much a boy, *understood* my destiny—even *when Father showed me?*"

Now his son's eyes gleamed. It could have been from what he was hearing, or from the intense cold.

"Your grandfather," said the old man, steadily, doggedly continuing, "stood me at the window to stare outside. It was black as midnight except for the porch light, and the drifting snow. Then he pointed silently at the snowy shapes of the topiary which lined the family walkway then, and now."

The younger Mann turned, expelling his warm breath, looking not at the lifelike sculptures of the topiary but to a nearly furtive grayness of untouchable clouds. He said nothing, but he seemed to hear Harley.

Frailer, it appeared, by the second, old Harley leaned against the windowsill to appraise the way his son stood, his back stiff. He detected a telltale shrug. "I know you don't wish to hear the rest, son. You believe I'm demented, but I fear this is nothing so lightly explained away." He paused, realized that the lessened visibility was only in part the fault of the gathering snowfall. "Daniel, hear me, please. I'm *dying,* Daniel."

His son, wiping a coat sleeve across his mouth, blinked as he turned. "That's quite enough!" Daniel Mann's eyes seemed red; his face was ruddy, suffused by blood. "I won't listen to more, Father. There is nothing wrong with you!"

"Then you weren't listening."

"Not any longer, I'm not." Taking Harley's arm, managing a conciliatory smile, he tried to coax the old man away from his house of memory. He succeeded for a few steps of the porch. "I should never have let you come here."

"You had no choice, Daniel. You're *my* son, not the other way around." He'd stopped at the bottom of the steps to lock his arm to the railing. "And now, damn you, hear me out! Let me explain the rest!"

Daniel Mann sighed, shook his head. "What is there to explain?"

"Much," Harley whispered, shuddering. Then without warning, he slipped down until he was sitting in a patina of snow. "There's much more, I fear."

"For God's sake, Father, it's snowing heavier by the minute!"

"Y'know, I used to walk through here. Frequently." He spoke absently, his gaze moving down the line of topiary figures, misshapen and twisted, haunted into unnatural forms by vagrant shadows. "Sometimes at night, with only the porchlight for illumination. And comfort. It frightened me, touching shoulders with a menagerie of sculptures in basic, *human* form; but I'd talked with Father and I needed to know them well." Eyebrows raised as he peered up to ask: "And you, Daniel? Were there times when fear stopped you at the sidewalk, or did you dare to venture farther?"

"They're shrubs. That's all they ever were to me, Father. That's all they are now."

Harley's eyes widened and he made himself say it, at least. "They are your *ancestors,* Daniel. And this front yard of the damned, with these perfectly manicured shrubs, is their cemetery — and their assignments in death."

"Father!"

"This is where your grandfather's *grandfather* came to be dead; and every son, after him; every son of a son. And this is where I have come, and where, Daniel, *you* must surely come one day."

"And if I don't?"

"It isn't — a matter of *choice.*"

The son sucked in a lungful of cold air and, with arms crossed on his chest as if he sought to hold himself together, he glanced over the misaligned deformities which were supposed to be his personal forefathers.

"Take this," Harley said, slipping the talisman on its chain from his neck, and holding it out to his son. "It will protect you until the day arrives when you are ready to die."

Daniel, turned to Harley, shook his head.

"You'll be the oldest now. The last descendant." He motioned for his son to come nearer, to claim possession of the pendant. "Now, Daniel."

"This is a lunatic business, Father." Slowly, grudgingly, he put out his open hand and watched as the old man dropped the charm into his palm. It felt warm, then, presumably from Harley Mann's pulsing throat. "Will you come back to the car now?"

"Daniel, you must place it round your neck, then *wear* it."

"*Then* you will let me take you back?"

"Please! Put it around your neck!"

"Only if you promise to come with me now, Father, with no further foolishness."

"I'm afraid I can't," Harley said, his voice all but inaudible, "leave." He buried his face in his hands, quietly shook his head. He seemed oddly ashamed. "I'm sorry, Daniel, but believe me, please. I cannot leave."

"Well, that is just great, isn't it? And what the hell am *I* supposed to do, Father? Leave you here to freeze?" Furious, his back to his father, he felt the pendant turning cold in his palm, numbing his fingers from the fine ridglets of the strawberry shrub pattern. Briefly, Daniel focussed his growing frustration on the familial talisman—then he screamed an echoing obscenity, and heaved the chained pendant into the air. It sailed above the path of the walkway, hit the Datsun's hood, and left miniature tracks in the thin film of snow.

Daniel saw it hit, and skid, and bury itself into a fist-sized mound of graying snow. And he spoke to the sky, incapable that moment of turning to face his father. "No more nonsense! No more about the pendant, *or* the shrubbery. Whether you like it or not, you're going back to the home!" Clenching his hands, he waited out the silence, then began to turn back. "Understood?"

And his father smiled sadly, a tear of abject, expectant loneliness sliding down the faded cheek. His eyes were grey-agate cold, grey-agate lifeless.

And Daniel's gaze was drawn to Harley's left foot, *tapping,* noiselessly, as if his Achilles tendon had been drawn up in a sudden spasm.

But Daniel realized as he stared that more, *much* more, was wrong with his father—

And watched as Harley's oxfords ripped along the stitching between vamp and arch, mudguard and collar. Eyelets popped; shoestrings slithered away. The leather *inhaled*—bulged, as if ready to explode—and *exhaled,* twitched and twisted until the material finally dropped away. The blood within the foot pumped full, fuller, the bulging followed riverlike trails up the calf and down to the foot at the same instant.

Daniel Mann jumped back—gaping—

And something *rootlike* erupted from the sole of his father's foot, tasted air with grubby feelers like antennae, then burrowed into the ground.

His father's clothing turned to ash—

And something branchlike, crisscrossing his father's leg, busily, briskly — foot, ankle, calf, thigh — in the canals of his blood vessels, ripped wide great quantities of skin.

Harley Mann's head lolled lifelessly back on his shoulders...

Daniel crept back another, sickened step, then another, before his legs gave way and he dropped to one knee. Peering over each shoulder by turn, he quivered internally before the nightmare presence of the unnatural, shrub-sculptured figures — each inquisitive statuary *leaning forward,* as if to whisper, and hiss, into his ear. And Daniel quickly scrambled to his feet, unwilling to hear what they might say. He looked down —

Piled upon the porchstep, where his father had been, was a misshapen mass of thick, raw branches, just beginning to bud.

He could not scream for the words reassuming shape in his memory: *You're* the oldest now, *you're* the *last descendant.*

Snow laced the delicate lines as the man-now-shrub grew, *formed,* head thrown back as real head had died, mouth gaping in silent, perpetual scream...a form not unlike the others, yet grotesque in its special way, not *quite* as unhuman, perhaps, as one might believe at first glance...

"Oh *Jes*us! Godal*mighty!*"

Daniel spun, repulsed to his soul, horrified by shame and the terror of the semi-human face which signaled his legacy. In the same motion, with the afterimage of his father's skeleton-of-wood a shadow at his back, Daniel sprinted for the Datsun. A thin layer of new ice coated the walkway. *The pendant, get the pendant!* He slid past the white picket fence, the last grotesque sculpture, and tripped forward over the hood of his car.

At once Daniel's left foot, toe to ground, trembled — *spasmed* — went out of control.

And he knew that something inside him, in his genes, cavorting wildly in his bloodstream, must explode from the sole of his foot to fasten him to the earth. His fingers, outthrust, touched the cold metal of the pendant —

His left shoe fell away.

A fragmented moment of wonder at the touch of winter, and

death, against his foot. Then the chain was in his fingers, he was lifting it over his head —

And the sole of his foot felt as if it had taken *root.*

The skin of his leg felt as if it were opening, splaying wide in fissures — felt as if his sap-gorged veins were turning fibrous.

And then the gold pendant was around his neck, in place, and everything went limp as Daniel passed out.

Conscious, Daniel Mann found himself sprawled upon the hood of his car, his jacket sleeves wet and coldly adhering to his flesh. The joints of his hands were brittle, stiff. Carefully, he lifted himself on one tender elbow, looked about for something familiar, and, in the midnight gloom, remembered the family heritage of which he had so recently learned.

In reflex, his shaking hand went to where the chain — the talisman — still hung from his neck. The dangling weight was reassuring; but it was also, he realized, ominous. Then he turned within from fright and loss to laugh, instead, and cry out to the nearby silhouette of the being who had sired him: "I'm alive, Father! Father, I'm *alive!*"

It was a scant moment later, when Daniel yearned to scramble back into the Datsun and flee from his horror, that he came to understand the delicate balance between past and present, death, and life.

His foot, no longer flesh and cartilage and human bone, had rooted.

The queer thing was, Daniel Mann experienced no pain. But he screamed, anyway, screamed as long as he could.

For his limb.

For his life.

And his new life, forever, in grotesquerie.

Soft

F. Paul Wilson

F. Paul Wilson is one of the Masques *writers who enjoys greater celebrity in science fiction circles; but unlike Gene Wolfe, or the other contributors, Paul knows science as a practicing physician. Maybe that's why he also writes spell-weaving horror; but here's a fair question: What kind of man finds time for a varied writing career when he's also one-fifth of a family-medicine group in Brick, New Jersey?*

Answer: The kind who plays three musical instruments (and writes music), jogs two miles daily, collects pulps, and raises two daughters. (He also tried to raise bonsai trees but his leafy patients didn't dig his bed-side manner.*)*

Born May 17, 1946, the good doctor was developed by the founder of modern sf, John Campbell. Often in Analog *and* Asimov's SF, *he also won the first Prometheus award — 7½ ounces of gold! His fifth novel,* Rakoshi, *is said to resemble the "Yellow Peril novels of the 20s and 30s."*

It was The Keep *which drew Wilson to your editor's attention. Lovers of horror who've only seen the movie do themselves an injustice, as reading the next yarn will establish. It arose from "two disparate scribbles in my notebook," and Paul, who likes turning clichés around, knew his storyline meshed when a body-builder said ruefully that the country was going soft.*

Then it occurred to F. Paul Wilson that he "had stumbled upon one of the most horrible lingering deaths imaginable." (The patient is ready, Doctor. . .)

I was lying on the floor watching tv and exercising what was left of my legs when the newscaster's jaw collapsed. He was right in the middle of the usual plea for anybody who thought they were immune to come to Rockefeller Center when—*pflumpf!*—the bottom of his face went soft.

I burst out laughing.

"Daddy!" Judy said, shooting me a razorblade look from her wheelchair.

I shut up.

She was right. Nothing funny about a man's tongue wiggling around in the air snake-like while his lower jaw flopped down in front of his throat like a sack of jello and his bottom teeth jutted at the screen crowns-on, rippling like a line of buoys on a bay. A year ago I would have gagged. But I've changed in ways other than physical since this mess began, and couldn't help feeling good about one of those pretty-boy newsreaders going soft right in front of the camera. I almost wished I had a bigger screen so I could watch 21 color inches of the scene. He was barely visible on our five-inch black-and-white.

The room filled with white noise as the screen went blank. Someone must have taken a look at what was going out on the airwaves and pulled the plug. Not that many people were watching anyway.

I flipped the set off to save the batteries. Batteries were as good as gold now. *Better* than gold. Who wanted gold nowadays?

I looked over at Judy and she was crying softly. Tears slid down her cheeks.

"Hey, hon—"

"I can't help it, Daddy. I'm so *scared!*"

"Don't be, Jude. Don't worry. Everything will work out, you'll see. We've got this thing licked, you and me."

"How can you be so sure?"

"Because it hasn't progressed in weeks! It's over for us—we've got immunity."

She glanced down at her legs, then quickly away. "It's already too late for me."

I reached over and patted my dancer on the hand. "Never too late for you, shweetheart," I said in my best Bogart. That got a tiny smile out of her.

We sat there in the silence, each thinking our own thoughts. The newsreader had said the cause of the softness had been discovered: A virus, a freak mutation that disrupted the calcium matrix of bones.

Yeah. Sure. That's what they said last year when the first cases cropped up in Boston. A virus. But they never isolated the virus, and the softness spread all over the world. So they began searching for "a subtle and elusive environmental toxin." They never pinned that one down either.

Now we were back to a virus again. Who cared? It didn't matter. Judy and I had beat it. Whether we had formed the right antibodies or the right antitoxin was just a stupid academic question. The process had been arrested in us. Sure, it had done some damage, but it wasn't doing any more, and that was the important thing. We'd never be the same, but we were going to live!

"But that man," Judy said, nodding toward the tv. "He said they were looking for people in whom the disease had started and then stopped. That's us, Dad. They said they need to examine people like us so they can find out how to fight it, maybe develop a serum against it. We should — "

"Judy-Judy-Judy!" I said in Cary Grantese to hide my annoyance. How many times did I have to go over this? "We've been through all this before. I told you: It's too late for them. Too late for everybody but us immunes."

I didn't want to discuss it — Judy didn't understand about those kind of people, how you can't deal with them.

"I want you to take me down there," she said in the tone she used when she wanted to be stubborn. "If you don't want to help, okay. But *I* do."

"No!" I said that louder than I wanted to and she flinched. More softly: "I know those people. I worked all those years in the Health Department. They'd turn us into lab specimens. They'll suck us dry and use our immunity to try and save themselves."

"But I want to help *some*body! I don't want us to be the last two people on earth!"

She began to cry again.

Judy was frustrated. I could understand that. She was unable to leave the apartment by herself and probably saw me at times as a dictator who had her at his mercy. And she was frightened, probably more frightened than I could imagine. She was only eighteen and everyone she had ever known in her life—including her mother—was dead.

I hoisted myself into the chair next to her and put my arm around her shoulders. She was the only person in the world who mattered to me. That had been true even before the softness began.

"We're not alone. Take George, for example. And I'm sure there are plenty of other immunes around, hiding like us. When the weather warms up, we'll find each other and start everything over new. But until then, we can't allow the bloodsuckers to drain off whatever it is we've got that protects us."

She nodded without saying anything. I wondered if she was agreeing with me or just trying to shut me up.

"Let's eat," I said with a gusto I didn't really feel.

"Not hungry."

"Got to keep up your strength. We'll have soup. How's that sound?"

She smiled weakly. "Okay. . .soup."

I forgot and almost tried to stand up. Old habits die hard. My lower legs were hanging over the edge of the chair like a pair of sand-filled dancer's tights. I could twitch the muscles and see them ripple under the skin, but a muscle is pretty useless unless it's attached to a bone, and the bones down there were gone.

I slipped off my chair to what was left of my knees and shuffled over to the stove. The feel of those limp and useless leg muscles squishing under me was repulsive but I was getting used to it.

It hit the kids and old people first, supposedly because their bones were a little soft to begin with, then moved on to the rest of us, starting at the bottom and working its way up—sort of like a Horatio Alger success story. At least that's the way it worked in most people. There were exceptions, of course, like that newscaster. I had followed true to form: My left lower leg collapsed at the end of last month; my right went a few days later. It wasn't a terrible shock. My feet had already gone soft so I knew the legs were next. Besides, I'd heard the sound.

The sound comes in the night when all is quiet. It starts a day or two before a bone goes. A soft sound, like someone gently crinkling cellophane inside your head. No one else can hear it. Only you. I think it comes from the bone itself—from millions of tiny fractures slowly interconnecting into a mosaic that eventually causes the bone to dissolve into mush. Like an on-rushing train far far away can be heard if you press your ear to the track, so the sound of each microfracture transmits from bone to bone until it reaches your middle ear.

I haven't heard the sound in almost four weeks. I thought I did a couple of times and broke out in a cold, shaking sweat, but no more of my bones have gone. Neither have Judy's. The average case goes from normal person to lump of jelly in three to four weeks. Sometimes it takes longer, but there's always a steady progression. Nothing more has happened to me or Judy since last month.

Somehow, someway, we're immune.

With my lower legs dragging behind me, I got to the counter of the kitchenette and kneed my way up the stepstool to where I could reach things. I filled a pot with water—at least the pressure was still up—and set it on the sterno stove. With gas and electricity long gone, sterno was a lifesaver.

While waiting for the water to boil I went to the window and looked out. The late afternoon March sky was full of dark gray clouds streaking to the east. Nothing moving on West 16th Street one floor below but a few windblown leaves from God-knows-where. I glanced across at the windows of George's apartment, looking for movement but finding none, then back down to the street below.

I hadn't seen anybody but George on the street for ages, hadn't seen or smelled smoke in well over two months. The last fires must have finally burned themselves out. The riots were one direct result of the viral theory. Half the city went up in the big riot last fall—half the city and an awful lot of people. Seems someone got the bright idea that if all the people going soft were put out of their misery and their bodies burned, the plague could be stopped, at least here in Manhattan. The few cops left couldn't stop the mobs. In fact a lot of the city's ex-cops had been *in* the mobs! Judy and I lost our apartment when our building went up. Luckily we hadn't any signs of softness then. We got away with our lives and little else.

"Water's boiling, Dad," Judy said from across the room.

I turned and went back to the stove, not saying anything, still thinking about how fast our nice rent-stabilized apartment house had burned, taking everything we had with it.

Everything was gone...furniture and futures...gone. All my plans. Gone. Here I stood—if you could call it that—a man with a college education, a B.S. in biology, a secure city job, and what was left? No job. Hell—no *city*! I'd had it all planned for my dancer. She was going to make it *so* big. I'd hang onto my city job with all those civil service idiots in the Department of Health, putting up with their sniping and their back-stabbing and their lousy office politics so I could keep all the fringe benefits and foot the bill while Judy pursued the dance. She was going to have it *all*! Now what? All her talent, all her potential...where was it going?

Going soft...

I poured the dry contents of the Lipton envelope into the boiling water and soon the odor of chicken noodle soup filled the room.

Which meant we'd have company soon.

I dragged the stepstool over to the door. Already I could hear their claws begin to scrape against the outer surface of the door, their tiny teeth begin to gnaw at its edges. I climbed up and peered through the hole I'd made last month at what had then been eye-level.

There they were. The landing was full of them. Gray and brown and dirty, with glinty little eyes and naked tails. Revulsion rippled down my skin. I watched their growing numbers every day now, every time I cooked something, but still hadn't got used to them.

So I did Cagney for them: "Yooou diiirty raaats!" and turned to wink at Judy on the far side of the fold-out bed. Her expression remained grim.

Rats. They were taking over the city. They seemed to be immune to the softness and were traveling in packs that got bigger and bolder with each passing day. Which was why I'd chosen this building for us: Each apartment was boxed in with pre-stressed concrete block. No rats in the walls here.

I waited for the inevitable. Soon it happened: A number of them squealed, screeched, and thrashed as the crowding pushed them at each other's throats, and then there was bedlam out there. I didn't bother to watch any more. I saw it every day. The pack jumped on the wounded ones. Never failed. They were so hungry they'd eat anything, even each other. And while they were fighting among themselves they'd leave us in peace with our soup.

Soon I had the card table beteween us and we were sipping the yellow broth and those tiny noodles. I did a lot of *mmm-good*ing but got no response from Judy. Her eyes were fixed on the walkie-talkie on the end table.

"How come we haven't heard from him?"

Good question—one that had been bothering me for a couple of days now. Where *was* George? Usually he stopped by every other day or so to see if there was anything we needed. And if he didn't stop by, he'd call us on the walkie-talkie. We had an arrangement between us that we'd both turn on our headsets every day at six p.m. just in case we needed to be in touch. I'd been calling over to George's place across the street at six o'clock sharp for three days running now with no result.

"He's probably wandering around the city seeing what he can pick up. He's a resourceful guy. Probably came back with something we can really use but haven't thought of."

Judy didn't flash me the anticipated smile. Instead, she frowned. "What if he went down to the research center?"

"I'm sure he didn't," I told her. "He's a trusting soul, but he's not a fool."

I kept my eyes down as I spoke. I'm not a good liar. And that very question had been nagging at my gut. What if George had been stupid enough to present himself to the researchers? If he had, he was through. They'd never let him go and we'd never see him again.

For George wasn't an immune like us. He was different. Judy and I had caught the virus — or toxin — and defeated it. We were left with terrible scars from the battle but we had survived. We *acquired* our immunity through battle with the softness agent. George was special — he had remained untouched. He'd exposed himself to infected people for months as he helped everyone he could, and was still hard all over. Not so much as a little toe had gone soft on him. Which meant — to me at least — that George had been *born* with some sort of immunity to the softness.

Wouldn't those researchers love to get their needles and scalpels into *him*!

I wondered if they had. It was possible George might have been picked up and brought down to the research center against his will. He told me once that he'd seen official-looking vans and cars prowling the streets, driven by guys wearing gas masks or the like. But that had been months ago and he hadn't reported anything like it since. Certainly no cars had been on this street in recent memory. I warned him time and again about roaming around in the daylight but he always laughed good-naturedly and said nobody'd ever catch him — he was too fast.

What if he'd run into someone faster?

There was only one thing to do.

"I'm going to take a stroll over to George's just to see if he's okay."

Judy gasped. "No, Dad! You can't! It's too far!"

"Only across the street."

"But your legs —"

"—are only half gone."

I'd met George shortly after the last riot. I had two hard legs then. I'd come looking for a sturdier building than the one we'd been burned out of. He helped us move in here.

I was suspicious at first, I admit that. I mean, I kept asking myself, *What does this guy want?* Turned out he only wanted to be friends. And so friends we became. He was soon the only other man I trusted in this whole world. And that being the case, I wanted a gun—for protection against all those other men I didn't trust. George told me he had stolen a bunch during the early lootings. I traded him some sterno and batteries for a .38 and a pump-action 12-gauge shotgun with ammo for both. I promptly sawed off the barrel of the shotgun. If the need arose, I could clear a room real fast with that baby.

So it was the shotgun I reached for now. No need to fool with it—I kept its chamber empty and its magazine loaded with #5 shells. I laid it on the floor and reached into the rag bag by the door and began tying old undershirts around my knees. Maybe I shouldn't call them knees; with the lower legs and caps gone, "knee" hardly seems appropriate, but it'll have to serve.

From there it was a look through the peep hole to make sure the hall was clear, a blown kiss to Judy, then a shuffle into the hall. I was extra wary at first, ranging the landing up and down, looking for rats. But there weren't any in sight. I slung the shotgun around my neck, letting it hang in front as I started down the stairs one by one on hands and butt, knees first, each flabby lower leg dragging alongside its respective thigh.

Two flights down to the lobby, then up on my padded knees to the swinging door, a hard push through and I was out on the street.

Silence.

We kept our windows tightly closed against the cold and so I hadn't noticed the change. Now it hit me like a slap in the face. As a lifelong New Yorker I'd never heard—or *not* heard—the city like this. Even when there'd been nothing doing on your street, you could always hear that dull roar pulsing from the sky and the pavement and the walls of the buildings. It was the life sound of the city, the beating of its heart, the whisper of its breath, the susurrant rush of blood through its capillaries.

It had stopped.

The shiver that ran over me was not just the result of the sharp edge of the March wind. The street was deserted. A plague had been through here, but there were no contorted bodies strewn about. You didn't fall down and die on the spot with the softness. No, that would be too kind. You died by inches, by bone lengths, in back rooms, trapped, unable to make it to the street. No public displays of morbidity. Just solitary deaths of quiet desperation.

In a secret way I was glad everyone was gone—nobody around to see me tooling across the sidewalk on my rag-wrapped knees like some skid row geek.

The city looked different from down here. You never realize how cracked the sidewalks are, how *dirty*, when you have legs to stand on. The buildings, their windows glaring red with the setting sun that had poked through the clouds over New Jersey, looked half again as tall as they had when I was a taller man.

I shuffled to the street and caught myself looking both ways before sliding off the curb. I smiled at the thought of getting run down by a truck on my first trip in over a month across a street that probably hadn't seen the underside of a car since December.

Despite the absurdity of it, I hurried across, and felt relief when I finally reached the far curb. Pulling open the damn doors to George's apartment building was a chore, but I slipped through both of them and into the lobby. George's bike—a light frame Italian model ten-speeder—was there. I didn't like that. George took that bike everywhere. Of course he could have found a car and some gas and gone sightseeing and not told me, but still the sight of that bike standing there made me uneasy.

I shuffled by the silent bank of elevators, watching my longing expression reflected in their silent, immobile chrome doors as I passed. The fire door to the stairwell was a heavy one, but I squeezed through and started up the steps—backwards. Maybe there was a better way, but I hadn't found it. It was all in the arms: Sit on the bottom step, get your arms back, palms down on the step above, lever yourself up. Repeat this ten times and you've done a flight of stairs. Two flights per floor. Thank the Lord or Whatever that George had decided he preferred a second floor apartment to a penthouse after the final power failure.

It was a good thing I was going up backwards. I might never have seen the rats if I'd been faced around the other way.

Just one appeared at first. Alone, it was almost cute with its twitching whiskers and its head bobbing up and down as it sniffed the air at the bottom of the flight. Then two more joined it, then another half dozen. Soon they were a brown wave, undulating up the steps toward me. I hesitated for an instant, horrified and fascinated by their numbers and all their little black eyes sweeping toward me, then I jolted myself into action. I swung the scattergun around, pumped a shell into the chamber, and let them have a blast. Dimly through the reverberating roar of the shotgun I heard a chorus of squeals and saw flashes of flying crimson blossoms, then I was ducking my face into my arms to protect my eyes from the ricocheting shot. I should have realized the danger of shooting in a cinderblock stairwell like this. Not that it would have changed things—I still had to protect myself—but I should have anticipated the ricochets.

The rats did what I'd hoped they'd do—jumped on the dead and near-dead of their number and forgot about me. I let the gun hang in front of me again and continued up the stairs to George's floor.

He didn't answer his bell but the door was unlocked. I'd warned him about that in the past but he'd only laughed in that carefree way of his. "Who's gonna pop in?" he'd say. Probably no one. But that didn't keep me from locking mine, even though George was the only one who knew where I lived. I wondered if that meant I didn't really trust George.

I put the question aside and pushed the door open.

It stank inside. And it was empty as far as I could see. But there was this sound, this wheezing, coming from one of the bedrooms. Calling his name and announcing my own so I wouldn't get my head blown off, I closed the door behind me — locked it — and followed the sound. I found George.

And retched.

George was a blob of flesh in the middle of his bed. Everything but some ribs, some of his facial bones, and the back of his skull had gone soft on him.

I stood there on my knees in shock, wondering how this could have happened. George was *immune*! He'd laughed at the softness! He'd been walking around as good as new just last week. And now...

His lips were dry and cracked and blue — he couldn't speak, couldn't swallow, could barely breathe. And his eyes...they seemed to be just floating there in a quivering pool of flesh, begging me...darting to his left again and again...begging me...

For what?

I looked to his left and saw the guns. He had a suitcase full of them by the bedroom door. All kinds. I picked up a heavy-looking revolver — an S&W .357 — and glanced at him. He closed his eyes and I thought he smiled.

I almost dropped the pistol when I realized what he wanted.

"No, George!"

He opened his eyes again. They began to fill with tears.

"George — I can't!"

Something like a sob bubbled past his lips. And his eyes...his pleading eyes...

I stood there a long time in the stink of his bedroom, listening to him wheeze, feeling the sweat collect between my palm and the pistol grip. I knew I couldn't do it. Not George, the big, friendly, good-natured slob I'd been depending on.

Suddenly, I felt my pity begin to evaporate as a flare of irrational anger began to rise. I *had* been depending on George now that my legs were half gone, and here he'd gone soft on me. The bitter disappointment fueled the anger. I knew it wasn't right, but I couldn't help hating George just then for letting me down.

"Damn you, George!"

I raised the pistol and pointed it where I thought his brain should be. I turned my head away and pulled the trigger. Twice. The pistol jumped in my hand. The sound was deafening in the confines of the bedroom.

Then all was quiet except for the ringing in my ears. George wasn't wheezing anymore. I didn't look around. I didn't have to see. I have a good imagination.

I fled that apartment as fast as my ruined legs would carry me.

But I couldn't escape the vision of George and how he looked before I shot him. It haunted me every inch of the way home, down the now empty stairs where only a few tufts of dirty brown fur were left to indicate that rats had been swarming there, out into the dusk and across the street and up more stairs to home.

George. . .how could it be? He was immune!

Or was he? Maybe the softness had followed a different course in George, slowly building up in his system until every bone in his body was riddled with it and he went soft all at once. *God*, what a noise he must have heard when all those bones went in one shot! That was why he hadn't been able to call or answer the walkie-talkie.

But what if it had been something else? What if the virus theory was right and George was the victim of a more virulent mutation? The thought made me sick with dread. Because if that were true, it meant Judy would eventually end up like George. And I was going to have to do for her what I'd done for George.

But what of me, then? Who was going to end it for *me*? I didn't know if I had the guts to shoot myself. And what if my hands went soft before I had the chance?

I didn't want to think about it, but it wouldn't go away. I couldn't remember ever being so frightened. I almost considered going down to Rockefeller Center and presenting Judy and myself to the leechers, but killed that idea real quick. Never. I'm no jerk. I'm college educated. A degree in biology! I know what they'd do to us!

Inside, Judy had wheeled her chair over to the door and was waiting for me. I couldn't let her know.

"Not there," I told her before she could ask, and I busied myself with putting the shotgun away so I wouldn't have to look her straight in the eyes.

"Where could he be?" Her voice was tight.

"I wish I knew. Maybe he went down to Rockefeller Center. If he did, it's the last we'll ever see of him."

"I can't believe that."

"Then tell me where else he can be."

She was silent.

I did Warner Oland's Chan: "Numbah One Dawtah is finally at loss for words. Peace reigns at last."

I could see that I failed to amuse, so I decided a change of subject was in order.

"I'm tired," I said. It was the truth. The trip across the street had been exhausting.

"Me, too." She yawned.

"Want to get some sleep?" I knew she did. I was just staying a step or two ahead of her so she wouldn't have to ask to be put to bed. She was a dancer, a fine, proud artist. Judy would never have to ask anyone to put her to bed. Not while I was around. As long as I was able I would spare her the indignity of dragging herself along the floor.

I gathered Judy up in my arms. The whole lower half of her body was soft; her legs hung over my left arm like weighted drapes. It was all I could do to keep from crying when I felt them so limp and formless. My dancer. . .you should have seen her in *Swan Lake*. Her legs had been so strong, so sleekly muscular, like her mother's. . .

I took her to the bathroom and left her in there. Which left me alone with my daymares. What if there really was a mutation of the softness and my dancer began leaving me again, slowly, inch by inch. What was I going to do when she was gone? My wife was gone. My folks were gone. My what few friends I'd ever had were gone. Judy was the only attachment I had left. Without her I'd break loose from everything and just float off into space. I needed her...

When she was finished in the bathroom I carried her out and arranged her on the bed. I tucked her in and kissed her goodnight.

Out in the living room I slipped under the covers of the fold-out bed and tried to sleep. It was useless. The fear wouldn't leave me alone. I fought it, telling myself that George was a freak case, that Judy and I had licked the softness. We were *immune* and we'd *stay* immune. Let everyone else turn into puddles of Jello, I wasn't going to let them suck us dry to save themselves. We were on our way to inheriting the earth, Judy and I, and we didn't even have to be meek about it.

But still sleep refused to come. So I lay there in the growing darkness in the center of the silent city and listened...listened as I did every night...as I knew I would listen for the rest of my life...listened for that sound...that cellophane crinkling sound...

House Mothers

J.N. Williamson

Ellery Queen, introducing another book I edited, thought I'd remain young—to him—even after my children were grown. And my close friend and then-co-editor, H. B. "Pete" Williams, called me "that closest thing to perpetual motion."

But that was over 30 years ago. I was in my teens; the Baker Street Irregulars—among them, Anthony Boucher, Vincent Starrett, August Derleth, Christopher Morley and Rex Stout— welcomed me as their youngest member (I was born April 17, 1932); and the seed was planted by them: I wanted most to be a writer.

The point is, I may be a late bloomer but I'm not a newcomer. And since I had the gall to edit Irregular notables—Associated Press exec Charles Honce, Professor Jay Finley Christ, and Latin scholar Morris Rosenblum as well—serving as your editor should surprise only those who can't believe in perpetual motion!

What bewilders me is that Boucher and Derleth were instrumental in boosting the careers of others in Masques, *when they seem to have been at it longer than I! It has a science fiction feel; it is simultaneously like being 17 again— and 104! Perhaps Tony and August invented time travel, after all!*

"House Mothers" is a layered, atmospheric tale meant to say somewhat more than we "genre writers," according to general reputation, are supposed to concern ourselves with. That *won't surprise anyone who has the sense to read, as often as possible, the other, distinguished writers in this anthology.*

In the moment before she discovered the house — at the paralytic instant she understood that the midnight woods concealed no shelter for a running and frightened woman — Pamela filled with second thoughts. Back in Barry's stalled Buick, God-knew-where off an unidentified dirt road, she'd been certain he meant to force her. She'd shrunk from him like a bottle-wadded bug in black cotton, then popped out into this spoon of a woods so complete unto itself that Pamela had half expected to spill over and fall forever into a shining pool of empty space.

Because the young or optimistically youthful fight terror simply by changing their minds, an inner focus, Pamela glanced back to the angry sounds of Barry's door slamming and his initial confrontation with the woods and wondered if she had let his hot ardor merge, in her expectations, with that of other men she'd known. True enough, she'd been raped two years before, that the humiliation afterward seemed even worse, in memory, than the attack. To this time it was her cherished belief, never once spoken, that rape victims urgently needed a place to go — somewhere peaceful, with people who said little, who never asked those questions which implied her complicity or worse, her seduction.

But she should not have let that have anything to do with Barry's relentless arms wrapping round her, his kissing her with unwarranted familiarity, his putting his moist hands where she had not wished them placed. They'd been acquainted only two years, all the time there was since... *what happened*; and he'd *known* about it, he'd even been the soul of gentle patience, until now. He should have understood it might take yet more time, before she was ready; or perhaps, from his viewpoint, he'd already waited longer than most men. Men's rhythms were different, the way they reacted to time's passage, and events.

Why is it, she wondered, brushing hair back from her forehead, again staring into the snaring clutch of the woods, *that we think we're individuals but mix up everybody* else — *stir them like a kind of social stew, till we can't tell them from one another?* A roof's corner was stroked by moonlight and she made out the window of a house; gamely, she pushed forward, mind in turmoil. *It's not just women who do that to men, we do it to other women.*

The flat-roofed, frame structure stretched before Pamela like a long, gray cat sprawled adamantly in the center of the clearing, softly ruffled by the pale, outreaching fingers of a matronly moon. It had a feline's undisclosed years and, in the house's hopeful mixture of styles, its unguessable origins. But the oddly languid grace appeared external and it was spoiled by vestiges of some old tension she imagined sensing. When she had half-crossed the clearing, drab weeds and drained autumn grass clinging damply to her trim ankles, she could see nothing whatever through the undraped window at the front. At first the seeming emptiness of the place suggested a beastly hunger, at best an unnerving hollowness. Then, nearer, all images of the cat were replaced by Pamela's fresh perception of a structure designed for institutional purposes, but long since abandoned.

Reaching the front door, she stopped, a recollection late in coming. *I passed this clearing before—or the edge of it*, she thought, lowering the hand she had raised to rap. She remembered her first burst of panic after bolting from Barry's car, her swift, breath-snatching rush over undetectable mounds and yielding hillocks, the damp branch that snapped against her cheek like a mother's palm. Hand at her breast, dislocated, Pamela glanced back the way she had come, remembering more.

Then—and again now, when she'd found the clearing—she'd had the impression of the sallow, slick-boned moon *receding* before her in the swirling skies, as though it had sought to draw her. . . here.

But that was foolishness! Close to the house, now, there was none of the apprehension she'd known from the woods. Pamela closed her fingers round the doorknob, concealing from herself a moment longer the temptation to go inside; and immediately she felt warmer, safer. If there was a queer readiness to what the house emanated, an unexplained projection of over-anxious *welcoming*, it was because it was intended to be a shelter—no, *more*, a sanctuary, *her* sanctuary! Placing trembling palms on the door Pamela shut her eyes, nodded gratefully. The people had meant it as sanctuary, they'd built it from a dream of service, from visions which *understood* her needs perfectly! It was right for her to enter, it was *proper*—

The door swung wide.

My weight, leaning, Pamela told herself promptly; *it wasn't entirely closed*; and entered.

"Hullo?" So dark, so bewilderingly dark in there! Pamela leaned forward, fingers locked to the frame of the door. As best she could tell, there was a narrow tunnel devoid of furnishings which channeled deep into the house, rooms to the right, and no signs of life. Cupping her brow as people do when they peer against the sun, she edged deeper inside, calling: "Is anybody here?"

At once a high-pitched sound flurried to her ears, so ill-defined it could have been a rodent's squeal, or the squeak of a floorboard bending beneath discreet weight. Pamela stopped, not breathing. It might, she felt, have come from below. Then it was gone so swiftly, and so thoroughly, it must have been nothing.

Shutting the door, putting out her hand to grope for a light-switch, she froze, eyes blinking furiously. While it was too dim to be the result of electricity summoned from elsewhere inside, a uremic trickle of adequate illumination—just that, she decided with some annoyance; adequate light—was unexpectedly provided. Fleetingly disturbed, Pamela turned back into the house's interior.

That first observation she'd made was correct, Pamela perceived. There were no furnishings—no discarded tables with broken legs, no pictures on the walls, no thumbtacks or crumpled papers or paperclips left on the gleaming wooden floors, *no* debris of any sort—in the hallway. Nor, she learned as she ventured forward, in the shadowed rooms leading to the left of the hall. The kitchen, she found, was the same; but when she glanced with shrinking curiosity through a window at the back, only the etched woods leaped into sight, imperturbably mammoth yet skeletally immediate against the house.

Disturbed, Pamela hurried from the kitchen, started back down the hall, aware for the first time how immaculate, how spotless, the place was. It was an absolute marvel, she realized, for a deserted house to be so tidy, so clean; it was all mute testimony to how dusty, even dirty, the city was, and —

She halted, confounded as she looked to her left. The front room — the area she had seen from the clearing, through the exposed window, and believed empty — was *filled with furniture!* She'd followed the natural line of the house's interior, up the hallway to peep into deserted sleeping spaces and one room she had conceived as a nursery, and had not glanced directly into this central living space.

But surely she'd been right in thinking no one was in residence; because nobody she'd ever known lived with all their furniture crammed into *one room!* It was, Pamela mused, entering and stepping slowly around the outer edge of the chamber, rather like a family had been told that a nuclear attack was coming, but was guaranteed that one region of the house — *this* room — would be spared.

Walking almost mincingly, cautiously touching things with her fingers, Pamela realized she had been wrong in believing the area was too crowded for her to move among the things. Paths, of a kind, had been left — narrow gaps wide enough for a slender person like Pamela to pass between tables stacked upon tables and chairs stacked upon chairs, to slip between several old refrigerators, and a miniature, child's rocker that creaked loudly as she did so. Across the room, she noticed three bookcases lining the wall like layers of growing skin, boned by books whose titles she yearned to scan; but that would require a different route, another path. A bed with several mattresses weighing it down was on another side of the front room, chests of drawers next to it and two television sets plus an old cathedral-style radio, strewn with cobwebs, waited there, too.

But her gaze had become temporarily fixed upon a pair of anomalies, items that seemed as out of place to Pamela as the dolls perched at high vantagepoint on an unlit floorlamp, glittering black eyes seeming to follow her movements.

One of the anomalies was a single well-padded, marvelously comfortable-looking easy chair, unlittered, left alone, close to the midpoint of the room — while the other, unexpected object was an intricately-patterned, surely costly, Oriental rug. There was clean, bare space around the edges of the rug and the big, cozy chair faced it.

Raising her head to look wonderingly back the way she'd come, Pamela noticed that all the paths between the old, abandoned furniture led directly to the ancient square of Persian carpeting...

"Pamela!"

The voice, distant, beyond the house, was familiar. Barry's, she realized without caring. He sounded as if he were outside the clearing, still thrashing about in the woods; he sounded both worried, and angry. What right did he have to be annoyed when it was he who had alarmed her, tried to —

Quickly she banished him and sat in the large chair, snuggled into it, imagined the contours striving to mold themselves to her. Smiling, she curled her legs beneath her and closed her eyes, suddenly so sleepy that she could not keep them open.

But it was the secure feeling, how *relaxed* she was, Pamela noted as her eyelids fluttered and she gazed sensually around her — not true sleepiness. Safe — and one thing more: Free to choose, that instant, what would pleasure her. Freed from the lusting, silly, dangerous male in the tangle of late-night woods she was starting to consider her own; freed from that old, terrifying fear that the man who'd raped her might return. Freed from other men who'd dated her, and the ones she'd worked for; from her older brother who'd always been their parents' major concern, and hers; freed from a father with a narrow, blinkered smile, who wanted "nothing for his little girl but her happiness" and who had never expected more from her than that her breasts would blossom "like a flower" and that she would marry a man, "intact."

But I was never intact, Daddy, she thought, drowsy and fretful, hugging the enormous chair's arm and shutting her eyes, *not even before the rapist, not even before your little flower blossomed. Because none of us were...*

...She awakened with the feeling that part of her mind had been left behind, and with the distinct but oddly unstartled impression of voices, muttering, speaking of her.

The Oriental rug which her chair faced lay now in a corner, folded neatly. Where it had been spread, a lid was raised above a missing section of flooring; and Pamela caught a glimpse of something firm, and squared-off, something just beneath the plane of the living room floor that looked like a step. A *top* step.

She leaned forward from her cozy chair, restrained from apprehension. The idea came to her that this place must be an old farmhouse, that what she saw before her was surely a trapdoor, leading to the cellar. How absurd she'd been to react, if marginally, with fear. All empty houses were scary at night and there was a reason why this room was cluttered with furniture. It seemed quite obvious, then, in a still-sleepy manner, what she had blundered into: A farm family'd bought a second home, possibly in town; not wanting to part with this fine house, they had carried everything they owned here, meaning to store it all in the cellar! It was probably an absolutely *huge* cellar lined with shelves containing bottles of jams and jellies, and things; the cellar probably ran the whole length of the house or longer — why, it could run the length of the entire county, if that was what it took to store the family furniture! There was still plenty of room *beneath* the earth, the only uses made of it were the foundations of houses — and cemeteries, of course.

She pressed slowly back into the great chair, gaze locked on the black, yawning hole at her feet. She tucked her legs more tightly under her. Why, then, *hadn't* they taken everything down into their cellar? And it couldn't be a farm, could it, when she'd seen nothing growing out front and nothing at the rear of the property but the hovering, mutely claiming woods?

"F'chris*sake*, Pamela!" The man's voice, from outside the house, nearer but from a different angle. "It's almost *morning!*"

She squeezed her eyes together, shook her head, looked again at the objects in this remarkable room, looking closer. That dining table, it was so beautiful! *I can almost see the ladies gathered around it, sharing the fine supper they prepared together, shyly yet wisely smiling and talking woman talk.* She paused there, remotely conscious of a mistake in what she had pictured, possibly an oversight; but when she refocussed upon the table, no one came before her mind's eye.

Perturbed, conscious of a prickling headache starting at the base of her skull, she followed with her eyes the route she had taken to her chair, saw again the child's tiny rocker, that peculiar way it had of moving, to and fro, driftingly, almost as if some small person, unseen and still, made it rock. *But the rocker is new,* Pamela saw, blinking, trying to concentrate. *Or—unused. No one alive ever sat in that miniature chair.*

Voices, talking—high, eager, discursive yet indistinct—*voices* drifted up, from the cellar. Or, whatever had been conceived deep in the darkness exposed by the lifted trapdoor. They made her jump, microscopically, because she had intentionally avoided thinking of the cellar, because she did not yet feel quite in full command of her thoughts. She became aware then of moonlight groping at the solitary windowpane in the living room, shedding unsteady illumination upon the hole gaping from the middle of the floor. It made unmistakable the fact that there were steps, leading out of sight—a simple means of reaching the source of the soft, far-off voices.

Pamela stood and the corners of her mouth twitched as if she knew, within, that a smile might be in order. A glad smile because, now, there was an end to her apartness; to her loneliness.

No. Pamela shook her head, knowing she'd again misread things. It was not that she was lonely or, really, ever had been. It was that she'd had certain *needs* which had not been fulfilled, could not be fulfilled by the men constantly seeking her out, absorbing her time and attention, her real purposes. And here, it appeared, was another kind of invitation, a different seeking after her, a new wanting. That surely was the proper interpretation of the timidly raised lid, the murmuring, high voices from the blackness. They wanted her to descend the steps and join them.

Fleetingly, her gaze settled on the spotless window, searched beyond. Soon it would be the start of one more day. The man — what he was called would not come to Pamela — had given up on her, driven away, it seemed. And that was...acceptable. She'd known somehow, since entering this place, that the time was coming when, at last, there would be no way back. But that, she assured herself, hearing a resumption of the whispered voices below, an undercurrent of excitement turning the sounds breathless, was no reason to fear. This feeling she had, in a way, was familiar. Pamela recalled being in restaurants during that quiet cusp when day is dying, remembered the other ladies who, looking knowingly at her from beneath partly veiled lids, asked that she accompany them to the restroom. To the Ladies; to togetherness.

They'd had a secret they desired to share with her which glowed beneath the frail, veined eyelids, and they had never shared it with her, before now.

Pamela's feet dipped into the darkness, her legs, then the entire, lower portion of her body was on the descending steps. She smelled something sweeter than sweet and wondered if it were the jellies lining the cellar shelves; and if they had spoiled.

He'd had every intention in the world of putting it to her, that was why he'd gone on seeing her; but he had never wanted it to look like rape to Pamela. Then he'd have had to see it that way. He had meant to *make* her want him, set out to persuade her the single way he knew; but she'd gone and gotten all bent out of shape.

What is so goddam *precious* about it? he asked himself for possibly the twentieth time, recognizing the big branch that had slapped him before and simultaneously dropping beneath it. It wasn't like she was a virgin or anything, and he had waited two whole years. He knew she needed it as much as he did, he sensed how fantastic she'd be once she got control of her crazy female glands. What the hell was she saving it for now? What did she have left *to* save?

Barry had jogged most of the way across the clearing before

it occurred to him to wonder why he hadn't caught so much as a glimpse of the house or the clearing. This *had* to be where she'd gone, dammit, but why she would seek refuge in a rotting, ramshackle heap like that, he couldn't imagine. Nobody lived there.

Pounding up to the door and rushing inside without knocking, it occurred to Barry that the bitch might've told someone he'd tried to rape her. The possibility possessed him until he had turned into the front room of this rickety shack and knew, with no question, that no one was in residence. The place was unbearably filthy; cockroaches scuttled into corners; spiderwebs veined his forehead and upthrown arm, causing Barry to shudder.

He was on the verge of leaving when he noticed something quite strange: An intricately-designed Oriental rug spread as neatly in the center of the room as if the lady of the house had just placed it there.

At first, he nudged it with his toe instead of touching it. He'd always hated the creepy old rags, and the pattern beneath his frowning gaze depicted an uncountable assembly of perfectly gowned women laboring at some unimaginable feminine task. It was offputting, and crazily so. At the same instant he wanted to stare deeply, probingly, into it and to kick it into a corner. But the ancient sucker might be worth a few bucks, it had been left behind and that made it fair game, so he ripped it off the floor, folded it crudely, and tucked it beneath his jacket. *Kinda odd,* he brooded, glancing at a corner of the Oriental where it protruded from his coat. *Not a single man in the whole damned picture.*

Then he detected the traces of a trapdoor, in the space which the rug had covered, and fell to his knees, following the line of it with an index finger. *I'd bet a ton a cellar used to be down there,* Barry reflected, *long before I was born. Womenfolk must have worked from dawn to dusk to stock it with good things, to satisfy their men. A different kind of women, not like modern broads who have it made, but gals who* knew *who was head of the family, king of all he observed. Gals who came across and knew their place.*

Abruptly he longed for those days, but the trapdoor was sealed, probably had been for decades. Passed up by time, the way it was with the clearing at the front — obviously a farm field — and the little graveyard at the side, each cold, gray stone bearing a faded date from more than a hundred years ago.

He wondered, straightening, what had happened to old Pam Neurotic. Must have slipped back to the road, hysterically hitched a ride. Hell with her, she'd never actually accuse him of anything after all the commotion she kicked up two years ago.

He paused at the door. He fancied that he'd heard something, something different, foreign — then another *calling* sound. Someone, or something, calling to *him*. A bogey chill spasmed. That was all crap, like a narcotic flashback; this ruined hovel held no life. Only memories, and maybe feelings.

Returning across the long-abandoned field as the sun struggled to supplant the pale, sapped moon, he realized he hadn't heard one woman's voice. He'd heard two, perhaps more, if he'd heard anything. Perspiring, he started jogging toward the woods; through it and beyond, his city, a conquerable place he knew like the back of his hand, teemed with men headed for work. But here it was like a cold, airless cemetery with the eyes of the dead on the back of his neck. No; more like some awful place *before* the cemetery: a church, maybe, an old-fashioned parlor where they used to lay you out, an enclosed and guarded place, as locked away and far-off as a sanctuary.

Before merging with the woods, Barry stopped to look back.

It was hard to concentrate with that hot rag of a rug inside his jacket, but he felt that he was remembering what the second, the last murmuring voice had said before he rushed from the room and the deserted farmhouse. It wasn't as high-pitched as the first, indistinguishable voice he'd imagined he heard. It might have belonged to an older woman, or it might have been the winds of dawn soughing through the branches of the naked saplings behind the house.

He knew he would remember until he could forget it the sinister, sibilant sounds of greeting: *"Welcome, sister. Welcome!"*

Party Time

Mort Castle

Mort Castle is that gifted writer who has a marvelous reason for not producing more fiction than he does: Castle is engaged in turning the young people of Illinois not only into readers but into potential writers. Free-lance, Crete's mustached master of the macabre is the guy despairing Midwestern educators shout for when students display the imagination to create stories, poems, or novels and said educators haven't the faintest notion what to do with budding Mathesons, Mayhars, and McCammons.

In March of '84, Mort evaluated over 1,000 papers for a writing talent contest, "each one getting a full half-page criticism." I've seen some of the material he uses, most of it written by this witty, caring teacher, and he restores the qualities of helpfulness and usefulness to the word "criticism."

Despite his teaching load, Castle, born July 8, 1946, has found time to write some 90 stories, articles and poems for such magazines as Twilight Zone, Green's, Cavalier, Mike Shayne's, *and* Dude, *in addition to the evocative chapbook* Mulbray *(1976) and two novels of breathtaking psychological insight:* The Deadly Election *('76) and Leisure's* Among Us, The Strangers *('84). The latter utilizes a fictive premise involving a certain kind of murderous mind that is genuinely shocking.*

Here, you'll encounter an example of one of the truly difficult forms in literature, the short-short story. Done properly, such tales have a sudden, devastating impact that lingers, and disturbs. "Party Time" is done properly...

Mama had told him it would soon be party time. That made him excited but also a little afraid. Oh, he liked party time, he liked making people happy, and he always had fun, but it was kind of scary going upstairs.

Still, he knew it would be all right because Mama would be with him. Everything was all right with Mama and he always tried to be Mama's good boy.

Once, though, a long time ago, he had been bad. Mama must not have put his chain on right, so he'd slipped it off his leg and went up the stairs all by himself and opened the door. Oh! Did Mama ever whip him for *that*. Now he knew better. He'd never, never go up without Mama.

And he liked it down in the basement, liked it a lot. There was a little bed to sleep on. There was a yellow light that never went off. He had blocks to play with. It was nice in the basement.

Best of all, Mama visited him often. She kept him company and taught him to be good.

He heard the funny sound that the door at the top of the stairs made and he knew Mama was coming down. He wondered if it was party time. He wondered if he'd get to eat the happy food.

But then he thought it might not be party time. He saw Mama's legs, Mama's skirt. Maybe he had done something bad and Mama was going to whip him.

He ran to the corner. The chain pulled hard at his ankle. He tried to go away, to squeeze right into the wall.

"No, Mama! I am not bad! I love my mama. Don't whip me!"

Oh, he was being silly. Mama had food for him. She wasn't going to whip him.

"You're a good boy. Mama loves you, my sweet, good boy."

The food was cold. It wasn't the kind of food he liked best, but Mama said he always had to eat everything she brought him because if not he was a bad boy.

It was hot food he liked most. He called it the happy food. That's the way it felt inside him.

"Is it party time yet, Mama?"

"Not yet, sweet boy. Don't you worry, it will be soon. You like Mama to take you upstairs for parties, don't you?"

"Yes, Mama! I like to see all the people. I like to make them happy."

Best of all, he liked the happy food. It was so good, so hot.

He was sleepy after Mama left, but he wanted to play with his blocks before he lay down on his bed. The blocks were fun. He liked to build things with them and make up funny games.

He sat on the floor. He pushed the chain out of the way. He put one block on top of another block, then a block on top of that one. He built the blocks up real high, then made them fall. That was funny and he laughed.

Then he played party time with the blocks. He put one block over here and another over there and the big, big block was Mama.

He tried to remember some of the things people said at party time so he could make the blocks talk that way. Then he placed a block in the middle of all the other blocks. That was Mama's good boy. It was himself.

Before he could end the party time game, he got very sleepy. His belly was full, even if it was only cold food.

He went to bed. He dreamed a party time dream of happy faces and the good food and Mama saying, "Good boy, my *sweet* boy."

Then Mama was shaking him. He heard funny sounds coming from upstairs. Mama slipped the chain off his leg.

"Come, my good boy."

"It's party time?"

"Yes."

Mama took his hand. He was frightened a little, the way he always was just before party time.

"It's all right, my sweet boy."

Mama led him up the stairs. She opened the door.

"This is party time. Everyone is so happy."

He was not scared anymore. There was a lot of light and so many laughing people in the party room.

"Here's the good, sweet boy, everybody!"

Then he saw it on the floor. Oh, he hoped it was for him!
"That's *yours*, good boy, all for you."

He was so happy! It had four legs and a black nose. When
he walked closer to it, it made a funny sound that was something like the way *he* sounded when Mama whipped him.

His belly made a noise and his mouth was all wet inside.

It tried to get away from him, but he grabbed it and he
squeezed it, real hard. He heard things going snap inside it.

Mama was laughing and laughing and so was everybody else.
He was making them all so happy.

"You know what it is, don't you, my sweet boy?"

He knew.

It was the happy food.

Everybody Needs a Little Love

Robert Bloch

During the 1960s, the odds were good that, if you were watching TV drama, it had been written by Rod Serling, Richard Matheson, Paddy Chayefsky, Charles Beaumont, Reginald Rose—or Robert Bloch. In winning awards from Screenwriters Guild and Writers Guild of America, his screenplays and scripts, many for Alfred Hitchcock, were beyond uncomputerized counting, and standard-setters for two media.

Yet Bloch, born April 5, 1917, in Chicago, has also found the invention and industry to write such hypnotically-named novels and stories as Out of the Mouths of Graves, Firebug, *"The Scarf,"* Spiderweb, The Couch, *"Yours Truly Jack the Ripper,"* Such Stuff as Screams Are Made Of, *"The Old College Try"—oh, yes, and* Strange Eons, Twilight Zone: The Motion Picture, Psycho, *and* Psycho II.

Robert A. Bloch sold his first story at 17 but earned his bread as a lecturer and ad copywriter, in Milwaukee, until the famous Psycho *did for him what most writers pray their books will do, and Hollywood beckoned. He's remained, since 1960. William F. Nolan remarked, as editor of his Bantam anthology entitled* The Sea of Space, *that Bob has "produced more than four hundred stories and articles, some two-dozen books, plus radio and TV scripts uncounted." But Nolan's anthology was published in 1970!*

Charles L. Grant, another anthologist, speaks of Bloch's fiction leaving an "afterimage." Stephen King, who admires the filmed Psycho *as much as most, reminds us (in* Danse Macabre) *that Norman Bates' dichotomous disposition was well-drawn in Bob's pre-Hitchcock novel. The surprising twists of "Everybody Needs a Little Love," your upcoming love-feast, are state-of-the-art Bloch, told, as always, in his quick-paced style. Quite often, I might add, Robert Bloch is the state of this art.*

It started out as a gag.

I'm sitting at the bar minding my own business, which was drinking up a storm, when this guy got to talking with me.

Curtis his name was, David Curtis. Big, husky-looking straight-arrow type; I figured him to be around thirty, same as me. He was belting it pretty good himself, so right off we had something in common. Curtis told me he was assistant manager of a department store, and since I'm running a video-game arcade in the same shopping mall we were practically neighbors. But talk about coincidence — turns out he'd just gotten a divorce three months ago, exactly like me.

Which is why we both ended up in the bar every night after work, at Happy Hour time. Two drinks for the price of one isn't a bad deal, not if you're trying to cut it with what's left after those monthly alimony payments.

"You think you got zapped?" Curtis said. "My ex-wife wiped me out. I'm not stuck for alimony, but I lost the house, the furniture and the car. Then she hits me for the legal fees and I wind up with zero."

"I read you," I told him. "Gets to the point where you want out so bad you figure it's worth anything. But like the old saying, sometimes the cure is worse than the disease."

"This is my cure," Curtis said, finishing his scotch and ordering another round. "Trouble is, it doesn't work."

"So why are you here?" I asked. "You ought to try that singles bar down the street. Plenty of action there."

"Not for me." Curtis shook his head. "That's where I met my ex. Last thing I need is a singles bar."

"Me neither," I said. "But sometimes it's pretty lonesome just sitting around the apartment watching the Late Show. And I'm not into cooking or housework."

"I can handle that." Curtis rattled his rocks and the bartender poured a refill. "What gets me is going out. Ever notice what happens when you go to a restaurant by yourself? Even if the joint is empty they'll always steer you to one of those crummy little deuce-tables in back, next to the kitchen or the men's john. The waiter gives you a dirty look because a loner means a smaller tip. And when the crowd starts coming in you can kiss service goodbye. The waiter forgets about your order, and when it finally comes, everything's cold. Then, after you finish, you sit around 'til hell freezes, waiting for your check."

"Right on," I said. "So maybe you need a change of pace."

"Like what?"

"Like taking a run up to Vegas some weekend. There's always ads in the paper for bargain rates on airfare and rooms."

"And every damned one of them is for couples." Curtis thumped his glass down on the bar. "Two-for-one on the plane tickets. Double-occupancy for the rooms."

"Try escort service," I told him. "Hire yourself a date, no strings—"

"Not on my income. And I don't want to spend an evening or a weekend with some yacky broad trying to make small-talk. What I need is the silent type."

"Maybe you could run an ad for a deaf-mute?"

"Knock it off! This thing really bugs me. I'm tired of being treated like a cross between a leper and the Invisible Man."

"So what's the answer?" I said. "There's got to be a way—"

"Damn betcha!" Curtis stood up fast, which was a pretty good trick, considering the load he was carrying.

"Where you going?" I asked.

"Come along and see," he said.

Five minutes later I'm watching Curtis use his night-key to unlock the back door of the department store.

Ten minutes later he has me sneaking around outside a store-room in the dark, keeping an eye out for the security guard.

Fifteen minutes later I'm helping Curtis load a window dummy into the back seat of his rental car.

Like I said, it started out as a gag.

At least that's what I thought it was when he stole Estelle.

"That's her name," he told me. "Estelle."

This was a week later, the night he invited me over to his place for dinner. I stopped by the bar for a few quickies beforehand and when I got to his apartment I was feeling no pain. Even so, I started to get uptight the minute I walked in.

Seeing the window dummy sitting at the dinette table gave me a jolt, but when he introduced her by name it really rattled my cage.

"Isn't she pretty?" Curtis said.

I couldn't fault him on that. The dummy was something special — blonde wig, baby-blue eyes, long lashes, and a face with a kind of what-are-you-waiting-for smile. The arms and legs were what you call articulated, and her figure was the kind you see in centerfolds. On top of that, Curtis had dressed it up in an evening gown, with plenty of cleavage.

When he noticed me eyeballing the outfit he went over to a wall closet and slid the door open. Damned if he didn't have the rack full of women's clothes — suits, dresses, sports outfits, even a couple of nighties.

"From the store?" I asked.

Curtis nodded. "They'll never miss them until inventory, and I got tired of seeing her in the same old thing all the time. Besides, Estelle likes nice clothes."

I had to hand it to him, putting me on like this without cracking a smile.

"Sit down and keep her company," Curtis said. "I'll have dinner on the table in a minute."

I sat down. I mean, what the hell else was I going to do? But it gave me an antsy feeling to have a window dummy staring at me across the table in the candlelight. That's right, he'd put candles on the table, and in the shadows you had to look twice to make sure this was only a mannequin or whatever you call it.

Curtis served up a couple of really good steaks and a nice tossed salad. He'd skipped the drinks-before-dinner routine; instead he poured a pretty fair Cabernet with the meal, raising his glass in a toast.

"To Estelle," he said.

I raised my glass too, feeling like a wimp, but trying to go along with the gag. "How come she's not drinking?" I asked.

"Estelle doesn't drink." He still didn't smile. "That's one of the things I like about her."

It was the way he said it that got to me. I had to break up that straight face of his, so I gave him a grin. "I notice she isn't eating very much either."

Curtis nodded. "Estelle doesn't believe in stuffing her face. She wants to keep her figure."

He was still deadpanning, so I said, "If she doesn't drink and she doesn't eat, what happens when you take her to a restaurant?"

"We only went out once," Curtis told me. "Tell me truth, it wasn't the way I expected. They gave us a good table all right, but the waiter kept staring at us and the other customers started making wise-ass remarks under their breath, so now we eat at home. Estelle doesn't need restaurants."

The straighter he played it the more it burned me, so I gave it another shot. "Then I guess you won't be taking her to Vegas after all?"

"We went there last weekend," Curtis said. "I was right about the plane-fare. Not only did I save a bundle, but we got the red-carpet treatment. When they saw me carrying Estelle they must have figured her for an invalid — we got to board first and had our choice of seats upfront. The stewardess even brought her a blanket."

Curtis was really on a roll now, and all I could do was go with it. "How'd you make out with the hotel?" I asked.

"No sweat. Double-occupancy rate, just like the ads said, plus complimentary cocktails and twenty dollars in free chips for the casino."

I tried one more time. "Did Estelle win any money?"

"Oh no — she doesn't gamble." Curtis shook his head. "We ended up spending the whole weekend right there in our room, phoning room service for meals and watching closed-circuit TV. Most of the time we never even got out of bed."

That shook me. "You were in bed with her?"

"Don't worry, it was king-size, plenty of room. And I found out another nice thing about Estelle. She doesn't snore."

I squeezed-off another grin. "Then just what does she do when you go to bed with her?"

"Sleep, of course." Curtis gave me a double-take. "Don't go getting any ideas. If I wanted the other thing I could have picked up one of those inflatable rubber floozies from a sex-shop. But there's no hanky-panky with Estelle. She's a real lady."

"A real lady," I said. "Now I've heard everything."

"Not from her." Curtis nodded at the dummy. "Haven't you noticed? I've been doing all the talking and she hasn't said a word. You don't know how great it is to have someone around who believes in keeping her mouth shut. Sure, I do the cooking and the housework, but it's no more of a hassle than when I was living here alone."

"You don't feel alone anymore, is that it?"

"How could I? Now when I come home nights I've got some-body waiting for me. No nagging, no curlers in the hair — just the way she is now, neat and clean and well-dressed. She even uses that perfume I gave her. Can't you smell it?"

Damned if he wasn't right. I *could* smell perfume.

I sneaked another peek at Estelle. Sitting in the shadows with the candlelight soft on her hair and face, she almost had me fooled for a minute. Almost, but not quite.

"Just look at her," Curtis said. "Beautiful! Look at that smile!"

Now, for the first time, he smiled too. And it was his smile I looked at, not hers.

"Okay," I said. "You win. If you're trying to tell me Estelle is better company than most women, it's no contest."

"I figured you'd understand." Curtis hadn't changed his expression, but there was something wrong about that smile of his, something that got to me.

So I had to say it. "I don't want to be a party-pooper, but the way you come on, maybe there's such a thing as carrying a gag too far."

He wasn't smiling now. "Who said anything about a gag? Are you trying to insult Estelle?"

"I'm not trying to insult anybody," I told him. "Just remember, she's only a dummy."

"Dummy?" All of a sudden he was on his feet and coming

around the table, waving those big fists of his. "You're the one who's a dummy! Get the hell out of here before I—"

I got out, before.

Then I went over to the bar, had three fast doubles, and headed for home to hit the sack. I went out like a light but it didn't keep the dreams away, and all night long I kept staring at the smiles—the smile on his face and the smile on the dummy's—and I don't know which one spooked me the most.

Come to think of it, they both looked the same.

That night was the last night I went to the bar for a long time. I didn't want to run into Curtis there, but I was still seeing him in those dreams.

I did my drinking at home now, but the dreams kept coming, and it loused me up at work when I was hungover. Pretty soon I started pouring a shot at breakfast instead of orange juice.

So I went to see Dr. Mannerheim.

That shows how rough things were getting, because I don't like doctors and I've always had a thing about shrinks. This business of lying on a couch and spilling your guts to a stranger always bugged me. But it had got to where I started calling in sick and just sat home staring at the walls. Next thing you know, I'd start climbing them.

I told Mannerheim that when I saw him.

"Don't worry," he said. "I won't ask you to lay on a couch or take ink-blot tests. The physical shows you're a little run-down, but this can be corrected by proper diet and a vitamin supplement. Chances are you may not even need therapy at all."

"Then what am I here for?" I said.

"Because you have a problem. Suppose we talk about it."

Dr. Mannerheim was just a little baldheaded guy with glasses; he looked a lot like an uncle of mine who used to take me to ballgames when I was a kid. So it wasn't as hard to talk as I'd expected.

I filled him in on my setup—the divorce and all—and he picked up on it right away. Said it was getting to be a common thing nowadays with so many couples splitting. There's always a hassle working out a new life-style afterwards and sometimes a kind of guilty feeling; you keep wondering if it was your fault and that maybe something's wrong with you.

We got into the sex bit and the drinking, and then he asked me about my dreams.

That's when I told him about Curtis.

Before I knew it I'd laid out the whole thing—getting smashed in the bar, stealing the dummy, going to Curtis's place for dinner, and what happened there.

"Just exactly what did happen?" Mannerheim said. "You say you had a few drinks before you went to his apartment—maybe three or four—and you drank wine with your dinner."

"I wasn't bombed, if that's what you mean."

"But your perceptions were dulled," he told me. "Perhaps he intended to put you on for a few laughs, but when he saw your condition he got carried away."

"If you'd seen the way he looked when he told me to get out you'd know it wasn't a gag," I said. "The guy is a nut-case."

Something else hit me all of a sudden, and I sat up straight in my chair. "I remember a movie I saw once. There's this ventriloquist who gets to thinking his dummy is alive. Pretty soon he starts talking to it, then he gets jealous of it, and next thing you know—"

Mannerheim held up his hand. "Spare me the details. There must be a dozen films like that. But in all my years of practice I've never read, let alone run across, a single case where such a situation actually existed. It all goes back to the old Greek legend about Pygmalion, the sculptor who made a statue of a beautiful woman that came to life.

"But you've got to face facts." He ticked them off on his fingers. "Your friend Curtis has a mannequin, not a ventriloquist's dummy. He doesn't try to create the illusion that it speaks, or use his hand to make it move. And he didn't create the figure, he's not a sculptor. So what does that leave us with?"

"Just one thing," I said. "He's treating this dummy like a real person."

Mannerheim shook his head. "A man who's capable of

carrying a window dummy into a restaurant and a hotel – or who claims to have done so in order to impress you – may still just have taken advantage of your condition to play out an elaborate practical joke."

"Wrong." I stood up. "I tell you he believes the dummy is alive."

"Maybe and maybe not. It isn't important." Mannerheim took off his glasses and stared at me. "What's important is that *you* believe the dummy is alive."

It hit me like a sock in the gut. I had to sit down again and catch my breath before I could answer him.

"You're right," I said. "That's why I really wanted out of there. That's why I keep having those damned dreams. That's why there's a drinking problem. Maybe I was juiced-up when I saw her, maybe Curtis hypnotized me, how the hell do I know? But whatever happened or didn't happen, it worked. And I've been running scared ever since."

"Then stop running." Dr. Mannerheim put his glasses on again. "The only way to fight fear is to face it."

"You mean go back there?"

He nodded at me. "If you want to get rid of the dreams, get rid of the dependency on alcohol, the first step is to separate fantasy from reality. Go to Curtis, and go sober. Examine the actual circumstances with a clear head. I'm satisfied that you'll see things differently. Then, if you still think you need further help, get in touch."

We both stood up, and Dr. Mannerheim walked me to the door. "Have a good day," he said.

I didn't.

It took all that weekend just to go over what he'd said, and another two days before I could buy his advice. But it made sense. Maybe Curtis had been setting me up like the shrink said; if not, then he was definitely a flake. But one way or another I had to find out.

So Wednesday night I went up to his apartment. I wasn't on the sauce, and I didn't call Curtis in advance. That way, if he didn't know I was coming, he wouldn't plan on pulling another rib—if it was a rib.

It must have been close to nine o'clock when I walked down the hall and knocked on his door. There was no answer; maybe he was gone for the evening. But I kept banging away, just in case, and finally the door opened.

"Come on in," Curtis said.

I stared at him. He was wearing a pair of dirty, wrinkled-up pajamas, but he looked like he hadn't slept for a week—his face was grey, big circles under his eyes, and he needed a shave. When we shook hands I felt like I was holding a sack of ice-cubes.

"Good to see you," he told me, closing the door after I got inside. "I was hoping you'd come by so's I could apologize for the way I acted the other night."

"No hard feelings," I said."

"I knew you wouldn't hold it against me," he went on. "That's what I told Estelle."

Curtis turned and nodded across the living room, and in the dim light I saw the dummy sitting there on the sofa, facing the TV screen. The set was turned on to some old western movie, but the sound was way down and I could scarcely hear the dialogue.

It didn't matter, because I was looking at the dummy. She wore some kind of fancy cocktail dress, which figured, because I could see the bottle on the coffee table and smell the whisky on Curtis's breath. What grabbed me was the other stuff she was wearing—the earrings, and the bracelet with the big stones that sparkled and gleamed. They had to be costume jewelry, but they looked real in the light from the TV tube. And the way the dummy sat, sort of leaning forward, you'd swear it was watching the screen.

Only I knew better. Seeing the dummy cold sober this way, it was just a wooden figure, like the others I saw in the store-room where Curtis stole it. Dr. Mannerheim was right; now that I got a good look the dummy didn't spook me anymore.

Curtis went over to the coffee table and picked up the bottle. "Care for a drink?" he asked.

I shook my head. "No, thanks, not now."

But he kept holding the bottle when he bent down and kissed the dummy on the side of its head. "How can you hear anything with the sound so low?" he said. "Let me turn up the volume for you."

And so help me, that's what he did. Then he smiled at the dummy. "I don't want to interrupt while you're watching, honey. So if it's okay with you, we'll go in the bedroom and talk there."

He moved back across the living room and started down the hall. I followed him into the bedroom at the far end and he closed the door. It shut off the sound from the TV set but now I heard another noise, a kind of chirping.

Looking over at the far corner I saw the bird-cage on a stand, with a canary hopping around inside.

"Estelle likes canaries," Curtis said. "Same as my ex. She always had a thing for pets." He tilted the bottle.

I just stood there, staring at the room. It was a real disaster area—bed not made, heaped-up clothes lying on the floor, empty fifths and glasses everywhere. The place smelled like a zoo.

The bottle stopped gurgling and then I heard the whisper. "Thank God you came."

I glanced up at Curtis. He wasn't smiling now. "You've got to help me," he said."

"What's the problem?" I asked."

"Keep your voice down," he whispered. "I don't want her to hear us."

"Don't start that again," I told him. "I only stopped in because I figured you'd be straightened out by now."

"How can I? She doesn't let me out of her sight for a minute—the last time I got away from here was three days ago, when I turned in the rental car and bought her the Mercedes."

That threw me. "Mercedes? You're putting me on."

Curtis shook his head. "It's downstairs in the garage right now—brand new 280-SL, hasn't been driven since I brought it home. Estelle doesn't like me to go out alone and she doesn't want to go out either. I keep hoping she'll change her mind because I'm sick of being cooped-up here, eating those frozen TV dinners. You'd think she'd at least go for a drive with me after getting her the car and all."

"I thought you told me you were broke," I said. "Where'd you get the money for a Mercedes?"

He wouldn't look at me. "Never mind. That's my business."

"What about your business?" I asked. "How come you haven't been showing up at work?"

"I quit my job," he whispered. "Estelle told me to."

"Told you? Make sense, man. Window dummies don't talk."

He gave me a glassy-eyed stare. "Who said anything about window dummies? Don't you remember how it was the night we got her — how she was standing there in the storage room waiting for me? The others were dummies all right, I know that. But Estelle knew I was coming, so she just stood there pretending to be like all the rest because she didn't want you to catch on.

"She fooled you, right? I'm the only one who knew Estelle was different. There were all kinds of dummies there, some real beauties, too. But the minute I laid eyes on her I knew she was the one.

"And it was great, those first few days with her. You saw for yourself how well we got along. It wasn't until afterwards that everything went wrong, when she started telling me about all the stuff she wanted, giving me orders, making me do crazy things."

"Look," I said. "If there's anything crazy going on around here, you're the one who's responsible. And you better get your act together and put a stop to it right now. Maybe you can't do it alone, the shape you're in, but I've got a friend, a doctor —"

"Doctor? You think I'm whacko, is that it?" He started shaking all over and there was a funny look in his eyes. "Here I thought you'd help me, you were my last hope!"

"I want to help," I told him. "That's why I came. First off, let's try to clean this place up. Then you're going to bed, get a good night's rest."

"What about Estelle?" he whispered.

"Leave that to me. When you wake up tomorrow I promise the dummy'll be gone."

That's when he threw the bottle at my head.

I was still shaking the next afternoon when I got to Dr. Mannerheim's office and told him what happened.

"Missed me by inches," I said. "But it sure gave me one hell of a scare. I ran down the hall to the living room. That damn dummy was still sitting in front of the TV like it was listening to the program and that scared me too, all over again. I kept right on running until I got home. That's when I called your answering service."

Mannerheim nodded at me. "Sorry it took so long to get back to you. I had some unexpected business."

"Look, Doc," I said. "I've been thinking. Curtis wasn't really trying to hurt me. The poor guy's so uptight he doesn't realize what he's doing anymore. Maybe I should have stuck around, tried to calm him down."

"You did the right thing." Mannerheim took off his glasses and polished them with his handkerchief. "Curtis is definitely psychotic, and very probably dangerous."

That shook me. "But when I came here last week you said he was harmless—"

Dr. Mannerheim put his glasses on. "I know. But since then I've found out a few things."

"Like what?"

"Your friend Curtis lied when he told you he quit his job. He didn't quit—he was fired."

"How do you know?"

"I heard about it the day after I saw you, when his boss called me in. I was asked to run a series of tests on key personnel as part of a security investigation. It seems that daily bank deposits for the store show a fifty-thousand dollar loss in the cash-flow. Somebody juggled the books."

"The Mercedes!" I said. "So that's where he got the money!"

"We can't be sure just yet. But polygraph tests definitely rule out other employees who had access to the records. We do know where he bought the car. The dealer only got a down-payment so the rest of the cash, around forty thousand, is still unaccounted-for."

"Then it's all a scam, right, Doc? What he really means to do is take the cash and split out. He was running a number on me about the dummy, trying to make me think he's bananas, so I wouldn't tumble to what he's up to."

"I'm afraid it isn't that simple." Mannerheim got up and started pacing the floor. "I've been doing some rethinking about Curtis and his hallucination that the dummy is alive. That canary you mentioned—a pity he didn't get it before he stole the mannequin."

"What are you driving at?"

"There are a lot of lonely people in this world, people who aren't necessarily lonely by choice. Some are elderly, some have lost all close relatives through death, some suffer an after-shock following divorce. But all of them have one thing in common—the need for love. Not physical love, necessarily, but what goes with it. The companionship, attention, a feeling of mutual affection. That's why so many of them turn to keeping pets.

"I'm sure you've seen examples. The man who spends all his time taking care of his dog. The widow who babies her kitten. The old lady who talks to her canary, treating it like an equal."

I nodded. "The way Curtis treats the dummy?"

Mannerheim settled down in his chair again. "Usually they don't go that far. But in extreme cases the pretense gets out of hand. They not only talk to their pets, they interpret each growl or purr or chirp as a reply. It's called personification."

"But these pet-owners—they're harmless, aren't they? So why do you say Curtis might be dangerous?"

Dr. Mannerheim leaned forward in his chair. "After talking to the people at the store I did a little further investigation on my own. This morning I went down to the courthouse and checked the files. Curtis told you he got a divorce here in town three months ago, but there's no record of any proceedings. And I found out he was lying to you about other things. He was married, all right; he did own a house and furniture and a car.

But there's nothing to show he ever turned anything over to his wife. Chances are he sold his belongings to pay off gambling debts. We know he did some heavy betting at the track."

"We?" I said. "You and who else?"

"Sheriff's department. They're the ones who told me about his wife's disappearance, three months ago."

"You mean she ran out on him?"

"That's what he said after neighbors noticed she was missing and they called him in this morning. He told them downtown that he'd come home from work one night and his wife was gone, bag and baggage — no explanation, no note, nothing. He denied they'd quarreled, said he'd been too ashamed to report her absence, and had kept hoping she'd come back or at least get in touch with him."

"Did they buy his story?"

Mannerheim shrugged. "Women do leave their husbands, for a variety of reasons, and there was nothing to show Curtis wasn't telling the truth. They put out an all-points on his wife and kept the file open, but so far no new information has turned up, not until this embezzlement matter and your testimony. I didn't mention that this morning, but I have another appointment this evening and I'll tell them then. I think they'll take action, once they hear your evidence."

"Wait a minute," I said. "I haven't given you any evidence."

"I think you have." Mannerheim stared at me. "According to the neighbors, Curtis was married to a tall blonde with blue eyes, just like the window dummy you saw. And his wife's name was Estelle."

It was almost dark by the time I got to the bar. The Happy Hour had started, but I wasn't happy. All I wanted was a drink — a couple of drinks — enough to make me forget the whole thing.

Only it didn't work out that way. I kept thinking about what Mannerheim told me, about Curtis and the mess he was in.

The guy was definitely psyched-out, no doubt about that. He'd ripped-off his boss, lost his job, screwed up his life.

But maybe it wasn't his fault. I knew what he'd gone through because I had been there myself. Getting hit with a divorce was bad enough to make me slip my gears, and for him it must have been ten times worse. Coming home and finding his wife gone, just like that, without a word. He never said so, but he must have loved her—loved her so much that when she left him he flipped-out, stealing the dummy, calling it by her name. Even when he got to feeling trapped he couldn't give the dummy up because it reminded him of his wife. All this was pretty far-out, but I could understand. Like Mannerheim said, everybody needs a little love.

If anyone was to blame, it was that wife of his. Maybe she split because she was cheating on him, the way mine did. The only difference is that I could handle it and he cracked up. Now he'd either be tossed in the slammer or get put away in a puzzle-factory, and all because of love. His scuzzy wife got away free and he got dumped on. After Mannerheim talked to the law they'd probably come and pick him up tonight—poor guy, he didn't have a chance.

Unless I gave it to him.

I ordered up another drink and thought about that. Sure, if I tipped him off and told him to run it could get me into a bind. But who would know? The thing of it was, I could understand Curtis, even put myself in his place. Both of us had the same raw deal, but I'd lucked-out and he couldn't take it. Maybe I owed him something—at least a lousy phone-call.

So I went over to the pay-phone at the end of the bar. This big fat broad was using the phone, probably somebody's cheating wife handing her husband a line about why she wasn't home. When I came up she gave me a dirty look and kept right on yapping.

It was getting on towards eight o'clock now. I didn't know when Dr. Mannerheim's appointment was set with the Sheriff's department, but there wouldn't be much time left. And Curtis's apartment was only three blocks away.

I made it in five minutes, walking fast. So fast that I didn't even look around when I crossed in front of the entrance to the building's underground-parking place.

If I hadn't heard the horn I'd have been a goner. As it was, there were just about two seconds for me to jump back when the big blue car came tearing up the ramp and wheeled into the street. Just two seconds to get out of the way, look up, and see the Mercedes take off.

Then I took off too, running into the building and down the hall.

The only break I got was finding Curtis's apartment door wide open. He was gone—I already knew that—but all I wanted now was to use the phone.

I called the Sheriff's office and Dr. Mannerheim was there. I told him where I was and about seeing the car take off, and after that things happened fast.

In a couple of minutes a full squad of deputies wheeled in. They went through the place and came up with zilch. No Curtis, no Estelle—even the dummy's clothes were missing. And if he had forty grand or so stashed away, that was gone too; all they found was a rip in a sofa-cushion where he could have hid the loot.

But another squad had better luck, if you can call it that. They located the blue Mercedes in an old gravel-pit off the highway about five miles out of town.

Curtis was lying on the ground next to it, stone-cold dead, with a big butcher knife stuck between his shoulder-blades. The dummy was there too, lying a few feet away. The missing money was in Curtis's wallet—all big bills—and the dummy's wardrobe was in the rear seat, along with Curtis's luggage, like he'd planned to get out of town for good.

Dr. Mannerheim was with the squad out there and he was the one who suggested digging into the pit. It sounded wild, but he kept after them until they moved a lot of gravel. His hunch paid off, because about six feet down they hit pay-dirt.

It was a woman's body, or what was left of it after three months in the ground.

The coroner's office had a hell of a time making an ID. It turned out to be Curtis's wife, of course, and there were about twenty stab-wounds on her, all made with a butcher knife like the one that killed Curtis.

Funny thing, they couldn't get any prints off the handle; but there were a lot of funny things about the whole business. Dr. Mannerheim figured Curtis killed his wife and buried her in the pit, and what sent him over the edge was guilt-feelings. So he stole the dummy and tried to pretend it was his wife. Calling her Estelle, buying all those things for her — he was trying to make up for what he'd done, and finally he got to the point where he really thought she was alive.

Maybe that makes sense, but it still doesn't explain how Curtis was killed, or why.

I could ask some other questions too. If you really believe something with all your heart and soul, how long does it take before it comes true? And how long does a murder victim lie in her grave plotting to get even?

But I'm not going to say anything. If I told them my reasons they'd say I was crazy too.

All I know is that when the Mercedes came roaring out of the underground garage I had only two seconds to get out of the way. But it was long enough for me to get a good look, long enough for me to swear I saw Curtis and the dummy together in the front seat.

And Estelle was the one behind the wheel.

Angel's Exchange

Jessica Amanda Salmonson

Admiring the title Tales By Moonlight *which Jessica Salmonson used for her anthology, we said so. She said she'd had a dream once of "the perfect title": "I awoke in the middle of the night thinking, 'My gosh! That's great! I've got to write it down or I'll forget it come morning!'" She did so, and "come morning, I had indeed forgotten . . . and looked about for the scrap, which said* very *clearly:* Night Skirt." *Seattle's gift to fantasy did a doubletake. "*Night *skirt? I threw the scrap away!"*

Salmonson, born January 6, 1950, finds time to see a weekly samurai film — surely an influence upon her novels Tomoe Gozen, Thousand Shrine Warrior, *and her newest,* Ou Lu Khen and the Beautiful Madwoman. *Her envelopes are decorated, too, with colorful images of Japan — plus pictures of strawberries which actually have a fragrance! Jessica . . . surprises.*

"Angel's Exchange," the prose-poem following, she "rather likes" because of "its oddness." The Strange Company has collected eleven of them in a chapbook entitled Innocent of Evil, *and also will be publishing her anthology of 19th century yarns,* The Haunted Wherry and Other Rare Ghost Stories. *To save you looking it up, a "wherry" was a broad, light barge. Salmonson has style!*

"Ah, my brother angel Sleep, I beg a boon of thee," said grimacing Death.

"It cannot be," answered Sleep, "that I grant a gift of slumber to you, for Death must be forever vigilant in his cause."

"That is just it," said Death. "I grow melancholy with my lot. Everywhere I go, I am cursed by those I strive most to serve. The forgetfulness of your gift brings momentary respite and would help a wearied spirit heal."

"I can scarce believe you are greeted with less enthusiasm than I!" exclaimed the angel Sleep, appalled and incredulous. "Despite the transience of the gift I bring to mortals, they seem ever happy to have had it for a time. Your own gift is an ever-lasting treasure, and should be sought more quickly than mine."

"Aye, some seek me out, but never in joyous mind," said Death, his voice low and self-pitying. "You are praised at morning's light, when people have had done with you. Perhaps it is the very impermanence of your offering which fills them with admiration; the gift itself means little."

"I cannot see that that is so," said Sleep, though not affronted by the extrapolation. "What I would give for your gift held to my breast! Do you think there is anything so weary as Sleep itself? Yet I am denied your boon, as you are denied mine; I, without a moment's rest, deliver it to others, like a starving grocery-boy on rounds. It is my ceaseless task to give humanity a taste of You, so they might be prepared. Yet you say they meet you with hatred and trepidation. Have I, then, failed my task?"

"I detect an unhappiness as great as mine," said Death, a rueful light shining in the depths of his hollow eyes.

"Brothers as we are," said Sleep, "it is sad to realize we know so little of the other's sentiment. Each of us is unhappy with our lot. This being so, why not trade professions? You take my bag of slumber, and I your bag of souls; but if we find our-selves dissatisfied even then, we must continue without complaint."

"I would not mind giving you my burden and taking up yours," said Death. "Even if I remain sad, I cannot believe I would be sadder; and there is the chance things would improve for me."

So Death and Sleep exchanged identities. Thereafter, Sleep came nightly to the people of the world, a dark presence, sinister, with the face of a skull; and thereafter, Death came, as bright and beautiful as Gabriel, with as sweet a sound. In time, great cathedrals were raised, gothic and somber, and Sleep was worshipped by head-shaven, emaciated monks. Thereafter, beauty was considered frightening. The prettiest children were sacrificed in vain hope of Death's sweet face not noticing the old.

Thus stands the tale of how Death became Sleep and Sleep became Death. If the world was fearful before, it is more so now.

Down by the Sea
near the Great Big Rock

Joe R. Lansdale

When writing is published under a pseudonym, there can be many reasons for it. Fame elsewhere and fear of a conflict of interests; a reputation in maudlin poetry while the pseudonymous work is pornographic; he (or she) places so much material in the same genre that the market appears oversaturated with his customary byline; he's ashamed of it but needs the money; etc.

There's this safe conclusion: The author adores writing so much that he's willing to relinquish the joy of seeing his real *name in print.*

Joe Lansdale's yarns have appeared under four pseudonyms — "Jonathan Harker," one example of this full-time writer's gall — and he's never had to be ashamed of anything. The one writer I know who may have *to write more than I is the Nacogdoches, Texas Terror, with over 60 tales of original, point-blank horror.*

He's young (October 28, 1951) yet he's sold to Twilight Zone, The Saint, Cavalier, *and such leading anthologies as* Necropolis of Horror *("The White Rabbit" — "one of the truly original concepts in the genre," said the editor);* Shadows 6 *("Hair of the Head");* Fears; Spectre; *and* Great Stories from the Twilight Zone *("The Dump"). Joe's psychosexual suspenser,* Act of Love, *subtly shows the influence of his confessed "role models": Matheson, Nolan, King, Bloch, and McCammon.*

"Down By the Sea" is a tale that makes you a quivering observer — not by keyhole but by camera close-up that puts you squarely there, *wringing your hands, screaming that* somebody must do *something. My inclination was to run...*

Down by the sea near the great big rock, they made their camp and toasted marshmallows over a small, fine fire. The night was pleasantly chill and the sea spray cold. Laughing, talking, eating the gooey marshmallows, they had one swell time; just them, the sand, the sea and the sky, and the great big rock.

The night before they had driven down to the beach, to the camping area; and on their way, perhaps a mile from their destination, they had seen a meteor shower, or something of that nature. Bright lights in the heavens, glowing momentarily, seeming to burn red blisters across the ebony sky.

Then it was dark again, no meteoric light, just the natural glow of the heavens — the stars, the dime-size moon.

They drove on and found an area of beach on which to camp, a stretch dominated by pale sands and big waves, and the great big rock.

Toni and Murray watched the children eat their marshmallows and play their games, jumping and falling over the great big rock, rolling in the cool sand. About midnight, when the kids were crashed out, they walked along the beach like fresh-found lovers, arm in arm, shoulder to shoulder, listening to the sea, watching the sky, speaking words of tenderness.

"I love you so much," Murray told Toni, and she repeated the words and added, "and our family too."

They walked in silence now, the feelings between them words enough. Sometimes Murray worried that they did not talk as all the marriage manuals suggested, that so much of what he had to say on the world and his work fell on the ears of others, and that she had so little to truly say to him. Then he would think: What the hell? I know how I feel. Different messages, unseen, unheard, pass between us all the time, and they communicate in a fashion words cannot.

He said some catch phrase, some pet thing between them, and Toni laughed and pulled him down on the sand. Out there beneath that shiny-dime moon, they stripped and loved on the beach like young sweethearts, experiencing their first night together after long expectation.

It was nearly two a.m. when they returned to the camper,

checked the children and found them sleeping comfortably as kittens full of milk.

They went back outside for awhile, sat on the rock and smoked and said hardly a word. Perhaps a coo or a purr passed between them, but little more.

Finally they climbed inside the camper, zipped themselves into their sleeping bag and nuzzled together on the camper floor.

Outside the wind picked up, the sea waved in and out, and a slight rain began to fall.

Not long after Murray awoke and looked at his wife in the crook of his arm. She lay there with her face a grimace, her mouth opening and closing like a guppie, making an "uhhh, uhh," sound.

A nightmare perhaps. He stroked the hair from her face, ran his fingers lightly down her cheek and touched the hollow of her throat and thought: What a nice place to carve out some fine, white meat...

— *What in hell is wrong with me?* Murray snapped inwardly, and he rolled away from her, out of the bag. He dressed, went outside and sat on the rock. With shaking hands on his knees, buttocks resting on the warmth of the stone, he brooded. Finally he dismissed the possibility that such a thought had actually crossed his mind, smoked a cigarette and went back to bed.

He did not know that an hour later Toni awoke and bent over him and looked at his face as if it were something to squash. But finally she shook it off and slept.

The children tossed and turned. Little Roy squeezed his hands open, closed, open, closed. His eyelids fluttered rapidly.

Robyn dreamed of striking matches.

Morning came and Murray found that all he could say was, "I had the oddest dream."

Toni looked at him, said, "Me too," and that was all.

Placing lawn chairs on the beach, they put their feet on the rock and watched the kids splash and play in the waves; watched as Roy mocked the sound of the JAWS music and made fins with his hands and chased Robyn through the water as she scuttled backwards and screamed with false fear.

Finally they called the children from the water, ate a light lunch, and, leaving the kids to their own devices, went in for a swim.

The ocean stroked them like a mink-gloved hand. Tossed them, caught them, massaged them gently. They washed together, laughing, kissing —

— Then tore their lips from one another as up on the beach they heard a scream.

Roy had his fingers gripped about Robyn's throat, had her bent back over the rock and was putting a knee in her chest. There seemed no play about it. Robyn was turning blue.

Toni and Murray waded for shore, and the ocean no longer felt kind. It grappled with them, held them, tripped them with wet, foamy fingers. It seemed an eternity before they reached shore, yelling at Roy.

Roy didn't stop. Robyn flopped like a dying fish.

Murray grabbed the boy by the hair and pulled him back, and for a moment, as the child turned, he looked at his father with odd eyes that did not seem his, but looked instead as cold and firm as the great big rock.

Murray slapped him, slapped him so hard Roy spun and went down, stayed there on hands and knees, panting.

Murray went to Robyn, who was already in Toni's arms, and on the child's throat were blue-black bands like thin, ugly snakes.

"Baby, baby, are you okay?" Toni said over and over. Murray wheeled, strode back to the boy, and Toni was now yelling at him, crying, "Murray, Murray, easy now. They were just playing and it got out of hand."

Roy was on his feet, and Murray, gritting his teeth, so angry he could not believe it, slapped the child down.

"MURRAY," Toni yelled, and she let go of the sobbing Robyn and went to stay his arm, for he was already raising it for another strike. "That's no way to teach him not to hit, not to fight."

Murray turned to her, almost snarling, but then his face

relaxed and he lowered his hand. Turning to the boy, feeling very criminal, Murray reached down to lift Roy by the shoulder. But Roy pulled away, darted for the camper.

"Roy," he yelled, and started after him. Toni grabbed his arm.

"Let him be," she said. "He got carried away and he knows it. Let him mope it over. He'll be all right." Then softly: "I've never known you to get that mad."

"I've never been so mad before," he said honestly.

They walked back to Robyn, who was smiling now. They all sat on the rock, and about fifteen minutes later Robyn got up to see about Roy. "I'm going to tell him it's okay," she said. "He didn't mean it." She went inside the camper.

"She's sweet," Toni said.

"Yeah," Murray said, looking at the back of Toni's neck as she watched Robyn move away. He was thinking that he was supposed to cook lunch today, make hamburgers, slice onions; big onions cut thin with a freshly sharpened knife. He decided to go get it.

"I'll start lunch," he said flatly, and stalked away.

As he went, Toni noticed how soft the back of his skull looked, so much like an over-ripe melon.

She followed him inside the camper.

Next morning, after the authorities had carried off the bodies, taken the four of them out of the bloodstained, fire-gutted camper, one detective said to another:

"Why does it happen? Why would someone kill a nice family like this? And in such horrible ways. . .set fire to it afterwards?"

The other detective sat on the huge rock and looked at his partner, said tonelessly, "Kicks maybe."

That night, when the moon was high and bright, gleaming down like a big spotlight, the big rock, satiated, slowly spread its flippers out, scuttled across the sand, into the waves, and began to swim toward the open sea. The fish that swam near it began to fight.

The First Day of Spring

David Knoles

It's interesting, if no longer news, that writers come from more varied and unexpected—sometimes contrary—vocational backgrounds than most people. Ben Jonson, celebrated producer of the masque, could boast that he'd cast an actor named Will Shakespeare in his own plays. Contributors to the present book are or have been racing drivers; teachers; master mechanics; cartoonists; lawyers; detectives; medical doctors; farmers; ad men; salesmen; singers and actors (one who cut records and starred in Kiss Me, Kate; *another who trained for grand opera); decorated servicemen; reviewers; parapsychology investigators; and taxi hacks. At least two are experts in martial arts.*

David Knoles, a Los Angelino born January 14, 1949, is cut from this versatile stripe. A new fiction writer, he's edited a Manhattan Beach newspaper and spent four years in the U. S. Air Force (1968–1972). An admirer of anything created by filmmaker Roger Corman, Stephen King, or Ray Bradbury, and currently managing editor of an automotive trade magazine, Knoles is one of those creative aspirants who, with encouragement, can produce much more fiction and see his career flourish.

*He writes all-out, revulsive horror—the kind non-fantasy devotees mean, when forced to confess that they "like a little gore now and then"—*knowingly. *This is the kind of yarn on which we all cut our supernatural eyeteeth—those that throb even when we believe they were pulled. "The First Day of Spring" makes one yearn for winter, when such* creatures *are safely skulking, or slithering, beneath the snow at our feet— creatures we only* think *have gone away forever...*

Years ago, at winter's end

It had been a particularly long, miserable winter for the eleven-year-old boy. In particular, a lingering ear infection of unknown cause had left him gaunt, and pale. Dad, who loved living in Arizona, had even suggested that "my little trooper has been swapped for a make-believe lad."

Until he'd seen his father's eyes twinkling, that had bothered Barry. Dad, and Doctor Roberts who made the ear infection go away, knew everything worth knowing.

On March twentieth, the sun came out again and the recovering child stood in the front yard of the family's suburban home, clad in a baseball uniform. He wore a mitt, crackly with disuse, on his left hand and knew, now, that nothing truly terrible could happen so long as Dad was near.

Pretending to pitch a fantasy no-hitter, Barry saw Dad from the corner of his eye, hurrying back and forth from the house. Into the trunk of the car parked in the driveway went all the exciting things the eleven-year-old had been expressly forbidden to touch: hunting knives, sleeping bags, a slender rifle sheathed in a pebbled leather case, and a cooler chest filled with beer. When Dad came out a last time, Barry was aware of an unfamiliar sound. Mickey Mantle would have to wait, bat frozen to his shoulder as the ace fastballer stepped off the mound.

Father was *whistling*. He never did that, the boy thought; not when he went off to the office in the city, not even to the restaurant with the family Friday nights.

"Where you goin', Dad?" He watched the man open the car door.

"Huntin', trooper!" The whistled tune broke off but the smile widened. "Special day for it, *real* special day."

"Yeah? How come?"

Dad spread his arms wide. "It's the first day of spring! Winter's done." He leaned against the car door, impatiently paternal yet seeming pleased to be asked. "Everything turns green. Hibernation ends."

"But what's that mean, Dad?"

"Hibernation? It's when all kinds of life starts going again; all kinds. It's. . .when the wild, hungry things come out." He grinned and slid behind the wheel of his big car. "Someday, maybe, I'll take you along. Nothing's finer!"

By the time the car was distant, the boy was ready to return to his fantasy batter. "It's the first day of spring, Mick!" he announced aloud. Then he blew his spinning fastball past the mighty slugger and jumped excitedly into the air. "*Wild!*" he cried.

But he was staring down the street, and toward the ravenous hills.

Two years ago

From atop the highest rock in the desolate mesa, Barry Locke imagined himself soaring higher — propelled by elation, a sense of coming into rightful power, and the uncounted beers he'd had for breakfast with Dad and his father's cronies. A hot, dry wind dusted his bronzed face and made his ear ache slightly, but that didn't matter.

Today he'd turned twenty-one.

"Hey, Barry!" A voice, from somewhere below. "Hotshot, you wanna come down here before you break your neck?"

He looked down at Herman Locke, his father, now an older version of himself. Dad's boots were hidden in purple sage; he was so at home, hunting, he might take root. "No way I'd ruin a special occasion like this, Dad," Barry called.

"Okay, okay." Strong hands were cupped to amplify his voice. "Stay there, then. But Pete, Harvey and me, we're gonna give what-for to some rabbit and coyotes. We can't wait for the likes of a silly young guy!"

Barry saw his father brush dust from his jeans and turn to depart. Hunting with Dad was an incredible gift; it meant he was becoming one of the boys and Barry didn't want to miss a minute of it. Sharing his only real passions was Herm Locke's way of telling the world his son was a man, now. Barry scampered down the face of the rock, doing his best to be athletic like the trooper his father enjoyed calling him.

Just to the left, he noted, lay a small creek. Sliding twenty feet into the soft sand at the base of the boulder, Barry jogged to the creek and scooped handfuls of impossibly cool water into his mouth. When he'd wiped his damp mouth with the back of his hand, Barry thought he caught sight of patterned color beneath the rock as he hurried after the older man. He knew Herm Locke meant what he said about waiting and so ignored the diamond design, even the unblinking eyes which watched his progress. All kinds of life springs up, Dad had said about spring, and the boy liked the way his father stoutly accepted the fact.

He was as unaware of the thing continuing to watch him as he'd been unaware that it had been beside the narrow stream from which he had drunk. And unaware of what the thing had aborted in its terror at seeing him, and left in the water.

March nineteenth — this year

He perched lithely on the naughahyde examining table, hands folded. He'd put off going to the doctor until two days ago and felt worse about being summoned for a second exam. When Doctor Roberts eventually entered, the *whish* of the opening door matched Barry's sigh.

"So." The middleaged physician stood before Barry. "The big day is about here."

He smiled into the clear, brown eyes he'd seen often since he was eight. Lance Roberts was the one his folks had turned to when he'd had the severe problem with his ear. Now, Roberts remained so youthful he was like a man half his age, made-up for a college play. "We tie the knot tomorrow, Doc. Do I get a big, purple lollipop from your file cabinet?"

Roberts grinned, glanced into his folder; cleared his throat. "How long have you been losing weight? Fifty pounds! You turned into an exercise nut?"

"I eat like a horse." Barry touched the shirt billowing from his waist. "Why?" He wasn't about to tell the physician everything.

"Any abdominal pains?"

Barry fidgeted. "Sometimes my belly rumbles if I even think of food."

"*Bad* pains?" Roberts pressed.

"This last year at school has been rugged." On occasion, the stomach pains made him think his churning insides were actually growing. "Pain, plus sleeping badly."

Thoughtfully, Roberts rubbed his chin. "So far, all we know is that your weight loss is abnormal. Stress, your plans to marry, can account for it. But I'd feel better with further testing. I can—"

Barry tried to muffle his agonized groan. He'd felt as if everything below the waist was turning end for end. He hadn't wanted to do this—his wedding was tomorrow—but the abrupt convulsions were all but unbearable that time.

Worse, Barry thought as he locked his arms around his middle, was the impression he'd had of a sound—a *chittering* noise—from the pit of his stomach.

"Let me see!" The doctor was on his feet, resting the flat of his hand against the patient's midsection. "This happens all the time, right?" he asked softly. Then he pressed down, firmly, finding organs that were more than normally firm even when relaxed. He strove to feel *past* them.

Palm in place, Roberts glanced up at the youth but said nothing. He didn't wish to be a wet blanket but he'd detected... *something*...in the stomach cavity, something resistive, and hard, which should not have been there.

Then he eased back against a low cabinet. From somewhere he produced a smile. "Don't begin anticipating cancer. For your peace of mind, we'll simply go ahead with the testing. I think I can get you into the hospital on Monday."

"*No.* I mean, I *can't!*" Barry adjusted his belt, frowned. "Plans are all in place for the wedding and our honeymoon in Hawaii. Couldn't you give me the name of a doctor in the islands, Doc? If nothing goes wrong, I can go in for tests a week from Monday."

Roberts' face was a grimace of professional disapproval. "If it is serious, well, the sooner the better." Then he saw Barry's young face and slapped his shoulder, affably, with his folder. "Very well; weddings are weddings." Frowning, he shook his head. "I'll set things up for a week from Monday."

Barry beamed his relief. "Thanks, Doc!"

"But one thing. I'd like to take some X-rays before you leave today. It'll delay you for only a short while and I can study them prior to your return." He fumbled a gown from his fullsized cabinet, handed it to Barry. "Slip into this and I'll fetch my nurse."

And stay away from luaus, Roberts thought, leaving the room. *Your belly already feels like you swallowed a roasting pig.*

Early the next day—March twentieth

While the pale, pink glow which sometimes gave detail to it had gone away long ago, the food opening still attracted the thing. Snug against warm, moist walls, it stared, anticipating.

The thing had no conception of itself; its appearance, its proportions, or the involuntary surges through its muscular system. It had no knowledge that its size was so great that it would soon be *wedged* against the walls which, since birth, had been its home.

Knowing only hunger, the thing had been moving steadily toward the membrane-covered opening for days, inching through a bloodied forest of twists and turns. It was precisely smart enough to have become weary of waiting for more and, wriggling and flexing another fractional inch of advancement, it headed for the opening.

Sharp pain brought Barry from light sleep and he experienced, at once, the waking nightmare he had not described to Doctor Roberts.

He had not wished to be urged to see a *different* kind of doctor.

Fleetingly, he seemed to be elsewhere, peering through eyes

other than his own—not hungry, but avaricious. The instant he focussed unblinkingly at a place his Barry-part did not recognize, yet salivated for nourishment, he was no longer human. He was savage; dedicated, exclusively, to self.

Then he was leaping from bed and racing downstairs to the kitchen where, in a cupboard, he found a nearly-full box of corn flakes. Barry did not care for corn flakes. Snatching a half-gallon of milk from the refrigerator, he started shoveling tablespoon-sized helpings of the breakfast food into his upturned mouth, washing it down directly from the bottle.

When he paused, gasping for breath, he saw internally bestial eyes looking back at him: flat, persistent, insatiable, unhuman.

He shoveled in more flakes as fast as he could.

Behind his splendid walnut-grained desk, Lance Roberts nursed a half-eaten sandwich and a pounding headache. The radio playing across the room didn't help but he lacked the energy to go turn it off. His patients so far that day had been children—screamers—and Roberts loathed what he was thinking about them. *Maybe I'm getting old,* he reflected. Sally had told him, joking, that he probably suffered from male menopause. Sally was just hilarious.

"Speak of the devil," he said, aloud, at the woman looking around the edge of the door. She'd knocked, opened it, and had her Important Look. "Melinda has yesterday's X-rays."

"Figures." The doctor lowered the sandwich from the nearby deli into its papery bed, motioned. "Come."

Sally rested the deep yellow envelopes on the lighted examining table and Roberts stood, balled his remnant of sandwich and scored Two in his wastebasket. *Another inspired luncheon,* he thought, going over to the panel and flipping on the light. He flipped past Myra Goldstein's likely gall stones and Eddie Fletcher's possible broken wrist, curious about Barry Locke's—

His *what?*

Some damned tumor, probably. Roberts sighed, affixed the first of the boy's X-rays. Herm Locke's "little trooper" had been an intense kid since Roberts first saw him with that ear infection. Ulcers could sometimes—

Lance Roberts gaped at the plastic photographic plate clipped to his light panel. He braced himself by putting palms on the wall, and leaning. He had to have been wrong, that first look. He looked again, and he hadn't been.

"Mother of God," Roberts said, swallowing.

What he saw was palpably impossible. Sure, something was growing inside of Barry, and it was lodged in the ribboning coils of the boy's small intestines.

It was not, however, a tumor.

"It's the first day of spring, folks!" exulted a disc jockey. "Time t'stop hibernating and get out here with all the other animals!"

"Always liked this place," Herman Locke declared from the sun-drenched veranda of the Seaview Inn. His son sat nearby, drinking imported beer and wolfing down a roast beef sandwich.

Barry mumbled around a large bite. "That's why you wanted Gail and me to get married here."

"Your little bride's father is dead. It was the least I could do."

Son appraised father, who did not catch subtle criticisms. Herm was a plain, companionable, well-meaning man—even when, Barry pondered, his judgment was a bit officious. The young couple had wanted a civil ceremony in Arizona, but Dad had brought them to this Victorian resort hotel on the Southern California coast for a formal wedding. Dad had to have his show, his productions, just as the twenty-first birthday hunting trip had been Herm's personal spectacular, presumably meant to win Barry's grateful love forever.

It was so unnecessary, thought the groom; he'd already love Dad forever.

Trying to fight against his health problems, Barry swallowed more beer and his gaze swept the veranda, drifted inside. They'd be married in the private chapel; then the reception would take place in the grand ballroom—that football field-sized hall just beyond the magnificent windows. Barry couldn't be comfortable in an "Inn" like this: Built around century's turn with blood-red roofs at forty-five degree angles, spirals and towers, those eighteen-foot high windows on every floor, it reminded him of all the haunted castles he'd heard of.

"I'm going to look in on Gail, freshen up. You'd better think about getting ready yourself, y'know." Dad winked. "Unless you're getting cold feet?"

Nodding, Barry saw his father saunter off, as outwardly unchanged as the endless Pacific streaming away from the base of the Seaview Inn—as solidly content with himself and obdurate as the cloaking cliffs rising above his Arizona hunting grounds.

Barry wasn't getting cold feet. But alone, seeking the strength to stand, he felt the rising agony anew in his stomach and again broke out in cold sweat. Barry gritted his teeth. "Not now, *please*—not *now!*"

Roberts took his seat on the commuter plane, hating the notion of flying, hating more what must happen when they touched down.

He had to try to help Barry Locke.

And he'd spent more priceless time getting Jerry Adams to agree to fly with him to Seaview. Adams, a professor at San Diego State, was a research specialist in...anomalies. Things that couldn't be, but were. Now, Roberts showed the X-ray to Adams, sitting beside him in the plane, who looked at it the best way he could: holding it up to the window and the afternoon sky. The doctor waited impatiently for a scientific remark.

"Dear God," Adams blurted, his hands holding the X-ray collapsing into his lap. "You're right; it's *there!* It isn't even *entirely* reptilian! *H-How?*"

Roberts was irritable. "What I need to know is how the hell do we get it *out?* How it *got* there can wait awhile. Correct?"

Professor Adams' lantern-jawed, slack expression said he wasn't listening. "Lance, I can't imagine how it...*survived.* Inside the man."

"I don't wish to imagine it," Roberts snapped. He had done that and it was too hideous to go over again while airborne. "I'd hoped you might be familiar with the phenomenon. I want a clue to how I can get that—that *thing*—out of my patient."

Adams was wide-eyed. "I suppose you'll have to excise it. Virtually a Caesarian procedure, I'd think."

Doctor Roberts faced the professor squarely. "Then I want *you* standing beside me," he muttered, "when it *pops out*—ready to strike!"

Everyone thought the wedding was romantic; that the new Gail Locke was the picture of a beautiful bride; that Barry was even more terrified and pale than the usual groom.

By early evening, the reception was still going strong, the remnant of the catered dinner had been cleared, and the band was playing. By no coincidence whatever, the bar was open. Gail, already changed into a pastel suit, took full advantage of it. Barry was acting peculiarly and had gone to change nearly forty-five minutes ago, so Gail was left to dance with her new father-in-law.

Having eaten so much that friends spoke of "the condemned man's last meal," Barry was sicker than he'd known possible. A torrent of pain had doubled him over on the carpeted hallway outside their suite. It was the third, and worst, of his wedding-day attacks; he'd had to crawl the fifty feet from the elevator to their fifth-floor rooms and had left the door ajar behind him.

He tugged himself somehow upon the king-sized bed, clothed but for his dinner jacket, abandoned on a chair somewhere downstairs in the ballroom. He knew then, with atrocious certainty, that his insides were being torn apart—literally. He had tried to gut it out the way Herm Locke would have wanted it; now it was killing him. On his side, Barry vapidly saw the ceiling, then that which the thing inside him saw: a darkened tunnel with a distant, barely discernible light at the end. Moaning audibly, trying not to cry even as the living entity within him stretched again, ripping at internal flesh—even as tears washed his cheeks, unfelt—Barry's tortuous hunger began to be exchanged for a hideous, bloated *fullness,* a swollen sensation which told him that his own blood was flowing everywhere, inside. He learned the dictionary meaning of intolerable pain.

His last shriek froze in his throat at the second of the internal *lurch,* and he stared, sightlessly, gave vision over to the parasitical thing; and then he tumbled end over end into a dark place of the spirit.

Gail flipped the switch inside the door and crossed her arms as she saw Barry sprawled on the bed. Drawn into a foetal position, his face was averted.

"So there you are!" Her words were somewhat slurred from the champagne she'd drunk. "Are you bored, sick, or simply eager?" Laughing lightly, she removed the jacket, let it drop with a theatrical gesture, and unbuttoned her blouse.

There was no response, aside from the impression of a sickeningly sweet scent in the air.

"Would you turn *around,* husband?" She unzipped her skirt, wriggled from it. "If I'm going to do a wedding night strip for you, the least you could do is watch!"

Still no answer but Gail, fuzzy-headed, let her blouse flutter to the floor and continued undressing until she wore only transparent lace panties. *He's playing his own little game,* Gail thought. Arms wrapped round her breasts, she kneeled on the bed beside Barry.

And heard, for the first time, gurgling sounds rising from his throat.

"Barry, what's wrong?" She shook his shoulder. *"Honey?"* With some difficulty, she rolled him over on his back, stared into an expressionless face. His open eyes were blank, his face ashen. *Oh no,* she thought, the horror newborn but growing fast, *my Barry's dead!*

His head *moved.* It craned from the stiff neck in a single, spastic jerking motion. When his lips parted, blood poured out, a geyser of it; it spilled down his cheek, was soaked up by the pillow. It splashed her reaching hands.

Screaming, Gail was off the bed—eyes never leaving his upthrust, gaping head, revulsed yet magnetized by the way it kept twitching, how the neck muscles corded like white hemp and the mouth stretched horrendously open. She imagined she heard tiny jaw bones cracking and, edging toward the door, stumbled over a chair. Immediately she looked back up at Barry.

The thing—struggling for room against the seeping, pinkened teeth that imprisoned it—came up from Barry's throat and surged out of his ruined mouth.

She fell to her knees, knuckles to her own lips, muttering syllables of prayer. Gail saw the entire head of the thing, then, saw the more-or-less triangular shape of it, the scaled snout and slitted, staring eyes on either side of it. She saw the thin, black forked tongue flittering, *tasting* the air—

Before she saw it pile forward onto the bed and then off it, moving forward on its slimy belly and partly upon miniature white appendages that could have been fingers, or merely the sundered shreds of Barry's sausage-shaped intestines. Miles of thumpingly-thick, heavy, diamond-designed body seemed to worm out of the dead man's mouth; and now, its blunt snout twitched, searching for and finding her. *Going* toward her.

Face in her arms, Gail screamed as she had never screamed before.

And Herm Locke was barreling into the suite, muscles knotted and his heart almost ceasing as he saw his new daughter-in-law, all but naked, cowering—and blindly screaming—feet away.

His eyes darted to the bed, discovering his son's remains, knew instantly Barry was gone. He'd seen a lot of dead creatures. Nothing could live, that way.

And then Herm saw the thing.

Dripping blood, some caked on it, its head and neck were a scalded question mark growing from its terrifying, deceptive coil. Tiny pale things below the head appeared to work, to clench and to beckon. The tail trembled, switched from side to side, *chittering*.

Locke had seen all kinds of reptiles before. Translucent snakes shimmering almost prettily on the surface of still water. Little ones, slithering into the flower bed, frightened by his lawn mower. Docile with the coming of winter, frenzied with the passion of midsummer in Arizona.

But Herm had never known such terror at the sight of a serpent before, nor seen such a serpent before — not even on dangerous hunting trips in late July, or on the first day of spring. The thing was on a direct line to where Gail crouched, and, "Get *out* of here," he hissed. The scream had become a monotonous whimper of fright. *"Gail — move it!"*

The thing, appearing to accept a challenge, turned from Gail and deliberately headed for Herm, at once slithering and scrabbling after him. He glanced left, right, questing for a weapon. No help, but he saw the massive windows, knew they were five stories up, formed a plan.

Stripping off his dinner jacket, he wrapped it round his left forearm and, sweating, backed toward the windows, motioning. "C'mon, come *on,*" he told it.

Then Herm lunged, from the left, meaning to draw the thing to his protected arm while he captured it behind the pyramidal head with his right hand.

It surged above the decoy, however, curved fangs slicing into the soft flesh of the human throat. Even then, it might have worked; but Herm had not been prepared for such massive weight. Off balance, driven backward, he stumbled toward the window above the magnificent ocean view, the thing trailing from his neck.

Striving to tear the razorish teeth away, feeling the serpent's enormous body coil suffocatingly around his own, Herm hurtled back through the window in a shower of splintering glass, the creature like a smothering, second skin.

For Doctor Roberts and Professor Adams, the Seaview Inn seemed to be one of the more well-appointed and classic structures on hell's immeasurable estate. They entered a world of horror and it took awhile before Lance Roberts could accept the fact that they'd come too late.

The men of science watched helplessly as the final ambulance left, no siren needed. On the Seaview veranda, enveloped by humid night, Jerry Adams kept prattling about the way they'd been too late to "see that thing in the X-rays." It had vanished, presumably borne away after, dying, it had crept to the ocean. Adams had looked everywhere for its traces.

Roberts ignored the professor, wished he hadn't brought him. Wished they hadn't been too late.

Wished a proud father had not passed along his own take-it-like-a-man, macho attitude, so that a nice youngster might have come sooner for help.

Roberts shut his eyes, crying, letting Adams chatter. No tears would show; years ago, the doctor had cried them out. Besides, it was quite dark except for a moon in its pregnant last quarter.

"Look." Adams, touching his elbow. Pointing. "Down there, on the beach."

Roberts followed the finger, wasn't sure, at first, he saw a thing.

Then he saw the apparent, enormous tracks of a great, serpentine being leading out to the ocean's edge where they stopped —

And its scaly skin lay crumpled: discarded, and outgrown.

Czadek

Ray Russell

You've written something Fine, but you're challenged, "Do you have a track record?" Modestly, you set the record straight: "Well, there are magazine sales to Esquire, Whispers, Midatlantic Review, F&SF, Penthouse, Amazing, *and* Ellery Queen's. *And nearly 100 appearances in anthologies ranging from Hitchcock collections and the Arbor House horror anthology, to Playboy's books of* Science Fiction and Fantasy, Crime and Suspense, Horror and the Supernatural—*plus* 100 Great Science Fiction Short Short Stories."

The man reels; you're relentless. "I wrote Incubus, Sardonicus, The Case Against Satan—*and yes, my writing has been translated. Into, I believe, eight foreign languages. Did I mention," you ask casually, "68* Playboy *pieces—or that I was Executive Editor of* Playboy *for its formative first seven years?"*

You and I don't do those things.

Ray Russell can.

Russell is another transplanted Midwesterner, from Chicago, born September 4, 1924, to Beverly Hills, where his creative garden has flourished since 1961.

"Czadek" might be the story he's known for from now on. This master of ironic humor begins with a grabber horror novelists would be ecstatic to use as a prologue, then turns in a "side-door" tour de force ala James, Machen, or RLS. "Unforgettable" is one of those overworked words. It applies to "Czadek."

"The gods are cruel" is the way Dr. North put it, and I could not disagree. The justice of the gods or God or Fates or Furies or cosmic forces that determine our lives can indeed be terrible, sometimes far too terrible for the offense; a kind of unjust justice, a punishment that outweighs the crime, not an eye for an eye but a hundred eyes for an eye. As long as I live, I'll never be able to explain or forget what I saw this morning in that laboratory.

I had gone there to do some research for a magazine article on life before birth. Our local university's biology lab has a good reputation, and so has its charming director, Dr. Emily North. The lab's collection of embryos and foetuses is justly famous. I saw it this morning, accompanied by the obliging and attractive doctor. Rows of gleaming jars, each containing a human creature who was once alive, suspended forever, eerily serene, in chemical preservative.

All the stages of pre-birth were represented. In the first jar, I saw an embryo captured at the age of five weeks, with dark circles of eyes clearly visible even that early. In the next jar, I saw an example of the eight-week stage, caught in the act of graduating from embryo to foetus, with fingers, toes, and male organs sprouting. On we walked, past the jars, as veins and arteries became prominent: eleven weeks...eighteen weeks (sucking its thumb)...twenty-eight weeks, ten inches long, with fully distinguishable facial features.

It was a remarkable display, and I was about to say so when I saw a jar set apart from the others that made me suddenly stop. "My God," I said, "what's that?"

Dr. North shook her head. Her voice was shadowed by sadness as she replied, "I wish I knew. I call it Czadek."

* * *

There used to be (and perhaps still are?) certain dry, flavorless wafers, enemies of emptiness, which, when eaten with copious draughts of water, coffee, or other beverage, expanded in the body, swelling up, ballooning, becoming bloated, inflated, reaching out, ranging forth, stretching from stomach wall to stomach wall, touching and filling every corner, conquering and occupying the most remote outposts of vacuous void; in that way creating an illusion of having dined sumptuously, even hoggishly, scotching hunger, holding at bay the hounds of appetite, and yet providing no nourishment.

Estes Hargreave always reminded me of those wafers, and they of him. Other things have brought him to mind, over the years. When, for example, I encountered the publicity for a Hollywood film (ten years in the making, a budget of sixty million dollars, etc.) and was able to check the truth of those figures with the producer, who is a friend of mind, the thought of Estes promptly presented itself. What my friend told me was that the movie actually had been made in a little over *one* year and had cost about *six* million dollars. As he revealed this, in the living room of my apartment, over the first of the two vodka gimlets that are his limit, the image of Estes absolutely took over my mind, expanding in all directions like one of those wafers. I saw him as he had been, a very tall but small-time actor, indignantly resigning from Equity, a move he'd hoped would be shocking, sending ripples of pleasant notoriety throughout Thespia. But it had gone unnoticed. The only reason I remembered it was because I'd been a small-time actor myself in those days, and I'd been present at the resignation. Where was Estes now? Was he alive? I hadn't heard of him in years.

"That stuff you see in the papers," said my guest, the producer, "that's the work of my P. R. guy, a very good man with the press. I asked him to pick me up here in about half an hour, by the way, hope you don't mind. He's set up an interview with one of the columnists for this afternoon, to plug the product. I wouldn't do an interview without him. He's great, this fellow."

Intuition flared like brushfire through my brain. "Did he used to be an actor?"

"As a matter of fact, I think he did, a long time ago."

(I knew it!)

"Is his name Estes Hargreave?"

"No. Wayne McCord."

"Oh."

Talk about anti-climax. My intuition, it seemed, was not so much brushfire as backfire. The reason I had homed in on poor old Hargreave was because he had always employed a Rule of Ten when reporting the statistics of his life. He just added a zero to everything. If he received a fee of, say, $200 for an acting engagement, he airily let it drop that "they paid me two grand," or, if a bit more discretion was advisable, he would resort to ambiguity—"they laid two big ones on me"—knowing that, if challenged, he could always claim that by "big ones" he had meant "C-notes." His annual income—which, according to him, averaged "a hundred G's, after taxes"—was, by this same rule, closer to $10,000 in the real world. *Before* taxes.

He applied the Rule of Ten to his very ancestry. His branch of the Hargreaves had been in the United States for a hundred and fifty years prior to his birth, he would proudly claim; but he and I had grown up in the same neighborhood, and I knew that his parents had arrived in this country just fifteen years before he had come squalling into the world, bearing their spiky Central European surname, which he changed after graduating high school and before being drafted into the Army (World War II). "First Lieutenant Hargreave" was another figment of his fecund mind: he never rose above the rank of buck private, and, in fact, took a lot of kidding with the phrase, "See here, Private Hargreave," a paraphrase of the title of Marion Hargrove's bestseller. I used to wonder why he didn't say he'd been a captain or a major, as long as he was making things up, but that was before I tumbled to his Rule. In the Army rankings of those days, First Lieutenant was exactly ten rungs from the bottom: (1) Private, (2) PFC, (3) Corporal, (4) Sergeant, (5) Staff Sergeant, (6) Tech Sergeant, (7) Master Sergeant, (8) Warrant Officer, (9) Second Lieutenant, (10) First Lieutenant.

The Rule of Ten was applied to his losses and expenditures, too. "I dropped a hundred bucks last night in a poker game" could safely be translated as $10. A new wardrobe had set him back "three and a half thou," he once announced; but his tailor also happened to be mine, and I quickly learned that Hargreave had spent $350 on two suits at $150 each plus a parcel of shirts and ties totalling $50.

There were, of course, areas that needed no amplification: his height, for instance, which was impressively towering without embellishment. It was to Hargreave's credit that he never felt compelled to *diminish* any numbers even when it might have seemed advantageous to do so: he never peeled any years off his age, and, to the best of my knowledge, was meticulously honest in his relations with the IRS.

Hargreave was clever. If Truth-times-Ten resulted in an absurd, unbelievable figure, he still produced that figure, but as a deliberate hyperbole. There was the time he was involved in a vulgar brawl with a person of slight frame who weighed not much more than a hundred pounds, and yet had flattened him. This was particularly humiliating to Hargreave because his opponent in that brawl was a woman. In recounting the incident, Hargreave first made use of another favorite device, simple reversal, and said that he, Hargreave, had flattened "the other guy." He did not, of course, claim that his opponent weighed a thousand pounds. Not exactly. But he did say, with a chuckle and a smile, "This bruiser tipped the scales at about half a ton." The Rule of Ten was thus preserved by lifting it out of the literal, into the jocular figurative.

When it came to matters of the heart, Hargreave applied a Rule of Ten to the Rule of Ten itself. For example, the oft-repeated boast that he bedded "two new chicks every week" (or 104 per year) was his hundredfold inflation of the actual annual figure, 1.4—the fraction representing misfires: couplings left unconsummated due to this or that dysfunction. Of course, I'm guessing about these intimate matters, but it's an educated guess, supported by the testimony of talkative ladies.

There were some Hargreavean inflations, however, that did not conveniently fit into the Rule of Ten or the Rule of Ten times Ten. The infamous *Macbeth* affair was one of these. That time, he utilized an asymmetrical variant somewhere between those two Rules—sort of a Rule of Thirty-Seven and a Half.

A summer theatre group had made the understandable mistake of booking him to play leads in a season of open air repertory — I say understandable because his brochure (a handsomely printed work of fabulistic fiction) would have fooled anybody. "Mr. Hargreave has appeared in over fifty Broadway plays" was one of its claims. He'd appeared in five, as walk-ons, or over five, if you count the one that folded in New Haven and never got to Broadway. "'OF OVERPOWERING STATURE... PRODIGY!'—*Brooks Atkinson*." Atkinson had indeed written those words about Hargreave, though without mentioning his name: "...But focus was diverted from Mr. Olivier's great scene by the unfortunate casting of a background spear-carrier of overpowering stature, who seemed to be nearly seven feet tall. It was impossible to look at anyone else while this prodigy was on stage." Hargreave was actually only six eight, but he may have been wearing lifts. (I've often wondered if he realized that Atkinson had used "prodigy" not in the sense of "genius" but in its older meaning of *lusus naturae* or gazingstock...)

Anyway, the brochure was an impressive document, and considering the fact that the prodigy it described was available for a reasonable $150 per week (or, as he later put it, "a thou and a half"), it was not surprising that the outdoor theatre snapped him up. There were half a dozen stunning photos in the brochure, as well, showing Hargreave in make-up for everything from *Oedipus Rex* to *Charley's Aunt*, as well as in the clear: he was a good-looking chap.

The first production of the summer had lofty aspirations: *Macbeth*, uncut, with faddish borrowings from other productions: a thick Scots burr (in homage to the Orson Welles film) and contemporary military uniform (shades of several Shakespearean shows, including the "G. I." *Hamlet* of Maurice Evans, but dictated by economy rather than experimentalism). To this outlandish medley was superimposed incidental music filched from both operatic versions of the tragedy, those of Verdi and Bloch (oil and water, stylistically), rescored for backstage bagpipes.

Hargreave wasn't to blame for any of this, of course, even

though he went on record as praising the "bold iconoclastic flair" of the production—which may have been no more than diplomacy rather than his own vivid absence of taste. No, Hargreave's transgression was the interminable interpolation he wrote into the classic script and performed on opening night, after first taking great care *not* to seek the approval of the director. What he did, exactly, was to apply the aforementioned Rule of Thirty-Seven and a Half to the familiar couplet—

> I will not be afraid of death and bane
> Till Birnam Forest come to Dunsinane

—bloating it up to a rant of seventy-five lines. If that doesn't seem particularly long as Shakespearean speeches go, be reminded that, of Macbeth's other major speeches, "Is this a dagger" is only thirty-two lines in length, "If it were done" but twenty-eight, and "Tomorrow and tomorrow and tomorrow" a scant ten.

The production, as I've said, was uncut, retaining even those silly witch-dance scenes considered by some scholars to be non-Shakespearean in origin. Hargreave's seventy-five leaden lines—delivered in no great hurry—made an already long evening in the theatre seem endless to the mosquito-punctured audience. I wasn't there, thanks for large mercies, but plenty of people were, and their reports all coincide to form one of the minor legends of contemporary theatrical lore.

The worst part of this depressing farrago was what happened after the seventy-fifth and final line had been bellowed. The spectators, mesmerized into mindless automata, to their everlasting shame gave Hargreave a standing ovation lasting a clamorous sixty seconds (ten minutes, according to him). Maybe they just wanted to stretch their legs.

The drama critic of the local paper did not join in the ovation. Although not enough of a scholar to spot the interpolation as such, he knew what he didn't like. Hence, he allotted only one sentence to the male lead: "In the title role, Estes Hargreave provided what is certainly the dullest performance I have ever seen in twenty-two years of theatre-going." There's a divinity that protects ham actors: the linotypist drunkenly substituted an "f" for the "d" in "dullest," resulting in a rave review that Hargreave carried in his wallet until it disintegrated into lacework.

Surprisingly, the unscheduled interpolation did not in itself cause Hargreave to be fired — or not so surprisingly, perhaps, considering the standing ovation and the lucky typo. What cooked his goose was his demand that, for the remaining *Macbeth* performances that season, the programs be over-printed with the line, "ADDITIONAL VERSES BY ESTES HARGREAVE." That broke the camel's back. He was handed his walking papers, and his understudy took over for the rest of the season. Hargreave, naturally, gave it out that he had quit. "I ankled that scene, turned my back on a grand and a half a week rather than prostitute my art."

But the director had his revenge. He reported Hargreave's behavior to Actors Equity (enclosing a copy of the seventy-five-liner that I've treasured to this day), and his complaint, added to others that had been lodged from time to time, not to mention the persistent rumors that Hargreave often worked for much less than Equity scale, caused him to be casually called on the carpet before an informal panel of his peers that included me.

"Sit down, Estes," I said chummily, "and let's hear your side of all this." He sat. With a grin, I added, "Preferably in twenty-five words or less. Nobody wants to make a Federal case out of it."

Hargreave did not return my grin. He looked me straight in the eye. Then he looked the other members straight in the eye, one by one. He cleared his throat.

"I stand before you," he said, hastily rising from his chair, "a man thoroughly disgusted with the so-called 'legitimate' stage and with this 'august' body. I am sickened by the East Coast snobbery that persists in promulgating the myth that the almighty stage is superior to the art of film. I have given my life, my dedication, *my blood* to the stage — and how have I been rewarded? Oh, I'm not saying I haven't made a good living. I'm not saying I haven't received glowing reviews from the most respected critics of our time. I'm not saying I haven't been mobbed by hordes of idolatrous fans. But all of this is Dead Sea fruit when I find myself here before a group of greasepaint junkies, none of whom are better actors than I, all of whom have the infernal gall to set themselves up as holier-than-thou *judges* of my behavior. Well, I am not going to give you the satisfaction. I hear they're preparing to do a remake of that classic film, *Stagecoach*, out there in the 'despised' West. Yes, I hear that clarion call, and I am going to answer it. I have been asked to test for the role John Wayne created in the original version. An artist of my experience and caliber does not usually deign to audition or do screen tests, of course, but I have no false pride. I will test for that role. And I will get it. You clowns will have my formal resignation in tomorrow's mail."

I never knew how he did it. Was it a kind of genius? Did he have a built-in computer in his head? I only know that later, when we played back the tape that one of our cagier members had secretly made of the proceedings, and had a stenographer transcribe it for us, I discovered to my wonder that Hargreave's resignation speech totalled exactly ten times the length I had waggishly requested of him: two hundred and fifty words on the button, if you think of "so-called" as two words. I had to admire the man. He was a phony, he had no talent, he was as corny as a bumper sticker, but he was so consistently and flagrantly appalling in everything he did that he was like a living, breathing, walking, talking piece of junk art. Whether or not he actually tested for the John Wayne role, I don't know. Maybe he did. I tend to doubt it. At any rate, the job went to Alex Cord.

The doorbell rang.

"That must be my man now," said my guest, draining his second and last drink. I got to my feet, opened the door, and looked up into a smiling, sun-browned, middle-aged but very familiar face, on top of a tall—prodigiously tall—frame.

"Estes!" I cried.

"Long time no see," he said, jovially, in the pidgin of our youth.

My intuition began brushfiring again, quickly making the John Wayne/Alex Cord/Wayne McCord connection, and I realized that Hargreave, after his *Stagecoach* disappointment, had taken on the names of both actors, probably in the hope that their good fortune would be mystically transferred to him. In a way, it had. He looked happy. He radiated success. He had found his true vocation.

"Come on in!" I boomed, genuinely glad to see him. "Have a drink!"

He shook his head. "No time. Can I have a rain check?" Addressing his employer, he said, "We'd better shake a leg or we'll be late. It's close to rush hour and we have to fight about ten miles of crosstown traffic."

"No, Wayne," the producer said with an indulgent sigh, "it's just eight short blocks up the street. An easy stroll. We could both use the exercise."

That was two or three summers ago. I ran into my producer friend again earlier this year, and asked about Wayne. He shrugged. "Had to let him go. He suffered a...credibility gap, I guess you could call it. People just stopped believing him. I suppose it was bound to happen. I mean, how long can you tamper with the truth the way he did, and hope to get away with it? There's always a price tag, my friend, a day of reckoning, know what I mean? Anyway, I gave him the sack. No, I don't know where he is now, but I'll bet a nickel he's still in show business."

* * *

"The gods are cruel," Dr. Emily North said this morning as she told me about the creature in the jar:

"Some friends of mine had mentioned it, how they'd seen it in a little traveling carnival. But I had to see for myself, so I drove to the outskirts of town and managed to get there just as they were packing up to move on. It was a real relic of a show, the kind of thing I'd thought had gone out of style. Shabby, sleazy, tasteless, probably illegal. But I did see what I went to see. Czadek was all they called him. Like the name of one of those outer-space villains on a TV show. But he wasn't rigged out in outer-space gear. He was dressed like a cowboy — Stetson hat, chaps, lariat. He twirled the lariat, and did a not-very-good tap dance. And he smiled — a desperate, frightened smile, full of anguish. I tried to talk to him but he didn't answer. He couldn't speak — or wouldn't, I never knew which. A few months later, when he died, the owner of the carnie phoned me long distance and asked me if I wanted to buy the cadaver for scientific purposes. So there he is. In a jar. Without his cowboy costume. Naked as a foetus, but not a foetus. An adult human male of middle age, well nourished and perfectly proportioned, quite handsome, in fact. But only eight inches tall..."

No, I can't explain it. I won't even try. But I think about those words "A day of reckoning" and "The gods are cruel" and "How long can you tamper with the truth the way he did, and hope to get away with it?" I recall some lines from Estes' awful amplification of *Macbeth* —

> For by this fatal fault I was cast down,
> Ay, to damnation, by mine own fell hand!
> None but myself to censure or to blame...

— and I think of Estes, who stood six feet, eight inches tall without his shoes. Eighty inches. Exactly ten times taller than the creature in the jar. The tiny dead man with the hauntingly familiar face. And I remember the original surname by which Estes was known before he changed it. A spiky Central European name...

The Old Men Know

Charles L. Grant

If you'd like proof that softspoken, considerate, gently witty and basically self-effacing workers with words can still succeed—both as writer and editor—let me introduce you to Charles L. Grant.

There are, however, two terms I omitted in describing Grant and each has, I'm sure, been instrumental to what he's achieved: taste, and an intimate kind of individualistic talent.

Where taste is concerned—a connoisseur's knowledge and approach to what he reads; a clear perception of what he wants that sidesteps the adamantine and settles upon advocacy— Charlie's has been good enough to win a World Fantasy Award for the first in his series of anthologies called Shadows.

Where intimate, individualistic talent is involved, again Grant's record speaks for itself: one Nebula for best short story, another for best novelette; a World Fantasy Award for a novella, another for Nightmare Seasons, *a collection of his own under-stated, alarmingly* real *short fiction. Stephen King, commenting on the 42-year-old Grant's novel* The Hour of the Oxrun Dead, *used two pertinent words in* Danse Macabre: *"Unsettling stuff."*

So, you're about to learn, is "The Old Men Know," a tale in which the principal characters are so seemingly genuine that you'll care about them from the start—a truly skilled writer's way of helping you to accept the numbing development of the story. I don't want to keep you another minute from learning, to your horror, precisely what *"The Old Men Know."*

There was an odd light in the yard in the middle of November. A curious light. And puzzling.

The weather was right for the time of the year: clouds so close they might have been called overcast were it not for the stark gradations of dark and light grey, for the bulges that threatened violence, for the thin spots that promised blue; a wind steady but not strong, damp and cold but only hinting at the snow that would fall not this time but too soon for comfort; the look of things in general, with the grass still struggling to hang onto its green, the shrubs tented in burlap, the trees undecided — some newly bare, others with leaves intact and tinted, colors that didn't belong to the rest of the land.

Those colors were precious now. They were the only break in desolation until spring, not even the snow promising much more than slush or the mark of passing dogs or the dark tracks of creatures mechanical and living. Those colors were loved, and cherished, and unlike the same ones that filled most of October, these were mourned because they marked the end of the end of change. To see them now meant the air no longer smelled like smoke, that the sunsets would be bleak, that the brown they'd become would fill gutters and driveways with work, not with pleasure.

But the light was curious, and so then were the colors.

From my second story study window I could see a maple tree in the middle of the backyard. It wasn't tall, but its crown was thick enough to provide ample summer shade, and a pile of leaves big enough for the neighborhood children to leap into after I'd spent an hour raking them up. Its color this year was a yellow laced with red, made all the more brilliant because the tall shrubs and trees behind it had lost their leaves early and provided the maple with a background glum enough to make it stand out.

Now it was almost glowing.

I looked up from my accounts and stared at it, leaned away and rubbed my eyes lightly, leaned forward again and squinted.

"Hey," I said, "come here and look at this."

A whispering of skirts, and Belle came to the desk, stood

behind me and put her hands on my shoulders. She peered through the window, craned and looked down into the yard as close to the house as she could.

"What?"

"Don't you see it?" I pointed to the tree.

"Yeah. Okay."

"Doesn't it look sort of odd to you?"

"Looks like a tree to me."

If she had said yes, I would have agreed, watched it a few moments more and returned to paying the bills; if she had said no, I would have pressed her a little just to be sure she wasn't kidding; but she had been, as she was increasingly lately, flippant without the grace of humor. So I rose, walked around the desk and stood at the window. The sill was low, the panes high, and I was able to check the sky for the break in the clouds that had let in the sun just enough to spotlight the maple. There was none, however, and I checked the room's other three windows.

"Caz, I think you have a blur on your brain."

"Don't be silly."

She followed me around the room, checked as I did, muttering incomprehensibly, and just low enough to bother me. And when I returned to the desk she sat on it, crossed her legs and hiked up the plaid skirt to the middle of her thighs.

"Sailor," she said, "you've been at sea too long. Wanna have a good time?" Her slippered foot nudged my knee. She winked, and turned slightly to bring my gaze to her chest. "What do you say, fella? I'm better than I look."

I almost laughed, and didn't because that's what she wanted me to do. When we'd met at a party five years ago, I had kept to myself in a corner chair, nursing a weak drink I didn't want, eavesdropping on conversations I didn't want to join. I was having fun. I preferred being alone, and I entertained the fantasy of my being invisible, a harmless voyeur of the contemporary scene, unwilling, and perhaps unable, to make any commitments. Then Belle had come over in dark blue satin, pulled up an ottoman and gave me the same lines she'd just spoken in the study. I'd laughed then, and surprised myself by talking to her. All night, in fact, without once thinking we might end up in bed. We exchanged phone numbers and addresses, and I didn't see or think of her again for another six months. Until the next party I couldn't get out of. This time we stayed together from the moment I walked in the door, and six months after that she moved in with me.

She didn't want to get married because she said it would spoil all her best lines; I didn't want to get married because then I wouldn't be able to be alone again.

"Caz," she said then, dropping the pose and readjusting her skirt, "are you okay?"

I shrugged without moving. "I guess so. I don't know. It's the weather, I imagine. It's depressing. And this," I said with a sweep of my hand to cover the bills, "doesn't help very much."

"That is an understatement." She stood and kissed my forehead, said something about getting dinner ready, come down in ten or fifteen minutes, and left without closing the door. I did it for her. Softly, so she wouldn't think I was annoyed. Then I went back to the window and watched the maple glow until the glow faded, twilight took over, and the dead of November was buried in black.

The next day, Belle dropped me at the park on her way to work. When I kissed her goodbye, I think she was surprised at the ardor I showed; I certainly was. Generally, I couldn't wait to be rid of her. Not that I didn't like her, and not that I didn't love her, but I still blessed those hours when we were apart. It not only made our time together more important, but it also allowed me time to myself.

To sit on the benches, to walk the paths, to leave the park and head into town. Listening to people. Watching them. Every so often, when I was feeling particularly down, hoping that one of them would come up to me and say, hey, aren't you Caz Rich, the children's book guy? They never did, but I sometimes spent hours in bookstores, waiting for someone to buy one of my books.

Well, not really *my* books.

I don't write them, I illustrate them. Mostly books about what I call critters, as opposed to creatures — silly monsters, silly villains, silly any bad thing to take the sting out of evil for the little kids who read them.

Some of the shopkeepers, once they'd gotten used to seeing me around, asked what it was like to be a househusband while the wife was out doing whatever she was doing. In this case, it was managing a string of five shops catering to those who bought labels instead of clothes. I used to correct them, tell them I was a commercial artist who worked at home, but when they smiled knowingly and kept it up each time they asked, I gave up and said that I liked it just fine, and as soon as I figured out what I was going to be when I grew up, my wife could stay home like a good wife should.

They didn't care much for that and didn't talk much to me again, but as I often said to Foxy, life in the fast lane has its price too.

I grinned at myself then, and looked around to see if Foxy was out.

He was, with his cronies.

They were sitting on the high step of the fountain in the middle of the park. The water had been turned off a month ago, and the marble bowl was filling with debris from the trees and passersby. Foxy and his men kept unofficial guard on it, to keep the brats from tossing their candy wrappers in it, and to keep the teens from pissing there whenever they had too much beer.

Only one person I know of complained to the police about the harrassment, and the police suggested slyly to Belle that unless she had mischief of her own up her sleeve there was no discernible harm done so please, miss, no offense but get lost.

Foxy grinned when he saw me, stood up and held out his hand. He was at that age when age didn't matter, and when a look couldn't tell you what it was anyway. His skin was loose here and tight there, his clothes the same, and his hair was always combed, and always blown by the wind. Unlike the others, he never wore a hat because, he'd once confided, he'd read in a magazine that using one of those things was a guarantee of baldness.

"Caz!" he said cheerily. His grip was firm, his blue eyes bright, his mouth opened in a grin that exposed his upper gums. "Caz, the boys and me were just talking about you."

The boys numbered five, all of an age, all of a color, and all of them smelling like attics in spring. They grunted their greetings as I walked around the fountain, shaking hands, noting the weather and generally not saying much at all. Chad was busy knitting himself a winter sweater with nimble fat fingers that poked out of fingerless gloves; Streetcar was reading; so were Dick O'Meara and his brother, Denny; and Rene didn't like me so he hardly acknowledged my presence beyond an ill-concealed sideways sneer. Once done with the formalities, Foxy and I headed off toward the far end of the park, where a hot dog vendor waited patiently under his striped umbrella for the offices to let out so he could feed them all lunch.

"So how's Miss Lanner?"

"Same. Fine."

Foxy nodded.

"You?"

Foxy shrugged. He wore a worn Harris tweed jacket buttoned to the chest, a soft maroon scarf that served as a dashing tie, his pants didn't match and sometimes neither did his shoes. "Could be better, but it's the weather, you know? Thinking about going to Florida before I get the chilblains."

"A trip would do you good."

He laughed. "Sure, when I win the lottery."

Foxy used to be an attorney, spent it all as he made it, and now lived on his Social Security and what other folks in their charity deemed fit to give him. He didn't mind charity; he figured he'd earned it. Age, to him, was a privilege, not a curse.

We passed few others as we made our way west. It was raw, and what pedestrians there were rushed along their shortcuts instead of admiring the views. And by the time we reached the stand, made our choices and turned around, the park was deserted except for the boys at the fountain.

"Any inspiration lately?" he asked around a bite of his lunch.

"Only that when I see you I want to open a savings account."

He laughed and poked me hard on the arm, shook his head and sighed. "Misspent youth, Caz, m'boy. You'd be wise to take a lesson from your elders."

Dick and Denny had finished their books by the time we'd returned and were attempting to find ways to keep the cold off their bald pates. Rene was pitching pebbles at the pigeons. Streetcar was dozing. Chad, however, looked up at Foxy, looked at me, and smiled sadly.

"Saw it again, Fox," he said. His face was more beard than flesh, his coat the newest of the lot. He should have been warm, but his teeth were chattering.

"You're kidding."

"While you were gone," and he pointed over my shoulder.

I looked automatically, and saw nothing but the grass, the trees, and a wire litter basket half-filled with trash.

Foxy didn't move.

"Saw what?" I asked.

"Gonna call?" Foxy said.

"Nope," Chad told him. "What's the use?"

"I guess."

"Saw what?"

Foxy patted his friend's shoulder and walked me up the path to the corner, stopped and looked back. "It's sad, Caz, real sad. Chad sees things. More and more of them every day. This week it's bank robbers."

"But you can't see the bank from—" I stopped, ashamed I hadn't picked it up right away. "Oh."

He nodded, tapped a temple. "At least he doesn't bother the police. If he did, I don't think we'd see him here much longer."

I was sympathetic, but I was also getting cold, so we spoke only a few minutes more before I headed home, taking the shortest route instead of picking streets at random; and once inside, I turned up the furnace to get warm in a hurry. Then I went upstairs and stood at my desk. I knew I should work; there were two contracts at hand, both of them fairly good, and the possibility I might get a chance to do a critter calendar for kids.

There was little enough wealth involved in what I did for a living, but there had been sufficient in the past five years so that Belle wouldn't have to worry if she ever decided to pack it in and stay home. I didn't know how I'd handle that, but since there didn't seem much chance of it, I seldom thought about it — only when I was feeling old-fashioned enough to want her home, with me, the way it had been for my father, and his father before him.

Being a liberated male when you're ten is easy; when you're over thirty, however, it's like mixing drugs — today it's cool and I don't mind because it doesn't limit my freedom or alter my perspectives; tomorrow it's a pain in the ass and whatever happened to aprons and babies.

And when I get in moods like that, I did what I always do — I worked.

So hard that I didn't hear Belle come home, didn't hear though I sensed her standing in the doorway watching for a moment before she went away, leaving me to my critters, and my make-believe children.

An hour later, I went downstairs, walked into the kitchen and saw that it was deserted. Nothing on the stove. Nothing on the table. I went into the living room, and it was empty, and so was the dining room. Frowning, and seeing her purse still on the hall table, I peered through a front window and saw her on the porch. A sweater was cloaked around her shoulders, and she was watching the empty street.

When I joined her she didn't turn.

"Chilly," I said.

It was dark, the streetlamps on, the leaves on the lawn stirring for their nightmoves.

"What are we going to do, Caz?"

"Do? About what?"

I couldn't see her face, and she wouldn't let me put an arm around her shoulders.

"I had lunch with Roman today."

Hell and damnation, the writing on the wall. Lunch with Roman today, several times over the past few months, a day-trip into New York to do some buying during the summer. Roman Carrell was the manager of one of her bigger shops, younger than both of us, and hungrier than I. If the husband is always the last to know, I wondered where I fit in. On the other hand, maybe he was only a good friend, and a shoulder to cry on whenever I got into one of my moods.

She pulled the sweater more snugly across her chest. "He says he wants to marry me, Caz."

"Lots of people do. You're beautiful."

Her head ducked away. "I am not."

"Well, I think you are, and since I'm an artist experienced in these things, you'll have to believe me."

Another one of our lines. Dialogue from a bad show that also happened to be my life.

Jesus.

I leaned back against the railing, looking at her sideways. "Do you want to marry him?"

Suddenly, there was gunfire, so much of it I knew it wasn't a backfiring car or truck. We both straightened and stared toward downtown, then I ran inside and grabbed my windbreaker from the closet.

"What the hell are you doing?" she demanded, grabbing my arm as I ran out again.

The gunshots were replaced by what sounded like a hundred sirens.

"Nosey," I said, grinning. "Want to come along?"

"You'll get hurt, stupid."

I probably was, but in a town this size the only shots ever heard came from the occasional hunter who thought a Chevy was a deer. This was something else, some excitement, and as I ran down the walk I hoped to hear Belle trying to catch up. She didn't. I wasn't surprised.

I reached the park about the same time a hundred others did, and we saw patrol cars slanted all over the street, their hoods aimed at a jewelry store a few doors in from the intersection.

An ambulance was there, and spotlights poked at the brick walls while a dozen cops strode back and forth in flak jackets, carrying shotguns and rifles and pushing the crowd back.

I made my way to the front in about ten minutes, just in time to see two attendants loading a stretcher into the van. There was blood on the sidewalk, and the shop's glass doors were blown inward. No one had seen anything, but from those I talked to it must have been a hell of a battle.

Belle didn't say anything when I finally got home; she was already in bed, the alarm clock set, and my pajamas laid out on my side of the mattress.

She left before I woke up.

"Well," I said to Foxy two afternoons later, "Chad's crystal ball needs a little polishing, huh?"

He grinned, turned to Dick and Denny who were feeding a lone squirrel from a popcorn bag, and asked if they'd mind holding the fort while he and I took a short walk. They said no, Streetcar was busy plucking leaves from the fountain, and Rene didn't bother to turn around.

Once we reached the far end of the path, Foxy stopped and faced me. "Chad's dead," he said.

"Oh hell, no."

"Yeah. Bad heart. Last night. His daughter called me. He went in his sleep."

I didn't say anything except to ask which funeral parlor he was in, then walked to the florist and sent the old guy some flowers. I didn't work at all that afternoon, and Belle didn't come home for dinner.

While I waited for her in the living room — TV on and unwatched, newspaper in my lap unfolded and unread — I listened to the leaves racing across the lawn ahead of the wind, and couldn't help hearing the sound of Chad dying. I paced until the wind died, then drank a couple of tasteless beers, waited until midnight, and went to bed.

Belle didn't return the next day either, which was too bad because that maple glowed again and I wanted her to see it before the clouds closed off the sun.

I called the shop, finally, all the shops, and kept just missing her according to the clerks. Roman was out as well, and I didn't need a plank across the back of my head to know I'd been deserted. Instead of bemoaning and ranting, however, I worked, which in itself is a sort of reaction—the yelling went into the drawings, the tears into the ink. It worked until I couldn't hold a pen any longer, until I was back downstairs and there was no one to talk to.

Alone was one thing; lonely was something else.

Still, I didn't lose my temper.

I decided instead to be noble about it all. After all, we weren't married, weren't even contemplating it, and if that's what Belle wanted then that's what she would have. Maybe she'd grow tired of the little prick; maybe she'd come back and maybe she wouldn't. So I didn't call again, and I worked as hard as I ever had over the next several days, only once going down to the park where I noticed Streetcar was gone, taken away, Foxy said, by the men in pretty white because he was talking about an atom bomb dropping into the middle of town.

"A crock," said Rene, and said nothing more.

Dick and Denny were nervous but they kept on reading, the same book, and I didn't ask why.

And a week to the day after she'd left, Belle came back.

I was in the kitchen fixing lunch when she walked in, sat at the table and smiled.

"Have a nice trip?" I said.

"So-so."

I couldn't help it—I yelled. "Goddamnit, Lanner, where the hell have you been?"

There was no contrition; she bridled. "Thinking, driving, screwing around," she said coldly. "You're not my husband, you know."

"No, but Christ, it seems to me I have a few rights around here. A little common courtesy wouldn't have killed you."

She shrugged and picked at something invisible on her lip.

"Are you back?" I said, sounding less than enthusiastic.

"No."

"A little more thinking, driving, screwing around?"

"I need it," she told me.

"Then get it." I turned my back to her, kept it there while I fussed with the skillet where my eggs were scrambling, kept it there until she got up and left. Then I tossed the skillet into the sink, threw the plate against the wall, picked up the drain where the clean dishes were stacked and threw it on the floor. I knocked over her chair. I punched the refrigerator and screamed when I heard at least one of my knuckles cracking.

Then I left without cleaning up, marched to the park and dropped onto a bench. Sat there. Blindly. Until Dick and Denny came up to me, twins in rags with paperback books in their hands.

"We saw it, you know," Dick said with a glance to Denny, who nodded. "We saw it yesterday."

"Saw what," I grumbled.

They hesitated.

"Gentlemen," I said, "I'm really very tired. It's been a bad day and it's not even two." I managed a smile. "Would you mind?"

"But we saw it!" Dick insisted as Denny tugged at his sleeve. "We really did see it."

"Yeah, okay," I said.

"So here." And before I could move they had shoved both their books into my hands. "They're really good," said Dick. "I won't tell you the end, though, it would spoil it, and I hate it when somebody does it to me."

Denny nodded solemnly.

Foxy came up then, put his arms around the two men's shoulders and looked an apology at me. "Let's go, boys," he said, steering them away. Another look, and I shook my head in sympathy. The sanity, not to mention the mortality, rate among the guys at the fountain was getting pretty serious. But they were all in the same decade, with the weather as raw as it was, and their health not the best, so it wasn't all that surprising.

It was, on the other hand, depressing, and I left before Foxy could return and tell me the latest from the geriatric book of fairy tales.

The newspaper I picked up on my way home didn't help my mood any. The Middle East was blowing up, Washington was squabbling, the state senate was deadlocked on a bill to improve education, there were a handful of murders, a kidnapping, and two bus crashes on the outskirts of town. Great. Just what I needed to read when I had twenty-one more critters to draw that needed the light touch, not a scalpel.

I tossed the paper onto the kitchen table and cleaned up the broken crockery; then I poured myself a glass of soda and sat down, hands on my cheeks, hair in my eyes, until suddenly I frowned. I picked up the paper, snapped over a couple of pages and read the story about the first bus crash. At first I didn't recognize the name; then I realized that among the eight dead had been poor old Streetcar Mullens.

"Well, shit," I said to the empty room. "Shit."

Two days later, Dick and Denny were dead as well, their boarding house burned down; they had been sleeping at the time.

I was on my way out the door when Belle drove up in front of the house. She didn't get out of the car, but rolled down the passenger side window. I leaned over and waited.

"Aren't you glad to see me?"

"I might be," I said flatly, "but a couple of friends of mine died last night. In a fire."

"Oh, I'm sorry." She polished the steering wheel with her gloved hands, then straightened the silk scarf tossed around her neck. "Anyone I know?"

"No," I said, realizing how much of my life she never knew at all. "A couple of guys from the park."

"Oh, them," she said. "For god's sake, Caz, when are you going to get friends your own age? Christ, you'll be old before your time if you're not careful." She looked at me then. "I take it back. You *are* old, only you don't know it."

"And what does that make you?" I laughed. "The world's oldest teenaged swinger?" I leaned closer, hearing the sound of dishes smashing on the floor. "He's too young for you, Belle. The first wrinkle you sprout will send him packing."

She glared, and her hands fisted. "You bastard," she said softly. "At least I'm getting the most out of...oh, what's the use."

She would have cheerfully cut my throat then, and I astonished myself in the realization that I wouldn't have let her. "You want a divorce then?"

She hesitated before nodding.

"And you want to be sure I'm not around when you and young Roman come by for your things because you want to spare my old man's feelings."

"You don't have to talk that way."

"No, but I am."

She swallowed. "If you had needed me, if only you had needed me."

"I did, don't be silly."

She shook her head. "No, Caz, you didn't. Not in the way it counted."

There were tears in her eyes. I don't know how long they'd been there, but they began to make me feel like a real bastard. She had a point, I suppose, but it had taken her a hell of a long time to find the courage to make her move. And to be truthful, I was relieved. When she drove away, I was almost lightheaded because someone had finally done something, taken a step, and now things would change. A selfish, perhaps even cowardly way to look at it, but as I made my way to the park I couldn't yet feel much guilt. Maybe later. Maybe later, in the dark, with no one beside me.

Foxy was sitting glumly in his usual place, and Rene was beside him.

"God, I'm sorry," I said as I approached them.

"Thank you, Caz," Foxy said without moving. His face was pale, his eyes dark and refusing to meet my gaze. In his lap his hands trembled.

Rene looked up. "Go away," he said sourly. "You ain't got no right here."

My exchange with Belle had drained my patience, and I grinned mirthlessly at him. "Shut up, Rene. I'm sick of your grousing."

"Oh, you are?" he said. "And how about if I'm sick and tired of you coming around here all the time, prying into what's none of your business? Huh? Suppose I'm tired of that?"

"Rene, hold it down," Foxy said wearily.

I was puzzled, because I hadn't the faintest idea what he was talking about, or why Foxy had suddenly lost his verve. Even after Streetcar's death the old man had managed to keep his good humor; now, his head seemed too heavy for his neck, and his hands still danced over the broadcloth of his lap.

"I'm not going to argue," I said, turning away. "I just wanted to give you my sympathy, that's all. I'm not being nosey."

But Rene wouldn't let it go.

"No? Then why are you all the time talking about what we see, huh? Why are you all the time asking about that?"

"He's a writer," Foxy snapped at him. "He's naturally curious."

"He ain't a writer, he draws pictures."

It was dumb, but I didn't leave. I had nowhere I wanted to go, and this for the time being was better than nothing.

"I illustrate," I corrected, almost primly, looking hard at Rene with a dare for contradiction. "I draw things for kids in books—which you're right, I don't write—and sometimes I do it for myself, all right? I draw houses and people and animals and critters and...and..." I looked around, feeling a surge of heat expand in my chest, and burn my eyes. "And trees, okay? The way they grow, the way they look in different seasons, the way they glow when there's no sun, the way they look when they've been hit by lightning. Christ!"

I stalked away and had almost reached the street when I heard Foxy calling. I looked back and saw him beckoning, while Rene yanked so hard on his arm that he toppled from the step to the concrete. I ran back, ready to exchange Belle for Rene and beat the hell out of both of them. But when I got there, Foxy was sitting up and Rene was sitting above him.

"What did you mean, about the trees?" Foxy said as soon as I was close enough to hear.

"Just what I said."

"Damn."

"Damn what?" I frowned. Rene wasn't talking, so I knelt and smiled. "Hey, is that what you guys have been seeing here in the park? A tree glowing sort of?" I poked Foxy's arm. "Hey, there's nothing wrong with that. It's the light. A break in the clouds, that's all. Hollywood does it all the time. Jeez, you didn't have to lie to me, the burglars and stuff. Good god, Foxy, I told you I saw it too."

He took my hand and held it; his fingers were ice, his grip was iron, and his eyes seemed farther back, black in his skull. "You see it for the dying," he said. "You see it for the dying."

He wouldn't talk to me after that, and Rene only scowled, and I finally went home after eating out. I felt, oddly, a hundred times better than when I'd left, and I even started to do a little work. Two hours later I was still at it, when I looked up and saw the tree.

It was dark outside; night had crept up on me while my pens were flying.

It was dark outside, and the maple tree was glowing.

The stars were out, but there was no moon.

And the maple tree was glowing.

I switched off the lights, and nothing changed; I hurried downstairs and stood at the back door, and nothing changed; I ran outside, and the tree was glowing. Gold, soft, and casting no shadows.

I was afraid to walk up and touch it. Instead, I went back in and sat at the kitchen table, watching for nearly an hour until the tree faded. Then I grabbed up a newspaper and began scribbling dates and names in the largest margins I could find. When I was done, I shook my head and did it again. After the second time, I had convinced myself that the old men in the park, if they had seen what I had, had been given glimpses of the future. Deaths. Accidents. And they were afraid of what they saw, so they made up stories to go with their age, with the failing of their minds. And they were afraid of what they saw, afraid of what it meant, and they died. A heart attack, a probable stroke, two men probably drunk in their rooms and not hearing the alarm.

"Jesus," I whispered.

And the telephone rang.

I thought it might be Belle, ready to tell me she'd be over to clear out her things.

But it was Foxy, and before he had a chance to say anything more than his name, I told him what I'd discovered and, if it were true, what it might mean.

"My god, Foxy," I said, fairly jumping with excitement, "think of what you guys can do, think of the people you can save."

"Caz, wait a minute."

"I know, I know — you don't want to be thought of as freaks, and I don't blame you. But god, Foxy, it's incredible!" I wound the cord around my wrist and stared grinning at the ceiling. "You know that, you know it's incredible, right? But look, you've got to tell me how you know where it's going to be and things like that. I mean, all I can see is the tree and nothing else. How do you know where the accident is going to be?"

"I don't."

"Impossible. Chad didn't just guess, you know. Do you *know* the odds on something like that?"

I wasn't making sense; I didn't care. Belle was leaving me, and I didn't care; the books weren't going right, and I didn't care. Something else was fine, and I was feeling all right.

"It was Chad in the store that night, Caz."

"So look, are you going to tell—" I stopped, straightened, blinked once very slowly. "Chad?"

"He needed the money. He knew he was going to die, so he decided to give it a try, to see if he could change it." There was a pause. A long pause to be sure I was listening and not just hearing. "It was Chad shot down that night, Caz. He was carrying a toy gun."

"Wait!" I said loudly, sensing he was about to hang up. "Foxy, wait. He *knew* he was going to die?"

Another pause, and I could hear him breathing as if he were drowning.

"*I* saw it today, Caz. I saw the tree. I know."

And he hung up.

I didn't want to go to the park the next day, but I did. Rene was sitting at the fountain, and he was alone.

"Where's Foxy?" I asked angrily.

"Where do you think?" he said, and pointed at the ground.

"He. . .he said he saw the tree yesterday."

Rene shrugged. And looked suddenly up at me and grinned. "So did you. A couple of times."

"But. . ." I looked around wildly, looked back and spread my hands. "But my god, aren't you afraid?"

"When you know it's done, it's done, right, old man?" And he grinned even wider.

There were a number of people walking through the park that day, but it didn't bother me—I hit him. I leaned back and threw a punch right at the side of his head, and felt immense satisfaction at the astonishment on his face as he spilled backward and struck his skull against the fountain's lip. He was dead. I knew it. And I knew then he had seen the tree and hadn't told me. So I ran, straight for home, and fell into the kitchen.

No prophesy except knowing when you'll die.

No change except for the method of the dying.

I had seen the tree glow, and I was going to die, and the only thing he didn't tell me was how long it was before it all happened.

There was fear, and there was terror, and finally in the dark there was nothing at all. Rene was right; when you had no choice, there was nothing but deciding you might as well get on with your work. At least that much would be done; at least there'd be no loose ends.

I started for the staircase, and the front door opened, and Belle came in.

I almost wept when I saw her, knowing instantly she'd been right—I'd not really needed her before, not the way it should have been. But I needed her now, and I wanted her to know it.

"Oh, Belle," I said, and opened my arms to gather in her comfort.

And gave her the perfect target for the gun in her hand.

The Substitute

Gahan Wilson

It is hard to imagine how anyone could enjoy a more brilliantly varied career than Gahan Wilson. While establishing a reputation second to none as a cartoonist of the highest calibre, his hilarious, strange, and oft-mordant work appearing in Playboy *as well as numerous other magazines, Wilson quietly set about the task of duplicating that success as a short story writer—usually dipping into the same dark, dank pool of Unlikely Things.*

If those accomplishments were not enough, Gahan has written "Screen" for Twilight Zone *magazine's "Other Dimensions" section since its inception in 1981, his commentary about new fantasy films among the most accurate and pertinent available in any medium.*

For those who believe that Wilson, who has become one of those rare cartoonists whose perturbing panels seem always to have been with us, is a newcomer to fiction in any sense, check this: The 1967 Playboy Book of Horror and the Supernatural *featured not one but* two *stories by Gahan Wilson. At that point, the editor noted, Wilson's cartoon connection with* Playboy *already stretched nine years into the past. One of those yarns, "The Manuscript of Dr. Arness," is still discussed almost two decades later.*

"The Substitute" is a daring story in concept, less because it blurs the genre lines beloved by many fretful editors than because of its theme and the important things it both says—and implies.

None of the children were in a good mood even to begin with. It was a foul November morning and every boy and girl of them had been forced by their mothers to wear their hated galoshes, and of course the galoshes hadn't worked, the snow had been too high (it was a *particularly* foul November morning, even for the Midwest) and had poured in over the tops so that their feet had got wet and cold anyhow, in spite of their mothers.

They took off their galoshes, and their soggy coats and hats, and put them in their proper places by the hook with the right name on it, and then they marched into room 204 of Washington School, Lakeside, where the sixth grade was taught, and were, to the last one of them, fully prepared to be horrid.

And it was only then that they realized that their troubles had just begun, for when they looked up at the big desk by the windows, behind which their blonde and pretty Miss Merridew, of whom they were all very, very fond, should by every right be sitting, there was, instead, a stranger, a person they had never seen in all their lives and wished they were not seeing now.

The stranger was a large, dark, balloonish woman. She seemed to be made up of roundness upon roundness; there was not a part of her that was not somehow connected with circularity from the coils of her thick, black hair, to the large, pearlish segments of her necklace and bracelets, to her round, wide, staring eyes with their dark irises set directly in the center of a roundness of white, which was a distinctly disconcerting effect since it made the eyes seem to stare at you so directly and penetratingly.

When the children were all settled at their desks and not one moment before, she stirred herself, making all those pearlish things rattle with a softly snakelike hiss, picked up the attendance sheet, consulted it very carefully with roundly pursed lips to indicate it was revealing many secrets to her, and when the class had become uncomfortable enough to make barely audible shifting noises, she looked up sharply and spoke.

"Good morning, students. I am Miss Or, that's O-R, and I will be your teacher for a time as poor Miss Merridew cannot be here due to an unfortunate, ah, accident. I am sure we will all get along just fine."

She paused to give a broad, rather fixed smile which the whole class disliked at once, and read off the attendance list, making little marks on the paper as she went along and studying the face of each student as they responded to their name. That done she stood, revealing that her roundness was not restricted to that part of her which showed over the desk, but continued through the length of her, down to a round, pearlish ball fixed to the toe of each of her black shoes, a decorative touch which none of the children ever remembered seeing on any Lakeside lady before, teacher or not. Her entire outfit, save for those pale, pearlish things, was black, unlike the colors of Miss Merridew's outfits which tended always to be cheerful and pleasantly sunny.

"Today we will have a very special lesson," she said, sweeping the children with another fixed smile and those strange, staring eyes. "We shall learn about a wonderful place which none of us have heard of before."

She moved over to the map holder fixed above the center of the blackboard, revealing a lightness of foot which was extraordinary in so large a person; she seemed to float from step to step. The map holder was an ingenious affair which contained an apparently inexhaustible supply of maps and charts of all descriptions which could be pulled down at choice like windowshades, and then caused to fly back up into hiding by a clever tug at their bottoms.

Miss Or selected a bright green tag which the sharper children did not remember seeing before, and unrolled a large, brightlycolored map new to them all.

"This is Aliahah," she said. "Ah-lee-ah-ah. Can you say that name, class?"

"Ah-lee-ah-ah," they said, more or less.

"That's fine. That's very good. Now, as you can see, Aliahah is extremely varied geographically, having mountain ranges, lush valleys, deserts, several large bodies of water, and an interesting coastline bordered by two different seas."

She paused and regarded the map with open affection while the children stared at it with varying degrees of disinterest.

"Mary Lou," said Miss Or, turning and fixing a thin, pale girl in the front row with her eyes which, now that the students had observed them in action, were seen to have the same near fixity in their sockets as those of sharks, "can you tell me how many major bodies of water there are in Aliahah?"

Mary Lou Gorman colored slightly, frowned, counted silently without moving her lips and answered, "Three."

"That is entirely correct," said Miss Or with a nod of her round head which made her thick hair float and weave in the air as if it weighed nothing at all, or was alive like so many snakes. "The most important one, Lake Gooki—"

There was the briefest of amused snortings from some members of the class at the sound of the name of Lake Gooki, but it was instantly silenced by an icy, vaguely dangerous glance from Miss Or's shark eyes.

"—is not only beautiful, but extremely useful, having no less than nine underwater mines, indicated by these pretty red triangles. The mines produce most of the radioactive ore needed for the war effort."

Leonard Bates rather tentatively raised a hand.

"Yes, Lennie?"

"Ah, Miss, ah..."

"Or, Lennie. My name is Miss Or."

"Miss, ah, Or," said Leonard, "I just wondered, was this going to be a test?"

"That's a good question, Lennie. No. There will be no test. However, it would be wise of you to remember as much as you can about Aliahah for the information will be most useful to you. Think of all this as a friendly attempt to familiarize you with a country which, I hope very much, you will come to love."

Leonard looked at Miss Or for a puzzled moment, then nodded and said, "Thank you, Miss, ah, Or."

Miss Or bestowed an odd, lingering glance on Leonard as she toyed absently with a pearlish thing or two on her necklace. Her nails were long and sharply pointed and painted a shiny black.

"Aliahah has only two cities of any size. Bunem, here in the north, and Kaldak in the midland plains."

She sent the map of Aliahah flying up into the holder with a smart pluck at its lower edge and pulled down a somewhat smaller map showing Kaldak, which she gestured at roundly with one round arm.

"Kaldak, being our main center of weapons manufacture, is levitational, if need be."

Harry Pierce and Earl Waters exchanged glances, and then Earl raised his hand.

"Yes, Earl?"

"Excuse me, Miss Or, but just what do you mean by 'levitational'?"

"Only that it can be floated to various locations in order to confuse enemy orientation."

Harry and Earl exchanged glances again, and this time made faces which Miss Or, turning back to the map with an alacrity which made her alarmingly weightless hair dance up from her skull in snakish hoops and coils, missed entirely.

"There are no less than two thousand, seven hundred and ninety four factories working ceaselessly in Kaldak," said Miss Or, a new note of grimness creeping into her voice. "Ceaselessly."

She turned to the class, and there was no trace of her fixed smile now. She seemed, almost, to be anguished, and one or two of the children thought they caught a glimpse of a large, round tear falling from one of her staring, dark eyes, though it seemed incongruous.

"Do you realize," she said, "how many of us that keeps from the fighting? The glorious fighting?"

She turned with a sweep and a rattling hiss of her pearlish things, snapped the map of Kaldak back into the holder, and uncoiled an involved chart whose labyrinthine compexities seemed to mock any possibility of comprehension, certainly from that of the sixth grade of Washington School.

"It is very important," said Miss Or, looking over her black shoulder at them with her pale face, "that you understand everything of what I am going to tell you now!" And something about the roundness of her face and staring eyes, and something about how her round mouth worked in a circular, chewing fashion as she talked, put them all so much in mind of a shark staring at them, sizing them up, or was it a snake? that they all drew back in their little seats behind their little desks, at the same time realizing it wasn't going to help at all.

And then she launched into a lecture of such intense and glorious inscrutability that it lost them all from its first sentence, from the first half of that sentence, from its first word, so that they could only boggle and cringe and realize that at last they had encountered what they had all dreaded encountering from their very first day at school: a teacher and a lesson which were, really and truly, completely and entirely, ununderstandable.

At the same moment Clarence Weed began, just began, to be able to see something peculiar about the long sides of the blackboard showing to the left and right of Miss Or's hanging graph. At first he assumed he was imagining it, but when it persisted and even clarified, he thought in more serious terms, thought about the light flashes he had seen just before coming down with influenza late last winter. But he'd only seen those lights out of the corners of his eyes, so to speak, as if they had been flicking far off to one side or even way around at his back, and the lights he was looking at now were directly in front of him, and besides, they didn't dim or blur if he squeezed his eyes shut for a second and then looked again, indeed, if anything, they seemed to get a little better defined.

"Of course," Miss Or was saying, following the spiraling curves of some symbol with the shiny, black, pointy fingernail of her left index finger, "density confirms with the number of seedlings loosened and the quantity surviving flotation to the breeding layer."

No, they did not blur or dim, nor, as he started harder at them, did they continue to be nothing more than lights. Now he could make out edges, now forms, now there were the vague beginnings of three dimensionality.

"To be sure they will sometimes gomplex," Miss Or explained

carefully. "There is always the possibility of a gomplex."

Clarence Weed looked across the aisle, trying to catch the eye of Ernie Price, then saw there was no need to give him any kind of signal as Ernie was leaning intently forward, studying the blackboard with all his might, so he went back to do some more of it himself.

And now he saw the shapes and spaces showing—what exactly was the process? Were these things showing through the blackboard? Or were they, somehow, starting to supplant it?—showing by their relationships a kind of scene. He was beginning to make out a sort of landscape.

"Any species so selected," Miss Or continued, "should count itself extravagantly fortunate."

There were things in a kind of formal grouping. He could not tell what the things were, nothing about them seemed familiar, but they were alive, or at least capable of motion. A kind of wind seemed to disturb them constantly, they were always fighting a tendency to drift to one side caused by some sort of endlessly pushing draft, and they reached out thin tendrils and clung to the objects about them so as not to be blown away. Clarence felt he could almost hear the wind, a sort of mournful, bitter sighing, but then he decided that *was* an illusion.

"The odds against such wonderful luck are easily several zahli sekutai. And yet you won!"

The beings, they were definitely beings and not things, were all staring straight out at him, at the class. He could see nothing which looked like eyes, could not even determine what part of the beings could be their equivalent of a head which would contain eyes, but he knew without question that they were looking, intently, at him and the other children.

He turned to see how Ernie was doing and in the process saw that all of them, every one of the children, were examining the blackboard with as much concentration as he had been, and then had what was perhaps the strangest experience of this entire adventure when he realized that even though he was looking at his classmates he was still seeing what they were seeing through the blackboard, exactly as if he were seeing it through all of their eyes, and he knew, at the same time, that they were seeing themselves through his eyes. They all seemed, somehow, to have joined.

"Though we have searched extensively," Miss Or was saying solemnly, "we have found no avenue of mental or psychic contact with the enemy. They are inscrutable to us, and we are inscrutable to them."

There had been all along something about the grouping of the beings which was teasingly near recognizable and at last Clarence realized what it was: their grouping was a mirror image of the class's grouping. They were assembled in four rows of five, just as the sixth grade was. And now he realized what else it was they reminded him of: balloons. They looked for all the world like a bunch of balloons of different shapes and colors such as you'd come across for sale in a circus or a fair.

Some were long and straight, some long and spiral; some, the majority, were almost perfectly round; some were a complex series of bulges of different sizes, and some were involved and elaborate combinations of some or all of these elements. In a weird sort of way this seemed to explain their lightness, their constant bobbing and sidewise slipping in the draft or wind which was so much a part of their world.

"Though there have been skeptics," Miss Or pronounced, "there is no doubt we shall eventually taste the fruits of victory, or at least of mutual annihilation."

But even now as Clarence watched them, the balloon beings were beginning some strange sort of group movement which, at first, he took to be an extreme change of posture on their parts; he even had a thought, though with no idea where it might have come from, that they were starting to engage in an elaborate magical dance ritual.

As the movements continued, though, he saw that they were much more extreme, much more basic than an ordinary shifting of parts, that these beings were involved in something a great deal more complicated than a changing of position. They were, he saw, actually engaged in a structural rearrangement of themselves.

At this point all the children of grade six gave a tiny, soft little sigh in unison, a sound so gentle that, perhaps very fortunately, Miss Or missed hearing it entirely, and Clarence Weed, along with Ernie Price, along with Harry Pierce and Earl Waters and Mary Lou Gorman blurred and lost their edges and ceased to be any of those separate children.

The species, threatened severely and seeing that threat, went quickly and efficiently back to techniques long unused, abandoned since the tribal Cro-Magnon, tactics forsaken since the bold and generous experiment of giving the individual permission to separate from the herd in order to try for perilous, solitary excellence.

Now, faced with an alien danger serious enough to hint at actual extinction, the animal Man rejoined, temporarily abandoning the luxury of individuality and the tricky benefits of multiple consciousness in order to return to the one group mind, joining all strengths together for survival.

Meantime the beings on the other side of the blackboard had progressed significantly with their transformation. Gone now were the smooth, shiny surfaces and come instead were multiple depressions and extrusions, involved modelings and detailings. No longer were they reminiscent of balloons, now they looked like animated creatures in a crude cartoon with simple, splayed hands and blobby eyes, but they looked somewhat like humans, which was not so before.

"Not a retreat," intoned Miss Or, "but an expansion. Not a falling back, but a bold exploration!"

She looked skyward, smiling and starry eyed, a figure in a patriotic mural. Around her the blackboard figures continued to take on something more like a structure based on bones and the fine points of the faces and fingers and even of costume trivia. Here was Helen Custer's belt with the doe's head buckle coming into focus, now, clearer and clearer, could you make out the round, black rubber patches pasted on the ankles of Dick Doub's gym shoes, and there was no mistaking the increasingly clear pattern of tiny hearts on Elsie Nonan's blouse.

But they were not Helen nor Dick nor Elsie forming there behind the blackboard. They were something quite else. Something entirely different.

"And if Aliahah, even sweet Aliahah, must perish in the flames and rays of war rather than fall into the power of vile invaders," Miss Or had now grown quite ecstatic in her posing before what she still took to be grade six of Washington School, one hand was clenched at her breast and the other raised to take hold of yet another tab from the map holder's inventory, her shark eyes glistening freely with sentimental tears, "its noble race shall survive, at whatever cost!"

The beings, now completely convincing simulations of grade six, began to form a column, two abreast, leading to the graph chart and, on perfect cue, Miss Or smartly sent the chart up into hiding in the map holder and pulling down a long, wide sheet, far bigger than even the map of Aliahah, a design altogether different from anything that had come before, a clearly potent cabalistic symbol which, from its linear suggestions of perspective and its general shape, could represent nothing other than some sort of hermetic door, a pathway for Miss Or's race—her identity with the ominous creatures on the other side of the blackboard was certainly now established beyond any shade of doubt—an entry for the invasion of our own dear planet, Earth.

"Let me show the way!" cried Miss Or joyfully, and all the round, pearlish baubles on her suddenly lit up brightly in orange and magenta, doubtless the colors of Aliahah, as she stepped forward, and with a broad and highly theatrical gesture of invitation to the beings which were even now advancing in step toward the sinister opening she had provided for them, shouted, *"Let me be th—"*

But, unfortunately for Miss Or, unfortunately for her approaching countrybeings, what had been the sixth grade of Washington School rose as one creature, strode forward, lifted her—she was, as her floating hair and prancing steps had suggested, extremely light—and flung her through the door where she impacted on her fellow Aliahahians much as a bowling ball strikes a line of ninepins, and the whole group of them no sooner gave a great wail of despair, when the sheet bearing the drawing of the door flew up into the map holder with a huge puff of smoke and a fine shower of sparks.

It was less than a quarter hour later that Michael O'Donoghue, the school's hard working janitor, experienced the greatest shock and surprise of his life since birth when he opened a storage closet of the main assembly hall with its biographical murals showing pivotal scenes from George Washington's life, and, sprawling with all the abandon of a Raggedy Ann, out tumbled the comely body of Miss Merridew, the regular and rightful teacher of the sixth grade.

Under the concerned ministrations of Mr. O'Donoghue together with the hastily-summoned school nurse, Leska Haldeen, and under the steady but alarmed gaze of Lester Baxter, the school principal, Miss Merridew was soon restored to consciousness and near to her regular state of health.

Her first thought, of course, was for the children, and so nothing would do but that she must hurry off with O'Donoghue, Haldeen, Baxter and a growing number of curious and worried others in tow, to see if her charges were safe.

They seemed to be, but a careful looking over of all of them showed that, without exception, they were in a peculiar, groggy state, blinking and gaping vaguely at nothing and looking for all the world, as Mr. O'Donoghue observed, "as if they'd been freshly born."

Of course they were asked many questions, not just that day, off and on for some weeks afterward, but none of the children ever seemed to remember anything at all about what had happened, or, if they did, none of them ever chose to tell.

It was noticed, however, that they all seemed to be very pleased with themselves, even if for no particular reason, and Lucy Barton did mention something vague to her parents just before drifting off to sleep that night, something about a nasty creature that somehow got into the classroom, but they couldn't find out from her whether it was a bug or a rat or what.

The next day Miss Merridew found she was unable to operate

the map holder so Mr. O'Donoghue took it to the basement to have a look at it and found that someone must have been tampering with it maliciously for it was indeed jammed and when he took it apart in order to repair it, he saw that some sort of odd conflagration had taken part in its interior. Apparently a flammable substance had been packed into it, set afire, and not only warped its works severely enough to put them beyond Mr. O'Donoghue's abilities to set it right again, but burnt all the maps so badly that there was nothing legible left of any one of them except for a small part of Iowa, and one other fragment which had peculiar, glowing colors in some strange, exotic design.

That was far from the oddest aspect of the little scrap, for Mr. O'Donoghue found that if he held it close to his ear with the designed part uppermost, he could hear a continual, complicated squeaking noise which sounded exactly as if a multitude of tiny beings were trapped in a confined space and endlessly crying in horror and panic as they unsuccessfully tried to escape.

Now from that description it might seem that the sound would be extremely disturbing and depressing to hear, but Mr. O'Donoghue found, quite to the contrary, that it gave him great satisfaction to hold the little fragment to his ear for minutes on end, and that the tiny screaming and turmoil, far from being in any way unpleasant, always gave him great satisfaction, and that the screams actually made him chuckle and never failed to cheer him up if he happened to be feeling gloomy.

After dinner that Thanksgiving he showed the fragment to his grandchildren and showed them how to listen to it, and when they heard it they begged him to let them keep it and he didn't, of course, have the heart to refuse.

They took it with them and, while they cherished it dearly and delighted in showing it off to all their friends, it was lost track of through the years and never seen or heard by any human being ever again.

The Alteration

Dennis Hamilton

Reversing the pattern of such Masques *authors as Bradbury, Nolan, Bloch and Russell, Dennis Hamilton was born in California (Long Beach, November 18, 1948) and moved to the Midwest—Indianapolis, to be exact. Whether that explains my favorite Hamilton anecdote or not is your call: As a transplanted teenager, athletic Dennis did a backbreaking stretch of yard work for a grouchy neighbor who then welched on the pathetic payment of their agreement. In the best tradition of vampires and assorted malcreants of midnight, Dennis borrowed a truck and proceeded to drive back and forth across said lawn until it was restored to its previous state—at least. "I did him a favor," Dennis promises.*

Written by a powerfully-constructed man who once was a match from making the Olympic wrestling team, "The Alteration" is a horror reader's reply to that deathless demand, "Where's the beef?" Hamilton himself is a gentle father of two, editorial executive for numerous computer software publications, a friend, ready with an answer to questions concerning horror's enduring popularity: "It is the least experienced of all emotions," Dennis says, stressing "pure, raw, wrenching horror" and adding: "There is not a sufficient amount of time for the brain to develop any psychological defense mechanisms against it."

Take my word: You've no defense against this bristling, brawny, convincing story by a tae kwando belt-winner. None. You'll find "The Alteration" has a lingering impact you can never quite forget.

The signal to take her came as they raised their glasses in toast.

Harry Crawley smiled warmly across the table to Lynn, radiating his meticulously crafted love. Their glasses clinked softly as they touched, and the two held the pose for an instant, the utterly indistinguishable gazes of forged and genuine affection locked over the brims.

"To us, alone," Harry softly intoned.

"Now and forever," the dark-haired beauty responded.

They sipped, Lynn Yager for the future, Harry Crawley for his thirst. He lowered his glass and a single drop of tequila rolled off it onto the table. Harry watched as the unwaxed wood absorbed it. Then his eyes wandered over the tales of the table. Spanish names, cryptic initials, revolutionary slogans and unintelligible scratches had been etched into its surface with the knives of El Lobo's coarse patrons. The graffiti of a thousand idle thoughts. Well, not all of them were idle. Eleven of the scratches were his. And Harry always had a purpose.

Harry glanced across the dark El Lobo barroom to Nuñez. His smile faded into a now familiar taut-lipped revulsion. Harry loathed Nuñez. Grotesquely fat, the Mexican's face reminded him of a sack of potatoes: skin the texture of burlap; pitted, formless, unsymmetrical. Nuñez had a constant, glistening coat of perspiration, and he reeked of the insidious stench of Puerta Valencia. Harry Crawley, a man of dark acquaintances, had never known a man more repulsive. Even for a compunctionless slaver.

Ramiro Nuñez was, however, a partner in business.

"Excuse me for a moment, darling," Harry said to Lynn. He nodded toward the tequila. "I'm going to see if I can't dig up a tamer wine."

Lynn smiled. "Don't be long."

Harry left and slipped between two faded, age-ravaged curtains that led to El Lobo's backrooms. A few moments later, a dark-eyed Mexican approached Lynn's table.

"*Por favor,* señorita, you're a friend of Señor Crawley's?"

"Why—yes," she said, half-rising from her chair. "Is something wrong?"

"He has taken ill, señorita, and wishes you to accompany me to him."

From behind a part in the curtain, Harry watched her start toward them without hesitation.

"Is it anything serious? Do you know what it is?"

"I do not know. It was sudden." The man walked ahead of her so as not to arouse her caution. He slipped behind her only when he opened the curtain and she stepped beneath his arm. Then in one practiced motion, he closed the curtain and covered her mouth so the other patrons in El Lobo wouldn't hear her scream.

The next moments always were frantic. The women inevitably struggled with Nuñez' zombies as best they were able. One image was always the same: the women, wide-eyed, moaning, weeping, looked desperately to Harry as they were being taken up the stairway to a second-floor room. How alike they all were, thought Harry. Did they want an explanation? Did they want help? Did they comprehend what was happening to them? Always they looked to him instead of their captors. The horror of his deceit, even when it became obvious, took time to sink in. He often wondered, were they not muted by their captor's hand, what they would say to him.

A few minutes later, Nuñez' men descended the stairs and walked past Harry and the sweaty beast that was Nuñez. They were breathing hard. Lynn had been a fighter.

"You guys getting too old to handle them?" Harry remarked.

One of them continued out the curtain after only a glance. The other, Raoul, the one who had approached Lynn, stopped, then stepped up to Harry. The Mexican's large ebony eyes glared contemptuously at him from dark sockets. "Maybe Señor Crawley would like to know if we could handle him."

Harry straightened, piqued. But Nuñez intervened with a grunt, motioning with his head for Raoul to leave. He cast Harry a last glance. Then he vanished between the curtains.

"They have no taste for you, Crawley," said Nuñez. "You watch what you say, eh? Raoul would cut out your heart and feed it to the fishes." He produced a bloated envelope and handed it to Harry. "Count it here," he said.

"I don't trust you enough not to," Harry replied, summoning an insolence he knew grated on the Mexican. It amused him the way Nuñez shifted on his massive haunches, glaring but silent. Physically, Harry wasn't a big man, and the disrespect somehow equalized them.

The money, four thousand dollars, was all there. He knew it would be. Nuñez was nothing if not a businessman. "See you next trip," Harry said.

The Mexican didn't answer him. He turned laboriously and started up the stairs. Each step required supreme effort for him to move his hulking mass: palms pressed hard just above the knees, right, left, right, left, wheezing breath from fat-choked lungs, muttering incessantly the grunt-language of the elephantine. Each rotted-wood step on the stairway creaked monstrously beneath his weight. The women always knew when he was coming.

Harry watched as the Mexican stopped at the top of the stairs. With a scarred, hairless forearm, Nuñez wiped sweat from his face; an instant later it glistened there again. He didn't look at Harry as he opened the door, then angled his body to squeeze through the frame. No, thought Harry, he wouldn't. He only was concerned with the woman now. Nuñez liked to have them first, before their minds were destroyed by the heroin, their bodies by the sailors. Harry listened. A moment later he heard the bed shriek as Nuñez lowered his grotesque hulk onto it.

On the way out of El Lobo, Harry used a penknife to make a twelfth notch in the table.

White slavery had been good to Harry Crawley. A dozen women in the past year, four thousand dollars apiece. It beat parking cars in Los Angeles, or groveling for walk-ons at scale wages in low-budget movies. This way he made good money and could constantly refine the artificial emotions an actor was required to summon. Just off-Broadway rehearsals, he often thought.

He stepped into Puerta Valencia's hot, stench-thickened night air, thinking about the solitary distraction in his otherwise lucrative set-up. Nuñez was the only pimp and slaver in Puerta Valencia. Until recently, Harry had been his only supplier. But he'd noticed unfamiliar faces lately among the women. Light-haired, light-complexioned faces—the kind which brought premiums from Nuñez and his clientele. That meant competition, but Nuñez wasn't talking about it. Next trip down, Harry thought, I'll look into it. Personally.

He started the long drive back to L.A.

Driving north along the coast, through some of Mexico's magnificent vistas and resort towns, Harry reflected on his system. Gaining intimacy with the women came easy for him. Although not strikingly handsome, he was a gifted charmer. And he could read lonely women. He could be assured and worldly or a lost, sullen, brooding child. He was able to perceive a moment's appropriate emotion and summon it accordingly. He was, he knew, a superb actor; his discovery by others as one was only a matter of time.

Harry had his routine down pat. He would ask the girls about backgrounds, families, avoided their friends and photographs, and like other prowling beasts, emerged only at night. He shunned girls with families, potential investigators. Only the alone or nearly alone served his purpose. Lynn Yager had had no one.

Harry limited his romances to a businesslike thirty days. A proposal of marriage or vacation, varying with the inclination of the girl, opened his next suggestion—"A little Mexican hide-away," he would say. "Let me surprise you." And he would tell them of warm moonlit nights on balconies overlooking the Pacific; hot, exotic Mexican delicacies; campfire dancing to Spanish guitars. When he spoke to them, it was softly; when he touched them, it was gently; when he loved them it was warmly. And it was all an act.

Vengeance never bothered him. The women were, he knew, captive forever. Or for as long as they lasted. Puerta Valencia was a dirty, reeking refueling depot for coastal freighters, an isolated cove of hell designed to quench the thirsts of ships and their crews. For sixty days, Nuñez force-fed the women heroin, keeping them in a constant, delirious stupor, addicting them hopelessly. Then he turned them out onto the docks to earn their rations. Only the freighter crews visited the village. No one ever stayed longer than it took to take care of business. It was, Harry often reflected, quite a perfect system. And at least for that, he admired Nuñez.

Back in Los Angeles, Harry followed custom and drove directly to Lynn Yager's apartment, which he entered using a key she'd given him as her fiancee. Hands gloved, he checked the apartment for jewelry, cash, and other untraceable valuables. He found some costume jewels, money in a change dish for the paperboy. Her bankbook said she had $132 in savings. Not enough to risk getting caught trying to retrieve it.

Harry, feeling a little cheated, resolved to start working a better breed of women. He ate a ham sandwich and drank a glass of milk before he left. As he was locking the door, he heard a voice from behind him.

"Excuse me, isn't this where Lynn Yager lives?"

Harry swallowed, straightened, composed himself. He turned and faced a stunningly beautiful woman. Full blond hair like a lioness, dusk-sky blue eyes, she completely took him aback. He smiled. His first thought was how she would look writhing beneath that great formless mass that was Nuñez.

Over drinks in a nearby bar, she told him her name was Carla Thomas. A friend of Lynn's from New York, she was a purchasing agent for a cosmetics firm, visiting L.A. on business. "I just thought I'd drop in and see her."

"Like I said, she's up in 'Frisco for a few weeks," Harry said. "I think she's going to relocate up there." His expression darkened a little. "I don't know what it means for us," he said slowly.

Harry watched her eyes react to his plight. Her hand moved a little, as if she'd momentarily considered placing it on his. She didn't, but the gesture told Harry a lot.

"Listen," he said, catching her eyes with a little boy's hopeful enthusiasm, "since you're here, why don't we have dinner one of these nights? I mean, if you're not busy..."

"I'm not, and I'd love to. I don't know a soul around here."

He smiled shyly. Then he delicately touched her forearm. "Great," he whispered.

The next night, they met again.

It was a candlelit Polynesian dinner at the Hawaiian Village. The atmosphere there worked for Harry. Like a drug.

He told Carla that he and Lynn had been sharing the apartment. "We just weren't sure about marriage yet."

She nodded. "So what do you do for a living?"

"Oh, this and that." He coupled his answer with a tiny shrug.

She smiled. "I had a friend in New York who used to tell people that," she said. "He was an aspiring actor."

Harry tensed a little, then slipped back into the moment. "Nothing so interesting. I'm a consultant. Management and finance, that sort of thing. The essence of dullness."

"So if, say, I wanted to call you for dinner before I head back to New York, you're in the book?"

"No," he said, "no, not exactly. I don't advertise. I get my clients by word of mouth. Not that ambitious, I guess." He paused and watched her eyes. They were soft in the gentle candlelight, luminous and lonely and hungering. Yes, she was ripe, he thought distantly. But there was something; something more to her; more than any of the others. Harry said, "But I have a private number you can use any time." As he looked at her, feeling suspended in her gaze, he felt her warm fingers close around his hand.

"Then I'm calling," she whispered, "now."

They spent the night at Lynn's apartment. And it was, in Harry Crawley's experience, unique. He'd never experienced any woman like her. Memories of the others faded into a feature-less blur. Now there was only Carla, and only that night. He found in her qualities he thought no woman could possess. The way she moved, the timbre of her voice, the way her eyes clung to him. He had made the others love him, but now he was being loved first. Loved with a soft, impossible intensity.

Yes, thought Harry, Nuñez would have to pay double for Carla.

Within two weeks, he knew all he needed to know. Or wanted to know. He decided to shorten the one-month schedule. Carla Thomas, he knew, was getting to him. It was getting harder to act out emotions because the real ones, the ones he'd never known, wanted to dominate. To Harry, it represented a flaw in his character; a potentially fatal one in his line of work. He'd always thought of himself as impervious to root emotion. Which is why he had to sell her sooner. He wasn't impervious.

And he was falling in love with Carla.

He made his move on their two-week "anniversary." He'd come to know her as capricious, ready to follow a whim on a moment's notice, and it was upon that weakness that he chose to play. For their anniversary he'd made reservations at an expensive downtown restaurant. Then he turned east when he should have turned west and drove up into the mountains, to a spot overlooking the misty city lights, and spread a white silk tablecloth over a low, flat rock. He set out a candelabra and poured 10-year-old Rothschild. She laughed exhuberantly as he cooked the chateaubriand on a skewer under a million winking stars. They ate and drank, he in a tuxedo and she in a gown, sitting on a blanket spread over dark, cool earth.

"I'll bet you've taken a hundred women here," she kidded him.

"You're the first," he lied. "I've come here alone before, just working things out. But with you—I wanted to share it. I wanted to show you off to the heavens."

She sipped her wine and shook her head, as if in wonder-ment. "The things you do say," she whispered. A gentle wind had blown her blond hair over one eye; candlelight danced in the other.

"Carla," Harry said after watching her for a moment, "I can't hide the way I've come to feel about you."

"And how's that?"

"I've fallen in love with you. I can't even think of Lynn anymore. And I don't want to. I think I've known from that moment outside the apartment when I turned around and saw you. I've never been so heady. Like every moment in my life had conspired to bring you to me." He stood and walked toward the edge of the overlook. Then he gestured to the universe overhead. "I've come up here thinking about us. About what to say to you. What to think about you. When I met you, it was as if my past had been erased. There was only the present, only you. Nothing else mattered. Now," he said in a softer voice, "I think that if I lose you my future will be erased as well. Gone before I live it because it won't be worth living." He turned to face her. She was still on the blanket, legs curled beneath her. Lights played on her features as a breeze brushed the candles. A solitary tear made its way down her face. "I know I could lose you by telling you all this. But we have to deal from a base of truth." He turned away from her and back to the distant lights. A moment later he felt her presence behind him. Then her arms snaked beneath his and wrapped tightly around him.

"So what do you want to do about it?"

The drive down through Mexico was hot. And every mile was an agony for Harry. He thought of Nuñez and the zombies, the drunken sailors, the lives abbreviated through the ravages of heroin; of the air and the odor, the way it was absorbed by the people of Puerta Valencia until they no longer noticed it, until they emitted it themselves, until, indeed, they passed it on to their offspring.

And there was Carla. Guileless, loving, innocent Carla. He thought of the things he'd said to her on the overlook. He'd said them many times before, to many women. But he had meant them for her. The others were — rehearsals. Now that his act had finally opened for real, he was going to give it up after one performance. To Nuñez.

The thought of returning there with Carla, of selling her, of leaving her to the nightmares of the cove of Puerta Valencia, finally became unbearable.

"We're not going," Harry said. He pulled the car off onto the shoulder of the road.

Carla had been riding along, head reclined, eyes closed, listening to the radio. She turned to Harry and said, "What are you talking about?"

"Let's head back to L.A. We can get married there. This is a miserable time of year for Mexico, anyway."

"What do you mean? It's green and warm, the sea is beautiful, we're together..." She let it trail off, then looked out her window, away from Harry. "So that's it, isn't it?"

"What's 'it'?" Harry asked.

"You're having second thoughts about us."

"Yes, I am," he said, "but not the way you think."

"How then?"

"Trust me, love," he told her. "There are better places for us to be."

She turned to him and studied him for a moment, as if trying to divine the truth. "You don't look like you feel well, Harry. Is everything all right?"

"I'm hot," he said, "and homesick."

"Okay," she relented; "then we'll go back. But I'll drive. You look horrid." She reached beneath her seat and produced a thermos. "Here's some iced tea I fixed at home. Maybe you'll feel better if you drink some."

They traded seats, and Harry settled comfortably back with a cup of tea. He drank it in one long swallow, then poured another and sipped at it. Out from behind the wheel he felt a drowsiness come over him. He didn't fight it. He hadn't slept well since the night at the overlook. Now things would be different.

Before he slumped into sleep, it occurred to him, only in passing, that during the entire trip he'd never seen Carla take a sip from the thermos.

It was a stiff, endless awakening for him, and though vision, hearing, speech and touch hovered collectively just beyond his reach, his olfactory senses were jarred awake by the acrid stench of fuel and oil. Harry cracked open his eyelids, breaking a seal of sleep that had congealed on them. Two featureless figures leaned over the bed on which he lay.

"Did you have a nice sleep, darling?" he heard Carla's soft voice inquire.

Harry tried to move, but stopped abruptly when he felt a pain tear through his abdomen.

"Lie still, sweetheart. You're in no condition to go anywhere." He felt her hand begin to stroke his hair. "Besides, you're home now."

Harry swallowed. The familiar stench grew stronger. "We're in Puerta Valencia," he said in a dry whisper.

"Indeed we are," she told him.

Harry looked at the other figure, forcing the image into focus. It was Raoul. His mouth was stretched into some hideous, toothy grin. It was then a bolt of fear tore through his body. Instinctively, Harry tried to get up, but he was bound spread-eagle by leather straps. And there was that pain in his lower abdomen again.

He tried to shout, but his voice was imprisoned in a whisper. "Damn you, what have you *done*?" His heart was beating furiously. "Carla, what's *happening*?"

"Don't get upset, darling," she soothed. "You've been through a trauma and have been sleeping for awhile." She smiled. "Almost three weeks now, in fact."

"Why?" The pain tore at him.

She glanced at Raoul, then back to Harry. "You've had an operation and needed time to recover."

He could barely form the word. "Operation?"

"Yes, Crawley," Raoul thundered, and grabbed Harry by his hair, jerking up his head to face down the length of his prostrate body. He held it long enough for Harry to see how they'd

mutilated him—his naked, hairless limbs and torso, the still raw scars near his crotch, the small, white, adolescent's breasts. Harry's scream was stifled when the Mexican shoved a gag in his mouth and knotted it behind his neck.

"There's a hospital in Zacetecas, about a hundred miles east of here, Harry," Carla said. "They're quite adept at this type of operation actually. Transsexual surgery has really become rather commonplace, although I admit we had to pay a premium since we didn't exactly have your consent. Fortunately the surgeon is a bit of a heroin trader on the side, so we were able to strike a bargain." She stroked his hair again. "Of course, this is just the beginning. There are a number of other treatments involved. Hormones and all that. But as you can see, the basics have been taken care of. I suspect you'll grow more amenable to the rest—out of necessity, if nothing else." She smiled that familiar smile, the one Harry had thought so full of love. "I could have just killed you, you know. But knowing you and your past, this seemed *so* much more appropriate."

Blue veins straining the skin on his forehead, Harry bellowed through the gag until he sank back, broken, weeping. Carla cupped his chin in her palm and turned his head toward one of his bound arms.

"As you can see, Harry," she said, indicating a large scabby bruise in the fold of his elbow, "you're being administered heroin. I'm sure you don't need an explanation as to why."

Eyes stinging with hate and frustration, Harry stared at his betrayer.

"Please understand it was business, Harry," Carla said with quintessential detachment. "You see, I'm Nuñez' other supplier. I can get closer to the girls—better girls—in a shorter period of time. I've even sold a few of them on making a living down here. It saves dear Ramiro on that staggering drug bill. And this business with you, this alteration—well, it was my idea, but Ramiro loved it. You really *didn't* have many friends here, you know."

Above the gag, Harry's nostrils flared at the stinging scent of Puerta Valencia.

"I do have to run, sweet. I'll be seeing you in a week or so. Do take care now." She turned and strode calmly toward the door. Raoul followed.

"NO!" Harry pleaded through the gag. *"Don't leave me!"*

"Goodbye, Harry."

"But I *loved* you," he bellowed, as if by the act he should be foreverafter immune to any violation.

Carla hadn't made out the words. "Isn't it amazing," she said to Raoul, "how they always look at you the same way when you leave. I always wonder what they're trying to say." She glanced at Harry, smiled, shrugged, and left.

Harry's head fell back to the hard, grimy bed. For minutes he wept quietly, and of all things he thought that now—*now*—he finally knew what the women had wanted to say to him.

Harry closed his eyes. He breathed the stench, felt it creeping into his flesh, into his mind, into his soul. He twisted, straining at his bonds. They held. Then he wept, agonized, praying for death. His sweat drenched the sheetless mattress beneath him. A hundred insects blackening the ceiling above him now drifted down to alight on him, his blood a new food source. Harry convulsed silently as they ate at him. His dizzying horror, his hoarse and hideous screaming, his tendon-tearing struggle with his bonds didn't begin until he recognized the grunted *step—step—step,* the monstrous groaning of the staircase, and he knew Nuñez was coming to have him.

Trust Not a Man

William F. Nolan

When Bill Nolan's first story appeared (1954), he'd already been a Hallmark cards cartoonist and water color painter. Since then, over 600 Nolan pieces have been published plus a varied array of 42 books: from the sf novel Logan's Run *(its co-written screenplay was one of Bill's three-dozen film/TV deals) to bios of hardboiled Dashiell Hammett, actor Steve McQueen and racing Speed King Barney Oldfield, to the line-blurring* Space For Hire *(Special Edgar award scroll from Mystery Writers of America in '71)—and its recent sequel,* Look Out for Space.

Born March 6, 1928, in "ole K.C.," Bill left the Midwest at 19 for California, where he stayed. While his first H&O collection (Things Beyond Midnight) *did not develop until 1984, Nolan vows, "Horror was my meat and potatoes as a kid." He became a close friend of Ray Bradbury, Charles Beaumont, and Ray Russell, whose yarns Bill reprinted in his 1970 anthology,* A Sea of Space. *Bradbury's* Long After Midnight *('74) is dedicated to Nolan. No writer in any genre today may have more loyal friends. His recollections of Beaumont, Bradbury, Richard Matheson and others were invaluable to Marc Scott Zicree's* Twilight Zone Companion *('82), which repeatedly quotes him—this delightful Good Guy who still sketches Creatures on his letters and all over his envelopes!*

If it's true that the line between horror and hypothetically "serious" fiction fades when the writer works effectively with psychological aberration, which someone surely must have written, I wonder why. Is it because the author eschews "real" monsters to enter the single realm science considers both sacred and presently unknowable— inner space? *More than other types of fantasy, horror encourages such explorations. Or could it be because writers were first to examine the human mind as it exists, and often do so better than psychologists?*

"Trust Not a Man" seems to support all these theories—with one exception. When William F. Nolan turns his talents to horror, the only things cast aside are the reader's incredulity and his last frail strands of courage...

For many years she had refused to believe she was pretty. She considered her nose too thin, her lips too full, her ankles too narrow. But a lot of people, mostly men, kept telling her how pretty she was and, in time, she came to accept it. She had *always* known she was bright. That was what Daddy always called her: "My bright little girl." She'd made top grades all through high school and college. She could have earned her degree, easily, if she had chosen to remain in college, but she got bored.

Professor Hagemann had been quite upset with her when she told him she was quitting at the end of her second year. He felt she could become a prize-winning botanist. She remembered how flushed and angry he looked: "Spoiled, that's what you are, Elise! Your father gives you too much, and you depend on him for everything. It's as if he *owns* you. Where's your spirit, your *incentive*? You've let him spoil you—and I say it's a damn waste!"

Of course, he was right about her; she *had* been spoiled by her father. All the stocks and bonds in her name when she was a child. The new Mercedes on her sixteenth birthday. The diamond necklace from Tiffany's for her twentieth. And, when she turned twenty-five, this large beach house in Malibu. It had cost $600,000 and was worth three times that much now.

After her evening shower, Elise sat cross-legged, in a yoga lotus position, on the woven tatami mat in front of the fireplace, listening to the ocean. To the surf coming in...going out...coming in...

Following her father's death she had remained in the house for a full month. Had groceries delivered. Ate alone. Saw no one. Just sat here, listening to the ocean, letting it talk to her.

Surf in..."Pretty," it said in a sibilant whisper.

Surf out..."Bright," it said.

And, finally, what it *kept* saying to her, over and over through the long nights: "Lonely...Lonely...Lonely..."

Daddy had been her world, entire and complete. He gave her everything. Love. Approval. Companionship. Knowledge. The void, after his death, was black and deep and terrible.

She'd sold the mansion in Beverly Hills, the Rolls, the inscribed Faulkner first editions, the Motherwell paintings, the collection of pre-Columbian art — even the *Elly*, the yacht which he'd named after her. Everything had been sold.

Except the plants. They were *also* his children — her brothers and sisters — and she would never abandon them. She had a special greenhouse constructed for them right on the beach. Plenty of sun. Controlled temperature and humidity. Special soils. And she had moved her father's lab, all of it, here into the house where she carried on his work.

Maybe *that's* why the advanced botany courses at UCLA had bored her. (Daddy taught me more about plants in his lab than any college professor ever knew.) She'd earned her *real* degree before she had ever set foot on campus. Her father had seen to that.

"Lonely..." the surf whispered to her. "Lonely..."

And she was now. Oh, God, she was!

Elise stood up.

Time to get out again. Into the real world. Time to make contact, meet a new man, explore a fresh mind.

She pulled the towel from her head and the shining red mass of her hair spilled loose. She combed it vigorously, put on a silk blouse, Gucci boots, and a pair of designer jeans, applied eye makeup and lipstick, and dabbed perfume between her breasts.

Ready for combat. That's how she thought of it. Field of battle: a singles bar. Opponent: male. His weapons: beach boy muscles, cool wit, blond good looks. Goal: seduction.

At least that always seemed to be *his* goal; she had others. Maybe some night, among all the eligible young men in this vast city, she'd meet someone like her father. Sensitive, warm, intelligent, caring.

Maybe.

Some night.

Fast Eddie's was crowded. Hazed with cigarette smoke. Noisy with punk rock and a frenzied cross-mix of alcoholic conversation. It was always this way on a Friday. She had liked the romantic atmosphere of the place when it was called *Starshadows*, before it had been so rudely converted from a quiet oceanside restaurant to a fast-action singles bar — but she just didn't feel up to driving into the city, and this *was* the best place in Malibu to make contact.

She needed to find a man tonight.

It was time.

"What'll yours be, hon?" asked the bartender. Female. Brassy and big-bosomed in a tight black leather outfit with her name silver-stitched over her left boob: Irma. My friend Irma.

"Johnnie Walker," Elise told her. "Ice — no soda."

"A hard John on the rocks comin' up," said Irma. And she began fixing the drink.

The bar was swarming with male predators. Why do I think of them that way? she asked herself. They're not *all* here to make a quick night's score. Some are just lonely, like I am. Decent guys. Maybe even a little shy. Looking for that "special" person. They're not *all* sharks, she told herself.

Elise was sipping her Scotch when she felt a hand touch her right shoulder. She turned.

"Hi, doll!" said a tall young man in a textured burgundy shirt, slashed low to display his matted chest hair. He was smiling at her from a wide, sun-bronzed face. His teeth were very white and even. Probably capped. "Mind if I squeeze in?"

"I'm a woman, not a doll," she told him coldly. "And I *know* what you'd like to squeeze into. Take a hike."

He muttered a sharp obscenity and drifted back into the crowd. Taut with anger, she finished her drink, ordered another.

The next two men who approached her were just like Mr. Bronze. Pushy. Obnoxious. Disgustingly self-centered. Sexually arrogant. One of them opened his hand to show her a white vial and asked her if she wanted to "powder her nose." She told him she didn't do drugs and he shrugged, moved away down the bar.

Elise was getting discouraged. Maybe she *should* drive on into Westwood or Beverly Hills. She'd heard about a new dine-

and-dance club that had opened on Wilshire, called *Harper's Hut.* Might be worth a try. She'd obviously made a mistake in coming here tonight.

"Are you...*with* anybody?"

Nice voice. Deep and strong. She looked up from her drink—into a pair of intense eyes so darkly-blue they were nearly black. She *liked* dark eyes; her father's eyes had been dark.

"Alone," she said.

"Well, I'm...I'm *glad.*" He smiled. Warm, sensitive smile. "I didn't see anybody with you."

"You've been watching me?"

"Yes, I have," he admitted. "You're a...very striking woman. I couldn't help noticing you. Hope you're not offended."

"At being called striking?" She smiled up at him. "That *was* a compliment, right?"

"Absolutely," he nodded. "You're really very attractive."

So are you, she thought. Tall. Good build (but not the over-developed beach boy type). Neat, casual clothes. No slash-neck cable-knit shirts or jock jeans. And that sensitive smile!

"How long have you been watching me?" she asked.

"Long enough to see you deal with those three creeps," he said. "They all seemed to get the message."

She grinned impishly. "You must think I'm hostile."

"Not at all. Just careful. And you *have* to be in a place like this. Most of these guys are on the hustle. That's all they're here for."

"And what are *you* here for?"

"Same reason you are, I guess. To meet someone worthwile."

"And what makes you think I'm worthwhile?"

"If you were just another beach bunny you'd be long gone by now. With one of those three guys. Simple, huh?"

She put out a hand. "My name's Elise Malcolm."

"Hi," he said, shaking her hand. "I'm Philip Gregory."

"Want to buy me another drink?"

"Sure do," he said, "but not here. This place makes me edgy. Can't we go somewhere quieter—get to *know* each other?"

"Don't see why not," she said. "But we'll never do that."

"Do what?"

"Know each other. Does anyone ever really know anyone else?"

And she stared into his dark eyes.

They took his car, an immaculate white 911-T Porsche, and she liked the way he drove—with courtesy and control. To her mind, he handled the Porsche the way a man should handle a woman.

He took her to *Carmen's* on Pico. The perfect choice. A dark corner booth. Spanish guitars. Candlelight. Good wine.

"So," he said, leaning back in the booth. "Tell me about yourself. First, I want to know what a classy lady like you—"

"—is doing at a pickup bar like *Fast Eddie's*, right?"

He nodded.

"I live near there, and I just didn't feel like a long drive. I've been lonesome. I thought maybe I'd get lucky."

He flashed his warm smile. "And *did* you?"

"Give me time to find out." She returned his smile. "But I *do* love your eyes!"

"Windows of the soul, huh?"

"Something like that."

He leaned toward her. "Do you really mean it, about my eyes?"

"I never say anything I don't mean."

"A toast," he said. "To honesty."

They clicked glasses, sipping the wine.

"I want to know all about you," he said. "Red-haired women are supposed to be mysterious."

"Really?" She grinned. "Well, the red hair came from Daddy. He was a scientist. A truly fine one. Along with my hair, I also inherited his passion for botany."

"Plants?"

"Right. I crossbreed them—like some people do Arabian horses. Daddy taught me a lot. He was a brilliant man. And very kind."

"Sounds as if you were close?"

She raised her eyes to his. "He took my virginity when I was fifteen."

Philip Gregory pressed back against the leather booth, staring at her.

She lowered her eyes. "I've shocked you. I'm sorry."

"No — it's just that . . ."

"I know. Incest is sick stuff. People don't like to talk about it or even *think* about it. But it happens sometimes."

He was silent as she continued.

"I guess it was my fault as much as Daddy's. I was trying out my budding feminine charms on him. Just to see what kind of power I could exert over a man. A lot of young daughters do that, consciously or unconsciously. They *tease* their fathers. And . . . it just happened."

He sipped his wine, then looked up at her. "How long did you . . . I mean, did it . . . continue?"

"No." She shook her head. "No, it didn't continue. Once it happened we both knew it was wrong. It stopped right there."

"And what about your mother? Did she know?"

"My mother died when I was eight, back in Ohio. That's where I'm from. Cleveland. Moved out here with my father when I was ten. He never remarried."

"I see."

"In Daddy's case that old saying applies — the one about being married to your work." The soft candlelight was reflected in her eyes. "When he died two years ago I suddenly realized that *I* had been, too. Married, I mean. Both of us — married to botany." She smiled. "Then, after he was gone. I began looking for what I'd missed."

"At *Fast Eddie's*?"

"There — and a dozen other places. You never know when you'll meet someone who is — as you said — worthwhile."

"Do I qualify?"

"In some ways, yes, or I wouldn't *be* here with you. In other ways . . . I'm not sure yet. How could I be?"

"Meaning you need to know more about me?"

"Right. Anyway, it's your turn to talk."

He had the waiter (who looked like an overaged matador) bring more wine before he began telling her about himself. Drifting guitar music from three strolling players accompanied his words. She couldn't help thinking how romantic it all was.

"I grew up in Berkeley. My father worked as a conductor on a cable car in San Francisco. Used to give me free rides. Mom stayed home to take care of me and my two little sisters. I'm a college grad—with a Master's in psychology from the University of California."

"Is that your profession?"

"My profession is gambling."

A strained silence between them.

"Now you're shocked," he said with a grin.

"Not really. Just surprised."

"I tried going into psychology. Even had my own office for awhile. But I made more money off the tables in Vegas than I ever did as a practicing psychologist."

"Gamblers always lose," she said.

"Not always. With me it's only sometimes. And I win a lot more often than I lose. Maybe I'm the exception that proves the rule."

"Well, maybe you are at that," she said. "What about marriage? I mean, were you...*are* you?"

"I was—almost. But I called it off at the last minute. Walked away from the lady when I realized I didn't actually love her. At least not enough to marry her. That was three years ago."

"And since?"

He shrugged. "Since then I've been involved once or twice. But nothing heavy."

They finished the wine.

"Hungry?" he asked her. "They have excellent food here. I particularly recommend the Steak Hemingway. That is, if you like steak."

"Right now I'd like a breast of turkey sandwich on two thick slices of pumpernickel."

He frowned. "I'm sure they don't—"

"Not here," she said. "My place. At the beach. I have some

turkey in the fridge. In a ziplock bag. Real fresh. How about it?"

"I say to hell with Steak Hemingway." And he pressed her warm hand.

At *Fast Eddie's* they switched to her Mercedes convertible, leaving his 911-T in the lot.

"No use taking both cars," she told him. "I can drive you back here later."

"Suits me," he said, sliding into the red leather passenger's seat.

"I can put the top up if it's too windy for you."

"No, I like open cars. You can smell the ocean."

"Ah," she smiled. "We have something in common."

"Open cars?"

"The ocean. I love it, too. That's why I live down here. To be near it. It's so *alive*."

And she accelerated the black Mercedes smoothly onto Pacific Coast Highway, smiling into the wind.

They were sitting in front of the fireplace with Segovia on the stereo (a night for Spanish guitars!) when he kissed her, taking her easily into his arms, fitting her body to his. The kiss was fierce, deep-mouthed.

She eased back from him. "Hey, let the lady breathe, okay?"

"Sure," he grinned. "The night's still young."

He glanced at the large oil portrait of a long-faced somber man over the fireplace. "Who's that?"

"The original mad botanist," she said lightly. "Professor Herbert Ludlow Malcolm, my father." Elise stood up, walked over to the painting. She trailed her fingers along its gold frame. "Daddy had some pretty radical ideas about plant life."

"Stern-looking old gentleman."

"Well...he took life very seriously," she said. "I guess I inherited *that* from him, too."

"You're sure a lot prettier than he was."

"Time to feed our tummies," she said. "Turkey in a ziplock, remember?"

"Whatever you say," he nodded.

"You *are* hungry?"

"Famished. But not necessarily for cold turkey."

"I'll let that one pass," she grinned. "Sandwich. Yes or no?"

"Yes."

He followed her into the kitchen, separated by a long counter-bar from the main living area. He sat down on a chrome bar stool, watching her fix the sandwiches.

"Know anything about botany?" she asked him.

"Only what I learned in junior high. And I can't remember much of that. To me, a plant is a plant is a plant."

Elise was slicing a loaf of dark bread. "Plants are like *people*," she told him. "Each has its own personality."

"I've heard about a rose screaming when you cut it," he said. "But that's a bit far-fetched."

"Not at all," she declared. "It's fact. Plants *do* have feelings. They respond to good or bad treatment. Even as a little girl I could feel their vibrations."

"I'm into vibrations," he said. "And I like the ones *you* put out."

She ignored this, arranging slices of turkey on their plates. "Daddy believed that plants could be developed far beyond what is perceived to be their present stage. He was always experimenting with them. When he died, he left me his notes. I've been carrying on his work. I think he would be proud of what I've accomplished."

She finished the food preparation, handed him his plate. "Turkey on pumpernickel. Fresh tomatoes. And some sliced papaya for dessert."

"Looks great."

"Let's eat in the greenhouse," she said. "I'll show you what I've been talking about."

They left the beach house and walked across a flagstone patio into a large beamed-glass building.

He whistled as the door clicked shut behind them. "Wow. This place cost a pretty penny!"

"Daddy left me a lot of pennies," she said.

The building was huge, much larger than he'd expected. An odorous riot of jungled growth stretched away from him in leaf-choked rows of midnight blues, deep purples, veined greens, brooding yellows. Colors were muted in the dim glow of over-head lights and the leafy rows lost themselves in shadow at the far end of the vast structure.

He loosened his collar. The odors were oppressive, suffo-cating — and the temperature was uncomfortably high. He felt sweat beads forming on his forehead and upper lip.

"I have to keep it warm in here," she said. "Hope you don't mind."

"I'll survive," he said.

"Put your plate down. I want to show you around."

"Okay, lady, but just remember, I *am* famished. And I'm not much for exotic plant lore. Keep the lecture brief and pithy."

"I promise not to bore you." And she kissed him lightly on the cheek.

She led him along one of the vine-and-leaf-tangled rows, talking animatedly. "There are up to half a million different plant species in the world. I have only a few hundred of them here, all classified according to their evolutionary development." She paused, turned to face him. "Did you know that plants are very *sexual*, that they bear sperm and eggs?"

"I do now," he said.

"They can be very exciting. Some are bisexual, having both stamens and pistils."

"Real swingers."

She looked angry. "You're making fun of me."

He shook his head. "Not really. I know you're heavy into all this leaf and stem jazz. It's just that I'm not goofy over plants. Is that so terrible?"

She smiled, relaxing. "I guess I *am* a little intense," she admitted. "But the more time you spend with plants — as you feed them, care for them — the more you learn to respect them. There's...real communication."

"To each his own," said Philip Gregory.

"The species along this row are all western herb plants —

Squawroot...Fireweed...St. John's Wort...Prairie Flax...In the Old West the Indians used them as medicines and as healing remedies for—"

"Hey!" He interrupted her flow of words. "You've just broken your promise. About not boring me."

"Sorry," she said softly. "I really came out here to show you Herbie."

"What's Herbie?"

"The end product of my crossbreeding. Herbie was Mother's special name for Daddy. She always called him that."

"Why don't we just forget Daddy?" he said, reaching out to gather her into his arms. "Let's concentrate on *us*." And he kissed her, forcing her head back.

"Don't," she said.

"Hey, c'mon, quit playing games. I know you want me. So I'm yours." He cupped a hand under her chin, looking into her eyes. "And you're *mine*."

Elise twisted away, pushing at his chest with both hands. "Stop it! I don't belong to you, or to anyone else!"

"Look, you invited me to your pad, and *not* just to show me some lousy plants." His tone was steely. "Now, do we proceed with things right here, on the floor, or do we go back inside to a comfortable bed? *You* call it, lady."

Her eyes flashed. "Do you actually think I'd let a *gambler* violate my body? Oh, you come on so smooth, easy talking, pretending to be so sensitive—but the truth is you're no different than all the others. On the hustle. Out to make a score. You don't give a damn about anybody but yourself."

"Who else *should* I give a damn about?"

He grabbed her, gripping her firmly by both shoulders. His face was hard, jaw muscles rigid. "You can have it easy or you can have it rough. Which will it be?"

"Herbie!" she called. "Now! Take him *now!*"

"You crazy bitch, what the hell are you—"

He didn't finish the sentence. A thick, leafy root snaked around his right leg, jerking him backward, away from her, with terrific force.

He struck the floor as three other spiny root-tentacles coiled around his body. One, encircling his neck, began to tighten. He clawed at it, gasping, choking, tearing his nails against its prickly barked surface.

He was dragged rapidly along the floor toward a corner of the greenhouse. Something tall and dark and fleshy lived there, in the gloom, pulsating, quivering... A sickening chemical stench filled the air.

"He's yours," said Elise. "Enjoy him."

She closed the soundproof door behind her and walked across the patio into the house, not looking back.

Elise sat cross-legged on the tatami mat, looking up at the portrait of her father above the fireplace...

It was too bad that Philip Gregory had turned out to be like all the rest of them. She really thought, at first, that he might be different, might be someone she could relate to, someone to share her life, to ease the pain of her isolated existence.

When she was a little girl her Daddy had quoted a line from a book written in 1851: "Trust not a man's words, if you please." And he'd been right, the author of that book. No man could be trusted. They were all corrupt. All foul and predatory.

She was glad that she had given her virginity to Daddy. As a special gift. It was only proper that *he* had made a woman of her. He'd been so gentle and sweet. No other man had treated her that way.

And, she was certain, ever would.

Elise Malcolm sat very still now, listening to the ocean. To the surf coming in, going out...saying what it so often said...

"Pretty," it whispered to her.

"Bright," it said.

And, over and over: "Lonely...Lonely...Lonely..."

Long After Ecclesiastes

Ray Bradbury

A few decades ago, book lovers spent uncounted enjoyable, silly hours trying to compile lists of the indispensable reads—books which, if one were dumped unceremoniously on a desert island, would keep one sane, even civilized. Being young, silly, a would-be writer and relatively civilized—the terms are not necessarily mutually exclusive—my version of the game had the old Doubleday Complete Sherlock Holmes *at the head of the list.*

Even now, I wouldn't remove Holmes and Watson, but I think the list might begin with The Stories of Ray Bradbury *(Alfred A. Knopf, 1981). My guess is that your editor is merely one of the few who would admit it, one of the great many who would put the collection there. Is anything, really, finer?*

In his introduction to Stories, *which he named "Drunk, and in Charge of a Bicycle," Bradbury observed that everyone "needs someone higher, wiser, older to tell us...what we're doing is all right." His commitment to* Masques *told publisher John Maclay and me just that; and who knows what influence it had upon the others here assembled? A suspicion: I think it told them the same thing about us.*

If "influencing" other wordsmiths means even unconscious emulation, however, I doubt that Ray Bradbury has influenced all that many authors; because imitating him is, I think, unthinkable. Like imitating Bill Russell or Larry Bird; Cole Porter; Shakespeare; Oscar Levant; Ella Fitzgerald; James Thurber. Yet in one way, writers who read Ray at his best are nearly bound to be influenced. His work is so overflowing with ideas that, inevitably, caught up in a Bradbury yarn or poem, the urge to tell a story one's own way—one's own idea-sparked connection—becomes inevitable.

How we take these spirit-soaring liberators of the mind for granted, whether they are writers or otherwise gifted! And how uncommon it is, in the throwaway society, for creators such as Bradbury to hold center stage for 10, 20, 30 years or longer! Rock stars and starlets are born, have their careers, thrust their young before a microphone or a camera—and something new, and wonderful, by Bradbury, has just been published!

Nonpareils generously span the decades with their gifts to us, bridging them above, undergirding that which is worth saving below; and a few carpers cannot egotistically cope with inferences they're left to draw: that titans at Bradbury's level are simply more extra-special than extraterrestrials, national treasures, giants who, while merely walking in our midst, seem surfacely *so much the same.*

Yet Bradbury, a modest and amiable man, describes himself in his Stories *introduction as a man whose "child inside . . . remembers all," even his moment of birth! And irrespective of his work's quality, Ray has produced more short stories than most authors. He tells how in his introduction to* A Memory of Murder *(Dell, 1984): "Starting back in the year when I left Los Angeles High School, I put myself on a regimen of writing one story a week for the rest of my life." He knew, Bradbury rebukes the insatiable revisionists, "that without quantity there could never be any quality."*

Now, having written The Martian Chronicles, Dark Carnival, Something Wicked This Way Comes, *and* Fahrenheit 451, *surely Bradbury does not* sustain *such a regimen? He does. In continuing to write between 18 and 32 pages weekly, he's even finished his first "mystery suspense novel,"* Death is a Lonely Business.

"Does Bradbury ever write horror?" That question was asked by several people I know, incredibly enough. Aside from a fact made quite clear by such expert practitioners as Dennis Etchison, Chelsea Quinn Yarbro, and Ramsey Campbell — namely that monsters and murderers are solely obligatory only to makers of horror movies — *the answer is:* Yes; *Ray Bradbury writes horror — some of the finest and most frightening, strangely imaginative, sometimes-beautiful horror ever written. In a way, that is where he began. Ray tells, in "Drunk, and in Charge," of writing his first stories "long after midnight," beginning at the age of 12 — tales about "ghosts and haunts and things in jars . . ." He recalls having used his relatives for vampires, and anyone who doesn't know such Bradbury characters as Uncle Einar have another treat in store.*

Point of fact, many yarns by the Midwestern master—born August 22, 1920, he has roots in both Illinois and Wisconsin— may be more at home in horror collections than elsewhere. Unless, of course, it's in a mammoth unpublished volume called The Very Best American Stories, period! *What monsters could be more effectively terrifying than the dinosaur in "The Fog Horn," basis for the motion picture "The Beast from 20,000 Fathoms"? And what about the individual chapters or tales comprising* Martian Chronicles? *Will anybody—it's almost everyone—who read "Mars is Heaven" forget Captain John Black, and the moment he realized that the "man" sleeping beside him was not his brother?*

Or—quickly now—what about "Small Assassin," "Heavy Set," "The Town Where No One Got Off," "The Crowd," "The Veldt," "The October Game," "The Lake," "The Coffin," "The Play-ground," or "The Black Ferris"? And don't write to tell me I forgot one; or 10; or 20—I know!

These dark mysteries Ray explores and describes are, in one sense, more disturbing than those written by writers (I am one) who set out primarily to create horror; and a disturbed or bothered or "things-aren't-right" feeling can anticipate and follow *the horrific outrage. The creative and pragmatic hemi-spheres of Bradbury's brain are ideally blended and work in healthy cooperation, you see, as he peers into unhealthy, illusory, evil, or fantastic realms. He quests in order to perceive what life and death are really about, so that we shall know which to celebrate, and when. He has the courage not of the curious, with one mental knee bent for a leap backward, to safety, but of the "child inside" who wants, as happily as possible, to* belong, *to* wonder, *and to* know—but not too much. *The poem which follows, written originally as a Christmas greeting to his legendary friends, aseasonally serves to ask questions about our eventual destinations. But being written by Ray Bradbury, the alternatives are* reversed—and not necessarily limited to hell, or to heaven.

Long after Ecclesiastes:
The First Book of Dichotomy,
The Second Book of Symbiosis,
What do they say?
Work away.
Make do.
Believe.
Conceive
That by the bowels of Christ
It may be true—
There's more to Matter
Than me and you.
There's Universe
Terse
In the microscope.
With hope find Elephant
    beyond—
God's fond of vastness there.
And everywhere? spare parts!
This large, that small!
His All spreads forth in seas
Of multiplicities
While staying mere.
Things do adhere, then fly apart;
The heart pumps one small tide
While brides of Time train by in
    Comets' tails.
Flesh jails our senses;
All commences or stops short
To start again.
The stars are rain that falls on
    twilight field.
All's yield, all's foundering to
    death.
Yet in an instant
God's sweet breath sighs Life
    again.

All's twain yet all is twin
While, micro-midge within,
Dire hairy mammoth hides in
    flea.
I hop with him!
And trumpet to the skies!
All dies?
No, all's reborn.
The world runs to its End?
No: Christmas Morn
Where my small candle flickers
    in the dark.
My spark then fuses Catherine
    Wheel
Which ricochets wild flesh in
    all directions;
Resurrections of hope and will
    I feel.
Antheaps of elephants do mole
    in me.
In good Christ's crib by shore of
    Galilee
We all step forth to feast
On star in East which rises in
    pure shouts.
We hug our doubts, but love,
For we're above as well as low;
Our bodies stay, our senses go
And pull old blood along;
We move to grave ourselves on
    Moon and Mars
And then, why not, the stars?
But always mindful on the way
    to sense
Where flesh and Nothing
    stop/commence;
Where shuttling God in swift
    osmosis

Binds abyss sea
In space born flea
And give us war-mad men some
    hope
To fire-escape psychosis,
Moves tongues to say
What's day is night, night-day,
What's lost to sight is found
The Cosmic Ground which
    shrinks us small
But dreams us tall again.
Our next desire? Space!
We race to leap into that fire,
To Phoenix-forth our lives.
God thrives in flame,
Do we game and play,
God and Man one name?
Under pseudonym,
Does God scribble us,
We Him?
Give up being perplexed,
Here's a text that's final,
God, the spinal cord,
We, the flesh of Lord.
In the Pleiades,
Read both, if you please.
Immortality's prognosis
Scriptured, shaped, designed,
Palmer penned and signed:
The First Book of Dichotomy!
The Second Book of
Symbiosis!

My Grandmother's Japonicas
(With Tributes)

Charles Beaumont

The "man who needs no introduction" is, likely as not, the man (or woman) who would win the Most Often Introduced award in his profession or purview. Editors do these things, I've found with mild horror, because it's always done—atrocious motivation for a maverick who spins fantasies. What, ultimately, can I tell you about the likes of Bradbury or Bloch that you are hungering to know?

The pity is that you probably will *benefit from some remarks about Charles Beaumont unless you're 40-plus or an attentive reader of names on the old* Twilight Zone *credit crawl. He wouldn't be 60 yet, if he were still with us, but he's been gone for almost 20 years.*

And not to know Charles Beaumont or his work is, for a reader of Masques, *akin to never having read or heard of Ray, Bob, or Richard Matheson. Or Peter Straub, Stephen King, Fritz Leiber, Ira Levin, or Tom Tryon. Or Serling, Dahl, Shirley Jackson; or Fredric Brown. Any experienced writer in* Masques; *or Dunsany, Lovecraft, Blackwood; O'Connor, Oates—*

Or James Thurber; Mark Twain; Herman Melville.

We are talking about the man whom Ray Bradbury *used as an* example *for new writers:* Write, *he told them,* write often, work at it, the way Chuck did.

But first, ah-h, first *you get an idea somewhere. Anywhere; read something or listen to two kids talking. Get it and poke at it, question and explore it, twist it around, enjoy it, work with it! For it was Bradbury's observation, in his introduction to Bantam's* Best of Beaumont *(1982), that nobody goes around telling Hemingway's ideas; or those of Faulkner, and Steinbeck. "Idea is everything," says Bradbury—please copy:* Ray Bradbury!—*and Chuck, somewhere, bobs his head and pounds on the table:* YES. *Along with, Bradbury suggests, Verne, and Hawthorne.*

I did not know Charles Beaumont. Yet within a day after John Maclay, Baltimore publisher, asked me to select writers for Masques, *I wanted—unreasonably, I assumed; Chuck's gone—something,* anything *unpublished, which he'd written. That was my idea. Or maybe it was Mort Castle's. Ardath*

Mayhar put me in touch with Joe Lansdale, who said William F. Nolan was one of Beaumont's best friends; Bill and I became chums and he told me, bluntly, to forget it. There was simply nothing.

What he'd forgotten, a few weeks before the anniversary of Chuck's death, was the extraordinary masterwork that is lovingly conveyed to you between the tributes of Ray Russell and Nolan. On one of those incredible Forever Days — the kind that reinforce your acceptance of zones, third levels, wonderlands — Bill's package arrived, his letter joyously announcing the contents: a photocopy of Charles Beaumont's last unpublished work, "My Grandmother's Japonicas."

Instantly I read it, then reread it. It occurred to me I might never have enjoyed reading anything else quite so much since my boyhood.

Bill ached to have his tribute to Chuck included. Matter of respect. Ray Russell did, too — and got my letter filled with raves for "My Grandmother's Japonicas" on that anniversary I mentioned. As Playboy *editor, it was Ray who* "ran *in to Hefner's office,* demanded *that he read"* Chuck's *"Black Country,"* then. *It was Richard Matheson who pointed out how we could obtain the rights to publish "Japonicas" for the first time. What those immensely talented gentle men got for their considerable trouble was the ineffably doleful joy of seeing their colleague's final work where it belongs: ready for you to read, and reread it.*

A Short, Incandescent Life

Ray Russell

When Charles Beaumont died on February 27, 1967, his friends and family were, in a sense, prepared. He had been dying gradually for years, of a rare disease. I happened to be out of the house, delivering the rough manuscript of a novel to my typist, when the news came. Ironically, the novel was *The Colony,* in which Beaumont appears in the fictional guise of "Chet Montague." When I got back from the typist's, I saw in my wife's face that something had happened. She told me there had been a phone call from a friend of ours. "Chuck died this morning," she added gently.

After phoning Chuck's widow, Helen, I sought the seclusion of my study, where I sat alone for quite a long time, communing with my memories. I heard Chuck's voice, and mine, overlapping in ebullient conversation, often raucous, frequently ribald; I heard shouted arguments about literature and drama (strangers "discuss," friends argue); I tasted the meals we had shared in restaurants all over Los Angeles, Chicago, New York; I saw again the first manuscript of his I had accepted as an editor, and felt its weight in my hands (10,000 words, typed on heavy bond); I remembered the grinding days we had spent collaborating on a screenplay. Outside my study, it was quiet; just a few birdcalls and the occasional soft plop of the red, berrylike fruit of the Brazilian pepper tree, falling to the ground outside my window.

Finally, I took the cover off my typewriter and tapped out a few paragraphs about Chuck, which I mailed to *Playboy* magazine in Chicago. Beaumont had been one of their best writers, and I felt sure they would want to publish a short eulogy. As a friend of his, and as the magazine's former executive editor, I considered myself amply qualified to write it. They surprised me by declining, giving as their reason: "We've decided to limit obits to full-time major staffers." Obituaries and eulogies of

Chuck appeared in many other quarters, of course: among them, *The Los Angeles Times, The Hollywood Reporter, Variety,* and a fine article in *The Magazine of Fantasy and Science Fiction,* written by William F. Nolan. [Published, following "My Grandmother's Japonicas," for the first time in book form. — Ed.] But the following words, intended for *Playboy,* were never published anywhere until now:

CHARLES BEAUMONT
1929–1967

Charles Beaumont is dead, at the age of 38. He was one of *Playboy's* most popular contributors for over a decade — from 1954, our first year of publication, to 1965, when the illness that was to be his last halted his typewriter.

That machine — a massive German "Torpedo," built to take rigorous punishment — was seldom silent, for Beaumont was a voluminous and variegated writer, equally adept at fiction and non-fiction. Such *Playboy* stories as "The Dark Music," "Night Ride," "The Hunger" will come to mind; and any number of his nostalgic articles — "Requiem for Radio," "The Bloody Pulps," "The Comics." Outstanding among the large body of his work for us is the novella, "Black Country" (September 1954) and the essay, "Chaplin" (March 1960). "Chaplin" won him our Best Article award. If we had been presenting awards in 1954, "Black Country" assuredly would have earned him the Best Fiction honor in that year.

Chuck Beaumont, however, was more to us than a talented writer. He was a close friend. From the beginning, when we gave him his first publication outside the science-fiction field, he was indelibly associated with this magazine, and proud of the connection. The feeling was mutual.

His home was in California, but he paid numerous visits to our Chicago offices, frequently staying in town for weeks at a time while he polished a piece for a pressing deadline. During such stays, many convivial glasses were raised with the editors, and many nights sped by swiftly, propelled toward dawn by good talk, high spirits and laughter.

Although much of his fiction dealt with the macabre, his personality was anything but morbid. He was full of wit and warmth, and was not ashamed of being a deep-dyed romantic. Given a choice between a long, drab life and a short, incandescent one, it is entirely possible he might have chosen the latter — and his short life truly was incandescent in its brightness and intensity. Chuck loved fast cars and often raced them in competition; he loved movies and comic strips and fine books and good music; he loved trains and travel; he loved language, our motley, marvelous English language in particular; most of all, he loved to write. Enthusiasm and a sense of wonder were his hallmarks — his greatest qualities as a man and his most valuable assets as a writer.

He left behind six books: *The Hunger, Yonder, Night Ride and Other Journeys, The Magic Man* (collections of his short stories), *Remember? Remember?* (his nostalgic pieces) and a novel, *The Intruder,* which dealt with the agonies of racial integration.

He also wrote several motion pictures and an impressive number of television plays, but he always admitted to being happiest "when I'm doing prose." We feel privileged to have published the best of that prose and grateful to have known its author. We mourn his death and the untimeliness of it; we mourn the unborn works he was not granted the years to create; but we do not mourn his spirit. That, and our memory of it, we fondly toast.

* * *

Chuck had often told me and his other friends about "My Grandmother's Japonicas." He had a special fondness for it. When we'd ask him why he'd never offered it for publication, he'd always reply, somewhat mysteriously, "I'm saving it," hinting that it would be an important chapter of a larger work, such as an autobiographical novel. I read it only after he died, and I do believe it to be wholly or in great part autobiographical.

It fits everything he ever told me about his boyhood in Everett, Washington, back in the days when he was still Charles Leroy Nutt — a name he wisely abandoned when he embarked on a career as a professional writer. I have no personal conviction — other than the most wishful of thinking — that Chuck is "looking down" on us at this moment; but I wouldn't dream of denying the possibility that he may be. And if he is, I think he's pleased that the story of his Baba's non-existent japonicas is being published at last.....................................

My Grandmother's Japonicas

Charles Beaumont

I've lost track now of the number of people who died in my grandmother's rooming house in Everett, Washington — but when I was going on sixteen the count stood at an even dozen — eight men and four women. They were mostly old folks: pensioned-off railroad workers, lonely widowed ladies of the town, a few from the heart of the family itself — my uncle Double-G, cousin Elmina — but some were not so old. Joe Alvarez, for instance, was only thirty-something when he breathed out his last. And there was a pretty young girl about whom I remember just that her face was very white and she had once taught school.

Death came to the house approximately once a year. Not unpresaged: you could smell it coming. For this was when Baba's — my grandmother's — garden broke into rich bloom and the roses grew where they could be seen from any window of any room. Other preparations were made, too; the house underwent a thorough cleaning, as if in anticipation of the arrival of rich relatives; the cemetery — some two or three miles out of town — came aswarm with aunts, all bearing new flowers and vases. They clipped the tall weeds from around the headstones, they polished the marble with soft rags, they berated the caretaker for his slothful inattention. I once watched Aunt Nellie spend over an hour rubbing the grime out of the wings of a white stone cherub that marked the resting place of somebody's stillborn infant, no one knew exactly whose. You could tell Death was coming by all these signs.

The doctor, whom I thought of as the house physician, was so frequent a visitor to our place that we all considered him part of the family. He was a tremendously fat man: his face was continually flushed and he panted a lot, which was to him an unmistakable symptom of coronary thrombosis. Each year, for as many years as I can remember, he would prognosticate with the authority of the practicing physician that he couldn't possibly last another six months. We always believed him. "I only wish one thing," Dr. Cleveland used to say. "When I go, I want to go here." That is, he wanted to die at our place. As things happened, he was one of the few in town who never did.

We were located second from the railroad tracks. A restaurant, a cannery, a hobo jungle and the town depot were on the immediate perimeter and they were all so disreputable that Baba's, with its fiercely shining coat of white paint, refinished each year, looked exceptionally genteel. It was an unusual house in that it was as perfectly square as a house can be: not one sliver of ornamentation, no balconies, no pillars, no filagree. It had two floors: four bedrooms upstairs, three below, plus an immense kitchen with a pantry as large as a bathroom. It was all kept fanatically clean.

The furniture looked antique, and could very well have been, except that antiques cost money and no one in my family had much of that and no one was quite old enough to have acquired antiques first hand. It was a mellow hodgepodge of styles.

The pictures on the walls were generally of large dogs. My grandmother had no fondness for dogs, however, and would never allow one in the house.

When my mother and I moved there from Chicago, where I was born, I was installed in one of the unrented upstairs bedrooms. This was about the time I had discovered Edgar Allan Poe, and it was therefore not much of an encouragement when Baba let it slip that a gentleman had only two weeks previously passed on "in this very bed." Like most of the others — at least one person had died in each room — the former occupant had been elderly; but, also like the others, he did not go quickly. No one went quickly at Baba's. They all suffered from a fascinating variety of ills, usually of a lingering and particularly scabrous nature. "My" gentleman, a retired lumberman, had contracted some sort of a disease of the kidneys or intestines and, as Aunt Pearl reminisced, it had taken him several months "in the dying."

Heart trouble was the most frequent complaint, though. It

seemed to me for a while that everybody in the house was going about clutching and reeling, catching at chairs, easing into bed, being careful not to laugh too hard.

Nothing could shake my aunts' firm belief that every disease, no matter what it might be, was contagious. When poor Mrs. Schillings was groaning out her last from advanced arthritis, movement had all but disappeared from our house. We creaked out of bed, we walked stiffly when we felt able to walk at all, and it was only after the funeral that the usual bustle was resumed. At the arrival of Mr. Spiker, who had come from his bachelor quarters across the way to die at Baba's, conditions reached a low point. Mr. Spiker suffered from, among other things, what my grandmother called The Dance: the old man shook and quivered horribly. It was, of course, not long before we had all begun to tremble in similar fashion. I used to spend many agonizing moments with my hands outstretched, trying to keep the fingers steady. Aunt Pearl, better than the rest of us at this sort of thing, fell completely apart this time. She took to her bed and stayed there for several weeks, shuddering in giant spasms which even Mr. Spiker couldn't match: he occasionally trembled his way over to comfort her. Later he died of an infected liver, a common sequel of drinking too much straight whiskey.

And yet, with Death as much a part of life as it was then, Baba's was certainly the most cheerful parlor in town. We would gather around the fire for hours every night and tell stories — generally in soft voices, so as not to disturb whoever might be dying elsewhere in the house.

The subjects of conversation seldom veered from Sickness, Death and the Hereafter. Baba would spend forty-five minutes to an hour telling how her husband died as a result of an accident in the sawmill where he worked; Aunt Pearl — as with all my aunts, a widow — would describe the manner in which *her* husband departed this earth ("Pooched out like a balloon and then bust!"); that would lead to someone's recollecting an article they'd read somewhere on how hypnosis was supposed to help cure cancer, and the next thing it would be time for bed.

I don't recall a completely easy moment I ever spent in the rooms they assigned me. Most often there was a peculiar smell, relative to the disease that carried off the former occupant: the sort of smell, like ether, that you can never quite get rid of. You can get it out of the air, but it stays in the bedsprings, in the furniture, in your head. My least favorite room was the one next to Baba's.

The walls here were a green stagnant-pool color and the bed was one of those iron things that are always making noise. Railroad calendars, picturing numerous incredibly aged Indian chiefs, hung lopsided on strings, and on the door, above the towel rack, there was a huge portrait of the Savior. This was painted in the same style as old circus posters, showing Him smiling and plucking from His chest cavity—realistically rendered with painstaking care and immense skill—a heart approximately five times the size of a normal one, encircled by thorns and dripping great drops of cherry-red blood.

Now what with *The Murders in the Rue Morgue* or *The Tell-Tale Heart*, the Indians on the wall and the portrait on the door, not to mention the atmosphere of disquiet, it seems odd that I should have decided just then to paint on the green iron flowered knobs of the bed's head-pieces—with India ink—a series of horrible faces. That is what I did, nonetheless, and as there were twelve such knobs, I soon had twelve unblinking masks staring at me.

At any rate, I was in no condition this night—a few nights after completing the heads—for one of Baba's pranks. She was a great lover of practical jokes, my grandmother, and her sense of humor ran to the macabre.

To give you an idea of what I mean, there was the time the lunatic escaped from Sedro-Wooley (this is where the insane asylum is). He'd been put there by reason of having cut off his wife's head with an axe one night, along with his mother's and some other relatives'. Now he was loose, and no matter how hard they looked for him, he simply wasn't to be found. The countryside was thrown into a delicious panic: I wish I had a dollar for every time my aunts looked under the beds.

Baba, then aged seventy-five, took this as a springboard for one of her most famous jokes. Here's what happened:

She went over to Mr. Howe's shack—he was a bachelor and there was gossip about him and her—and borrowed some of his old clothes. Then she put these on, covering up her hair with a cap and dirtying her face, and got the short-handle hatchet from the wood-house. She waited a little while—it was quite late, but we were all light sleepers: the drop of a pin would have made Aunt Myrtle and especially Aunt Dora sit bolt upright—then she crept into the house and stationed herself inside the closet of Aunt Myrtle's room.

Now Aunt Myrtle frequently got frightened and would literally leap at the sight of her own reflection in a mirror, so you can understand why she was chosen. It isn't hard for me to see Baba now standing there in the dark, clutching the axe, grinning widely. . .

She waited a minute, and then, from the closet, came a series of moans and shufflings that could easily have roused the adjoining township.

Frankly, it's a wonder they didn't empty the family shotgun into Baba, because when someone finally got up the nerve to open that door—I believe it was my Uncle Double-G—there were Goddy-screeches that would have terrified any real lunatic. "Goddy!" they yelled, "Goddy! Goddy!"

It all gave my grandmother immense satisfaction, however, and she never tired of telling the story.

There was also another favorite little prank of hers. It was the day I accidentally broke off the blade of the bread knife. We managed to make it stand up on her chest so that the knife appeared to be imbedded almost to the hilt in her. Then I was commanded to rip her clothes a bit and empty a whole bottle of ketchup over her and the linoleum. Then she lay down and I ran screaming, "Somebody come quick! Somebody come quick!" It was gratifying that Aunt Dora fainted away completely, though the others saw through the joke at once.

Baba was an extremely good woman by and large, I've decided. I never heard a cross word out of her. I never saw a beggar come to the door but that he went away with a full meal and frequently more — with the single exception of one old man who happened to have a dog with him. He wouldn't leave the dog outside and Baba wouldn't let it track up the house. She fretted for days about the man.

But there was still that sense of humor.

Observing my reading material at the time, she would say to me: "Now sonny, I'm old and one of these days I'll be dead and gone. I'm just telling you so that when you feel a cold clammy hand on your forehead some night, just reach out and take it: it'll be your old Baba, come to visit." That put me in a sweat: I still can't stand, to this day, wet rags on my brow.

The oddest, most unsettling experience of my life took place a few nights after I'd finished painting the horrible heads on the bed.

I had been reading *The Facts in the Case of M. Valdemar* and the concluding bit about the mound of putrescence in the bed lingered long after the light had been put out. I kept trying to *imagine* it. The whole upper floor was deserted at this time, aside from myself and Baba's room, Mr. Seay having been plucked from this mortal sphere two days earlier owing to sugar diabetes and his fondness for candy bars. The window was open. I was just dozing, thinking about putrescence, when there was this soft *thud-thud* as of someone advancing very slowly up the stairs. The tread was so slow, however, that I recognized it as Baba's — she was going on eighty now. I waited, knowing what to expect. And I was partially correct. The footsteps got closer, I could hear my bedroom door opening; the *thud-thud* came across the room and someone sat down on the bed. I braced myself. It was Baba, of course, in a puckish mood. Shortly she would let out a blood-curdling scream or cackle like a witch, or worse. But — nothing happened. There was a heavy asthmatic sort of breathing in the room — I couldn't see, as there was no moon — but nothing happened. Tentatively I nudged the weight on the bed with my foot: as nearly as this sort of test can tell, it was Baba all right. Minutes passed. And more minutes, the breathing regular as ever. Still nothing. No movement, no sign; only, the breathing got heavier and I could hear a kind of thumping, like a small animal hurling itself at a dead-skin drum.

My mother came in and calmed me down. Questioned suspiciously, my grandmother denied having put a toe in my room all night.

Now I realize what had happened. I'd no way of knowing then, however, and for years I told the story of the midnight ghost that sat on my bed.

What had happened was, Baba had come to scare me and just plained worked herself into a heart attack from sheer excitement. No one must know about this, so she'd sat there waiting for the pain to pass.

We all thought of Baba as several evolution-phases beyond being a mere human. Uncomplainingly and resolutely she had for years tended to the sick and dying of the house, but never once had she succumbed, actually, to a single germ. The rest of us might go about clutching our hearts or trembling or duplicating the death-agonies of whatever tenant: not Baba. And it finally got so that we believed she was immortal as George Bernard Shaw. We thought of the world with everybody in it dead but my grandmother and George Bernard Shaw, and them walking hand-in-hand among the littered corpses, seeing to proper burials and trying to make things nice for the departed. I don't know what Mr. Shaw would have thought about that.

There was a particular reason why I was unhappiest in the room right next to Baba's. It was because she never let anyone, not even her own daughters, enter this room and I was continually overwhelmed with curiosity. Yet, I knew I must never violate the rule, for I had more than a suspicion it would make Baba sad — and most of us would have jumped in front of a locomotive before seeing that happen. Also, who knew? the room might have contained mementoes of past indiscretions, or she might have been hiding a mad sister there — for myself,

I inclined to the latter view.

Neither was correct, however, as it evolved.

The truth was, Baba had a heart condition. And this was where she went whenever she felt an attack coming... In a way she sensed it was only her apparent immunity to Death and illness that allowed us to take the horror and the fear away, as we did. If we'd seen her sick even once, we were sure things would change; it would have become merely a big house where a lot of people died.

Things did change when she had her stroke.

Fortunately, no one else was dying at the time. Mr. Vaughn, the former town stationmaster, was bedridden, but this was more due to laziness than anything else: his groans, which had been filling the air, ceased abruptly when the news was out.

Baba had been taking tea with Mr. Hannaford, the undertaker, and red-faced Dr. Cleveland who was in the habit of stopping by in between calls. It was morning. I knew she was feeling good, because she'd put a partially asphyxiated toad in my trousers pocket — to my terror, as I despised and mortally loathed toads and like creatures. I found it on my way to school. When I got home from school no auguries were in the air, except I noticed idly that the roses were in exceptionally fine bloom — the yellow ones particularly were everywhere. And the air was full of a natural sweetsyrup fragrance, unsuggestive of the slumber room.

But things were powerfully quiet.

My first thought was that Mr. Vaughn had died. But then I saw the old man seated on the back porch, holding his battered old felt hat in his hands and revolving it slowly by turning the brim. He looked far from happy. He stared at me.

At first they wouldn't let me see Baba. But I pleaded and bawled and finally they gave in and I went into the downstairs bedroom Aunt Nell used for her patients (she was a masseuse).

I expected something hideous, judging from the way everybody was carrying on. A mound of putrescence in the bed would not have been unnerving: I was ready.

But, aside from the fact that she was in bed where I'd never seen her before, Baba looked little different — except perhaps more beautiful than ever. Her hair had been taken down and combed against the pillow and it looked silver-soft even against the spotless Irish linen slip. Her face was lightly rouged and powdered and she wore a pastel blue shawl over her gingham gown. Her eyes were closed.

I asked everyone else to please leave the room. Surprisingly, they did.

Poor Baba, I thought. The stroke had come without warning; it had knocked her to the floor and when the doctor finally arrived, there was nothing to do. Her entire left side was paralyzed, for one thing. It had hurt her brain, for another. She would suffer a short time and then die...

I looked at her, feeling as empty as I'd ever felt before; I knew I must say something, try to be of comfort in some way, difficult as it was.

I walked to the bed and, gulping, touched her folded hands, as if to make this awful dream seem somehow real.

Baba's left eye opened. "Somebody," she suddenly screamed, "come and help me! This young man is trying to feel of my bosom!"

My grandmother "suffered" for three years, which fact confounded medical science as represented by Dr. Cleveland and restored our faith in her immortality.

She never got out of the bed, but few people have done more traveling than Baba did after her stroke. Mostly she returned to her birthplace in North Carolina, though frequently she would chronicle personal experiences with the wild savages of Montana and Utah. She spoke several authentic Indian dialects fluently, we knew that (though not where she picked the knowledge up) and for whole days running there would not be a word of English heard from her room. It was a fact that she'd never in her life been to Utah and visited Montana only once, to see William Hart's statue — on second thought, that might have been Wyoming. Anyway, it was all a long time after the last wild savages disappeared.

Once she spent a day calling out the sights of Chicago like a tourist guide: "Now this here is the famous Art Institute; to your right you see the Shedd Aquarium; over there is the Planetarium; we are now passing old Lake Michigan." Of course, she'd never been there.

Time took precedence over space in Baba's travels: she was a different age every day. It wasn't easy to keep up.

"Get your damn hands off of me, Jess Randolph!" she yelled one night, waking the whole house. "I am entirely too young for these kind of monkeyshines."

Another night we were startled to hear: "The Great! Letty's chopped her hand off with the axe!" This referred to the time my mother inprovidentially severed the third finger of her left hand whilst cutting up some kindling wood. Baba had held the finger on so tight that when Dr. Cleveland finally arrived it was possible to effect a mend-job. It had happened fifteen years before my birth.

Baba's appearance never got any worse, but this was the only thing that remained static in her new life. In addition to her trips around the world, back and ahead through time, she developed one day no different from any other day the notion that she was pregnant.

Nothing could dissuade her, either. Because of her heart there was nothing but to humor her, so for almost an entire year we would ask her if she felt it was "time" yet; she'd listen, poke her stomach with her good hand, and answer no, but soon, and we'd all better stick around.

Then one day I stopped in her room for a visit and, as had become customary, inquired whether she thought it would be a boy or a girl. This used to delight her.

She just looked at me.

"Gonna name it after me, are you?" I joshed.

She rolled her eyes. "Letty!" she called. "Come and get your young'n. He's gone completely crazy!"

After that the subject of grandmother's pregnancy never came up.

By this time we had stopped taking in boarders and Death and Dr. Cleveland became infrequent callers. At least, in their official capacities. And with the absence of these two, a pall slowly descended which none of us seemed able to lift. It wasn't exactly a gloomy or joyless house, but the lively spark that pulls each moment from the level of the ordinary to something a little finer, this was certainly gone. And it would never come back.

On a nicely chill September morning, with many of the roses still left in the garden, Baba called us all into her room and announced calmly that she was going to stop living. Now since she was the only one of us who had never previously issued such a statement — Aunt Dora always said "Goodbye, goodbye" and squeezed my arms even when she was only going to the movies — we were impressed. Unconvinced, but impressed.

Baba asked Pearl and Nellie to take her to the window so that she might have a last look at her flowers: she was there fully forty-five minutes and got to see them all, plus a lot no one else could see for she remarked how lovely the japonicas were and there had never been japonicas in the garden.

I remember it all very well. I was standing by Baba's side at the window and, since it was true — it was early in the morning — I commented that the hoarfrost looked like diamond-dust on the grass.

Baba jerked her head around. "Young mister," she said, "I'll thank you to remember there's ladies present!"

For some reason that made me cry. I wanted suddenly to pray, but we all changed religions so often, I could only apologize. They sent me out for an ice cream bar, then: my grandmother always had a great fondness for ice cream bars.

When I got back she was dead.

I spent that night in the room with the horrible heads. But they didn't scare me a bit.

I imagine they're still there, if the ink hasn't faded.

Charles Beaumont:
The Magic Man

William F. Nolan

He was an adventurer.

A thousand passions shaped his life. He was always discovering new ones, remembering old ones. My phone would ring at midnight in California: Chuck calling from Chicago to tell me he planned to spend the day with Ian Fleming and why not grab a plane and join them? By morning I was in Illinois. We flew to Europe that way, spurred to action by a wild Beaumontian plan to see the 1960 Grand Prix at Monte Carlo. ("I'll write it up for Playboy!" And he did.)

He loved King Kong, trains, pulp magazines, Vic and Sade, Oz, Steinbeck, old horror movies, late-night coffee shops...All his pores were open; he absorbed life with his body, mind and spirit. He moved through the world like a comet. This is not hyperbole; it is fact. Sleep was an enemy — to be endured for a few hours each night. Chuck was almost never at rest; there was so much to see, to learn, to experience, to share with others.

Racing driver, radio announcer, musician, actor, cartoonist, multilith operator, statistical typist, film critic, story analyst, book and magazine editor, literary agent, teacher at UCLA, freight expediter, the father of four children...he was all of these. But writing was the blood in his body, the stuff of dreams put to paper, the driving force which gave ultimate meaning to his life.

Chuck could never write fast enough to catch up with his ideas, and he always had many projects planned: a play with Richard Matheson, a novel of his youth, a World War I flying spectacular, a comedy record album with Paul DeWitt, a film on auto racing, a novelet about a cowboy he'd met in Missouri...

A technical virtuoso in prose, he utilized many styles, but the distinctive "Beaumont touch" was always evident, whether he was telling us about power-hungry Adam Cramer in *The*

Intruder, jazzman Spoof Collins in *Black Country,* the perverted lovers of *The Crooked Man,* the tough stock car veteran in *A Death in the Country,* or the gentle little man who rode stone lions in *The Vanishing American.* And although he wrote in many fields, it was fantasy and science fiction which shaped him as a creative writer. "I lived in illiterate contentment until spinal meningitis laid me low in my twelfth year," he once declared. "Then I discovered Oz, Burroughs, Poe—and the jig was up."

He spent his childhood on Chicago's north side, and in Everett, Washington, with his aunts—publishing his own fan magazine, *Utopia,* in his early teens and writing countless letters to sf/fantasy publications. Radio work led to his leaving high school a year short of graduation for an acting career in California. It didn't jell, and soon he was inking cartoons for MGM in their animation studio and working as a part-time illustrator for FPCI (Fantasy Publ. Co.) in Los Angeles.

And starving.

His father obtained a job for him as a railroad clerk in Mobile, Alabama—where, at 19, he met Helen Broun, and scribbled in a notebook: "She's incredible. Intelligent *and* beautiful. This is the girl I'm going to marry!"

When Chuck moved back to Los Angeles, Helen went with him as his wife.

I met him (briefly) for the first time late in 1952, at Universal. Ray Bradbury, then working there on *It Came From Outer Space,* introduced us. I recall Chuck's sad face and ink-stained hands; he wanted to *write* for Universal, not run a multilith machine in the music department. Ray was certain of the Beaumont talent, and had been helping Chuck with his early work—as he later helped me. The first Beaumont story had already appeared (in *Amazing*) and within a few more months, when I saw Chuck again, half a dozen others had been sold. Forry Ackerman, then Chuck's agent, got us together early in 1953, and our friendship was immediate and lasting.

I found, in Chuck Beaumont, a warmth, a vitality, an honesty and depth of character which few possess. And (most necessary) a wild, wacky, irreverent sense of humor; Chuck could always laugh at himself.

The Beaumonts were in disastrous shape in '53; Chuck's typewriter was in hock and the gas had been shut off in his apartment. I remember his breaking the seal and turning it back on; his son, Chris, required heat, and damn the Gas Co.! Chris got what he needed. Later, as his other children, Cathy, Elizabeth and Gregory came along, he loved them with equal intensity. Chuck's love was a well that never ran dry; it nourished those around him. No one was happier at a friend's success; Chuck had a personal concern for what you were, what you were doing, where you were headed in life. He would encourage, bully, insult, charm—extracting the best from those he loved. You were continually extending yourself to keep up with him; happily, he kept all of his friends at full gallop.

Chuck's last hardcover book was *Remember, Remember*...and there is so *much* to remember about Charles Beaumont: the frenzied, nutty nights when we plotted Mickey Mouse adventures for the Disney magazines...the bright, hot, exciting racing weekends at Palm Springs, Torrey Pines, Pebble Beach...the whirlwind trips to Paris and Nassau and New York ...the sessions on the set at *Twilight Zone* when he'd exclaim, "I write it and they create it in three dimensions. God, but it's *magic!*"...the walking tour we made of his old neighborhood in Chicago...the day my first story was published ("See, Bill, you *can* do it! You're on the way!")...the enthusiastic phone calls, demanding news ("Goodies for ole Bewmarg!")...the fast, machine-gun rattle of his typewriter as I talked to Helen in the kitchen while he worked in the den...the rush to the newsstand for the latest Beaumont story...

He was 25 when he wrote *Black Country* and began his big success with *Playboy* and his close friendship with editor Ray Russell. He was 38 when he died, after a three-year illness. It is trite to say, but true, that a good writer lives in his work. Charles Beaumont was a very good writer indeed. His full potential was never realized; he might well have become a great one.

The Magic Man is no longer with us, but his magic still

dazzles, erupts and sparkles from a printed page, shocks us, surprises us, makes us laugh and cry — and, finally, tells us a little more about the world we live — and die — in.

That's all any writer can hope to do. Chuck did that.

For us, the Beaumont magic will always be there.

Master of Imagination
(Interview)

Richard Matheson

That original writer and perspicacious editor Ray Russell, in an uncredited introduction to his friend's frightening yarn "First Anniversary"[1], *said, "Richard Matheson is almost too good to be true."*

As he generally is, Russell was right. There's been no one since the development of television—in or out of movies or so-called "category fiction"—like the author and *scripter of such dissimilar unforgettables as* Duel, What Dreams May Come, The Shrinking Man, *and* Bid Time Return.[2]

Possibly Matheson, a modest man, senses it. Perhaps he has never considered himself a science fiction or a horror writer but a "realistic fantasist" because he knows nature challenges Olympian versatility, and Richard prefers to remain a moving target. No one medium appears to maintain a lasting grip on him; he is or has been at home writing short stories, novels, theatrical and TV scripts, and stage plays. While no less knowledgeable a personage than Stephen King regards him as one of the two writers to affect the modern horror story[3] *and it was this dignified son of Norwegian immigrants with whom Rod Serling first shared writing chores on TV's* Twilight Zone, *Richard Matheson now means to produce work that uplifts (as this interview reveals)—writing that stimulates a less-horrified and -fictive interest in fundamental questions of life and death.*

"An enormous man, luxuriantly bearded and pale-eyed, like a seer of old," Ray Russell said of the man who adapted the "unadaptable" Bradbury masterpiece, The Martian Chronicles, *and the Jack Palance-starring* Dracula, *to television, and spoke of Richard's "deep and abiding belief. . .in everything super-, preter-, extra-, or un-natural." Here, Matheson clarifies those beliefs and politely explains why he adheres to them but is no sermonizer. The also-bearded Russell and William F. Nolan, who has called Matheson "Mr. Dependable, Mr. Resolute, Mr. Solid," agree with him that he was born to write (that first event happening in New Jersey, February 20, 1926). He wrote* Novel One, The Beardless Warriors, *following combat duty in World War II, and the fact that it may loosely be termed a "war*

novel" does not seem surprising to Matheson — nor should it be, since such men become interested in a great many things and are always hard to pigeonhole. His first published short story, "Born of Man and Woman," opened the world of fantasy to him — and it was as if lovers of fantasy had been waiting for Richard. After that publication, in 1950, science fiction mags welcomed him and, in common with most 20th century writers, he went where the fiction sold.

But what Matheson offered was something different, or special: Oft-terrifying tales in which all appears normal, possibly small-townish of milieu, but for an ever-spreading stain of the fanciful, the unexpected, or the alarming. No more did readers have to mumble the names of foreign characters or locations, then settle for another rehashing of the time-honored but ancient myths. Now, as H. P. Lovecraft once hoped, horrors could be really "original" and the "illusion of some strange suspension or violation of the galling limitations of time, space, and natural law"[4] might be happening down the block or around the corner — or deep inside a character not surfacely unlike the spellbound reader.

The writers of horror and the supernatural who came next, know it or not — among them, his good friend and sometimes-collaborator Charles Beaumont — were in a way liberated by the influence which Richard Matheson subtly exercised through his prose — and perhaps, most of all, on television. It is a fate he takes with seeming ease that his most permanent renown may reside in those stories he devised or adapted for that impermanent, often-unfaithful creature sometimes called "the tube." Consider his Night Stalker adaptation[5] or Night Strangler original; The Morning After; or such Twilight Zone Matheson originals as "Little Girl Lost," "Steel," "Death Ship," "The Invaders," "Nick of Time," or "Nightmare at 20,000 Feet."

Maybe it's simpler to accept a videotape, electronic future when you know that, so long as television itself exists, uncountable people will be delighted by your impressively varied, creative output and knowing you are the Master of Imagination.

1. *The Playboy Book of Horror and The Supernatural,* 1967.
2. Called *Somewhere in Time,* starring Christopher Reeve and Jane Seymour, in the motion picture version.
3. The second was inventive Jack Finney, author of *The Third Level* and *The Body Snatchers.*
4. *Some Notes on a Nonentity,* by H. P. Lovecraft.
5. This surprising and exciting blend of horror, detection, humor, and clever special effects with reporter Carl Kolchak at the center — an inspired characterization by actor Darren McGavin — was, to that point, the highest-rated television film of all time.

On Being Richard Matheson: His Work and Defining It

JNW: Do you feel there is greater freedom in writing fantasy than other kinds of writing? Are you comfortable when you're termed a "fantasist"?

MATHESON: There is, to be sure, a certain freedom a fantasy writer has. He is not bound by reality. If he wants to write a story about someone traveling through time, he does so without regard for the scientific realities which make such travel impossible in the literal sense. If he wants to have vampires prowling suburbia at night, he does so. If he chooses to have his main character *shrink* until he disappears from sight, he does not hesitate to do so. I have, of course, done all these things — and enjoyed it very much. I doubt if I enjoyed, as much, following the progress of a teenage infantryman through Germany in World War Two or writing suspense or murder mysteries or westerns, for that matter... It does the creative spirit good to shift gears and go from zero to sixty in seconds flat, fantasy-bound.

At the same time, I regard myself as a *realistic fantasist*... I like my fantasy firmly entrenched in contemporary reality. It occurred to me just today that, in the realistic soil of our times, I enjoy inserting one minor seed of fantasy. How that seed grows and what it grows into is the usual substance of my work. It is my nature — half dreamer, half conservative. It is the most pleasurable way for me to function creatively. In the past, I certainly came to the conclusion that writing terror worked best (for me, anyway) when it took place "in the noon-day sun." This phrase either came from Anthony Boucher's mind or he quoted it in a review of my novel, *A Stir of Echoes*.

I don't care to write terror any longer. Not *per se*, at any rate. If what I have to say includes areas which are necessarily frightening, I do not short-change them. But to scare readers for that reason alone is no longer of interest to me. Doing so is a venerable literary tradition and I do not condemn it. I just have lost my interest in doing it personally. ... I feel I have other things to do now. God knows that, where the world and its conditions are concerned, I am virtually a cynic. When I see who runs society and what they do to it, I usually shake my head, cast my eyes heavenward and mutter a curse under my breath. I see, in our world, a reenactment (in many cases literal) of the Roman Empire. Mankind — at least, this stage of it — is coming to a point where major decisions have to be made, the primary one being: Do we go on or do we blow it again? By this, I mean that I think prior civilizations on earth reached similar points and made the wrong decision. I hope we do not.

JNW: Joyce Carol Oates once said that all writing is experimental. Agree? And what seems to you to be the primary distinction, if any, between the *avant-garde* so many critics extol, and the fantasy writing so many readers read?

MATHESON: I am not exactly sure what Joyce Carol Oates meant... In the sense that an experiment is a trial or a test conducted to find out something, of course almost any human endeavor is experimental. This includes writing. When we write, we are trying out something. ...The elements being tested are psychological. Memory. Emotion. Aspiration. Our brains come up with ways in which to take these ingredients and, hopefully, cook them into a new, tasty stew...

The difference between *avant-garde* and fantasy? I feel that *avant-garde* has more to do with form and/or technique than thought content. Not to mention the fact (a fact, to me) that fantasy is more difficult in that there are certain guidelines to follow; at least, in the kind of fantasy I prefer. I don't think there is, in *avant-garde,* any point the practitioner reaches beyond which he or she cannot go. Fantasy, I believe, does have that point. Call it logic. Whatever it may be, that willing suspension of disbelief always spoken of hardly comes into play in *avant-garde* literature. The author — or artist; whatever — has a point to make and will use *any* means to make it. And without regard for the question, "Am I going too far?" In fantasy, I think, it is a question which the creator must constantly be aware of, if not constantly asking himself or herself. If you go too far in *avant-garde,* you will probably get a pat on the back from the coterie which loves *avant-garde.* If you go too far in fantasy and break the string of logic, and become nonsensical, someone will surely remind you of your dereliction. I am not against *avant-garde.* I just think, pound for pound, fantasy makes a tougher opponent for the creative person.

JNW: Mr. Matheson, some writers confess a heavy debt to their mates. My wife, Mary, has certainly been *indispensable* to my career. You?

MATHESON: In many ways. For one, she always believed I would be a success. I cannot tell you how many women — who seem to be supportive and encouraging — actually don't believe, deep within themselves, that their mate will ever make it as a writer — an actor, composer, whatever. This is, most often, not even deliberate. It is buried in the subconscious. . . . My wife never doubted, for a second, that I would succeed. And that is an immense support for a beginning writer.

From a more practical standpoint, she ran a house and four children's lives in the company of a *writer* — not the easiest task in the world. She accepted what I was and helped me in every possible way to accomplish it; a wondrous thing for a wife to do. Also, with all her other work, she read manuscripts and commented on same — very valuably. Of especial value is the fact that most of what I believe she *doesn't* believe and, representing that standpoint, she helped me to avoid overdoing things — (kept me) from becoming a proselytizer instead of a story teller.

Lately, getting her Master's Degree in Psychology, she has taken on an entirely new — and extraordinarily valuable — role in my writing. I have never been a master at characterization. I have gotten away with my stories because I *felt* them strongly and, more often than not, the characters were me or parts of me; so they were, to that degree, realistic. Now I can discuss character and motivation with my wife and it is, hopefully, opening up new vistas of possibility for characters in my stories or scripts to come.

Valuable? More *in*valuable, I would say.

JNW: Tell me, is your work better with deadlines or unsupervised?

MATHESON: I hate deadlines. I have never really worked to one. Never. I always had my TV assignments done on time when I did series TV. If I hadn't, it wouldn't have mattered, they'd have filmed something else instead. I don't recall ever having to complete, for instance, a *Twilight Zone* segment in a special period of time. Or any script. I also discovered. . .writing something fast doesn't mean much if it isn't good. If it's good, they'll wait. They may kvetch a little but even that doesn't happen too often. I was supposed to finish an outline for a mini-series by last May. I didn't finish it until September. No one pressured me about it. Of course, it is so monumental, maybe they were hoping it would go away and they wouldn't have to make a judgment on it! But they didn't pressure me. No one ever has.

In prose, I have done everything on spec. One book I got an advance on; *Hell House*. If I hadn't, I probably would never have finished it; my conservative side, you know. I didn't want to give them back their money. So, I struggled. It took me ten years to finish. Ray Russell said that it reads like it was written by three different writers. He was right! I *was* three different people during that decade. I kept changing. And my style and approach kept changing. I hated that pressure. I'd rather write on spec.

Of course, in TV and movies, you don't do that. So there is the personal, psychological pressure you put on yourself. Not time-wise; quality-wise. Will I do a rotten job they'll have to pay for, anyway? That disturbs.

JNW: How does a writer start out today? Is it harder than it was when you began?

MATHESON: Money is the answer to that. You (hold a job) full-time or part-time until you can afford to quit and write full-time. There is no other answer. I don't know if it's any harder...

There are still the book markets. Still the motion picture markets. Still the magazine markets. Still the television markets. And, most importantly, I think, still the same lack of good writers in any market. I am sure that beginning writers are still told, as I was, how many millions of people are trying to write and how impossible it is to make it because of these odds. The fact is that, out of these millions, only a handful *can* write and, more importantly, will keep writing day after day. Frankly, I don't know of one good writer who has not "made" it to whatever degree his or her talent — and psychological drive — took him (or her).

JNW: Is there any sign of receptivity at the network level to the idea of a *TZ*-type program? And do you believe there'd be writers willing to produce that much, week after week, as you, Rod Serling, Chuck Beaumont, and the others produced?

MATHESON: There is little reception to the idea of putting a *Twilight Zone*-type program on TV. Commercial TV, anyway; I don't know where cable TV is — not very far, from what I hear. If there *was* reception... I'd have been involved with one a long time ago. Dan Curtis and I did two anthology-type films which were both directed toward series. One problem is that "half hour" is now synonymous with comedy on commercial TV. And the *Twilight Zone*-type story works best at a half hour. They have tried some (similar in kind) at an hour — even doing several stories within the hour — but it doesn't seem to gel. And although there are writers who can do this kind of material, the *Twilight Zone*-type story is different from the published type of story. Dan Curtis and I, in looking for material for what we hoped would be a series, ran through every copy of *The Magazine of Fantasy and Science-Fiction* — which should have been an ideal source. We found few for the simple reason that the structure

of the *Twilight Zone*-type story calls for the immediate introduction of a fantasy notion followed by the working out of same,
with a final twist at the end desirable. Most fantasy stories lead
up to the fantasy notion, do not start with it instantly. This
makes a difference.

Also — a kind of side track but, perhaps, interesting — Richard
Maibaum and I tried to create a series called *Galaxy*.
H. L. Gold was to be the story editor. We planned to use only
the "classic" science-fiction stories. In reading through them,
we discovered that the science fiction short story world is a
rather bleak one. The power of most of the stories comes from
the power of hopelessness.

Maybe cable TV will come up with a series. I doubt if
commercial TV will ever come up with a *Twilight Zone* again.

JNW: In the two-part *Twilight Zone Magazine* interview
(September, October 1981), referring to the film version of your
novel *Bid Time Return,* you said you "believe that there literally
is no audience for that type of picture anymore." Do you wish
to clarify that?

MATHESON: I over-simplified. What I should have added is
that the typical theatrical audience is not open to films like
Somewhere in Time. Even that might have been ameliorated
had they released the film in a very slow way — one theatre in
each city — and allowed it to build its audience. There were
people who were sorry they missed it but it was gone before
they knew it was around. That there *is* an audience for it was
proven when the film was shown on cable TV. It was, for a while,
the hit of the Z channel here in L.A. People watched it again
and again. It was a special Christmas Day presentation. Also,
the film sold well in cassettes. So I have to alter my stance somewhat. A mass theatrical audience for the film? No. But an
audience? Yes.

JNW: Does the atmosphere hostile to such films have anything
to do with an obsessive emphasis on "relevant" issues?

MATHESON: *Relevant* issues? Bloody "law and order" films? Teenage "crotch" films? Inane comedies? Gory horror films? Not much relevance there.

When they try to make something like *The Right Stuff*, it pretty much fails at the box office. A pity and a crying shame. No, look to *television* for relevance, generally speaking.

JNW: Television?

MATHESON: Glossy and superficial more often than not. But at least they're trying. Take away *Silkwood* and *Testament* and what relevance is there in films today? And did they make a lot of money? They did not.

JNW: Richard, you said that your first published story, that jewel "Born of Man and Woman," was taken partly because "it had a mutation in it," and became sf. Do *you* regard yourself in any manner as an "sf writer," as a fantasy/horror writer, or simply as a professional writer?

MATHESON: I think I have written some genuine science fiction. Not in the scientific sense, although the research I did for *I Am Legend* has a lot of sound material in it. ...I think a story like "The Test" is genuine science fiction because it deals with a problem existing in our world which I carried into the near future and tried to resolve, as it might be resolved in a governmental (and awful) way. To me, science fiction takes an already established fact or facts and extrapolates them into the future—or the present, for that matter. Which is why a western on Mars is still a western, not sf.

I am a *story teller.* That is how I regard myself. I have written terror stories when I was moved to do so...western stories... suspense stories. Murder stories. A war novel. A love story. And, of late, I am trying to write things which I hope might be helpful to mankind in some way.

A professional writer? I guess. The first agent I ever had said that I wanted to write like an amateur and be paid like a professional. Maybe he was partly right. Maybe I cherish a kind of amateur status. *Not* in the area of craft, of course; I value craft very highly and try to practice it as carefully as I can. But if "professional" means "looking to the market first" I guess I will live and die an amateur.

JNW: Then Steve King was right, in *Danse Macabre,* that you have little interest in "hard science fiction"?

MATHESON: None at all. I find science fascinating but I have no desire (and little ability) to combine it with fiction.

JNW: Do you think some magazines draw too fine a line between fantasy, sf and horror?

MATHESON: I think the line between science fiction and fantasy *is* definite. One extrapolates the known; or should. The other deals with the unknown... Horror and terror are different in my mind. Terror affects the mind. Horror affects the stomach.

JNW: King also suggests that certain writers are basically conservative.

MATHESON: I think, if we are talking about terror or horror —which I assume that Stephen is referring to—I agree. That is one reason I have chosen to back off from the genre. Very little in the way of morality is ever mentioned in this genre...the basic function of which seems to be to scare the wits out of people.

Perhaps I might use the example of the third sequence from *Twilight Zone—The Movie.* It was based on Jerome Bixby's story called, I believe, "It's a Good Life." This is a genuine terror story in that it begins in terror, takes place in terror and ends in terror. No change. No attempt to change. On those terms, it works extremely well.

I tried to make two basic changes in my approach to the story. One was the purely story-telling device of not beginning in terror but beginning on a more normal level and edging into terror. My second basic change was to try not to end in terror but to veer, however possible, into some kind of positive direction. It would have been the easiest thing in the world to remain firmly fixed...and give the viewers a little parting chill. I've done it, I know how, it's not that difficult when you have the right elements. I chose to try and take a frightening situation and see if there was any resolution to it, however slight. Clearly, it didn't work out to anyone's satisfaction but I'm not sorry I tried it. I think it was a step forward. So the step becomes a stumble? Better that than never trying at all.

JNW: I've offered the opinion that pre-Ira Levin writers of horrific fantasy were less inclined to preachment, to attribute blame to a literal source of evil—that sometimes there was more attention to sheer *story*.

MATHESON: I think that almost the reverse is true. Early terror and horror fiction abounded in blame to literal sources of evil. I think Ira Levin was going back to a literary tradition, not deviating from it. I think that writers today are more likely to find "evil" in ourselves rather than in outside agencies. We are, after all, living in the age of psychiatry. It seems to me that fantasy writers today are more likely to ascribe terrors and horrors to that which goes on inside the human psyche. Of course, they haven't given up on the Devil or demons or possessing spirits, *et al.* But, if nothing else, I think they are trying to blend it with the dark regions of the human psyche rather than ascribing blame to outside agencies exclusively, which fantasy/terror/horror writers did habitually in the old days.

JNW: By "pre-Ira Levin writers" of horror, I meant those *immediately* preceding him, and William Peter Blatty, but I didn't make myself clear. But speaking of demonic forces, I've lost a friend because, according to his faith, my work in occult and horror seemed to him a Meddling in Things which Don't

Concern Me. Yet they *do* concern me, Richard. Do you think writers who use the Satanic concept as part of storylines are assisting some force or forces of evil?

MATHESON: No... I think the centering of blame for any kind of evil in the world on outside agencies is a mistake, however. Let me add, quickly, that, from a story-telling point of view, it is often enjoyable to read or see such stories. But actually to blame any of mankind's woes on outside agencies is pointless, I think. There is only one cause of "evil" in the world. Mankind. I find these endless discussions of the "problem" of evil to be a waste of time. I mean, in the sense of trying to find someone to lay the blame on other than ourselves. I don't think God (whoever or whatever He/She/It may be) is sitting around in the clouds either interceding or ignoring us.

We were given, by some machinery, one hell of a planet to live on. Wherever we came from originally (and I have various thoughts on that), we are *here,* now. It's our world. However we got it, it was in fine shape when we did. We're the ones (and I mean mankind, going back to whenever mankind started on Earth) who goofed. *We* screwed up. We made the evil: the hatred and the greed, the wars and pollution and horrors. We designed and built the bombs and the missiles. Not God. Not the Devil. Any attempt to remove ourselves from the responsibility for the world and what it is today is escapism.

Of course, the mass population of the earth is rather helpless now, bound in by an anti-progressive system of haves and have nots. But this system wasn't invented by God or Satan. Mankind invented it and allowed it to flourish. *It's our world.* Now we have to lie in it, incinerated, or discover what really matters, and make a difference.

JNW: Then our stories have neither harmed nor helped any church, synagogue, or other religious institution?

MATHESON: I doubt if our stories have made any appreciable

dent in any religious institution. Unless, it is to help them foster the notion that outside agencies are responsible for evil, and that, to deal with these outside agencies, we must turn to the church.

I don't believe this. I believe that each man and woman must turn to himself/herself. Anything any man or woman does to lift responsibility from his or her own shoulders and give to an institution which, in time, invariably abuses that power, is a dreadful mistake.

I don't want to sound too harsh... I think that religious institutions do have the positive effect of organizing human thought toward the end of spiritual awareness. Some of them do it well. Some of them don't. But in the end, each man and woman will have to come to this awareness *personally.* I believe this.

We can't count on tour guides to get us to paradise. We have to get there on our own.

Writing As a Career: The Matheson Viewpoint

JNW: More talented youngsters turn to film instead of the printed page. How awful is this, Mr. Matheson?

MATHESON: I think film—and especially television and, hopefully, cable TV—is the media of our time. Do you doubt that, if Dickens were alive today, he would be the biggest miniseries writer in the world?

People (once attended the theatre) because there was nothing else, and they wanted diversion. When books...and magazines were printed, they read because it was the media of the time and they wanted diversion. They kept going to the theatre, too, of course! But I suspect a lot more stayed at home and read...

Then the camera was invented and the theatre and books were, in a sense, doomed. *Not entirely.* They never will be. But can it be denied that major city theatre is dying?...

Films took over from books. People went *en masse.* Every week; it was a family habit. Then television came along and people could stay home again, and be diverted. *Now* they don't even have to think, as they did when they read the books and magazines. And therein lies the problem: TV reaches—can reach—one hundred million people *in one night.* The thing is, what is allowed to reach them is rarely that worthwhile.

JNW: You like writing scripts, then.

MATHESON: I have been very frustrated by the majority of what I wrote in script form, how it all turned out, I mean. *Very* frustrated. I am...not alone in this. Virtually every script writer feels the same way. I have had, actually, far more satisfaction from television (scripts), commercials and all.

If I can say the things I want to say in television—mostly through long form programs, although possibly from series—I will choose television. If I can't say what I want to say, then I will have to start writing books again. We keep trying to talk, us writers. Make someone listen.

JNW: What was most challenging to you in 1960? And today?

MATHESON: What was challenging in 1960 was to try and make a successful living out of writing without giving up what I enjoyed writing. What is challenging today is to try and make a successful living out of writing, and say things which are *important* to me. A much bigger challenge. Not, I hope, an ill-fated one.

JNW: On the lighter side, in *On Becoming a Novelist,* the late John Gardner made a list of a typical writer's characteristics: Irreverent wit; strong visual memory; criminal cunning and childishness; a lack of sensible focus. Richard, *is* there anything about you, or me, different than what makes non-writers tick?

MATHESON: I think writers are possessed of constantly functioning *doppelgangers.* No matter what happens in their personal lives—and I mean no matter *what*—their creative doppelganger stands aside, and observes; comments; takes down ideas and schemes from a distance. It is, at once, a terrible and wonderful gift.

I can stand in a group at a party, conduct one conversation and listen to three or four others, and pick up not only sentences and thoughts but feelings and character revelations of the people involved in the other conversations. It's like being an ace spy. Except you didn't *ask* to be an ace spy. It just happened. So you live with it and try to make the most of it... not to let too many people know that you are this rather questionable person.

I don't mean that writers can't suffer as people too. It's just that this schizo condition permeates their lives. They live and they observe their living, at one and the same time.

JNW: Why?

MATHESON: They have to; no choice. They are writers.

JNW: Are "genre" and "mainstream" writers different? How difficult would it be for a King, a Rick McCammon or Bob Bloch, to write a novel about ordinary people in ordinary circumstances — and find similar success?

MATHESON: I don't think Stephen King, for instance, would have the least trouble writing a so-called "mainstream" novel. Why should he? He already writes about people, and does it so that the reader is utterly convinced of what is happening. It just so happens that what he wants to convince them is happening is scary and occult. But that is his choice. ... If he wanted to write a mainstream novel, he would do it just as successfully. Why not? So would Bob Bloch; he's come close to it many times.

A good writer writes about recognizable human beings undergoing believable circumstances. These writers do that in their work. All that requires change is subject matter. The approach would be the same.

Anyway, the word "mainstream" is a lot of crap. What makes *1984* a mainstream novel rather than a science fiction novel?

Quality? If so, a lot of so-called science fiction novels should be considered mainstream novels. A lot of fantasy novels.

JNW: Agreed, but what of *placing* the novels? Try this: If King, or Ray Bradbury, or you, wrote a Follet/LeCarre/Buckley/Ludlum sort of novel — would that be easy to place and for the publisher to promote?

MATHESON: Probably harder — except in the case of Steve King or Ray Bradbury, whose fame has transcended genre qualifications. People would read what they wrote out of interest in their writing. The rest of us would have a harder time. We are "expected" to write a certain way. We chose to write that way in the beginning, and we are happier writing that way. But *if* we decide we are not happy writing that way, we would have a lot more trouble breaking away from it. From an initial standpoint, that is. If we wrote a *classic* "mainstream" novel, no one would care what our name was.

JNW: Well, when Richard Christian Matheson began writing, did he naturally move into realms of interest similar to yours? And did you discuss discipline, how hard writing can be?

MATHESON: My son Richard is not as bound by the fantasy genre as I have proven to be. He is not interested in science fiction.

JNW: As you were not.

MATHESON: I wasn't either but I went into it because my conservative side saw all those sf magazines in the '50's and decided it was more feasible to write for them than for fantasy magazines.

Richard's idea interests are broader than mine. And he has skills I never had. He has an editorial-producer skill which I will never possess. He deals with people better than I do. I have always, essentially, "hidden out." Richard is right in the hurly-burly of television at the moment and conquering it. (*Editor's note:* The younger Matheson, whose fine short story is part of this volume, is a story editor for television's *The A-Team.*) Naturally he has desires to retreat sometimes and "hide out," like me. But he is more involved than I ever was. More capable of being involved.

As far as discipline, I think he saw how I functioned and decided it was workable. He believes, like me, that the writing counts, not the writer. In a professional sense, of course, not a human sense. He knows that if you write something and it's good, there will be a kind reception of it. It is important to be a good human being, as well—and Richard is that, absolutely, one of the kindest young men I have ever known and that is not just the father talking. But, in TV, no matter how great a guy you are, unless you "write good," you don't last too long—as a writer anyway. And he and his collaborator "write *real* good!"

And Richard writes good in prose, too. I am very proud of his accomplishments, both human and professional. Every father should be so lucky.

JNW: Do you, sir, think there's too much emphasis placed on the commercial prospects of a novel or story?

MATHESON: I don't identify with that kind of thinking. Unfortunately, this may have held me back from more commercial success. I was astounded, some years ago, when my agent sent me a note—it was sent to all his clients—saying, in essence, "Think about that book before you write it. Do you really think it's a saleable idea?" That was the gist of it.

I hate to think this is justified. But it probably is. I have written a lot of things that got nowhere. But then, I have always gone on the premise of writing what fascinated me at the time. That's *not* commercial thinking. And I really don't write very commercially. I don't think I could if I tried. Once, I wrote a science fiction story with the market in mind. I managed to sell it but I still sort of cringe inside that I "thought of the market" first. That cringe makes me an inferior professional, I guess.

But maybe a better writer.

JNW: Richard, Isaac Singer is quoted by *Paris Review* as saying, "I liked that a story should be a story. That there should be a beginning and an end, and there should be some feeling of what will happen at the end." Agree?

MATHESON: Of course I agree with Singer. A story has to have a beginning, middle and end. I still have trouble with the two-act form of plays. Which did they eliminate, the middle or the end? Of course, I realize that they combined them into two acts. But why? To avoid two intermissions? It was such an ideal breakdown for a play.

JNW: What advice about full-time writing do you always give a person who has just written a novel or yarn he, or she, considers saleable?

MATHESON: I don't think you have to give too much advice to someone who has actually written a novel. A story maybe. Just *keep writing,* that's the advice. Get better by writing *constantly.* Keep submitting. Don't submit and *wait.* Submit and write something else. Stay with it. If you have talent, you'll make it. Simple as that. There simply are not that many good writers around. There are openings, believe me.

JNW: Ms. Oates declared, in *Paris Review,* her agreement with Flaubert's remark that "we must love one another in our art as the mystics love one another in God. By honoring one another's creation we honor something that deeply connects us all, and goes beyond us." Your comment? And isn't there slight distinction here, since our art is given us by God to discover and nourish?

MATHESON: I think we should compete only with what we

can become; our potential. We are not in competition with other writers. At least, we shouldn't be. We should respect what they are trying to do and hope that they respect what we are trying to do. And, certainly, I believe that creativity is more than a cellular emission from the right side of the brain. Very often, we are conduits for ideas that seem beyond us. Of course, there's the subconscious and everything we have read and been exposed to, all our lives. So who knows where it all comes from?

But, ultimately, thought itself comes from some power beyond; I believe that. And since thought is rather essential for writing, I guess our "art" is given to us. How well we take care of what we have been given is up to us.

Richard Matheson — His Personal Views and Values

JNW: You took care of your gift beautifully, in the writing of *What Dreams May Come,* I think; it's my favorite Matheson novel, possibly because of my Meddling Concerns. And you said in *Twilight Zone* that a friend has sought financing for a film version; correct?

MATHESON: *What Dreams May Come will* be filmed, with Stephen Deutsch as its producer and me as its script writer. It will be made by 20th Century Fox. When this will happen exactly, I know not...

JNW: I felt that novel was a personal religious statement, seriously delineated. Is it ever hard these days to recover the beliefs you so beautifully expressed?

MATHESON: ...The views in *WDMC* are personal ones. I could never have completed the book otherwise. Even so, there were a number of times when I stopped and said to myself: "Forget it, no one is interested." I actually put it aside and started on another project. But I couldn't leave it unfinished, so I went back... I'm glad I did. As I have said, it is the most valuable thing I've written (to me) because it moved people and gave them comfort.

JNW: I remembered and referred to it when my father Lynn died a few years later.

MATHESON: Good, Jerry, I hope it helped. As to your previous question, though, I have no problem in recovering the conviction. The problem—if it is one—is that, as one goes on reading and thinking, the views alter. But the basic belief is unshakable. I am sure we survive death in some personal form. What the exact nature of that survival is, I am no longer as sure about. The (circumstances or events of the) moment of death seems pretty well established by eons of similar reports. What happens *afterward* is something else again. I may have over-simplified, in my novel. On the other hand, I *did* call it *What Dreams May Come*—and if it turns out that survival after death is just that—an individual dream after physical death, said dream ending when the next incarnation commences— what differences does it make?

JNW: What, indeed?

MATHESON: Dreams seem totally real to us when they are taking place. The survival experience would seem just as real even if it were only a dream. And, being a dream, it would, of course, vary from person to person. But the basic conviction is set in my mind. We came from some higher place, and, via incarnational steps, are trying to get back to that place. Or maybe most of us are *not* trying, that may be the problem on Earth. But we *should* try. It's a return trip worth taking—and, I believe, an inevitable one.

JNW: Don't some of your views, integrated, less fully-formed than they became, show up at times in your yarns and *TZ* scripts?

MATHESON: I'm sure that traces of all these existing or

impending beliefs show up in my work through the years. Certainly the notion that there is more going on around us than nuts-and-bolts reality is a constant in my work. How each *Twilight Zone* I wrote reveals these things and to what extent, I don't know...

I have had a number of essays written about the psychological background of my work. "Paranoia" seems to be a favorite word. Daniel Riche, in an essay in a French collection of my stories, started by saying, "The key word is anxiety." This was probably more true then than it is now though I am not without anxieties to this day. The odd thing is that I have this schizophrenic type of philosophy.

JNW: In what way?

MATHESON: Regarding my overall view of the universe, the meaning of life, etc., I have a belief system which, for me, anyway, is comforting and keeps my mind at peace. About the world we live in (however), the anxieties remain. To bring it down to its simplest level, I am not afraid of dying but I don't want that death to be painful or lingering or anything that would make it less than agreeable. Just this morning, I told my father-in-law that my choice would be to die in my sleep at the age of 85. I'm sure it is a wish that everyone would have if they thought about it. Conditions that prevail in the world make this possibility somewhat less than certain. Even young people— even *children,* for God's sake! — do not foresee long, comfortable lives for themselves anymore. That is one of the deepest horrors of our time.

JNW: I've thought for quite awhile that "afterdeath" is both a nagging question and passion-laden, ongoing curiosity to many writers of fantasy and the occult. Yet it is rarely faced directly. Richard, is this because of timidity; childhood awe; respect; fear? What?

MATHESON: The Bible—I suppose, Jesus—said that the last

enemy to be destroyed is death. Seems perfectly true. Even at funerals, people avoid the topic. They turn themselves off. Why? Simple. They are afraid of thinking about it. Mortality is frightening to them. Even religions confront it only in the vaguest terms. Most people do not confront it at all. Except occasionally, when a book like Dr. Moody's comes out and becomes a best seller for a little while. It's always there, though. Check the *National Enquirer* and the other tabloids; *New Evidence That Proves We Survive Death!* is a headline (seen weekly) on the check-out lines of your neighborhood supermarket. Everyone wants to believe it. And, interestingly enough, a poll by Gallup Jr. proves that about 70% of the population state that they *do* believe it. I hope that's true. I suspect that a lot of their belief is wishful thinking.

Stephen Deutsch, my producer and friend, and 20th Century Fox—and I, of course—are hopeful that we can do something to disseminate a little positive thinking on the subject through the filming of my novel.

JNW: But I sense *embarrassment* in many people when death, or an afterlife, is broached—do you?

MATHESON: Writers, by and large, want to feel as though they are the sophisticates of the thinking world, the true intellectuals—and in a very real way, they are. But that means you don't stick out your neck on subjects which might give you a faceful of scorn or a diatribe in the eye; someone looking at you with a smirking smile, and saying, "You don't *really* believe that, do you?"

JNW: That happened to me two weeks ago in Chicago when I replied, "Yes, I believe in God."

MATHESON: Most writers dread this. I don't dread it anymore. I don't care. I don't ever try to convince anyone of anything. No way to *do* that. I said that every person's pilgrimage to truth must, eventually, be a personal one. I present my ideas to the public in as entertaining a way as possible; period. I will not then take on a defensive posture and wait to deflect the blows. If you don't want to see or read what I write, don't. You've got a lot of company.

JNW: But you — and I confess, it's true for me, as well — consider reports of dying persons in tunnels of light, being retrieved by long-dead kinsmen or religious figures, quite persuasive?

MATHESON: This evidence is the strongest for survival. It doesn't tell anything about what happens afterward but it certainly indicates a commonality of experience at the point of death and for some little time after. The rub is that these people have to "come back" and tell us about it. The ones who *don't* come back could tell us a lot more.

Here again, I don't care to argue with people who insist that this experience is hallucination, brought on by a number of causes: drugs, fear, re-living the birth experience, etc. I used to carry around some slips of paper on which I had counter-arguments to the hallucination theory. I even had it all memorized, once, when I was going to appear on *Good Morning, America*.

By God, I was primed for that appearance! My mind was alive with information. So I went on the program and a very chatty heart doctor talked so much that, suddenly, our appearance was at an end and I had said about 2% of what was flying around in my skull. I couldn't believe it. I have gotten over it by now and the heart doctor went on to write a book on the subject, so he's on our side. But, boy, I had a lot to say that morning, America, and I never said it! Now I am not interested in saying it. Not in the role of torch bearer, anyway.

JNW: The reflective Ms. Oates has suggested that it doesn't matter greatly "*what* states of mind or emotion we are in" when we write, if it's actually transcendental, a "rise out of" customary moods. I know that holds true for my own work, quite often.

MATHESON: I think it is as simple as this: by constant writing — *daily,* that is — we keep open a channel to whatever source supplies us with all that stuff that comes out of our pencils or typewriters or processors which we look at afterward and think, "Did *I* write that?" What that source is, we must leave to discussion. Much of it is subconscious, of course. I think it goes further than that, but that is my personal view — and that of many other writers, too.

However, since this constant effort toward keeping the channels open is what counts, the *state* of mind in which one begins...on any individual day matters not at all, as Ms. Oates states. And, of course, as you have indicated, we are all escape artists. Reality obviously oppresses writers. Otherwise, why do they keep attempting to re-form it? Freud said that. I say it, too!

Did you know that he also said, near the end of his life, that if he had his druthers, he would devote his life to parapsychology?

JNW: No, I didn't. That's fascinating. I think that the mightier the mind, the wider the gap in simple apprehensions lesser people automatically achieve — some kind of compensatory blindness.

MATHESON: Jung, of course, was always at least semi-involved in the world of parapsychology and mysticism. (I always preferred Jung.)

JNW: So did I, until recently, when I've become aware of Abraham Maslow's gigantic contributions. Both Maslow and his friend Colin Wilson mention the "peak experience," when work really flows. Do you have peaks, and valleys?

MATHESON: There are clearly times of the month when things flow faster — and that is not a bad pun, although the Moon may be behind both phenomena. I have noticed, beyond equivocation, that, at times during the month, the words come easy, the ideas come easy. At other times, you work just as hard and dross comes out. We are obviously. . . "tidal" creatures. . .a part of a living entity; what exists around us. Sometimes we are in harmony with it, sometimes not. That is man's problem, I think, as I have said. Mankind is basically out of harmony with life itself.

JNW: You believed, in 1981, that horror had "played itself out for now." What about cycles in art?

MATHESON: I find it remarkable—and somewhat distressing—that some "cycles" seem to have died out entirely. The western cycle in films, for instance. The swashbuckler cycle. . . Where did they go? Almost literally, none are made. They were popular forms. (Now) the form of horror films—and horror literature, I suppose—is altering, too. Why this is so, I don't know. Maybe the true horrors in our world are just too immense for horror fiction to permit us a vicarious escape from the *real* scary stuff, the chief of which is the ability of man to split atoms at will.

JNW: How is horror differing?

MATHESON: Horror seems more teeth-gritted, these days—as though people are saying, "If you are going to make me forget what I'm *really* afraid of, you're going to have to increase your horrors geometrically until my flesh crawls, my stomach gurgles, and my screams become semi-human."

It sort of reminds me of De Sade's *120 Days in Sodom.* (I read that as research for the film *De Sade;* that's carrying research pretty far, I'd say.)

JNW: True devotion!

MATHESON: These guys in this castle can't maintain their excitement with the simple perversions. They get worse and worse, until they are so abominable that sex has been left far behind and *only* horror continues. And continues—and continues. I see this tendency in movie audiences these days.

And in a lot of writers happy to provide a full measure of gut-wrenching horror; all the market will bear.

JNW: Sometimes without the slightest originality of idea.

MATHESON: A similar thing is happening with the plethora of horror novels, I think. I don't read them but I see the covers on the book racks and they get more ghastly all the time. For some reason, children seem to be fixated-on these days; why, I don't know. I suppose Blatty started it with his book. Are children now the outside agency of all evil? One would think so to look at all the covers with those crazy-eyed kids lurking in attics, on the verge of committing some atrocity. What happened to the age of innocence? Psychologists talk about the pity that young people are being deprived of their childhoods, being forced prematurely into the adult world.

JNW: Which isn't what it's cracked-up to be, even when it *is* cracked-up!

MATHESON: Horror writers seem to be laying a guilt trip on children. Plus, they don't think they're going to live very long because of the atom bomb. Poor children! It is no comfort to me to believe that, whatever happens. . . they will survive. While they're here in our world, it should be a little nicer for them, a little more nurturing.

JNW: Covers to my own books underline what you've said about "crazy-eyed kids," but largely, Richard, the covers have had little to do with what's *inside* the books. My first novel, *The Ritual,* shows on the cover a sort of young Buddha with a single growing horn. My Playboy book, *The Banished,* depicts zombie-like children with glowing eyes. And my Dell title, *Babel's Children,* pictures one nasty-looking small boy and a ghost-like double. But in all cases, in the novels themselves, the children were *victims,* not catalysts of evil. I believe this happens to a large number of writers in horror, but whether it's the artist's fault or an editor's, I don't know. What about another cycle of horror? Will publishers and filmmakers be more selective next time?

MATHESON: When they dominated the market—when the public sought its diversion through books and magazines, then weekly movies—publishers and filmmakers could afford to be more selective. They were always in business to make money—isn't that the American Way?—but they didn't always have to stoop to the lowest denominator, appeal to the lowest in man's nature in order to make that money. Now television has forced their hands. Predictably, they are going for the guts. They want to stay in business. Not all (are tasteless). There are men of honor in this world now, as there have always been. But *most* of them? Greed, man, *greed!* The single human motivation which, I believe, has brought more misery into this world than any other.

JNW: Does Richard Matheson see himself as "typecast"?

MATHESON: Of course. Articles refer to me as "Science fiction writer Richard Matheson." I'm not . . . but categorization is always rampant. People need to pigeon hole. Not just writers. Everyone. In every way. I happen to accept a good deal about astrology, but where is this pigeon-holing more apparent—and cringe-making—than when you meet someone at a party and they ask what sign you are, and you tell them and they smile smirkingly, and say, "Oh. One of *those*"? End of conversation. You have just taken up residence in a pigeon hole.

JNW: I believe it has to do with a practical need to have a line about another person while simultaneously evading the obligations arising from real friendship.

MATHESON: There's a wonderful song in the show *Working.* A young woman sings, "Just a Housewife." It's a sad song and very telling. Another vivid example of categorization. I'm not trying to say categories don't exist. What I am railing against is categorization based on prejudgment, with a total lack of full evidence. In that world, I am "Science fiction writer Richard Matheson."

JNW: Have you made peace with that kind of thing?

MATHESON: No.

JNW: I've never made peace with the way fine supernatural novels by Peter Straub, Anne Rivers Siddons, and Herman Raucher were considered "genre" books but some novels with such elements are treasured by the lit-crits.

MATHESON: To me, there are no genres. There are good stories and bad stories. The genre idea is an afterthought by publishers or editors. . .a bad afterthought.

JNW: Hurray!

MATHESON: But people need it. They understand the world better if everything is on a ready-made shelf. So why fight it? Writers should write the best material they can, then hope they can escape categorization with it. Or, like Stephen King, elevate the category to such a height that it lives right alongside of "mainstream" and usually beats it out, certainly from the standpoint of popularity.

JNW: TV programs made for sheer entertainment also come under fire. And by the way, isn't your son's program another, different kind of fantasy?

MATHESON: *Everything* on television is fantasy-adventure. Or fantasty-comedy. Or fantasty-reality.

JNW: The quantity of violence which offends certain sensibilities doesn't disturb you?

MATHESON: I find it amusing that no matter how violent the action, no one ever gets so much as a bruise — from eight to nine o'clock anyway; the magic TV hour when no one gets injured in accidents or fights. That is certainly fantasy!

JNW: Have you considered writing for *The A-Team*? Or, knowing another passion of yours, sir, acting on the program?

MATHESON: No, I haven't thought of writing for (it); I couldn't. I don't know how. It isn't that simple. And my acting is confined to local theatre groups. I know how difficult it is to be a really good actor and would not attempt to venture out of my shallow depth. I think I *could* have been a fine actor — just as I think I could have been a fine songwriter or a fine composer. But... I never "paid my dues" in these areas. ... I wish the day of the Renaissance Man were still with us. But I think it went out with royal sponsors. If you have to support four children without a monarch to give you ducats for your work, you tend to narrow your output to those areas which are the most feasible from a commercial standpoint. I did, anyway. My conservative side. So I do the rest as hobbies. I enjoy them immensely but I know my limitations. I regret them but I know them.

JNW: As an avocational actor, you're better equipped than many writers to evaluate performers. With what actors would you begin your own ensemble company of players? William Shatner?

MATHESON: While spending a year and a half preparing my mini-series outline, I took occasional pleasure visualizing performers in various parts... Richard Chamberlain. Jane Seymour. Peter Ustinov. Christopher Plummer. George Hearn. Derek Jacobi. John Saxon. Fritz Weaver. Leslie Nielsen. Cloris Leachman. Julie Harris. Jose Férrer. Robert Stephens. Sian Phillips. Burgess Meredith. David Wayne. Jessica Tandy. Viveca Lindfors. Hume Cronyn. Olivier; Gielgud. Ron Moody. Robert

Foxworth. Timothy Dalton. Pat Hingle. Barbara Harris. Lee Grant. Janet Suzman. Martin Balsam. Jason Robards. Michael Learned. Norman Lloyd. Kate Nelligan. Uta Hagen. Dan O'Herlihy. Maureen Stapleton. Peter Straus. Richard Jordan. Patty Duke. George Grizzard. And, of course, William Shatner. With an ensemble company of these brilliant players, one could conquer the dramatic world!

JNW: How lovely, hearing so many of my own favorites cited! I think Stapleton, Phillips, Tandy, Hingle, that glorious Kate Nelligan and Chris Plummer — well, their work should be preserved permanently. Richard, what does "immortality" as a creative artist mean to you?

MATHESON: I have never thought about immortality as a writer. I would like to contribute something worthwhile to this world as a creative person before I toddle off to the next phase...

Sometimes, I pass my short story collections or novels, on a shelf, and actually start, and think, "Oh, yes, I wrote those, didn't I?" I never think of them, never reread them. I have a tendency to forget everything I wrote and think only about what I'm doing now. What I wrote in the past is of little interest to me. I enjoy the actual act of writing; that is where the most pleasure comes from. After that, it is detail and business, and hoping that people will like what I've done.

JNW: How would you like to be remembered?

MATHESON: I would like to be remembered as a helpful human being and as one of the better story tellers. I've tried. I've failed a lot. For the failures, I feel regret. I try not to repeat them.

J. N. WILLIAMSON is the author or editor of nearly 30 books, 20 short stories, and 15 articles, all *published since 1979. Among them are such specials and lead books as* The Evil One, Death-Coach, Hour, Playmates, *the hilarious* Death-Angel, *and the supernatural novels* The Banished *(Playboy),* Ghost Mansion *(Zebra), and* Ghost *(Dorchester). William F. Nolan compared the latter to the work of Stephen King and Peter Straub and, with reviewers, called Williamson "a born storyteller." Williamson's second novel,* The Houngan, *won a Best Fantasy award from* West Coast Review of Books; *his most recent novels include* The Dentist *and* Babel's Children *(Dell) and* The Offspring *(Leisure).*

A native of Indianapolis, Jerry Williamson attended Shortridge High School from which Kurt Vonnegut, Jr., graduated. Prior to writing novels, while rearing six children with his wife Mary, he wrote stories for Ellery Queen's Mystery Magazine *and was thrice an editor-in-chief in Indiana.*

Williamson's chapter on the art of horror writing is part of the 1984 revised Writer's Handbook. *In his introduction to J. N. Williamson's* Anomalies, *author Thomas Millstead wrote: "He has blended fantasy, mythology and terror in striking ways that have earned a permanent niche in the ranks of American fiction."*

JOHN MACLAY was born in Pennsylvania in 1944, received his B.A. and M.L.A. from Johns Hopkins, served in the Army, and has been advertising director of a biomedical company and a billion-dollar bank, president of an historic preservation group, master of a lodge, the publisher of 15 books on local architecture and history and 10 short novels, the author of a dozen published stories, and a collector of books, coins, antiques, and Civil War items. He lives with his wife and partner Joyce and two sons in Baltimore and on a farm near Gettysburg.